LIBERA, GODDESS OF WORLDS

Andrew Sweet

Any time, any time while I was a slave, if one minute's freedom had been offered to me, and I had been told I must die at the end of that minute, I would have taken it—just to stand one minute on God's airth [sic] a free woman— I would.

— Elizabeth Freeman

To my wonderful wife end final editor, Hollee Sweet - I love-you-like-you.

1

Prologue

Monday, September 4, 2237

Lyra Craevis, Deseret - Mijloc

Ordell Bentley descended wide, thick-carpeted stairs in his modest townhome that marked the center of Lyra Craevis and the beginning of the exodus of slaves from off-world into Lyra Craevis. Software updates had smoothed the edges of his virtual body, blending his angles into smooth arcs. As well, years of solitude in the virtual prison known as Inferiere had smoothed his personality so much that any connection to what earthlings called the "real world" had long since dwindled to nothing in his heart. Everything he needed had followed him here anyway, like Monica who, from the smell of bacon sizzling on the level below, prepared something resembling breakfast in the kitchen below. His world was complete enough for him, despite the fact that if he picked any direction and walked a few "miles" then the city and surrounding foliage diminished into empty white space.

He rounded the corner at the bottom of the stairs, hands secured in the pockets of his plush alabaster robe - a comfort about which Monica often teased him. After a hundred and eighteen long years of existence, he felt entitled to a few luxuries. A few more steps brought him into the kitchen where Monica Caldwell tried her best at the ancient art of cooking on an actual stove. Had it not been for the limitations set in their virtual home, she would have failed. Ordell could tell by the odor that the bacon had already been on too long. When that happened, the flavor and texture defaulted to in-world 'cooked bacon' flavor, losing all nuance of her involvement in the process. She twisted her head to look as he transitioned with a heavy step down to the hardwood.

"You're up," she told him, smiling. "Finally."

"I love sleep," he commented to her without apology. "If you'd been in …"

"Inferiere for years unable to sleep at all, I would love it too. They fixed that before you even left. Sit over there."

She motioned to one of four stools flanking the counter - a counter which hadn't existed the day before.

"More changes?"

Monica nodded.

"What do you think? The old open dining area grated on me."

Ordell nodded and grunted as though he approved, but he'd become used to the old dining area. He made his way across the empty floor to her, and when he was close enough to catch a whiff of her perfume, he picked up his pace and closed the gap between them, ending the stride with his arms around her lifting her from her place.

She grinned as he did, looking down into his face. They'd almost gotten her right, except they'd missed a mole that should have been on her left ear. Her bright red hair shot up around her head in something that resembled a frizzy halo, and he loved the way it looked on her. She leaned forward to kiss him as he spun her around and then deposited her back where she'd stood.

"In a good mood?"

"Safe. I have you here. What else would I need?"

"You *do* have me here." The words might have echoed his joy, but he knew the heaviness they held. Her smile faded first from her lips and then from her eyes as he began to regret having brought attention to the fact that she was *here*, in Mijloc, instead of off-world working with the Humanity in Crisis Council, spiriting former slaves called models into the city. Her countenance quivered. The way it still got to her after forty years brought a lump to his throat. He'd missed the worst of it, having been dead in the real world and a ghost in Inferiere for most of the bloodshed.

"I'm sorry." It was the same thing every time, and as usual, his apology seemed insufficient compared to what Monica had lost. She swiveled her head from side to side, and the familiar pattern played itself out to the same logical end.

"There's nothing to be sorry about. *You* didn't firebomb HCC headquarters. *You* didn't level the Village in New York. *You* didn't kill a thousand models."

"No, I didn't."

She tried to lift the pan holding the bacon, but instead pulled it to a different burner, and then put her hands on the counter by the stove with her back to him.

"I didn't mean to bring up ..." He tried to extend the apology. Ordell should have known better after so many attempts at comforting her, but since he lacked the strength to stand idle while she suffered before him, he took up his part of the dance with a pinch of self-loathing.

"It's so *frustrating*, Ordell." She turned to him and her eyes had gone gray. "*So* frustrating. How many years of our lives went to pursuing freedom? *Nothing changes*. Polli still hate us, police still kill us for less than looking at them. Politicians even run on re-instating the Madison Rule. It's almost like nothing changed at all."

"Something did," he assured her. "We have Lyra Craevis." She seemed to relax then, and he held up his wrist before her. "See? No barcode. And I'm only twice the size of a normal person in here."

Monica laughed. "You're right. And we have Kelleigh."

He stepped back from her and checking the belt on his robe.

"We do. Still sleeping somewhere, I guess."

"She learned to love sleeping from you."

On cue, he heard Kelleigh's drowsy shuffling as she followed down the stairs he'd just been on. Ordell moved to the side to grant her access to one of the counter chairs. Rubbing the collected grains from her eyes through a stifling yawn, Kelleigh entered the kitchen and sat at the counter beside him without acknowledging he existed. He smiled at her anyway, and watched her settle into her seat. Instead of the thirty-year old woman that she was, he saw the little girl he'd first met twenty-six years before. He recalled the tears streaming down her face as she stood there, alone and motherless.

Twenty-seven years earlier…

Lyra Craevis, Deseret, Mijloc

He'd expected to see an expansive and complete world when he arose from his bay-borne slumber, but the moment his eyes were able to perceive anything, there was nothing to see. This confused him, as did the violation of his other expectation: Bodhi Rawls was nowhere to be seen. The gangly man with light-swallowing dark hair should have been the first to greet him. Being almost an inch taller than Ordell, who loomed over most men, the creator of this virtual world would have been difficult to miss.

"Bodhi said you'd be up soon," he heard a woman's voice, and realized that he'd materialized with his back to someone. His groggy mind tried to place the tenor, and when he did he took a slow turn, soaking in first the edges of crimson hair and then pale skin that emanated light, creating something of a halo. A smile pushed its way onto his lips - until he held her full face in view. Eyebrows furrowed together, jaw clenched, and lips drawn into a tight line told him that Monica Caldwell, his lover for over fifty years, barely kept herself together. Beside her lingered a child with sandy-brown hair clutching tightly to Monica's clothes, eyes closed against the whiteness. The little girl's eyelids puffed around the edges, and tear tracks decorated her cheeks.

"What's the matter?" He asked Monica as his heart raced in his chest in a programmed response to his body mirroring her anxiety.

"Fire. From the sky, from the streets. They *bombed* us Ordell. Where did they get the bombs? The Village. It's ..."

She couldn't even talk. Her hand went up to block her mouth, but she didn't have to say anything else. He could tell from her empty stare that whatever had happened at the Village, there wasn't much left of the planned community for freed models. The Village had been her sole obsession since his assassination, even when it had become overrun with models after slavery was once again deemed to be unconstitutional. Just beyond Monica's stoic features, a figure materialized, and beyond him, other bodies started to appear in as well.

"Ordell. Sorry to bring you in before things are set yet, but as you can see, things have gotten bad out there. We're starting to funnel models in and we don't have a place for them yet. Since you've got experience, would you mind showing folks the ropes. There will be a developer in here in a few minutes to put together a few more homes and start expanding.

"We've got something like a virtual conference room going. HCC members are going through rubble recovering whoever's animus module back-ups we can."

"How bad is it?"

"Between the Village and HCC headquarters, maybe lost a few thousand altogether. Haven't even started looking at the other communities outside of New York yet."

Now aggregating the details in his mind, he understood that there had been multiple attacks, but he still didn't understand why. His attention was draw to people from the crowd, some with stock avatars and others with more refined ones, who began to disperse into the white emptiness.

"Come back, you'll get lost," he said. The whiteness was almost alive. Too far in one direction and everything behind disappeared, a jarring experience for anyone but probably worse for these people, half of whom he guessed from their wide-eyed gazes knew nothing about where they were.

"Clone flue," Bodhi said. "Influenza X escaped from the Village and into New York City. After that, it didn't take long for sentiment to change. Mom says it was like watching the tide come in off the harbor. Suddenly, polli were everywhere."

Polli were the term that models, genetically-modified clones like Monica and himself, and the little girl as well as the now twenty or so others staggering about lost, used to talk about non-models. As such, it was a bit out of place for Bodhi to use the term, but he'd been working with them for so long he was almost an honorary clone.

6

"They took souvenirs," Monica interrupted, her hands pressed tightly around the girl's ears. "Kelleigh's mother, they burned her and handed out bits of her body, Ordell. I don't know how I ever believed we could exist among people who see us as a hobby. Her physical *body* Ordell."

She released her hands from Kelleigh's ears and swooped her arms around Kelleigh's body, pulling her tight against her.

"And then they killed *me*," she said, stumbling over the words that came out of her mouth. In a quieter voice, she continued. "Killed me with one shot. Better treatment than others."

A shiver worked its way through her tensed muscles.

Back to Tuesday, February 2, 2237

Lyra Craevis, Deseret, Mijloc

"Ordell, are you going to join us?"

His mind snapped back to the present to find the table set and Monica and Kelleigh both seated already. Ordell crossed the kitchen and stepped around the new counter to the table, where the feast had been moved during his inattentive remembering. There, he reached out and grabbed Monica's hand. She returned his gesture and then glanced over to Kelleigh, who had already dived into her food.

"Good morning," he said to her, and she nodded in acknowledgement. "Any plans today?"

"Going out with some friends," she said. "Not sure where we're going yet. Maybe down to play some video games."

In the "real world" someone Kelleigh's age would have to find a job to support herself. In Mijloc there was no rush, because survival didn't depend on it. Kelleigh still lived with

Monica and Ordell, even well past the age that off-worlders, people on Earth, would expect.

After her first twelve years, Kelleigh had come to see this as her world, and her existence. By now, there was no other reality. Ordell had personally witnessed the few memories from Earth Kelleigh had that didn't include fire and bloodshed fade over the years. Her historical experiences were still there somewhere, recorded forever in her animus module memory banks. But it had been ages since they'd been replaced in her forward memory. Instead, the friends she had gained in the tiny city now occupied her concern and time. For her, there had never been an Earth to lose. It was a small thing that he found himself thankful for so many times over during his life. He reached across the table to tousle her hair, which she shrugged off with mock annoyance soon chased by a smile.

"Ordell, I'm not ten."

"You should see what I see."

She deftly changed the subject.

"What about you two lovebirds?"

Plans? Ordell thought about the day ahead of him. There was some vegetation around the side of the house that probably needed to be trimmed back. He could have halted the plants at the right age and height with an in-world mod, but he enjoyed the experience of working with his hands.

"A bit of gardening," he suggested as his fork hung in the air. "Possibly work on the house where repairs are needed. Maybe explore or do a bit of building on the edge of town."

The city had grown out from his house, and along the edges, volunteers extended the city outward as they had time, adding shops and more homes for additional models that sought for refuge. Most of Mijloc was developer-built. Lyra Craevis was the only one that occupants were allowed to build on - a habit formed from the early days when there was nobody else to do the work.

Ordell caught a flash of movement from Monica.

"Bodhi's stopping by this afternoon," she said, nodding toward Ordell. "He's got another panel of developers applying and he wants our help to look through them."

"Bodhi's coming?" Kelleigh asked as she took a five-second break from shoveling food into her mouth.

Monica smiled at her. "Does that change your mind?"

"Uh- no. Not really, just curious. When's he getting here?"

Ordell cleared his throat and then cut into a piece of bacon.

"*Curious*, Ordell. That's it." She flung the words at him in mock offense.

"Not obsessing any more?"

"I have a girlfriend, remember? No, I'm not stuck on Bodhi. It was a passing thing from when I was twelve."

"But he was dreamy," Monica cooed, fluttering her eyelashes over sky-blue irises with a smile on her face.

"I've got to go," Kelleigh said, pushing herself back away from the table. "If you're not going to tell me, fine." Ordell could tell from her demeanor that her patience faded quickly. Monica picked up on it too and let the joke die.

"Three o'clock," Monica said. "Do you want us to wait for you?"

She shook her head, swishing her brown hair around her ears.

"No, I'll pass. Too much to do. I do want to talk to him though. Can you let him know?"

Ordell nodded as he watched Kelleigh rise from the table, wondering how busy video games could keep her. He guessed she had a project that she wasn't ready to tell them about quite yet. A minute later she was gone, leaving her plate half-filled with eggs but deficient in bacon. Monica placed her fork down, plate empty, and Ordell swished his hand through the air in a clearing motion. Within a second, the dishes and extra food dissolved away and the counter, stove, and table were as clear as they had been the night before. He shifted his eyes over to Monica's, and waited patiently for what he knew came next. Her day was planned already, he knew, though he didn't yet know what role she expected him to play.

"What are you into today?" He asked.

"News," she told him, grinning beneath eyes that suddenly seemed exhausted. "I need to catch up with what's going on out there. More models should be coming in soon."

They'd been bringing in models ever since those early days, wave after wave. Now over seven-hundred thousand occupied the oasis-like city, but there never seemed to be an end to it. Monica stayed engaged, monitoring violence against models off-world, and directing the Humanity in Crisis Conference on where to expend resources. Ordell lacked the motivation to keep things going ever since the Reversal that had begun with the Village in New York, and spread through HCC headquarters and then throughout the rest of the United States shortly after the Madison Rule went in. A spate of anti-model laws followed the violent attacks, spewing forth from all states at once, imposing zoning rules limiting where models could live, shoving them all together on undesirable dumping grounds and into flood zones, creating instant and self-perpetuating slum housing. Free or not, models were no more accepted after the repeal of slavery than before. The negative consequences exposed expectations that he didn't know he had about a rational, reasonable resettlement program and an engaged and helpful public.

Gardening was easier and less heartbreaking than continuing the fight. And so, Ordell spent most days doing mundane, household things like groundskeeping. He found peace in trimming the hedges and watering the plants around their home. While he worked on the hyacinth bushes, she kept up on world news through their television set, a thin wall-mounted device that hung above their mantle vomiting information from Earth directly into their living room. He worked his way around the house, cutting as he went and watching leaves and branches fall into little piles. The sun drifted overhead, pounding more and more virtual photons into his neck and exposed arms, but they stayed their normal pale brownish complexion.

There were no sunburns in Mijloc.

Ordell clipped a wayward branch to watch a clump of leaves fall together to the dirt, then noticed that a new creature made tiny tracks in its shade. Bending forward, he grabbed a previously cut branch and held it in place for the insect to board. Pulling it up to his face, he examined the creature up close.

"Hello, little guy," he said, not expecting a response (and not getting one). An abdomen and pinchers told him it was an ant, but not one that he'd ever seen before. The developers were an ambitious bunch paying so much attention to detail.

"Happy birthday, old man!"

Ordell blinked and then, realizing the voice came from behind him instead of from the insect before him, twisted his torso to see a tall figure silhouetted in black against the sun.

"Old man?"

"By my calculation, you're about a one-eighteen, right?."

Ordell stood from his hunched posture, grinned and extended his hand. Bodhi moved in quickly and pushed Ordell's hand aside for a hug instead.

"Does age matter in here?"

Both backed up a bit and Bodhi shrugged.

"The sun in here tracks the Earth's rotation, so kind of, I guess. At least the years are the same if you're interested in counting. Not sure yet what will happen if off-world trade is approved. So far nobody's asked that question."

Ordell raised one eyebrow.

"You think that'll happen soon? Off-world trade?"

They already had some trade, mostly to allow Paivana Thoughtforms to shuttle currency into Mijloc and back out again. All transactions had to be funneled through Paivana Thoughtforms though, as there was no such thing as direct person-to-person trade across world boundaries. With more and more models as well as polli now arriving all the time, many doing innovative things in-world, the need to open trade up became more pressing by the day, and Bodhi had been heading up conversations for more than a decade already. Eventually a decision would have to be made.

"It only takes one vote going our way," Bodhi said, face stony and serious.

"Could be years still."

"Maybe. I'm thinking a couple of weeks though. Emergent Technology and Prescient are both backing us."

"Really? What changed?"

"Money. The United States economy is taking a hit right now. Hundreds of thousands of models now have to be paid and can't be killed arbitrarily. The World Bank will end up picking up the tab unless the GDP grows somehow - a *lot*. Naturally, the two leading modeling agencies would rather that deficit come from Mijloc instead of from them, but that can only happen if people there can trade off-world. Monica's inside?"

Ordell nodded toward the house.

"She's been watching news all day. Might be in a mood."

"Smart woman. There's still a world out there, Ordell. Off-world keeps in-world working."

Bodhi waved a stack of manilla folders in his hands.

"Coming to help parse through the applicants?"

"I guess. Good selection this time?"

"One. I think she's going to be amazing. The rest are

mediocre, but good enough. This one, though," and he held up a manilla folder. Across the top a label read 'Aida Lothian'. "She's going to make Mijloc world-class."

"Let's take a look," Ordell said, and followed as Bodhi crossed into the townhouse, turning to catch one last glimpse at his gardening work, and taking in a deep, satisfied sigh.

2

The Creator

Wednesday, October 4, 2237

Seattle, Washington - Earth

Aida Lothian coaxed a land mass from the depths of the infinite ocean forty feet below the spot where she hovered against the algae-colored sky. The salty smell of the water permeated her nostrils and a fine mist of spray intermingled with the humidity to soak her through her clothes even in the lower stratosphere. Escaping water cascaded from an emerging mountaintop as ripples expanded outward to atrophy and die. The peak rose miles into the sky, pulling with it large, flat areas and expansive muddy fields, each which she shaped with a thought, tugging it higher and higher against the skyline.

When she felt enough ground cleared the mirrored surface, Aida wove her hands through the air, making modifications with each movement, feeling the edges of the island with her hands as they formed intricate patterns, yanking at the shore in some places, pushing it back in others. Eventually the land gave way to the form she'd anticipated, an exact replica of Pangea.

She gave herself two breaths of a break. The time allowed the newly-aerated ocean floor to cast off the remnants of water, drying before her eyes. Then she formed reptiles and amphibians with her thoughts, spreading them across the shorelines and distributing them out into the shallower parts of her nascent Panthalassic Ocean. With a flick of her wrist, Aida dropped four humanoid families down onto the coast along the Tethys Sea. She felt under the ground for limestone and other stone to pull them up into a rocky ridge, separating her people from the dangers of the nascent jungle. They would be safe from the more hostile creatures, though winged beetles as large as dogs could clear the fortification if inclined. Aida wanted her people to survive unattended for at least seven generations, which would give her enough time to build the rest of her planet, an effort that had spanned multiple weeks in planning and setting gravitational conditions. In the beginning, there had only been a gas nebulous. It was Aida who summoned errant rocks together to create a fiery, molten ball, and then cooled that into something livable.

Human laughter drew her attention to the shoreline.

The people she'd made ran around naked. That was going to be a problem. She watched, irritated, as the beachside frivolity quickly degenerated into a mass orgy. If she could entice them to invent clothes, then perhaps they might stop shagging long enough to evolve into an actual society. But perhaps she had ways to force that evolution more quickly. Aida turned down the heat, and watched as the change rippled through her world. Declining temperatures worked through Pangea as a severe icy front, causing the cold-blooded Sauropsids to become lethargic targets for faster moving thermo-regulating creatures. She had now deviated from history. A few Permian-Period animals, the ones who could clear the cliff wall, became dinner for her humans. Warm-blooded Therapsids, smaller creatures more capable in the cooling climate, began their reign. Years passed in minutes while she watched on.

She'd guessed there would be a die-off, but she hadn't foreseen the storm that materialized around her, nipping at her dangling feet. As Aida elevated herself higher to be free from it, her lime green hair whipped about in the increasing winds. Her humanoids scattered from the sea beach to hide in nearby caves, and she grit her teeth in disgust. She knew what they would do there, naked and free from predators or the impact of weather. Her plan to force them to invent clothing hadn't worked at all.

The storm gathered force and the swirling clouds and gusty winds formed into a typhoon large enough to cover half of the global landmass. The spectacle was as intriguing as it was dangerous, and easily could kill her humans and everything else on her planet. Aida pondered whether to react as her self-directed anger roared up inside. Of seventy-three variables controlling weather patterns, twenty of them changed related to temperature and she had done the equivalent of turn down all twenty at once. A chip-less android would have known that such a drastic temperature swing could tank her entire climate balance. But it was too late now. In the immersion game Event Horizon, time only flowed one way. The storm couldn't be un-made, not quickly and not without consequences.

A flash caught her attention as a bright neon green ball of light penetrated her upper atmosphere. Aida made out the ball to be an orb-shaped spacecraft barely larger than she was. The vessel came to a stop in the air beside her and the top slid open like a helmet shield lifting, revealing a man who she hadn't invited and who would inevitably distract her from her work. The worst part of it was that he probably wanted to be friends. She could tell by the over-exuberant way he greeted her.

"I saw your storm from space – awesome!"

Yep, friends.

She didn't acknowledge him at first, hoping that he would leave her alone. Still, she felt his stare as the hairs stood on the back of her neck, prompting her to record a mental note to turn down physiological responsiveness in her haptic suit. But he had been friendly, so the rules dictated that she should reciprocate, even if she hated small talk.

"Thanks," she replied. "It's an accident."

She played for modesty. People usually responded well to that. Besides, it *was* an accident.

"I'd keep it," he grinned with his brown eyes sparkling in the ambient light. "Early planets can get pretty boring. Your storm spices it up."

She thought about what he said, now watching him with her peripheral vision. The storm seemed stationary, like the one on Jupiter. Even though it took up half of her planet, and the air currents had stabilized. She could leave it there for a while and see what became of it. It might be interesting to watch the patterns unfold and chart out the hundred or so variable changes that they impacted. Then she remembered that it was essential to respond to people when they talked.

That was a rule.

"Interesting idea, maybe I will."

Perfect. Not a commitment, but not a complete dismissal either. Her mother would be proud.

"Jordan," the man provided his name without her having asked for it. "Jordon Helm."

She cringed. She would have to introduce herself now.

That was also a rule. Aida assumed it was his real name, though it matched his avatar handle so could have just as easily been fake. People didn't normally use real names in Event Horizon. She wouldn't know without doing some searches and then it would be obvious that she was checking up on him as he sat there awaiting her response. Too much work and too little control. Instead, she decided to provide her own name in reciprocation - mainly since 'Libera, Goddess of Worlds' was very obviously not it.

"Aida Lothian."

"Great to meet you, Aida."

As quickly and quietly as he'd arrived, Jordan closed the shield and elevated back up through the atmosphere out into what passed for space in the game. She hovered there a moment, watching the storm spin and feeling the airborne water molecules spritz against her skin. She hung motionless as she processed the preceding events. For a moment she attempted to recapture the serenity she'd felt in the flow of creation, but it was lost, stolen from her by the man's interruption. Scowling, she flipped her hand's quickly to pull up the in-game menu and left.

Aida pulled down at edges of her skin-tight haptic suit at her midsection, where the top and bottom joined. As it came free, she scratched at the pink indentations it left across her belly while she did her best to wriggle free from it's vacuum seal. Even a seventh-generation Thoughtforms Special couldn't quell post-immersion itch. She next unbuckled the fully-sensory lockout helmet that kept distractions at bay during gameplay. Then she peeled away her extensile gloves, comprised of the same silicone-like material as her shirt and pants.

Once removed, the suit only weighed about as much as a portable replicator, without its protein packs, so it was easy for Aida to toss it across the room into the box-like cleaner, another Thoughtforms special. Even in the darkness, she hit her target and the box sealed with a hiss and began processing, bringing a smile to her face and memories to her mind of her previous rig, which had consisted of cheap gloves and a light aluminum resistance body-frame. All of her efforts to hack that into something resembling a full-immersion suit made gameplay easier, but the lingering odor of sweat and bacteria became an in-game character, testing her resolve with every round. Far too bulky for the sanitizer, she'd had to clean it all by hand and even with a chemical bath, bacterial contamination remained about 0.8 colony-forming units where she could reach. Hidden surface bacteria lingered around 2.1 c.f.u. and growing all the time. The Thoughtforms Special with the pulse xenon ultraviolet light sanitized to about 0.9 c.f.u., including the places she couldn't see. The net result: no more odor with a side effect of better gameplay as the few motion-assisting servos didn't get clumpy and grind.

Clear of her gear, Aida gathered together her previously discarded work clothes, black vinyl shorts, platform heels, and a purple velour jacket with the white halter top, before cracking the door to step back out into her master bedroom, feeling the plush carpet beneath her itchy toes. She turned left into the bathroom to redeposit her pile of today's work-clothes atop the mounds of the unclean. After a quick shower, she slipped into a fluffy faux-fur robe and pulled down her worn copy of the *Celestial Bodies Connecting*, the only novel she'd ever owned in print. She settled into her magnetic-suspension reading chair and pressed backward to recline. Aida twitched her fingers in the motion command to summon her lamp from across the room. Wrapped tightly in the robe, she engrossed in the tactile sensation of turning pages and the sultry smell of slowly decaying trees.

The man named Jordan Helm gnawed at her subconscious, drawing her thoughts back to the game. In Event Horizon, people sometimes did trek the cosmos to find her avatar Libera, Goddess of Worlds, and extract secrets about achieving in-game godhood. Aida Lothian never met their expectations. Her rules weren't complete enough to get through actual human interactions most times, even if Jordan had asked no difficult questions. The nonchalant way he had treated her made her think that he didn't know who she was, which was, of course, impossible. Planets shared her name across the virtual cosmos. He couldn't have been unaware. Otherwise, the entire interaction had seemed fairly mundane.

Why did he bother her so much? She searched her mind for references to his name. She hadn't recognized it at first, but her animus module would remember anything her forward memory didn't. That strange hybrid of physiology and technology, 'installed' via a nanite-filled capsule by mouth, and had long ago made its way into her brain and its network had taken over higher-order cognitive function. Along with it came the extended memory, though her forward memory bordered on eidetic, so she didn't often find use for the module's additional storage. But sometimes it came in handy. Once she recalled that she had it, accessing the module was as seamless as thinking. Very quickly, Aida found her answers about who Jordan was - but not in her persistent memory. Images spun up of explosions at cloning worksites and wanted postings throughout Labyrinth, the virtual web that connected the entire planet. She assessed that most likely the owner of the avatar was a teenage boy with delusions who had picked up the name because it was edgy. Thousands of others probably shared that same controversial name on every virtual platform in existence. Problem solved.

Aida picked her book back up and delved into the world of the slowest burning alien invasion she had ever read about.

She particularly loved the imagery of nature and the world that existed three-hundred years before. The romantic notion of countries wrestling for global control, spying on each other, fighting wars - all things which didn't happen anymore - appealed to her. The Globalists eventually won, so now there was only the single government, the World Government, which regulated the relationships between nation-states. There hadn't been a war for nearly a hundred years since individual national armies dispersed. Unlike in the story, no alien invasion had been necessary.

Focus eluded her. As pleasant as it was to recall globalism's historical origins, Aida's progress in her novel stalled as she re-read the same page repeatedly. With a heavy sigh, she tossed the book onto her empty dresser surface, opting to try sleep instead. She wiggled free of her robe, which soon joined her book, and crossed the few feet to her bed. Then Aida pulled herself onto the floating mattress and let it mold to the contours of her body, in a cocoon-like embrace. The temperature in her room jumped to a comfortable seventy-eight degrees Fahrenheit as she lay, working on stilling her chaotic mind. The lights dimmed for her, and calming violin music played thin notes in the background.

Sleep wouldn't come. The incident with "Jordan" bounced around in her brain until she gave in to her curiosity again. She arose from the prone position, and in response her room lightened to three-hundred and seventy-five lumens, allowing her to see the plain white dresser against the far wall that housed all of the clean clothes she owned, and the fluffy robe she'd discarded across it's top. For a quick second, she lost herself in the light and shadows of the robe and the dresser. Then she searched the Labyrinth again.

"Jordan Helm, Event Horizon"

Her animus module returned information like memories surfacing, each of which contained more details about the link between the man and the game. He was known to play the game often and used it as a recruitment tool for his activism. Her heart quickened and she lurched bolt-upright when she received another memory, an image of his in-game avatar. The avatar looked similar to what she'd seen, though she learned from the accompanying information that he was supposed to be a level seventy in Event Horizon, which meant he didn't need a ship at all. He'd attained godhood so long ago that he had the power to apparate between worlds and didn't even have to fly between them if he didn't want to. A sense of relief spread from her head to her toes until she read on. Even though he didn't *have* to, Jordan enjoyed flying in his orb-shaped ship through the virtual cosmos.

The sound of a landing drone caught her attention and made her jerk her head to the right. At first, she thought it had come from somewhere in her master bedroom, perhaps a joke from one of her flatmates who had snuck it in to spy on her sleeping. That wasn't something they would have done so she dismissed the notion quickly. When the sound reoccurred, she realized it was from her animus module, and what she'd been experiencing wasn't a drone but an incoming call. She sucked in her breath as she checked the caller. Jordan Helm. Allegedly.

He couldn't have gotten her animus a.p. address from her in-game character or even 'looked her up' anywhere public. Aida was more careful than that. She tried to convince herself that she was impossible to find, and the caller had to be a coincidence. But as she thought about that, she realized the obvious truth. *She* could have gotten the information. It wouldn't have taken more than a few minutes because the people she had known before she joined Paivana Thoughtforms had tendrils everywhere. If she could do it, he could too.

Answer the call, she told herself. It's a rule.

"Aida, thanks for answering. How are you?"

People always ask that. When she was younger, she responded to the question with an enumerated list of good and bad things that had recently happened to her. She now had a rule against that. Conversations meant reciprocity, though, so she responded.

"Jordan?"

"Yes, it's me. Sorry, is this a bad time?"

It was always a bad time for her to talk to people, but her rules indicated that she should never say that. Instead, she kept to her usual pattern of avoided answering the question altogether.

"Why are you calling me?"

"I've been thinking about you since we met."

He hadn't. When Aida was twelve, a little boy had told her that she was pretty, and she'd thought that might be true. For two days, she had believed that it was real and asked her mother to help her with her hair every day, brushed forty times on each side. It wasn't until a pep-rally two weeks later when he claimed ignorance of her that Aida had realized she'd been lied to. Oh, her mother swore she was pretty every day for two months afterward because she cried every single day.

That became the first rule that Aida created for herself: don't believe people who say nice things. Most of the other rules were donated by her mother.

Jordan was an extremist, a man who believed in his cause so fervently that other humans had become expendable. He was a criminal, which made him interesting. But he was also a person, so any nice thing he had to say to her was probably a lie. She wouldn't argue with him about that, though. There never was any point.

"Why?"

"Why have you been searching for me on the virtual web?"

And there was that. Of course, Jordan knew about that. Aida would have known if she were him.

"Not the same."

"That's fair; it's not. I have a proposition for you, Goddess of Worlds. That job you did in Gqeberha was impressive."

It was worse than she thought.

"I don't do that anymore."

"I know you're clean. If the answer is no, I won't bother you anymore."

"No."

"But I haven't even asked the question yet."

"Fine. Ask the question."

"I need to disappear."

In an earlier life, Aida had hacked into global government organizations, banks, and military bases. It had been interesting - so she had done it, and so far hadn't been caught by anything but rumors. Network protocols and the interconnections called to her. Aida could still feel the tug to explore the plethora of patterns that formed and evaporated every day as endless signals were born, aged, and died in a silence that only she seemed to observe. Interactions were endless and ethereal, all layered on top of basic communication rules. She knew those rules and how to use them. Of course she could make him disappear. But should she? She wondered why he couldn't do that job himself. He'd tracked her down quickly enough.

As she pondered all of the reasons why helping him would be a horrible idea and would likely end in catastrophe, she heard her voice as though someone else worked her mouth.

"I'm listening."

And she knew that conversation would change her future forever.

3

The Lost Soul

Friday, January 18, 2256

Lothania, Deseret, Mijloc

Lincoln Montague shoved the door to the family farmhouse open wide, happy to have an evening free of band practice. Marching contest lingered just around the corner, and her free time dwindled as a result. The favored winner was expected to be Lyra Craevis, a bustling metropolis several orders of magnitude larger than their sleepy little town. Lothania stayed competitive though, even if only in their marching band. The football team of Lothania high school remained an embarrassment, and the games offered no wins all season, and only provided a delivery vehicle for the halftime show. She hummed along to the classical opera music that had been streaming nonstop in Sarah's family car on their ride home, so much that she didn't notice the quiet until she finished a line of melody in the pause before the next. Then she noticed.

An oppressive silence seeped out from the rooms of the normally bustling farmhouse. Her father wouldn't be there, of course. His car was gone and he often worked late in the city. Friday traffic was the worst out of Lyra Craevis. She didn't expect him home for at least another half-hour. The silence she felt was the absence of her mother's endless rattling of dishes or cleaning or some other chore. The only sounds she could hear were that of her own breath and the incessant creaking of the hardwood floor beneath her feet. Dropping the white and orange bag in her just inside the foyer, Lincoln noticed the overturned chair first, then the shadow beside it, and oblong shape with strange extrusions jutting out at the edges. The shadow rotated slowly against the floorboards and her eyes rose up to see what cast it. Shoes, an obscene green that bordered on vomit-colored, hovered in the air inches from her face. They spun slowly, caught in a glacial revolution that took them half a turn one way, then nearly as far the other.

It took her a moment to connect the disjointed shoes to the shadow and then to the decorative exposed rafters over the foyer where she stood. Even when she made out her mother's outline against the dim light piercing the windows, she still didn't believe for five seconds, and her mind rationalized that her mother only played on the rafters the way that Lincoln had done as a child. She recalled climbing and sprinting around the home, and using her father's old ladder to mount the rafters until she was tall enough to jump up and grab them herself. Then she used to swing down and land in a super-hero pose on the floor, but her mother didn't dismount.

Lincoln finally dropped her dance bag to the floor and sprinted over to her mother. She grasped the woman's calves and shoved up as hard as she could, trying to loosen the rope that suspended her - rope and not fingertips - from the rafter above. At first, it seemed to slacken, until her mother's knees buckled. Lincoln fell, losing her grip, and she met the floor with her chin, crying out, but there was no response to her pain. Sucking in a deep lung of air, she screamed for her absent father through a mouth bloodied by the collision. Reigning in the panic and pushing down her feelings, Lincoln did the only other thing that came to her frazzled mind and called the emergency line.

"What is your emergency?"

Lincoln screamed between sobs.

"My mother - somebody killed her. I need help."

"Lincoln, is that you? What do you mean somebody killed her?"

"Send someone to the farmhouse. I can't get her down."

Lincoln disconnected the call and hurled herself toward the kitchen. She returned with a giant carving knife, and lunged up to catch the rafter with her left hand, but as she reached back to swipe at the rope her fingertips slipped and she found herself careening backward toward the ground. A moment later, her chest heaved as she tried to suck in the wind that had been knocked from her body, twisting on the floor, bleeding and crying and screaming. Again and again she tried, failing with the same result. She wasn't strong enough to control the blade and hold herself to the exposed board. Lincoln changed tactics, and grabbed her mother's spinning body across the thighs and then hoisted her up again, holding her as long as she can, and then falling. Over and over she did tried, only stopping when the paramedics arrived and forced her to let go.

Dropping into a heap of tears, she lay alone on the floor while they cut her mother down and carted her away. By the time her father arrived, the only occupants remaining were her and Sheriff Albert Grisham, sitting in the living room in the unnatural silence.

At first, the sheriff opened an investigation and called in witnesses all around the town. Having been the only death within city limits in the town's entire history, the event became the central point of gossip for everyone. It flared up like a lit match to fresh gasoline at first, and for several months Lincoln's dazed presence at school was followed relentlessly by whispers and hidden glances. But it didn't take long for the town to move on. In fact, rumors about the town's next new resident replaced the news of her mother's death so quickly Lincoln wasn't even certain that a story of the incident made it into the newspaper. Open and shut, Sheriff Al said, a clear-cut suicide. Her mother had been unhappy, according to his investigation. She buried her mother and her father at the same time: her mother in the ground, and her father in the bottle.

Then, suddenly nobody had time to talk to her about it. She was told, not in words but in shrugs and derisive glances followed by wide berths on the Main Street sidewalk, to get over it. Life goes on.

But not hers. And two years later, her life still hadn't progressed past that fateful day.

Friday, November 12, 2258

Lothania, Deseret - Mijloc

Lincoln studied her mother's death, pulling at the edges of her memories and tugging any exposed threads she could find. She examined the clippings on her evidence board. A green shoe stared at her, pinned next to a photograph of those bulging, bloodshot eyes that always made her cringe. But she always looked. Something on that board was a clue that would tell Lincoln who had stolen her mother away. But still groggy from waking, her mind could only stumble through the possibilities and she couldn't consolidate her sporadic thoughts into a single useful idea. The dark gray chair in which she sat swallowed her up. In an echo of a memory, she remembered her mother's light, airy laughter and the way it used to fill the house.

She refused to be defeated.

Lincoln stretched her sore back, stood from the tiny writing desk that doubled as her investigative lab and sighed loudly. The change in perspective brokered no new information. If she was candid, there hadn't been anything new in nearly six months. There *couldn't* be new evidence because she'd alienated most of her friends and nobody wanted to talk about her dead mother anymore. Lincoln even hated her own myopic obsession.

Not bothering to shower, she slid out of her pajamas and pulled on a wool sweater and some blue jeans. She added thick socks and duck boots in case she wanted to cross the creek to see the only friend she had left. Sufficiently bundled, she poked her head through her door and surveyed the area. It was far too easy to run into her father in the tiny farmhouse. After determining his absence, she cut across the living room as quickly as she could and made her way out through the front door, stumbling over the first brick in the entryway and colliding with the moist earth face-first. The ground tasted like iron and clay and she spit out a mouthful of muddy saliva. As she pulled herself to her feet, she saw something shiny glint beside the gray-silver sedan which hadn't moved in weeks. She pulled herself to her feet and walked toward the object. The sandy dirt reflected brightly as the silicon crystals in the sand reflected the sunlight, each crystal shimmering like a tiny star. There, embedded in the crusty dirt, lay the source of the persistent gleaming. The thin sand partially concealed an earring shaped like a lotus flower.

Tire tracks led to the spot where it lay, were worn by sand and time. She'd never seen that style of earring before, but she could still could hear her mother's voice explaining the meaning of the lotus flower.

"Stability and enlightenment, and the true nature of beauty," her mother had told her, brushing her ten-year-old hair behind her ear and smiling down. "The flower grows up from the mud in the bottom of lakes and streams. It forges itself into a beautiful blossom, despite its humble origins."

Lincoln retrieved a sandwich bag from inside of the house, careful to check for her father who meandered the halls like a zombie. A tear rolled down her left cheek as she sealed the earring away and placed it into her front pocket. She pulled her jacket tightly closed and began a brisk walk to help organize the disconnected thoughts in her mind. Evidence or coincidence, she now had something new to obsess over.

"Lincoln?"

She took another step. Her foot slid a centimeter into the sand before she realized that someone called out to her. Turning toward the sound, she saw Sarah Douglas climb up from the bed of Althaus Creek, smiling. Lincoln smiled back as best she could, happy enough to have the company and a conspirator with whom to examine her findings.

"Hi, Sarah!"

In Sarah's presence, Lincoln always felt plain. It didn't help that Lincoln's inherited heterochromatic eyes from her mother - one green and one blue - jarred people when they first saw her. Unlike her mother's slim triangular face and sandy-brown hair, which made the eyes a beauty accent, Lincoln had her father's round face, which made her seem to squint when she focused on anything and those eyes brought attention right to that. Her reddish-brown hair frizzed up with any humidity of greater than one percentage point. Sarah was from a magazine, with her full lips and square, inquisitive features. Blue eyes and blond hair combined with impeccable clothing that only the Douglases could afford to create the town's Aphrodite.

Even in the stony, narrow creek-bed, Sarah walked with the confidence of a model.

"You're up early," Lincoln said.

"I wanted to catch you before everything starts moving. Walk with me?"

Despite her desire to blurt out the details of her new discovery, Lincoln respected the unusual subdued tone of Sarah's words and followed her towards a hidden animal trail tucked behind some short bushes nearby. She followed Sarah's head and ducked past a low oak branch near the path entrance. Once clear, the trail opened up into a thin dirt road, littered with the debris of storms past.

"I've been doing a lot of thinking," Sarah began. The words immediately forced Lincoln's mind back over the years that she'd known Sarah, picking at the possible ways she may have mis-stepped. To reinforce her burgeoning insecurity, Sarah's smile slowly morphed, forcing her thick lips into a single thin line. Lincoln watched as Sarah inhaled, avoiding eye contact, then exhaled deeply with resignation. Lincoln shifted her weight from her left foot to her right and studied Sarah's body movements for clues about her future.

"Are you okay?"

"Yeah, this is just harder than I thought."

Lincoln's heart thrust, forcing its momentum into her unwilling body and sending involuntary shivers through her tensed muscles.

"Are you going somewhere?" she asked, shocking herself with the idea which until that moment hadn't been a possibility. Sarah's lingering silence gave the idea substance. Of course *Sarah* would leave. It was a crime to keep someone like her from the world, cooped up in this tiny town delivering the gift of her beauty to unwilling patrons. Lincoln's teeth dug into her bottom lip until she winced.

"Nothing like that. I'm trying to..."

"You're going to Lyra Craevis to finish your degree, aren't you?" Lincoln decided and turned her face away from Sarah to hide the tears she felt collecting already in her eyes.

"Stop. I'm just trying to ask you out."

"Out? Like on a date?"

Lincoln had never considered Sarah a potential romantic partner. Attractive, smart, and funny, Sarah came with undying loyalty to her friends and unrelenting hostility toward those who hurt them. She also exuded femininity in a way that rendered her invisible to Lincoln's typical heterosexual attraction. Besides, Lincoln had a murder to solve. She tried to say no, but each time she opened her mouth to speak the words seemed wrong, and the longer Lincoln didn't answer, the more severe Sarah's continence became until she morphed into a statue carved from granite.

Lincoln's mind stopped. The energy sapped from her body, and tears clouded her vision. It was unfair, *completely* unfair, that Sarah would ask her such a thing. Instead of a offering response, Lincoln turned away and focused on the woods ahead, staring in silence as the wind caressed the leaves and seeped unwelcome into her clothes.

"That's okay. I'm sorry I asked. I don't know what I was thinking."

Lincoln stared furiously at the woods in front of her, unable to understand how Sarah thought it was a good idea to ask her that question. Now. When her mother's death still permeated the air around them.

"Um...okay, no problem," Sarah said, not waiting for a response. "I have to get back."

Lincoln's anger turned to guilt over the new pain she

caused. She turned to ask Sarah to stop, but the girl had already turned away and made her way back up the path toward the creek that separated their family properties. Lincoln didn't pursue, not knowing what to say, even though she knew that she should say *something*. What remained of her energy disappear and she sat down on a nearby log, alone among the insect sounds, which slowly recovered from the silence of her presence. The forest loomed around her like a grotesque, misshapen animal that had swallowed her up completely. She slid off of the log to the ground, then lay her head back, ignoring the pain of the scratches that ran down her back as she leaned into the thick bark of the forest's insides. Wanting just a few minutes of peace, Lincoln closed her eyes.

4

Building Mijloc

Friday, October 6, 2237

Seattle, Washington - Earth

Aida's heart maintained a slow, steady rhythm that other people took for granted in their perpetual ignorance of the glaring interruptions life hoisted upon them. In the darkness of the private changing chamber she felt safe, cocooned in a dim light and a silence that locked the rest of the world out. She smoothed her hair back with her left hand, pulled a helmet over her head with her right, and fastened into place the sleek purple head-gear that was aesthetically more appropriate for riding a hover bike than engaging in a haptic experience. The last component of her work uniform in place, she sighed as she considered that now, she had to thrust herself back out into the chaos. Aida quickly wiped down every surface she could reach with a moist towelette. 1.8 c.f.u. of bacteria no matter how many times those surfaces were wiped. It would be closer to 6 c.f.u. in the corners where nobody bothered to inspect. She tossed her used napkin into the tiny round trash bin and slid her hand over the black glass front of her locker to tell it to latch. Her pulse already pounded in her ears, but she exited the room anyway, senses back on full alert as she anticipated all of the people she would crash into during the short jaunt from the privacy of the changing room and the virtual reality work station.

The air in the private dock smelled like old sweat, a consequences of an endless parade of workers using the room to port into the virtual world of Mijloc. The odor didn't bother her as much as the knowledge that it wasn't really *sweat* she smelled, but bacteria in the sweat, breeding, eating. Every day she had to talk herself down from running away screaming, with the knowledge that she would forget all about it when she immersed into Mijloc and the mixtures of odors from the sealed chamber began to simulate the virtual world, overpowering the stench. She slipped the visor down over her eyes. As she connected to her corporate network, the first step in accessing Mijloc, an alert flashed bright green across the bottom of her visual display.

She wasn't expecting any messages. Ever.

Aida examined the light with curiosity, then decided to ignore it, which given her hyper-awareness, there was a good fifty-percent chance that she probably couldn't. As she navigated the interface to enter into the Mijoc, the message indicator flashed again and she realized that ignoring it wasn't actually a possibility. She selected the message with her eye movements and brought it forward. The subject of the message read "Thank You", and attached to it was a tiny file that her system seemed to think was a Ceta program, the language at the heart of virtual world creation. Everything virtual was based on Ceta...including viruses.

She quarantined the file and began a suite of virus checks

against it on top of whatever corporate had done to it in its journey to her inbox.

Habits.

The scans verified the file to be virus-free with a tiny bell ring, but just to be sure, she flicked the bytes as hex up into her visor display for visual inspection. Hundreds of lines of code floated in the air before her head. Her mind compiled the code into images as the building blocks stacked on top of each other. Green here, a seed there, and a growth distribution function way over there. Flowers. Specifically giant flowers that looked and spread like dandelions. Western Salsify, the perfect addition for the mid-western twenty-first-century town she created in Mijloc.

Her stomach churned as the meaning of the email congealed.

The inner workings of Mijloc were trade secrets, and nobody had access to them who wasn't a direct Paivana Thoughtforms Employee. Aida dropped out of the code and examined the message metadata again. In the sender field there were only two initials - JH. She felt her pulse quicken and perspiration gathered under her helmet. Jordan Helm. He was too much of an unknown - those flowers could be a gesture of amiability ...or a thinly veiled threat. But she was at least satisfied that they weren't a virus.

Her mind skipped forward. Those types of flowers would be perfect for an empty lot next to an abandoned mission in her town. With a quick flip of her wrist, Aida saved the file to the transient storage that would be with her when she crossed over into virtual reality. She planned to have nearly fifty of the plant, and spread with the wind into other lots. It would be interesting to see how they distributed throughout the world. The gift was both thoughtful and perfect, but considering that she hadn't told Jordan what it was that she worked on at Paivana, it felt like as much a threat as an expression of kindness.

Not trusting people who were friendly, after all, was a rule. And Jordan had been *very* friendly.

She shifted her focus to world-building. Designing worlds was comfortable and exciting, and it required enough concentration that she didn't get bored. Hundreds and sometimes thousands of variables vied for control. With development spread over multiple software tools, all of which were accessible only through the virtual reality interface, Aida spent most of her day in a haptic suit. Unlike the world in Event Horizon, this virtual world adhered to precise parameters given to her from project officers. When people were finally available to populate the area, they needed to believe that the world was real. That was core to the Paivana Thoughtforms mission.

When she'd started the month before, she had been placed on a wide flat plane devoid of color. No walls, and no horizon line, only her avatar, a scanned three-dimensional version of herself, existed in the bland void. She couldn't resist a minor hack to tweak her hair color, adding a bit of green, but otherwise she followed corporate rules.

Back then, she'd created the tiny bed and breakfast first, a lone building in the middle of an empty field. Other creators were dots in the far distance. Allegedly they were her partners or accomplices in building the massive new world. Still, she'd never actually met any of them, and very quickly she'd surpassed all of them in capability. Now, they were mainly inconveniences.

Bodhi Rawls had named the world Mijloc before the first building went into it, because of its multiple meanings which intersected to mean 'wealthy middle way".

She knew from onboarding that the world was a hail-mary by Paivana Thoughtforms to expand into the commercial sector from the government contracts. Though global arrangements were steady income for a company that ran the first virtual prison, Inferiere, the market was so small that the price negotiations had always been one-sided. Mijloc would be the second certified global world in existence and an alternative source of income for the company. People who couldn't afford sub-models, or bodies within which they could transfer their consciousnesses, still craved immortality, and Mijloc would bring it to them. Eternity to the masses by way of creating a virtual world.

Paivana Thoughtforms and Jordan Helm could have been natural allies. Jordan hated the sub-model cloning industry, and Paivana competed with them indirectly, or if rumors were true, more directly than any other company in existence.

The town had grown since then. She'd created a bed and breakfast and added a lake, a community building near what should have been city center, and a Sheriff's office. The latter two she put close enough together so that the Sheriff could attend community meetings with minimal inconvenience. She placed cars into the streets, some older ones, and some newer, but all consistent with the late 21st century. Her favorite was a bright yellow sports car with tailfins and thick tires. Some day, she would find the right owner for this object of her affection, which brought a smile to her face whenever she saw it. Sometimes, in her seclusion, she loaded into it for a ride across the open, nothing plane.

The town wasn't enough of a distraction to keep Jordan from her mind, though. As confusing and potentially threatening as the gift he'd given was, it would still save her nearly a week of development and trial-and-error. That was the only reason why, during her lunch break, she accepted another call from an undetermined caller through her animus module. As soon as she accepted the invitation, Aida found herself in a room seated at a small table. Jordan sat across from her, looking as he had when she'd seen him on her planet.

The animus module had sensed that she was in a haptic suit and used that knowledge to spin up the room. Based on the granularity, she had some theories on network speed - private network with end-to-end encryption. The background was choppy, but she saw him in exquisite detail, complete with chiseled jawline and the nonchalant flop of wiry purple hair across his forehead. Perfect teeth too - so perfect that they made her want to smile just because he did. She had the good sense not to though. He was still not to be trusted, even more so after the flowers. Besides, it was a rule.

"Why are you calling me at work?"

"Have you decided whether or not to help me?" His tone seemed flustered but his smile never wavered. She wondered how much of his avatar was a patch to conceal his true emotions.

"It depends. You have other people I'm sure who would do this for you. Why me?"

"From what I understand," he replied, "you're the best. I've been asking around for months. Your name keeps coming up."

She didn't believe that. Years had passed since she'd worked helping SNO operatives disappear to start new, less-exciting lives as the Siblings of the Natural Order faded from prominence. She was the best, or at least one of the best, at manipulating the various virtual worlds in which she had a presence. She knew that empirically – it was part of why she'd gotten her job.

"Does the fact that I'm retired come up?"

"Yes, all the time. But I ignore the bit about retirement," Jordan replied, his grin cracking open a bit wider.

"Maybe you should pay more attention."

"I don't have that luxury. I'm nearly twenty-two, and I don't want to spend the rest of eternity in Inferiere. Can you help me or not?"

She detected a trace of irritation in his voice and thought that it was okay because she was irritated as well. Better that it made him less nice, which made her trust him a bit more. Still, she felt herself regretting ever answering the call.

"Maybe," she offered, still undecided. If she stalled enough, she thought, perhaps Jordan would go away.

"I need this by next Wednesday if you're going to do it."

"Why Wednesday?"

His image began to break up then. His movements became jerky, and his face blurred over with static.

"Nothing. I need it then. Will you help?"

She was just about to change her maybe to no when his face disappeared, and the room began to shiver as though it were developing hypothermia. Warnings went off in her mind as she considered the possibility that someone might have been eavesdropping on the conversation. Monitoring privately networked calls was challenging to do, but the right government agency could. The telltale signs were all there, from the choppiness to the latency and intruding static. But those could also have been signs of a bad connection too. Don't take unnecessary risks - also a rule. She willed herself out of the virtual meeting and talked herself down from removing the haptic suit altogether and calling it an early day. Mijloc work had to be done, and it wasn't as though she'd said yes, or even had information on Jordan Helm that anyone else didn't have.

She was bulletproof if anyone asked, so she had to ask herself why she was nervous. The answer came as she began another round of plantings, this time wild onions. Her fears were about him. She liked him, much to her dismay, and that was something that irritated her more than the fact that he thought himself important enough to interrupt her workday. But along with the fear was a touch of hostility, which she'd traced to something he'd said. The next Wednesday was just over a week away, and that wasn't enough time. If she was going to help him, she would have to start that evening and put her virtual world on hold. The storm still raged, and if she ignored that to deal with him, she might risk the lives of her humans. Another generation had begun already, and although they nodded and smiled at her amiably when she told them about clothes in their emergent language, nobody had so far donned any. They still fornicated like rodents.

She decided not to help him. Something was happening in a week, and whatever it was, it spelled trouble for him, and probably for her, if she got involved. Wednesday couldn't be arbitrary. That was a rule - there is no such thing as coincidence. She decided that she wouldn't accept his calls any longer, and let the whole thing go.

For the remainder of the day, Aida received no more calls from Jordan. She wasn't entirely sure how firm her no was, so it was better not to test it. Something about him made her feel tingly and warm, and like she could trust him despite the rules, which was a thought that caused her heart to race and her eyes to go wide. *That* was losing control involuntarily. Weakness.

The day came to a slow close after several more grueling hours of wondering what next Wednesday truly held in-store while trying to get her locality configurations right. Finishing her least productive day in months, she gave up and stripped out of her suit, wrapping in a thin towel to cross the floor to the showers. There, she found a handful of others had beaten her there so she waited for a room to become available.

The office emptied of people while she waited, which suited her as it relieved her of the obligation to social niceties. Since she genuinely didn't like most people, so came into the office before anyone else and left after everyone else. Her *early day* was normal closing time for most other employees.

Whenever she did run into actual real-life humans, they asked the same questions.

"Hey, aren't you that girl who Bodhi hired from a run-in in Event Horizon?"

To *that* question, the answer was yes, and sometimes she would give them the response quickly and quietly and try to slip by. Inevitably they would then engage in small talk. This was a waste of her time and theirs because she loathed the waste of time and energy called actual conversations, especially in a world writhing with distraction. She would shut her eyes to diminish the noise sometimes, but her assailant wouldn't understand.

The fact that she struggled with a severe personality quirk wasn't nearly as widely known as her Paivana origin story, or even her rumored background as a gray-hat hacker. In virtual reality, she toned down the symptoms that had plagued her for a lifetime. She had no nervous tics in virtual life. Her avatar only occasionally stuttered, trying to come up with the right word sometimes. Her animus module corrected her language more quickly in virtual reality than in actual reality because the time synchronization was better tech-to-tech. And virtual worlds are quiet, so that helped her too. Even the busiest virtual worlds lacked the soundscape of real life due to the exponential cost in sound development. Frivolous things such as insects, unless central to the world ecosystem, were absent. For Aida, virtual life was real life, and her real-life was an uncomfortable prison that she had to suffer through.

The rules helped some. Her devoted mother had turned every point of confusion in her life into rules that she could follow. If she followed the rules, usually everything in her life continued to work as expected. She got up in the morning, came home in the afternoon, and played Event Horizon until sleep. Some rules were more comfortable to follow than others. Like, let people talk was a simple rule to follow, as it required only being quiet. She rarely followed the rule that 'you should make eye contact when talking to someone' because it was challenging. When she did it, she was so focused on her eyes that she often forgot what it was that was being discussed.

These were the things she thought about as she walked carefully through the hallways of the modern office. Only a single robot tried to greet her, but she didn't have to worry about responding to it.

She had timed her journey home right. Her roommates surrounded the dinner table and predictably extended her an invitation, which she declined with a forced smile and a wave before climbing the stairs to the master bedroom she occupied at the very top. Then, a few minutes later, she was back into her haptic suit and plugged into Event Horizon. The storm was still where she'd left it – and four days had passed so nearly a lifetime for her humans. She soared above the storm high in the atmosphere, staring down into its eye. Then, on a whim, she let herself fall toward its center. The wind swung her around in wider and wilder arcs until it threw her miles across the gray sky like a jet piercing into the clouds. With all of the force of gravity, she plowed into the surface of the earth, carving out a rocky pit with her body. She stood and dusted off her faux-clothing without a single scratch, only meters away from the entrance to the cave in which the humans had taken up residence.

Something caught her attention. By the entrance sat the little round spacecraft that had first brought Jordan Helm into her world. He walked around with her humans and communicated with them even though they only spoke a language that had evolved with them. Three of the women donned woven skirts, and the men wore sock-like woven bags covering their genitals strapped to their midsections with strings. There were no new children, so it seemed that they'd slowed their fornicating enough actually to have some future as a society. Her heart jumped at the possibility that the civilization may last after all. Though she'd created many worlds, she had previously had to invite and allow other actual humans to populate them. This time, though, Libera Goddess of Worlds created the world as a whole and its life from bytecode. She'd genuinely earned her goddess title.

Jordan waved, and not thinking, and she waved back at him before traversing across the wet sand. The question about helping or not helping didn't enter her mind. Instead, she immediately went to work beside him, without looking at him once but helping her people learn to fashion more complicated clothes and tools. As she did, she couldn't help smiling, and the two of them stayed working side-by-side for so long that Aida realized that she'd entirely forgotten about eating. He finally tried to engage in conversation.

"I love your world. I promise I'm not stalking you," Jordan told her, "it's just, you're building a civilization on the same planet with a massive storm on one side. How cool is this?"

She couldn't tell whether he was authentic – she didn't have the cognitive tools. He had a massive grin across his face, but she couldn't tell if 'it made it to his eyes,' as many books had described to her that real smiles did. He didn't have to be very good to trick her, she knew, because others' mannerisms were something she struggled with even in virtual reality. For her, every interaction was a coin flip. She decided to accept that he was truthful this time, despite violating her rules.

"It's amazing," she responded, "this is my first real god-world."

"You should see mine sometime. It's a train wreck. Have you ever seen that dystopian holovid Hostile Intentions a few years back? It was kind of like that."

She hadn't seen the movie but had heard of it. She remembered something about cannibalism and people skinning each other, so the holovid hadn't topped her list of experiences to which to subject herself. That, and as a source of entertainment, holovids paled in comparison to world creation and design.

"Sounds bad," she agreed. It was essential to be polite - that's a rule.

"It was. But in fairness, I was running from three countries at the time while building it. That was just after Bentley."

Bentley had been a sub-model cloning facility. It "had been" because Jordan had destroyed it with a bomb.

"After you blew up Bentley?" she accused without emotion, and without looking at him still.

"What? No, I didn't blow that place up. That exploded because one of the cloning tanks ruptured and spilled noxious chemicals into the heating system."

"I remember the headlines. You were there protesting, and it exploded. People from your faction even went on the news to take credit for it."

"Yeah, that was an opportunity we couldn't let go. Fear is a great motivator. But truth be told, we didn't blow up anything. It fell in our laps."

He smiled at her again, and she believed him a little bit more, knowing the entire time that it was dumb to listen to the criminal denying his crimes. The smile could have meant anything.

"Is that why you want to disappear?"

He didn't answer, but the smile faded. He stared in the direction of the storm.

"Life is about to get very hard for me," was his only response.

They passed the time watching the sunset she'd manufactured in the sky, side by side in the wet sand. She had grown comfortable with Jordan. The way he'd helped to take care of her humans mattered to her and made him more relevant in her eyes. He may have known that and may have been trying to gain her confidence, but she'd never know for sure. Don't trust nice people. That was the rule. But she didn't have to trust him to enjoy the companionship that his strangely calming presence brought. She lay her head on his shoulder as the sky turned pink and orange from the storm's atmospheric disturbance.

"I'll help," she told him. She thought she felt him swallow, and was sure that she felt his shoulder relax slightly as soon as the words left her mouth. He seemed friendly and familiar now, and he smelled like Sandalwood.

5

The Gift of Speech

Tuesday, October 9, 2237

Seattle, Washington - Earth

When she had first created her humans, Aida had intended to teach them English. However, it had taken them so long to learn just how to put clothes on their bodies that she found she didn't have the time to spend on the intricacies of speech, though the game had such rules to allow them learning. For most of their existence, they communicated with grunts and hand gestures. After work one day, she realized that some of their grunts had begun to repeat and sounded very much like actual words. A gangling man with a limp made a sound that seemed like 'catwoo', while pointing to the ocean behind her. There, among the waves, she made out the dorsal fin of some sea creature.

"Catwoo," she told him, nodding to let him know that she understood, realizing that she hadn't kept close enough track of the animals evolving in her oceans and any sorts of creatures may lurk beneath its surface. She pondered momentarily how much the storm would influence their evolution.

"Hi," came Jordan's voice from the mouth of the cave.

She looked up to see his thick beard and animated features coming into the light from the darkness. Jordan was stalking her. He showed up far too often. Jordan might have set up some alert she didn't know about that let him know when she was there. Sometimes he was there already when she arrived, such as when she had come across him building a canoe with the tribe. She ignored him, instead focusing on the one major thing she wanted to do today - name her planet. Now that she knew it was stable and wouldn't self-destruct, the time had come to christen it.

"Oduduwa," she said, without hesitation or explanation. The African creator god, Oduduwa had taken advantage of his drunken brother's absence to create a world that he could enjoy. To her Pangea continent she gave the name Obatala, Oduduwa's drunken brother, and the people she chose to call the Obatali.

"I love the names," he Jordan said. "What are they for?"

The question sent shivers up her spine. Jordan kept insisting on conversation as though it wasn't enough that she'd already committed to his escape kit. She didn't answer, directing her attention instead to one of her Obatali close by.

"Ktalo," he said, marking their hundredth word.

"Shark," she replied Jordan, explaining the term before she realized she did it. "Can you b-believe how quickly they're l-learning?"

She clamped her mouth shut, embarrassed to have stumbled over the words. Sometimes the haptic settings that preempted her stutters struggled if her emotions rose too quickly. She became too excited about every new word that the Obatali added to their lexicon, the suit had difficulty keeping up with her rapid emotion spikes. Jordan seemed not to notice as she watched him through the corner of her eye.

"It is amazing," he assured her, and took her hand, sending alarm signals cascading up her wrist and kick-starting her heart. "Building this world with you is amazing. The people you've created are perfect, Aida."

He stared at her eyes. He couldn't stare into her eye because she skillfully dodged him. Then she remembered a rule that she'd forgotten. People like to make eye contact when they talk. The haptic gloves and embedded nanites created the sensation of pressure, sweat, and heat where their hands touched. She turned her eyes toward his slowly, cautiously, and then saw his clearly for the first time. She smiled at him while she gazed into his green eyes and wondered if they were his real eye color. Hers were natural, though she sometimes corrected her heterochromia, depending on how sensitive she felt about it.

"You're perfect, Aida," he continued, never breaking her gaze. She blushed as he said it, and her avatar blushed too. She didn't know everything about Jordan, she understood, but she believed his feelings toward her. No, she chose to think that his feelings were real and that she had better than a fifty-percent chance of being right. The way he'd helped bring the Obatali, her children, out of the cave, and helped train them, he was a patient and thoughtful man. The stalking was a bit of a problem, but nothing about what she witnessed in him told her that he was a man who was capable of blowing up a cloning facility. When she looked at him, she found that she believed that it had been an opportunistic move to claim credit for the explosion, as ill-conceived as it was.

"Are you okay?" he asked, staring at her. She felt her anxiety spiking again and knew that her haptic suit worked hard to keep all of her symptoms hidden from him. She fought the urge to avert her gaze as a knot of tension in the back of her head grew larger by the second, expanding into her prefrontal cortex. Part of her wanted to share with Jordan that she wasn't quite normal and that her accomplishments had been attributable in part to that fact. Part of her believed that he probably already knew more about her than she could divulge.

"I-I'm f-fine," she struggled to say as her anxiety continued to climb. The world seemed too bright as the sunlight on the Obatala-side of Oduduwa pierced her eyes. She felt the sand against her skin, millions of tiny particles bouncing off, and some working their way into her loose-fitting woven dress, a gift from the Obatali. Sea-spray at her back, slapped against her exposed skin between the shoulder straps. It was all too much. She felt her eyes tearing up as she looked at him and realized that he didn't believe her.

"I have trouble with overstimulation," she told him. "Being with you … or anybody… i-is extremely hard for me."

"I wouldn't have known."

"I compensate with my suit and avatar mods."

"But you don't seem that bad."

She didn't respond to that. It was the same response as always. Everyone with whom she'd ever disclosed her personality problems told her the same thing. It was as though they suddenly became experts in her condition, and there was a required set of behaviors that she wasn't properly displaying. Soon, Jordan would likely ask her to turn off the padding to see what she was really like, turning her into a zoo animal. Never mind that Aida had already designed who she felt she was really like in Event Horizon. From that point forward, he would probably start looking at her funny, trying to guess when she had her out-of-control moments. It was an exhausting pattern she'd experienced her entire life.

"I'm sorry, I don't mean it that way. I meant you are so

amazing; it seems impossible that there's anything like that wrong with you."

"The suit compensates."

"No, you don't understand me. Look at you. You've created this entire world, and you're famous in the Event Horizon. I mean, you're Libera Goddess of Worlds. During the day, you're working on Mijloc..."

He continued, but she stopped listening. He knew. He knew the name of the project she worked on and had just confirmed it.

"Stop Jordan."

"...amazing, wonderful... what?"

"We have to talk."

She pulled her hand from his and stepped back, maintaining eye contact, as tricky as it was. It was a rule.

"How do you know about Mijloc?"

"Really? I thought it was obvious I knew when I sent flowers. It's not exactly a secret that you work for Paivana Thoughtforms. Nor is it a secret that they're building Mijloc. And.. I mean, look around you. What else would you be doing?"

It didn't explain how he knew the type of world Mijloc would be, but a Ceta plant program? Thinking about it the way that he explained, it could have been a good guess. She couldn't prove otherwise, so she moved on.

"This whole disappearing thing. Why? What are you planning?"

"Nothing, Aida. I'm not planning anything. It's just time to leave Jordan Helm behind so I can have a life. I'm just so tired of fighting, you know?"

"You know who my friends are, right?" She didn't wait for him to confirm. Of course he did - he'd been stalking her. "The people who help me say you're planning something big."

"Really? Like what?" he asked her, smiling with his eyes and slightly curving up the corners of his lips.

"You tell me."

"I can't just yet, Aida. But I will, I promise. I just need a little more time."

He grabbed her hand back and pulled her to him. To her surprise, she let him do it. She felt her body press into his chest as he squeezed her in. Suffocating, Aida turned her head away, facing the ocean. Every second that she spent trapped between his arms she fought the urge to pull herself away. Her heart pounded against the inside of her chest and her breath worked hard to keep up. Aida couldn't separate her fear from her longing, and stood statuesque in his embrace.

"Aida," he told her, "I want you to be part of everything I do. You are such an amazing woman. I promise I'll tell you, just not yet, okay?"

His beautiful eyes matched the green-blue of the sky as he moved his face closer to hers. He tilted his head sideways for what might have been a kiss, she supposed, except that nobody ever kissed her. Not a real person anyway. She felt his lips against hers and let herself fall into it as her body and mind conspired to betray her. They breathed together as their lips joined more and more firmly, and something new took over. The embedded nanites and synchronized cognitive experience of her animus module went to work. She felt his tongue probe at the entrance of her lips. They stood in their unplanned embrace, with the ocean waves pounding behind them until Aida realized the Obatali had gathered into a rough circle around them. The crowd emanated noises that she considered jeers or laughter - she wasn't sure yet about some of their sounds. Jordan would tell her, eventually, what it was that he was planning. In the meantime, she had this. The red pushed back from her mind as Jordan's presence filled its void. She pulled away from him slowly, saddened to feel his body warmth experience degrading from her haptic suit, and his lips disappearing away from hers.

"I love you," he told her.

She left the game.

Aida pulled her helmet off too quickly and scratched herself across the forehead. There was no blood, which she confirmed by touching her haptic glove to the spot and then rubbing her fingers together, testing the texture. The lights remained off so that she couldn't see anything. She tossed her helmet to the floor and breathed in apartment air, taking a lungful of the oxygen-nitrogen mix that could only occur in real life and never in the filtration of her full-immersion suit.

Her hands shook. Aida's body trembled as the thought of Jordan poked at her around the edges. She didn't want his attention. Nobody had ever loved Aida except her mother, but even she had disappeared when Aida was too young to understand why. Aida assumed that her mother must still love her, wherever she'd gone. But this man, this stranger, could not possibly love her. He was lying, as she should have known the moment he was kind to her. Because kind people can't be trusted.

Even if she wanted to love, she didn't know if she could. As she turned the idea over, she tugged at the edges. He lied to her. He stalked her. Of the few guidelines her mother had given, Aida had no rules about love. Her mother hadn't expected that to come up, she supposed. Aida definitely hadn't expected such a thing.

Aida removed the suit and dropped it into the cleaning box. Her skin felt slick and hot, where Jordan had touched her. The warmth of the apartment chilled her skin as the sweat evaporated.

She walked into the bathroom and looked at herself in the mirror. One blue and one green eye stared out from beneath her sandy brown hair. Those eyes were genuinely happy. Her smile reflected at her, and she wondered why he wouldn't love her.

Nice people were not to be trusted. It was a rule.

The voice of reason penetrated her mind as it always did and shattered the illusion. She felt angry adrenaline spread like buckshot through her body. Her teeth chattered against one another as she flashed through ways that she could get rid of the man. As her eyes squinted and channeled her hostility, somewhere deep inside was a tiny whisper that maybe he wasn't so bad. After all, if she wanted to find out what he was hiding, all she had to do was allow herself to search for the answer.

After her shower, Aida reclined in her floating chair as she often did, only instead of reading a book. She closed her eyes and dialed out with a thought to connect with someone she hadn't heard from in years.

"Who is this?"

"Emily, it's me."

"Libera? It's been a damn long time. How are you?"

"O-okay," she stuttered, anxious about what she was about to ask.

"You don't sound okay, girl. You sound like shit."

"I-I'm f-fine, really," she spluttered, fighting through her impulse to not speak.

"What's the matter?"

"D-do you have time for a private conversation?"

Her stuttering worsened.

"Okay."

A second later, she was in her private virtual meeting room, a copy of a planet from the timeless classic The Little Prince, complete with a single red rose under a dome of glass. A larger woman stood near, dressed an iron-meshed tunic in a domed helmet and a brass breastplate. Emily Jensen straddled the rose on firm, thick legs, and usually seemed as though she were ready to punch somebody in the face. From beneath the helmet flowed her long thick dreadlocks, each nearly the thickness of a sapling. Pudgy cheekbones pushed out fleshly beneath the metal helm.

"Wow, you are a mess, aren't you? How can I help?"

"I-I don't know," she said, now herself without her haptic suit support, so her mannerisms were prominent. The one saving grace was that her animus module didn't allow her avatar to go wild-eyed, but her rocking was prominent. She hated the physiological responses that manifested around anything in which she invested her emotions. The more important to her something was, the more her symptoms spread like the lingering aroma of rotting flesh from an amorphophallus bloom. Like the flower, she became a pretty, flawed thing.

"Tell me, who's bothering you. We'll solve the problem."

"It's not that," she said, the words becoming more manageable now. "D-Do you know Jordan Helm?"

"I know *of* Jordan. You know better than to ask those questions."

"Sorry, I-I'm rusty."

"What about him?"

"I think that he's planning something, and I want to know what."

"You want me to spy on that crackpot?"

"He's not a crackpot, Emily."

The words leaped from her mouth uncontrolled, and she realized that she was defending the very man she was in the process of asking Emily to investigate. That was not a good sign. Her emotions had no link to reality since she couldn't read people well. Her mind based her feelings on wrong information. Her heart was no less vulnerable than anyone else's, despite her physiological shortcomings. It was making the wrong decision.

"You know he blew up that cloning factory, right? That's crackpot behavior."

"He said he didn't do it on purpose."

She slapped her hand across her mouth. She couldn't defend him, because that meant that the answer to her question, the one she was still in the process of asking, might not matter anyway.

"You *are* out of practice. What do you mean, 'he said'? Did he do something to you?"

"No. Just... I need to know."

"Why?"

"I'm not *that* out of practice, Emily. My business, but don't worry. I can pay."

"I don't want your money and don't need your secret. Just remember, you were my friend first. If he messes with you, tell me, okay?"

Emily wasn't large in real life. Aida had met her once, ages ago. The woman was one of only a handful of people that made it past Aida's trust barrier. Emily was a skinny little girl with dark-brown, almost black, skin - skin so black that her smile was like the sun shining in a night sky. She'd hacked her animus module when she was twelve to build the stocky warrior princess that she presented as in private chats. That sort of tampering with the animus module was risky, and hacking her own was unheard of, but Emily had done it. She was like Aida in her understanding of the underlying technology.

Emily had her following of warrior princess admirers. Very much interested in self-promotion, Emily maintained an avatar clothing line and trademarked everything aspect of her look. In truth, the clothing line was more a way to clean the money she got from for-hire animus module hacks than an actual enterprise, though she did have some innovative fashions for anyone pursuing the warrior-princess look. It was because of Emily that Aida's darting eye movements didn't manifest in private chats. Emily had done that voluntarily for her after meeting in person and understanding from that interaction how bad Aida's symptoms could get. Aida remembered the overwhelming cacophony of sounds at the coffee shop, which had caused her to turn away at the entrance and almost miss the meeting altogether. Emily had run out after her and waited with her as Aida worked through the overstimulation. After the fit passed and the duo were safely secluded from additional stimulus in a nearby park, Aida learned that Emily wanted help tracking down and harassing an abusive ex-boyfriend. Aida had, of course, done that for free.

Their call ended the same way it always did, with the huge warrior princess picking up Aida in a bear hug and nearly crushing her avatar. Then, Aida was in the silence of her room again, with the ambient lighting at fifty percent. She picked up *Celestial Bodies Connecting*, which she still hadn't finished, and turned to the second chapter when she felt the buzzing of an incoming animus call.

"Libera," an encoded voice said when she answered. "We're ready. We'll leave a package on Azeroth near the blue dragon. Do you have our payment?"

"Sent. Pick up on Hyboria."

The voice belonged to a representative to Siblings of the Natural Order. The group hacked for hire, precisely the sort of firepower Aida needed to make someone disappear since she wasn't technically in the business anymore. The 'package' was Jordan's escape kit, which would, when triggered, initiate the slow destruction of any Jordan Helm references in the virtual web. It didn't have to be Jordan. Anyone who executed the kit would disappear, which meant that she could always find a buyer if Jordan turned out to be planning something she couldn't stomach. Other than the questionable legality of the industry, escape kits were decent investments.

For now, Aida would leave the package in place on Azeroth, because it was one of her worlds anyway, and she knew what kind of security she'd created there. Whether she relinquished the box to Jordan or not, she determined, would largely depend on what Emily discovered. Trust was good, but when dealing with people like Jordan Helm, trust wasn't the best approach to survival.

6

Spurned Love

Friday, November 12, 2258

Lothania, Deseret - Mijloc

For several minutes, Lincoln sat motionless against the half-decayed log, long enough for a trail of ants found their way onto her back, foraging for new food. One of them bit into her neck, soon destroyed by an instinctual slap of her hand. Other stings followed in a unified response as what she now understood were fire ants attacked from where they'd breached her clothing, a handful on her shoulders and pinching sensations along her lower back. Lincoln dragged herself to her feet and wipe the insects away, shaking her entire body while flapping the bottom of her sweater to expunge the more enterprising ones exploring her clothing. Still dazed by Sarah's rapid departure, Lincoln half-stumbled and half-walked her way back to her house, fighting back tears. She slammed the bedroom door shut behind her, and let herself fall to her bed as the stress of the morning pressed down on her.

Two long, lonely days passed before she thought of the earring again. Instead, she obsessed over the silence of her mobile phone. Lincoln battled internally over whether or not she should call. Would Sarah even answer? If Sarah did answer, what should Lincoln say? It was Sarah who unfairly toppled the balance between them, and now, Lincoln couldn't decide whether she wanted to recover their friendship or try to build a romantic relationship from its ashes. Whatever the future, their old connection died with Sarah's question.

Bereft of answers, Lincoln searched for some other distraction, and the earring screamed for her attention. It fit somehow. If Lincoln could prove that the earring mattered, that would be something worthwhile. The sherriff might help. He'd stopped returning her calls ages ago, but he was still polite enough whenever they met, and she felt sure that he would at least talk to her. Sheriff Al had done so before. In the weeks just following her mother's death, he had even assigned men to look into a few of her suspicions. She'd found a footprint by the back door that she hadn't recognized. The impression belonged to a paramedic who snuck a cigarette after securing the body into the ambulance. Regardless of the result, she'd never forgotten that the Sheriff had taken her seriously, and she saw in his eyes then that he wanted her to be right.

Lincoln parked at the free lot near the Sheriff's office just after mid-day. She'd timed her arrival for when he returned from lunch, hopefully in a good mood. The air had a chill in it, and the leaves on the poplar trees which graced each side of the entrance were bright orange and red. The wind blew in short bursts as she approached the glass door with his name and title displayed prominently across the front. The giant sticker letters looked like they hadn't changed since the late

2230s, except maybe to fade a little.

He sat behind his desk, finishing up a hamburger and dripping mustard onto his desk. Lincoln crossed the open office floor over linoleum tiles as cautiously as though she traversed a worn rope bridge. When he smiled that warm smile he sometimes got after a good sandwich, she took the seat next to his desk.

"Ms. Montague," he greeted her, in his slightly patronizing way, "how may I help you?"

"I found more evidence."

His smile faltered, and as effortless as it had seemed just seconds before, suddenly appeared to take a great deal of work for him to maintain. Lincoln didn't hesitate to drop the sandwich bag containing the earring on the table in front of him.

"That's an earring. And judging by the design, probably your mother's. What does that have to do with her closed case?"

"It's not hers. I have all of hers, every single one. This one I haven't seen before. It belongs to someone else."

The swish of the door brush against the linoleum floor caught Lincoln's attention, and the bench by the door creaked as someone sat upon it.

"Could belong to anyone," he told her as his attention shifted from her to whoever had entered. Lincoln turned around on the plastic seat as best she could, and felt flush as she recognized the woman who had entered. Bright blue eyes and golden hair framed a smile flush with straight, white teeth. She regained her composure and quickly flashed a smile of her own.

"Lincoln!" the woman said, "I didn't know you were here. How are you, dear?"

"Fine, Katy, just trying to convince the Sheriff to re-open my mother's case."

"Same as usual, then? I hope you find what you're looking for," Katy said, and then scrunched her eyes up as they fell on the plastic bag.

"Is that what will do it?"

"It's an earring. Lotus flower – do you know whose it is?"

Something flashed across Katy's face as she stared at the contents in the plastic bag, or so Lincoln thought. It could have been that Katy recognized it, but Lincoln guessed the look had more to do with Sarah.

"Listen, dear," she said, "Sarah told me about the other morning. She finally worked up the courage to tell you how she feels. Did you know she'd been practicing all summer?"

"I'm sorry?"

Lincoln felt her legs begin to weaken, and her heart thumping loudly in her chest.

"Are you sure that this thing you're doing is worth losing her?"

"I don't want to talk about that here, Katy. You can understand?"

"Sure, dear, I'm just saying that perhaps you should consider her feelings."

Lincoln could feel her cheeks flush with a mixture of anger and embarrassment. She grabbed the bag from the table and stood up abruptly. Anger flowed through her veins like scalding lava, leaving behind the red flush of shame as it exploded from her heart to her skin.

"I'm sure Katy has more important things to talk about than my mother's murder," she scolded, and exited the office without waiting for Sheriff Al's response.

"Thank you, dear."

Lincoln heard Katy say something else, but she was through the door and out on the sidewalk by that point. Directly in front of her, seated in the passenger's seat of the Douglas' truck, sat Sarah, staring straight at her. Lincoln turned quickly to the right and headed down the street toward the free lot where she'd parked, thinking that she might spend some time in the city center shops. Now, as she felt the heat growing around her ears, she wanted to go home. She made her way toward the free lot, trying to ignore the prickly feeling in her neck telling her that Sarah's eyes never left her.

In truth, there was nothing about Sarah that she didn't like. Lincoln had never been herself attracted to women, but had she been, Sarah was the best human being Lincoln ever known, hands down. Loyal to a fault, gorgeous, but not arrogant, and confident about everything in her life, Sarah was precisely the antithesis of Lincoln, who ran hot and cold by the second. Until that morning, they had complemented each other perfectly. Not one of the available men in town could hold a candle to her dedication. In fact, had it been any other day, Lincoln would have called Sarah complain about her bitchy mother's overuse of the word 'dear.' Lincoln visualized a mental image of her and Sarah laughing together. Instead of decompressing from the stressful encounter, Laura now stomped across the sidewalk, poisoned by Katy's words. The lot approached rapidly, and Lincoln fished her keys from her pocket, only to have them slide to the ground by her car's front passenger door.

That was the last embarrassment she could take. Her resolve melted as the keys bounced and jangled against the pavement, and tears rushed to her eyes as she bent down to pick them up as casually as she could. If she kept her back to where she'd parked the truck, then at least Sarah wouldn't see her crying. She struggled to reach the keys through tears when she saw that they lay just beneath the front tire, about where she had found the earring in relation to the car, back on the farm. That sparked a thought that the earring may have fallen out of the automobile. She opened the door and slid into the driver's seat. Then, she leaned her head back in part to regain her composure, unsure that the embarrassment had passed yet. She attempted to visualize the automobiles that were there when she had arrived home from school that day. She didn't remember seeing any cars when she got home. Was it possible the earring had belonged to her mother after all?

No. Lincoln wouldn't admit that. The earring was essential to discovering the cause of her mother's death.

Thinking further, her father was off running errands at the time. Her mother's car wasn't there either because it was in the auto shop behind the school. Her mother had dropped the car off that morning, and it was going to take a couple of days to get back. The mechanic? He was a single man named Keven Wright who had opened the shop a few years prior. The Sheriff had already investigated him. It turned out that he'd returned to the shop in time to work on a couple of additional cars that day. Besides that, the earring wasn't the type he would have worn in his single pierced ear.

She struggled to remember. Wake and all, there had been hundreds of people on the property. Since her mother's death, there had been even more. Maybe it wasn't a lead at all. She bristled at that because she had nothing else. A voice broke through her thoughts.

"Do you have a problem with me?" Sarah asked through her open window.

"What do you mean?"

"You walked right past me and didn't even stop. I've followed you for like a block, and you didn't turn around. Are you avoiding me now?"

"I'm not avoiding you, Sarah," she said, "I just wasn't ready."

"Ready for what? It's still me, Lincoln. Remember, Sarah? Your friend for your whole life? I took a chance and knew it would be weird, but you're not even trying."

"It's not you, Sarah. I'm not even sure how I feel about what you said. It's just, my mother..."

"It's always your mother, Linc. She's dead. I love you, and I'm alive and right here. I've always been here."

Lincoln gasped and rolled the window up hastily, blocking out any more of Sarah's words. Every single day, Lincoln woke up feeling the hole in her life that her mother had once filled. Every. Single. Day. She went to bed most nights feeling the same emptiness that kept her at arms distance from her birth community. It was as though Lincoln lived in a completely separate universe, a universe that stopped all movement when her mother died. *Her* universe had killed itself, and all that she had left was the decreasing expulsion of heat as all motion slowly came to a stop. And Sarah, of all people, knew that and knew how hard it was some days for Lincoln to get out of bed.

"Bitch," she muttered.

Lincoln revved the engine once to warn Sarah to back up, because even if Sarah had hurt her, Lincoln still didn't want to run over her feet. Lincoln was fucking thoughtful that way. She shifted into gear and backed the sedan out of the parking spot, close enough to scare Sarah but not to hit her. Then she drove, but only for a block before pulling into a back alley and placing the car into park. Her hands shook. She was in no condition to drive, and she knew it.

Trapped in the automobile, Lincoln bit back her tears, unsure if they were tears of rage or anguish. She wouldn't let them fall. She gritted her teeth tightly and breathed in and out through her clenched jaw. For a moment, she believed that the building anger would overwhelm her and force loose the tears that she resisted shedding. But as she sat, she thought about the earring, and how much closer she might be to finding her mother's killer. Sarah or no Sarah, she had a new lead. This knowledge lifted her anxiety and pulled her spirits up enough so that she no longer had to worry about crying. However, she was still too flustered to drive.

Perhaps she was right the first time about Katy's reaction. The woman was a gifted actress. Perhaps the earring belonged to her, and she'd recognized it. That would explain the excessive cruelty with which she'd treated Lincoln. Then again, Katy never needed a reason to be cruel. Lincoln remembered her first sleepover at Sarah's. Katy, so desperate for attention, had tried to coax them into a party game involving positioning themselves on a plastic sheet with markings for where each hand or foot would go. All Lincoln and Sarah had wanted to do was lay in bed and gossip together. At first, they complied out of politeness, though both had been miserable. Sarah eventually saved the evening by pulling Lincoln upstairs to her bedroom, locking the door behind them.

Lincoln didn't want to think about what it would mean if the earring was Katy's. She wasn't sure what it would mean above the fact that her father may have been with Katy that day or someday after. Lincoln couldn't remember seeing another set of tire tracks she didn't recognize that day, though. Too much time had passed for Lincoln to be sure of anything, anymore. The idea wouldn't quit, though.

She would have to get into the Douglas' bed and breakfast to search for the other earring. That meant talking to Sarah, who she'd just called a bitch, and nearly ran over with her car. It would take some doing to get through the door now.

Her mobile phone rang in her pocket, interrupting her thoughts.

"Lincoln," came a man's voice on the other side, "there's something you should know."

"Who is this?"

"Has it been that long? Sheesh, I guess so."

"Scot Beck?"

She got a mental flash of his bright yellow sports car with two black stripes down the center over the hood and extending to the tail fins. He loved that car.

"Are you still investigating?"

"I am," she said and tried to settle her breathing.

"You know how I'm friends with David McGinnis? We were talking about - well, I don't remember. There may have been drinking involved. Anyway, he said that there was a note."

"David the a paramedic?"

"Yes, that's him. He said it wasn't for your father or you. He said your mother addressed it to someone named Jordan Helm. They kept it in evidence without opening it. He said that they were going to open it if the coroner said somebody committed a crime, but he said it was - oh, I'm sorry - I'm insensitive."

"No, continue...please – I'm sure I've heard it all before."

"Coroner said it was suicide. So the note stayed in evidence. Lincoln, it may still be there."

7

Worlds

Monday, November 15, 2258

Lyra Craevis, Deseret - Mijloc

Bodhi Rawls, owner and founder of Paivana Thoughtforms and the first virtual prison the world had ever seen, squinted through the reflective sheen of his office window overlooking the city. Blinding sunlight bounced off of people picnicking on the rooftops of the lower buildings while the interspersed high-rises casted shadows down toward the streets below, offering pockets of darkness nearing pitch black. From his perch, Bodhi could make out the streams of models flowing through the sidewalks and streets in pursuit of their daily errands. This perspective, staring down at the humdrum of everyday existence, brought him a sense of peace - an ease shattered by someone pressing the buzzer on his office door, demanding entrance. The door buzzed once again and then popped open.

"Things are going well," his mother's voice assured. He turned to see her dark-black hair tinted with brown laying over her tan shoulders. Her piercing hazel eyes captured his attention.

"Hi Harper," he said, trying to remember when it had been that he'd changed calling her mother to calling her by her first name. He guessed it was about the time that she had finally decided to move into Mijloc full-time.

"The developers think it's possible," she continued. "Look."

With that, a white panel materialized before her holding the embedded image, and he saw what she was talking about. On the display, he saw a fetus and the digital projection below read "3 mo".

"Is this happening in here?"

"Only in a lab so far, but it's definitely happening. Torrent says that the digital model is so close to reality that with the five-hundred attempts, forty of them are showing birth defects from heart valve problems to brain development issues."

His eyebrows shot up into concern, which she immediately picked up on.

"That's *good*, Bodhi. That means that we have the algorithm right. None of those defects will actually manifest into births."

The sparkle in her eyes made his heart float. It had been decades since he'd seen that level of determination and ambition in her face. And if he was honest, there was a lot to celebrate in the success she reported. Scattered throughout Mijloc's million residents were somewhere around thirty thousand who had transitioned to Mijloc in their primes, as he had, without ever having conceived a child.

"All five-hundred pods were successful?"

"Every single one. It worked exactly as we expected."

"Are we finished?"

The program wasn't cheap, and there were other things to spend money on, like the intensive certification process it would take to assure any children born in Mijloc would also be recognized to trade off-world.

"Not yet, Bodhi. This is only part of it. What about the *pregnancy*?"

"Why would anyone *want* to be pregnant?"

"You died too young. Many people don't just want a child - they want to feel the child growing and connect during the prenatal experience. They want to feel the child kick and share that experience with their partner."

He wasn't buying it.

"Nobody wants morning sickness."

"Some people do. Even the pain of childbirth is something that some of us would want to have gone through at least once in their lives."

He sighed and cracked his neck, satisfied with the loud popping noise that erupted from his non-existent vertebrae. It was a nice touch.

"Okay, so more to do," he acquiesced as she nodded vehemently.

"Yes, more to do," she said. "Torrent and I are working night and day on it. We activated the sleep hack to do it."

"Torrent is in here full time?"

Being the CEO of both Paivana Thoughtforms in-world and Paivana Thoughtforms off-world took so much of his time that he found that he missed out when keeping tabs on his friends - or in this case, his father. The look she gave him though told him that this wasn't the first time they'd had the conversation.

"He has been since August."

Of course he had. But not once had Bodhi been to see him, or had Torrent come to see Bodhi. His mother seemed to pick up on his discomfort.

"He tried to visit you about a month ago, but you were in off-world conferences all week. Then we got bogged down with the last phase of this experiment. I'm sure he'll be to see you soon."

Maybe. There weren't guarantees with Torrent, especially when he was working on a project, which seemed to be his perpetual state. Bodhi had inherited that quality, and between the two of them and their respective obsessions, neither had made time for the other in years.

"It's not important."

"Come for dinner. Torrent's coming over tonight and Kelleigh and Cliodhna are bringing some food from the deli and Ordell and Monica are coming. It'll be nice to get everyone together again."

"Cliodhna?"

"You don't listen do you? That's from Torrent. Cliodhna is Kelleigh's new partner."

"What happened to Chibundu?"

Harper shook her head.

"Break-up. Chibundu kept trying to make Kelleigh quit the shop. Eight o'clock tonight at my home. Do you at least remember how to get there?"

"Autonav."

"But you should remember these things. What if autonav stops working sometime? Then you'll be lost and alone out here."

He smiled at that response, getting a glimpse of the woman whose anxiety had molded the first fifteen years of his life.

"If autonav fails in-world, then we'll have a lot larger problem than me getting to your house."

"Take Main out of town, then turn into the Claymont subdivision. Three streets in, turn left and my house is the first one on the right."

"I'll be there."

By the time he arrived at his mother's home, there was nowhere left to park. Kelleigh's hot-pink two-seated Chramer Eagle, the only one of its kind in Mijloc, sat next to the steps leading up to the door. Bodhi and Ordell had worked hard to surprise her with that particular present the year she turned eighteen. Beside that sat the precursor to Ordell's favorite volantrae in the form of a wide-fronted 2164 Falcon, red with black stripes down the front of it. Monica's motorcycle leaned casually on its spokes behind the automobile, a vehicle she loved with the same intensity with which Ordell loved his Falcon. Bodhi could already imagine the lengthy conversation that resulted in them taking their separate cars instead of riding together in Ordell's. Torrent's car, a very practical but ostentatiously colored lime-green sedan, took up what was left of the wide driveway.

Dropping his own wayward automobile on the curb beneath the wide leaves of an oak tree, Bodhi slid the keys into his pocket and made his way across the yard. He looked at the automobiles one at a time, recalling the moment each owner joined him in Mijloc. He made his way through the thickening evening air, pregnant with dew drops ready to be released. Bodhi listened for a second to the noise on the other side of the door before letting himself in. Aiden's weak laughter filled the air until a coughing fit took over and a moment later, when it quieted, there was nothing but silence until Bodhi made out his mother's voice followed by an uncomfortable laugh that trickled through the group.

Bodhi knew that type of laugh. It was the same laugh he'd given his mother before she finally made the decision to come into Mijloc for good. The physical body's limitations follow people into Mijloc when visiting, limited by the haptic gear's slow throughput and expensive translation into avatar motions. Her wheelchair-confined legs didn't work right in-world back then. Even when she could get around okay, she had often been so winded that simple in-world tasks were too difficult, like simply traversing a room. Aiden was getting close to that, but he had refused to admit that his eighty-year-old body was beginning to fail him.

Taking a breath, Bodhi pushed his way through the door, cognizant that as he did so, the voices fell off. Harper practically ran across the room to help him out of his coat, assistance which he shrugged off as he pulled his arms through his sleeves, thinking how ridiculous it was that he wore a coat at all. But he had done that for a reason. Each person in Mijloc could have been a temperature of their own choosing. It wouldn't have been hard to give each person that level of control over their own immediate environment. Maybe some day, he would start adding conveniences like that, but the important thing for those waking into Mijloc was the willing suspension of disbelief. At least at first exposure, it had to be as real as possible.

"Come in, have a seat. This is..." Aiden took a breath mid-sentence and looked as though he might cough again before Kelleigh interrupted him and took over.

"This is broiled pheasant and chickpeas," she said. "That's greens." She motioned to a pot with steam lifting off, then continued. "I think your mother wanted you to sit over there."

It was the only empty seat left, so Bodhi guessed that was probably true, a guess supported by his mother's hand in his back pushing him toward it.

"I'm so glad you came," she told him as he took his seat. "It's not the same without you here."

Smiling faces all looked up at him, expectant faces that

waited on him to say something, though he wasn't certain what. Then Monica broke the silence.

"When are you going to find a life partner?"

He felt the blood flush into his cheeks and lowered himself into the seat as the the bitter smell of collard greens invaded his nostrils. Without answering, he scooped some onto a heaping pile on his plate, placed it before his seat, and then ducked his body down as though he used it for shelter from Monica's scrutiny, eliciting laughter from the group.

"Leave him alone," Aiden said in his frail voice. "Without him, you'd all be dead now."

This statement wiped the grin from Monica's face, and Bodhi felt compelled to answer her question now that Aiden had injected more tension into the atmosphere. Ignoring Aiden, and wishing he would finally decide to give up on Earth so that the could get past his physical and growing mental limitations, which would be more expensive to fix than if he came in defect-free, Bodhi chimed in with an answer and a smile.

"I'm too busy for that," he commented. "Besides, I would feel really strange trying to forge a romantic relationship here when I created this world. It would be unfair pressure on whoever I tried to date."

"Please," said Kelleigh, grinning at him. "You know better than that. Everyone loves you here. There's got to be *someone* out of the entire population of Mijloc who strikes your fancy?"

"Strikes my fancy? What a peculiar phrase."

"She's been reading a lot," chimed in a voice from a girl who Bodhi didn't recognize, but who he could tell from the way her gaze never left Kelleigh, even when addressing the rest of the group, who she had come with.

"Cliodhna? It's a pleasure to meet you," he said as he scooped out some of the chickpeas onto his plate, and nodding at her.

"Likewise, Bodhi," she answered, breaking her gaze for long enough to make eye contact before shifting back to Kelleigh again. He forced his shoulders to relax.

"My name is on the contracts. Every single one has my digital signature on it. It would be inappropriate for me to pursue a romantic interest in anyone here."

"And his heart was tragically broken by Ms. Christine Barnett," Kelleigh summarized his story to Cliodhna, whose eyes took on that glassy look that comes with unwelcome pity. "How many years ago was that?"

"Only about fifty. It hasn't been long enough yet."

Bodhi smiled at his mother's response. She didn't look a single day over thirty years, but this conversation had been going for at least that long.

"It's not Christine," he protested. "It wouldn't be appropriate. And can you imagine the scandal out there?"

"Is this a real world, or isn't it?"

She didn't let up.

"Officially recognized as of this year. Trade is open."

"And you are the president and CEO of Paivana Thoughtforms in Mijloc and Earth?"

"So far, yes. They haven't asked me to stop doing either. That may just be because they haven't gotten that far yet."

"Did anyone hear about the situation in Lothania?" Ordell chimed in, breaking up the scrutiny and Bodhi shot him a look of thanks. Lothania was about thirty minutes away by highway, the small town that Aida Lothian had created before her tragic accident.

"What situation?" Harper turned her attention to Ordell, and Kelleigh did too. Aiden kept his focus on Bodhi, but Bodhi couldn't be sure that he actually saw him or knew that he stared.

"Do you remember when that poor woman killed herself

all those years ago?"

Bodhi's lips creased into a tight line. He remembered, and he would always remember the first and only in-world death. Before that happened, he hadn't realized it was even possible for someone to die in-world.

"Her daughter is convinced that it was murder."

"Murder?" Bodhi asked. "Was she brought in-world as an infant?" Sometimes people that young had problems believing that it really was impossible, practically impossible, to kill in Mijloc. Ordell shrugged.

"I just learned about it in the paper today."

"They do things a bit differently there than we do here in the city. They don't tell their children the truth about their world at first," Harper said.

"Why?"

Harper shook her head. Bodhi's head still spun around the notion that someone had died in Mijloc. Inferiere, maybe. But Mijloc wasn't designed that way.

"Should I get involved?"

"No," his mother. "They're not doing anything wrong and they'll have to tell her the truth sooner or later."

"When did this happen?"

"Two years ago," Aiden said, breaking his long silence with a voice that seemed like it might disappear before the words were all clear of his mouth. "The woman who died was Aida Montague, husband Niles, daughter's name Lincoln. Lincoln and her father -"

He took a deep labored breath.

"Lincoln and her father live in a farmhouse on the edge of town. We accessed the woman's animus module and tried to save it, but it couldn't be recovered, and we couldn't find it to send it to tech services."

"You couldn't find the bay?"

"The bay was empty. It was the strangest thing, looked like

the it had never been used."

Aiden stopped and wiped his head, where perspiration had begun to accumulate from the effort of talking.

After dinner, Bodhi took the short drive to his understated single-family home on the opposite side of Lyra Craevis. His mind didn't stop when his head hit the pillow, but still digested the idea of the girl, stranded alone in Lothania, not having other relatives or anyone who might help her. It was a situation he hadn't planned for, making death nearly impossible as they had.

He considered how the death may have happened. There were ways to overload the animus module using software, of course, but it wasn't possible from in-world. Having been the initial creator of the in-world interface, he mulled over the potentiality of doing something like that, and decided that it would have to have been a software glitch or something beyond the bounds of Mijloc.

But how, then, had someone initiated it? Off-world communications were only allowed through specific communication rooms within Paivana Thoughtforms Headquarters. This lock-down had come after his falling out with Christine illustrated to him the dangers of allowing on-demand point-to-point cross-world communication. Instead, at least for the early days, he'd commissioned the creation of various points from which communication could originate, and these he'd buried within the massive Paivana Thoughtforms complex.

There were too many questions to which he didn't know the answers. Bodhi closed his eyes but sleep wouldn't come. A death in the system, and it had never been brought to his attention. His guess was that it had occurred just after the split between the in-world and off-world Paivana Corporate Entities. With all of the work going into that, and little fallout from the death, it was possible that he was overworked at the time and lost track. But even searching his animus module and its on-board eidetic memory didn't yield any information about Lincoln Montague - not even signing an entry form for her. It was as though she'd never existed, and yet she was busy disrupting life in the small town of Lothania.

Did it matter that an uncommon name like Aida was shared between the town's founder and the dead woman? He pondered that question for a long time, staring up into the darkness. His mind navigated back to the discovery of the young woman's body connected to life support. Was it possible that the biggest mistake of his life still haunted him all these years later?

8

Libera, Goddess of Worlds

Tuesday, November 16, 2258

Lothania, Deseret - Mijloc

Lincoln awoke in darkness, still seething at Sarah for minimizing her mother's death. Katy's added condescension evoked bitterness in the back of Lincoln's throat, and the events altogether had made for a miserable day with no investigative progress. Teeth clenched into a straight line, Lincoln glared at the ceiling and then at the table, seeing neither. Then her lips softened and her eyes sunk down to the carpet. Whether Lincoln was angry or not, Sarah wasn't the cause of the hostility raging in Lincoln's heart. Sara had only asked a simple question, and had even handled Lincoln's silence as gracefully as implied rejection could be handled. Lincoln's insides went cold when she thought about Sarah now, and her throat felt clogged, locking down all of the emotions that she couldn't name to tumble through her insides. Lincoln stared at the battery indicator on her mobile phone, watching the bars slowly tick down to nothing without any calls.

A naval star that had been converted into a wall clock told her that the night had progressed to only four in the morning. The peace of sleep was denied to her. With a sigh, she pulled herself from beneath her down comforter and slipped on practical brown slippers. She must have looked silly in them with silk shorts on and a thin cotton tank-top. Doubtless, anyone who had seen her would have laughed. Sarah would have positively rolled on the floor, making the dramatic most of the situation.

Lincoln took two deep breaths and blew out slowly and steadily.

Sarah's mother crept into Lincoln's mind like a brown recluse emerging from a wood pile. At first, Lincoln tried to dismiss the memory as a residue of the exchange from two days prior. She made another attempt at sleep which also failed. Then she finally re-examined her mental image of Katy Douglas, and something became startlingly clear. The woman, when she had switched to go on the verbal attack, had been staring at the earring. At the time, Lincoln had been so frustrated and self-conscious that she hadn't paid attention. She'd interpreted Katy's actions as being pure Katy and had waffled on the underlying motive. Lincoln looked back through her memory. She recalled that the woman's eyes hadn't left the earring once. She knew something about that piece of jewelry, Lincoln was confident, but Lincoln couldn't tell what the something was.

She went through the image once more, and then another time, looking for a moment, a second, that would reveal what Katy's involvement with the earring was. She played the scene over and over in her head. Katy had entered the building, taken her seat, and then had started chatting with

Lincoln casually. Then the conversation switched, and Katy had attacked Lincoln for her lack of reciprocation for Sarah.

If only the woman knew how much Lincoln needed Sarah in her life then that conversation wouldn't have happened. But of course, Katy would have found some other way to disapprove of Lincoln's personality. It was a pastime for the woman.

Lincoln re-focused on their exchange, and finally saw what she'd missed before. In the corner of her eye, she had seen the movement. As soon as she and Sheriff informed Katy of the earring, her left hand had sought her ear. The earring must have been one of Katy's, and she had known it. The fact that she had seen it and recognized it meant that if the mate of the earring still existed, it wouldn't for long. Lincoln would have to act now if she wanted any chance of seeing it.

Lincoln visualized Katy's jewelry box, something she'd seen many times over the years while playing with Sarah. When Sarah's mother entertained guests, the pair of them would often try out different items from it, from her pearls to her gold and silver chains. She smiled as that memory returned and then felt herself tearing up. Lincoln turned her head and swallowed, keeping the tears at bay for the moment. She struggled to focus on the box again - small and wooden, with carvings of angels along the sides, and sanded smooth to the touch.

Her mind turned to investigative mode, blocking her tears and guarding Lincoln against other unwelcome emotions. Instead, she worked on how to get to the box, now that she'd complicated her relationship with Sarah. Being warned, it wasn't very likely that Katy would let Lincoln through the door, and without Sarah as an excuse, Lincoln didn't have a way to argue that Katy should. A guest's presence might keep Katy occupied for most of the day and allow Lincoln to sneak in and have a look, if she could gain entrance and, of course, avoid Sarah. But after the night that Lincoln had, it seemed that if she ever wanted to sleep again, she would have to clear the air between the two of them and apologize anyway, and that might be enough to gain Sarah's assistance.

An unwelcome twist of pain slammed into Lincoln's gut and wrenched her sideways. Tamping down the feelings didn't work, and the overwhelming feeling was obvious in nature. She missed Sarah. She missed Sarah so much that it crippled her. The tears finally surfaced, easily overpowering Lincoln's will as she lay curled up on the bed. She couldn't help but picture Sarah's face, glowing with concern, and holding her as she had so many times when Lincoln had felt overwhelmed in the face of life. Hours they'd spent together in embrace after her mother's death, and the emotionally stunted Lincoln had even lashed out at Sarah in her pain. But now, Lincoln's pain was all about Sarah, and for one brief moment, a realization teased at her mind - that Sarah was already more than just a friend to her, but Lincoln had been too caught up in herself to understand. Her body heaved as she let the tears fall, stifling her cries as best she could into her pillow.

Three hours and no additional sleep later, Lincoln found herself parked in the tiny lot in front of Sarah's home. The lot was barely large enough for four cars, and the fourth automobile, which Lincoln's had the unfortunate pleasure of being, had to park at an incline that required a firm, functioning parking brake. She pulled up on the lever in the central console. Then she sat in the driveway, and slid her head down between her hands, resting it against the steering wheel. After several seconds of controlled breathing, Lincoln pulled her head back up, gathered her courage, and she stepped out of the vehicle. Then she stumbled to her knees on the steep incline. She didn't have far to fall since her parking angle ate up a lot of what otherwise would have been free-fall space for her. Lincoln scraped her knee on impact, splitting her pants and turning them red around the new wound.

Great.

She stood up slowly, checked for further damage, and then gingerly picked her way along the steep driveway toward the front door. There, just beyond the screen, she saw Sarah, stifling a laugh with the inner hardwood door ajar. All of the tension seemed to melt away at that moment, as Lincoln too felt herself begin to chuckle then laugh outright. Sarah pushed the door open, and Lincoln passed through the opening and wrapped herself in Sarah's arms. She squeezed as tightly as she could with her head nestled into Sarah's hair and whispered to her.

"I'm sorry. I've been a bitch to you. Can you forgive me?"

"I already have."

Lincoln pulled back a little from the embrace so that she could see Sarah's piercing blue eyes.

"I do want to try this with you. I don't know what I was thinking before."

Then Lincoln heard the water running in the kitchen. That had to have been Katy. Sarah was saying something back to her, but the sound of the water ate at Lincoln, distracting her from the conversation. If Katy was in the kitchen, then now was the time. She pondered whether to tell Sarah her intentions or not. Given what they'd been through, Sarah might misinterpret and assume that Lincoln only used her to access her mother's jewelry. Lincoln needed that access but needed Sarah too. She pulled in Sarah again to continue the hug. A moment later, her decision made, Lincoln asked to be excused.

"Bathroom," she said. "Sorry, I'll be right back."

Sarah nodded and let go of her body, allowing Lincoln to slip past and up the stairs towards Katy's room. The stairs stretched around as she followed them, and ended in the hallway at the top. On either side hung images of various founders of Lothania, starting with the earliest near the stairs to the most recent at the end by the bathroom and Katy's room. Lincoln followed the hallway in earnest. When she reached the end, she could have turned left to go into Katy's room and find the truth, or right and keep her word. With a brief sigh, she turned left and twisted the knob, hoping against hope that a locked door would turn her around. It swung quietly open.

The room smelled of must and fabric. Lincoln entered and pulled the door behind her, but didn't close it for fear of the sound attracting attention. She scanned the room for a sign of the jewelry box but didn't see it anywhere. Lincoln scrambled quickly to look under the bed, but it wasn't there either. What she did see was a pair of fuzzy handcuffs that had collected nearly an inch of dust. That was good gossip to share with Sarah if Lincoln ever told Sarah about this. She scooted herself back away from the bed with her hands and stood back up. Then Lincoln saw a writing desk against the wall, similar to her mother's. As she approached, she feared that the desk would be locked and thwart her. She opened the rolling top without resistance, and she breathed a sigh of relief.

Just in front of her sat the smooth lid of the ornately carved little jewelry box. She flipped the lid open and began rummaging through the various pieces of jewelry. When she came upon the pearl necklace that she and Sarah used to wear as children playing dress-up, she felt the smallest pang of guilt materialize in her gut but pressed forward in spite.

Then she saw it. Down near the box's bottom was a tiny lotus earring, just like the one she had in her pocket in a sandwich bag. She pulled it free and placed it naked into her other pocket. Then she saw something else beneath it. Just below, scrawled in her mother's handwriting, was a note labeled "To Jordan, My Love."

Reading that line was like a punch in the chest. She staggered backward and slammed down onto the musty blanket covering the bed. The obvious question was who was Jordan, and close behind that one was the question of whether the letter got her mother killed. But even here, with the potentially direct evidence, Lincoln couldn't imagine her mother cheating on her father. They were two halves to the same coin, as her mother had always said. This self-assurance made her feel better - enough better to raise to her feet again. She walked to the box and grabbed the letter to place it into her pocket too.

"Did you find what you were looking for?"

A voice penetrated her focus, and she turned to find Sarah standing in the doorway. Angry, hostile eyes had replaced her earlier happy and enthusiastic demeanor.

"I didn't want you to know..." Lincoln began, starting to explain that though she was in Katy's room, that Sarah was essential too. But then, would she have come to see Sarah if not for the earring. She slumped her shoulders and began to walk towards the door, not even bothering to finish.

"You could have talked to me about this. I would have looked for you, Lincoln."

Sarah's tears fell quickly now, and Lincoln wanted to hold her and to confess everything she'd ever done and tell her it would be okay. She tried to reach out for Sarah's hand as she neared, but Sarah pulled away through the doorway.

"I think you should leave."

As frustrated as she was, Lincoln nodded and decided that it was probably better to walk away than try to explain again.

"I meant what I said," she told Sarah as she passed, "about us. I do want to give us a try."

"I'm not sure I do anymore."

The words were the second shot to the chest that Lincoln had experienced in the last few minutes. As much as it hurt, she kept walking.

The drive back home passed in silence. When Lincoln arrived, she knew that her father was very likely awake and staggering through the house in his underwear since it was nearly eleven. Not didn't feel emotionally ready to cope with him, whatever stage of grief he had decided to wear for the day, Lincoln parked on a the driveway plywood and processed her feelings. She took the letter out and placed it on the dashboard in front of her. Lincoln felt the anguish of losing her best friend was over her like a scalding shower. No matter what she tried, the trajectory for the two of them had been off since Sarah had asked her to begin dating. She wanted that moment back, and she desperately wanted to say the right thing this time.

"Yes, a thousand times, yes. I absolutely would love to take this journey with you."

A thousand times, yes. Maudlin much?

In her mind, replaying the moment, that's what she said, though, like it or not. And after that in her imagination, the two were inseparable, just like before, only more so. Together they braved the rumors and judgmental stares of friends and family. She blinked back her sadness and focused instead on the letter.

"To Jordan, My Love," it read across the cover.

She burned to know its contents, but right now, if she took it and the earring back, would Sarah still be there?

"To Sarah, My Love," she thought as she imagined the letter a different way. Maybe Jordan was the love of her mother's life, and somehow years separated them. Given that context, and the pain she now felt, suicide seemed like less of a crime. Lincoln could let it be suicide if that were the case. She could drop the charade of investigating a murder, a willful self-delusion that she'd adopted so that she wouldn't have to hate the woman. There was no justification better than forbidden love.

It all rested on the contents of the letter in her hands, and who Jordan was. She wiped her eyes and peeled the envelope open, centimeter by centimeter, ripping as she went. Then she pulled out a folded piece of paper.

Jordan, my love,

I have treated you so unjustly, and I can't even explain to you how we ended up in such a mess together. You should know that we have a daughter. She's not a transplant, like the other children, but an offspring that you and I made together. She's real, and she's got the spirit you used to have. I carried her in my womb for us and brought her into this world. She's the first of her kind, Jordan. If you only knew her, you would be so proud of what she's become.

I have to leave. I can't tell you too much about it, and you wouldn't understand anyway the way you've become, but I can't help you from here.

I hope you never know the pain of sharing a bed with someone who doesn't love you. I hope that you never understand the feeling of unrequited love. I'm not angry. I broke you somewhere along the way, but I will love you always.

Your Wife,
  Aida Lothian Montague
  Libera, Goddess of Worlds

Goddess of Worlds. That was the strangest way Lincoln could ever imagine a letter ending, especially a suicide note. That's what this was, though, she was sure. And, in a way, she felt relieved that her mother had done it for love. If the letter was right, and Lincoln thought it had to be because when someone died, what was the point in lying any further, then

Niles wasn't even Lincoln's birth father. Somewhere, out there, in the world, existed a man named Jordan who, according to the letter, didn't know he had a daughter.

9

Betrayal

Wednesday, October 11, 2237

Seattle, Washington - Earth

Her humans had exploded in population and already had begun farming. Jordan's presence still set her teeth on edge, but she'd so far been able to talk herself down from the red. Aida only put in that much effort because Jordan's influence seemed to be improving her civilization. She'd come to realize that their latest advances weren't accidents. Jordan had been spending his time here teaching them to fish or helping them build simple tools. Once she'd calmed herself enough to focus, the pair worked side-by-side, her organizing the town leaders, and him playing with the children. Loud giggles and occasional screams of laughter erupted from the Jordan's group, tugging at her attention until she finally looked and saw him crawling on hands and knees with children hanging from his sides. They were failing to tickle him into submission. Then the serenity of the moment was crushed when Jordan finally shook free of the children and approached her, spiking her adrenaline.

"Any news on my escape kit?"

Aida hadn't expected him to ask. Now she realized that of course he would. Instead of offering a response, she posed a challenge.

"What happens after Friday?"

He only smiled. She hadn't expected an answer. Her calculated exchange was effective in limiting the conversation to only a few sentences.

Aida turned her attention back to the Obatali with whom she was attempting to form a council while working through their language barrier. The Obatali still spoke no English, and her use of their language, though expanding, was limited by the delay since her previous visit. During the week that she wasn't here, they'd gone through several generations and as many dialect changes.

Jordan closed the distance and touched her arm before she realized what he was doing. The skin-like material of the haptic suit amplified the pressure of his touch so that she could almost distinguish his fingerprints. Ripples of energy spread from the contact and throughout her body.

Aida pulled away from him by teetering backwards. Within the feathery pressure of his fingers lay an invitation that she almost missed, as red obscured her vision and mind. Almost too late, she returned to him, rotating in time to catch an offered kiss. Swept up by the sensations, Aida returned his kiss, pulling him tightly to him as they both descended into the warm sand.

The Obatali gathered, fascinated with the idea of their gods making love. Some lingered back, obligated to the priority of work to support their fledgling society, but others formed a large circle around the couple on the beach. Time slowed as the two grasped at each other, intertwined in the sand, while the ocean waves crashed behind them occasionally sending shivers of cold water against their naked skin.

Afterward, as Aida stuffed her haptic suit into the cleaner, every nerve ending on her body hummed with nervous energy. She felt the heat rise to her face, dissipate, then rise again. Jordan was the first real person that she'd ever been with. Her personality hang-ups became too intense far before the point of physical intimacy with anyone else.

It wasn't real.

All of the sensations were the results of nanites and wire mesh working together to convince her body that something intimate had occurred. As much as it meant to *Aida* to experience even that level of connection with another human being without being overpowered by her disorder, for all she knew others had such experiences multiple times a day. Besides, he only stuck around because he *needed* something from her. The thoughts refused to be placed aside as she ruminated over and reveled in the experience.

Her arms shook as she turned the shower knob, letting water fall into her hair. The slow drip of the water off of her took with it the lingering sensations of his touch as the heat seared her flesh, a welcome distraction from her obsessive mind. As she finished showering and stepped out into her main room, she felt a buzz in her animus module and recognized the a.p. as belonging to Emily.

Aida's heart dropped. Emily would only call if she had found out what Jordan was up to. Aida could leave the call unanswered. She was no longer certain she wanted to know, especially as the memory of her recent experience hovered just out of reach. She answered anyway - it was a rule.

"Girl, you have got to listen to this. I found out what your man is up to."

Emily's "you'd better sit down" tone was so crystal clear

that even Aida could understand what it meant.

"W-what d-did you f-find?"

Damned stutter.

"Trouble, Aida. Do you know that plant in New York? Emergent Biotechnology's flagship where the Briggs models are produced?"

She was familiar. The flagship was one of three in New York. Two of them had long since closed down after the Madison Rule was overturned. The Briggs factory had been converted to create sub-model clones, back-up bodies for immortals.

"Yes, I know it."

"It won't be around in two days."

"It's closing?" she asked.

"Closing? No, it's Jordan Helm-ing. Massive explosion. This one is in the middle of New York, and millions will likely die because of it. You're his escape plan."

His escape plan. She hadn't told Emily about the kit that she'd been working on, so for Emily to come to this conclusion was startling. The words echoed inside her brain and settled into the dark animal nether-regions of her consciousness. Hostility flared in her, and then grew into anxiety and fear, and finally into the persistent fight-or-flight that made her rock back and forth on her bed while her avatar rocked similarly in the meeting room.

She could hang up, and had it been anyone except Emily, she would have. But Emily knew what was happening in Aida's real life. The real life Aida had wild, wide eyes that struggled to focus, overlaying her virtual animus-constructed private chat room with artifacts from the master bedroom. Embedded halfway through Emily's leather-clad body was suspended a desk which had no business being there. But, Aida couldn't close her eyes any more than she could prevent the repetitive motion of her body, or pull her arms from around her legs.

"Are you okay girl?"

She struggled to say yes, but nothing came out except a guttural "yaaaaawwwwp". Her brain flashed red and her thinking had slowly diminished until she felt more feral than human. She wanted to scream, and so she did scream. Emily took her arm in the private room, but without the haptic suit, she couldn't feel the gesture, and so the motion did little to stave off her attack. Somewhere in the background she heard a banging on the door, and at first, she thought someone was knocking to enter the private chat, which was an impossibility. Then she realized that the screaming she had been doing was happening in the real world as well. With all of her remaining willpower, she slowed her rocking to a stop and managed to squeak out a word of comfort to whoever loomed outside of her bedroom door.

"I'm okay," she said. "J-just burned myself that's all."

True enough. The heat in her mind cooled slowly. She could finally see again as the animus module re-asserted itself over her vision causing the desk jutting from Emily's side to disappear from view. Aida breathed slow measured breaths as she attempted to pull her symptoms back under control.

"You're not okay, are you?" came Emily's voice, to which Aida simply shook her head rapidly.

"Do you want me to … stop him?"

"N-no. I can handle it."

"And you don't want me to do it for you? One-time offer?"

She didn't really know how she could possibly explain to Emily the ridiculous idea that Aida had become obsessed with the man, possibly even loved him. Emily had been a consistent and loyal part of her former life, a life during which Aida would have admired Jordan for his ideological purity, no matter that people would die. A former version of Aida wouldn't have cared about innocent people's lives being sacrificed in the battle of ideals. That version of her was gone though. Yet here she was, harboring lingering feelings toward a mass murderer, at worst, and a would-be mass murderer at best.

"I've got to go."

"I know girl. Let me know if I can help."

Aida opened her eyes to see the room before her, unchanged and unassuming. Millions of lives rested in the balance of whatever decision she might next make. Her apartment wasn't the apartment of someone who held so many peoples fates in her hands. Adorned with a plain wooden dresser, plastic chairs with floating cushions, and the single twin bed with a floating mattress, it hardly seemed like the home of a would-be savior.

Her animus module buzzed once more, and she accepted the offered private chat. Emily wasn't there, even though it was the same room they had shared before. On the table sat a piece of paper. Aida moved her body to get a closer look, and on it she saw the numbers 3:44:309:87:23:42:9983. She recognized it immediately as an a.p. address. If Emily left it for her, it could only mean one thing. The address had to be his. Now, she could contact him as easily as he contacted her. She grabbed at the paper using her animus module to direct her body movements, and as she touched the paper it dissolved into her mind. There was only one thing left to do. Aida dialed the emergency number for the New York Police Department - using audio-only this time.

"New York Police Department," the highly-administrative voice came over the audio.

"I need to report a crime,' she said.

"What crime?"

"The day after tomorrow in your city, a massive bomb will go off. I can give you the man responsible. Can you stop it?"

Through gritted teeth, she disclosed all she knew about

Jordan, including the fact that he'd hung out near her planet in Event Horizon. She left out key details, such as the fact that it was *her* planet, and the fact that she'd built an escape kit for him at his request.

Then she pulled on her helmet. Aida slid her nanite-lined suit back onto her skin, struggling with it as it gripped her newly-cleaned flesh. Then she let herself back into the virtual world, willing her senses as dull as she could. The real world washed away as she submerged deeper into the blackness. Light began to form in small firefly-like clusters that swarmed and then came together into a solid circle of brightness. Aida moved toward it, swimming through the blackness of nothing. The entire universe of Event Horizon existed in that bright spot, a singularity in an otherwise nondescript void. She kept it like this on purpose. The space was empty of all stimuli, and for her type of personality disorder, sensory deprivation was peace. Aida floated down to the light and as soon as she touched it, she found herself at her last save point in Event Horizon, hovering near the surface of the beach on Oduduwa where the Obatali lived. They raised their hands in celebration of her return, and she would have joined, except this time, though, she needed to find Jordan.

"Behind you," came his voice, strong and confident. She turned to find him standing with his legs shoulder-width apart, poised in such a way that he reminded her of the ancient Greek Colossus. Her anxiety spiked as his words bounced around in her head. She steeled herself and painted a glare across her face, intending to stare him down. Aida's body betrayed her, and she couldn't keep eye contact, so she glared *near* him instead. She posed her question in a frantic rush of sentences.

"Now's the time. I have your escape kit. Tell me what you're using it for."

"To disappear," he quipped, but she maintained her stoic

demeanor until he finally threw up his hands.

"Emergent Biotechnology has been growing again. New York is still their largest concentration of clone development. If I can destroy that, it'll take them at least five years to rebuild.

"Five years..." she said to herself quietly. It was the kind of setback that she would have dreamed about once.

"How many will die?"

"Not many," he assured her. "The bomb will be contained."

It was a lie. She knew that he told it to make her feel better about her complicity, though it did say something that he seemed to measure the morality of his action by how many people would die as opposed to that *any* people would die. Not killing was a rule.

"Couldn't you EMP it?"

"Too temporary," he said, "and a blast that big would still have casualties anyway. What's the matter, Aida? You knew what I do when we started this adventure.

"I never..."

"Never what?"

"I've never felt the way about anyone that I feel about you."

She said it, and she hoped that he believed her. What was to happen next would be a much softer blow if he believed.

"Neither have I," he told her, and took her hands in his. Then he leaned in for a kiss, but this time, her lips were nowhere to be found. She pushed away from him and walked toward her tribe. At first he followed her, but then the Obatali formed a spear wall behind her as she passed. It was a gesture, as his god-level would have allowed him to wipe them all out with a thought. He respected her boundary though, and boarded his ship to leave.

Within the confines of the cave, she sat alone, and

motioned everyone else out. She listened to the swishing of the waves and the children playing in the sunlight beyond the cave's entrance.

For the next three days the news of his arrest was inescapable. If he knew it was her who turned him in, he didn't act on it. Thanks to an "anonymous tip", the police had been able to track his physical a.p. down to a location in Brooklyn. Jordan had been working as a barristo in a coffee shop, and using their virtual reality equipment at night. Using a false name a false personal identifier code, and had managed to steal enough explosives to level the entire neighborhood of Briggs. It would have been a wasteland, and rebuilding on that scale would have been impossible. He had lied about that as well, which didn't surprise her. After all, he had been very nice to her.

Jordan never disclosed how he planned to escape. She guessed that much because no police ever showed up to ask her pointed questions about escape kits. He faded from her life and into the headlines. In response, she worked. For the next several weeks, she went into the office earlier and stayed later. With every day, Aida added to Mijloc and Lothania. She neglected Oduduwa and the storm, unsure that she would ever return to Event Horizon again. The game had become a reminder of what she had sacrificed, and she wasn't even sure that the sacrifice had been worthwhile. No matter how much on the straight-and-narrow she remained, she always had the impulse to follow her ideals wherever they might lead. This, and the very real fact that she had turned Jordan in, left her stranded on an island of betrayal with no escape from the guilt she faced.

Days turned into weeks, and eventually, Jordan faded from the headlines into the far recesses of her animus module, to remain tucked away as a reminder of why nice people can't be trusted.

Mijloc replaced her obsession with Oduduwa. She built churches and pubs, single-family homes. Eventually real people would need to live there, so she prepared for them farms, goats, and vegetation. Aida dug wells and stood up electrical grids. Reality faded away as she spent more of her time in virtual life. She began to sleep there as well, and her life became one unending virtual reality session.

She slept in Mijloc. She woke in Mijloc. Aida learned how to trick her body into skipping meals by eating plants in the virtual world. The act of chewing helped stave off her stomach's complaints. Aida skipped bathroom breaks so much that she developed a urinary tract infection. Everything she could do to stay in Mijloc and not interact with the world, she did. Aida lost thirty pounds, which gave her a skeletal look that seemed to terrify the people she passed in transit when she did make the occasional trip home. Aida confined herself to the dark of night for travel to minimize the stimuli in her fragile emotional state. She felt and looked like a ghost in the city, floating to and fro. Even then, the city beat at her with florescent lights, flying cars, and random street entertainers. The world was a cruel place.

It was as though she poured her life force into Mijloc. With her decline, cities formed and stretched toward the skies, and ponds sprung and mountains sprouted. Like Gaia, she gave of herself until the world hummed with animal, plant, and insect life. Unused cars popped up on the roads and driveways, and weather patterns started to form and stabilize. She formed the ice caps of the world, and the deep ocean trenches. The world had to be perfect, and it was slowly becoming so with every breath she lost.

In her frenzy, she'd almost managed to forget about Jordan. Work and sleep provided little opportunity for rumination. Her lack of proper sustenance kept her mind focused on only the most critical of tasks as the rest of her life faded away. For

Aida, it was the closest she'd managed to a blissful time. Work kept her both entertained and distracted.

That bliss shattered with a news headline that she happened to see while walking home. She'd stopped in front of a store at the sight of Jordan's face, huge and rotating in a store window. Beneath his disembodied head was a ticker that displayed the title of the content. There, in bold letters, it stated that Jordan had been sentenced to life in Inferiere.

Life. That didn't really mean life. Inferiere was a virtual prison. Life in Inferiere was eternity. She knew and understood Inferiere. It was a world created for torture and pain. She gasped and staggered backwards. Failing to account for the weakness of her starved and atrophied muscles, Aida crashed to the ground in a heap of useless bones and flesh. The last thing she remembered before her consciousness left her was the date of confinement. Her new deadline, she remembered thinking as the world faded, was one week from today.

10

Reconciliation

Thursday, November 18, 2258

Lothania, Deseret - Mijloc

The letter sat opened on her writing table, the most damning piece of evidence she had acquired during her entire two years. It was an answer, and yet, wasn't. Her mother had loved someone else. That part was easy to understand, but the letter had seemed more of something that someone would write before embarking on a long journey, than to end their time on the earth. And there was the relentless question of how such a letter had fallen into Katy's hands. Another mystery was why Katy's weathered earring was sunken into the sand just outside of their farmhouse door when as far as she knew, Katy and Lincoln's mother hated each other. Lincoln couldn't see a way to an answer to either question though, not anymore. As tempted as she was to continue her belief in her mother's murder, the letter was close enough to a suicide note to dissuade her of the idea.

As Lincoln pondered all of this, the wall behind the writing desk disappeared. It wasn't absent for long, but that brief second was long enough for her to make out the outline of the community center downtown. When she focused on the wall, she saw that it had returned, still showing the fine ridges of expensive wallpaper, a waste in the farmhouse, but a nod back to a time when owning a farm actually paid money.

She chalked the disappearance to an illusion and returned to her ruminating. Jordan was a name, she realized, and that had to be something. Sheriff Al had to at least consider looking for him, and helping her to find him. Jordan was her real father, after all, if any of the letter could be believed.

Lincoln rose to her feet and paced the room over a well-worn path that had depressed the carpet into a miniature racetrack. She wore fuzzy socks with tiny dancing elves on them that jutted out under her lengthy striped two-piece pajamas. She'd passed most of the last two days in a similar manner, except perhaps changing the socks to her others with Santa's happy face embroidered into the sides.

The phrase "Libera, Goddess of Worlds" must have meant something. She looked up the reference on her laptop computer via the internet and landed on a site dedicated to pagan holidays. "Libera" was known as the free goddess, the wild one who was unrestrained by the boundaries of expectation. This description was nothing like her mother at all. The woman she had known was reserved, polite, and very adept at the her use of manners. Her mother had worked hard to be loved by all, every day of her existence. There wasn't anything about the woman that even remotely resembled freedom, but then, she wouldn't have assumed her mother to take a lover either.

"Goddess of Worlds" was the next phrase she turned over

in her mind as she began to take another lap around the worn loop that took her to the writing desk, to her bedside lamp, in front of her door, and finally back to her bed post. That added another dimension that Lincoln was afraid to consider too closely. If her mother had been losing her mind, then perhaps that would explain the letter completely. Jordan might have been a completely fictitious entity, and her mother might have considered herself a deity. Then, the suicide could have potentially been accidental, because her mother might have believed that she would be able to actually come back from it.

Or she might not have.

Goddess of Worlds could have been a really strange term of endearment. As little as Lincoln liked to admit it to herself, the former was more likely than the latter. The sound of a large metal door closing against rubber seals stopped her in her tracks. Her father had probably closed the stainless steel refrigerator. Then she heard a loud 'thunk' and 'fucking bullshit'.

He would know, but what would it cost her to talk to the drunkard. She'd been empathetic at first, and for over a year. After that, she'd given up. The man spent his farm subsidies on alcohol except for what she'd managed to siphon away before he spent it all. She kept food on their tables by beating him to the mailbox. One time she'd even kept drinking money from him, only to have him attempt to kill himself by slitting his wrists with a table knife. It was a botched, dumb effort and probably he hadn't intended to actually do it, but he could have ended up dead just the same. As much as she'd grown to hate his company, she hated the idea of being alone even more.

And now, she needed to extract information from his boozy head. She took a deep breath, and picked up the letter, then decided better and put it back down. He was an unpredictable drunk, and the letter might not survive the encounter. Lincoln took another breath, and walked cautiously toward the door, mentally reprimanding herself for voluntarily walking into what she'd normally be trying to avoid. She cracked the door to her room, and stepped out into the abyss.

Niles had been handsome once. He had a square jaw that his emaciated condition made look skeletal. His eyes were a deep piercing auburn, and his hair, even unkempt as it was, maintained a glossy shine and lay in waves over his formerly broad shoulders which now stretched out barely past the width of his hips. He wore a tattered t-shirt that used to be his favorite, and which he wore now as his only one, with beer stains marking the passage of days and weeks since it had been washed. He smelled of alcohol and sweat, and his skin was tight like a filled ballon. Rosacea lightly touched his cheeks.

"Lincoln, how are ya doin?" he shouted to her as soon as she emerged fully into the family room where he lurked.

"Dad, I have some questions about mom."

"Sure, sweetie," he slurred, "what questions?"

She gulped and paused while she thought out whether she would really be willing to ask him. The sweet demeanor he now held was as transient as the blowing wind. Perhaps she could start with her mother's mental state – that wouldn't suggest anything to set him off. Asking if she had been cheating on him would have triggered him for certain, and if he hadn't been aware, then she might have had to go back to suicide watch as she had after his first attempt.

"Mom...was she...okay?"

"Okay?"

"Yeah, was she, like, mentally okay?"

Tears loaded into his eyes preparing for launch, and she mentally made ready to escape back into her room if necessary.

"Your mother," he began, "was a saint and a genius. She worked so hard for everyone to be happy. She worked for me to be happy, for you to be happy...."

He trailed off as he talked, muttering to himself quietly, then he chimed up again.

"...my fault. She should never have left us," he told her. "Well, you. She should never have left you."

"So she didn't have, you know, mental problems?"

"What? No, she's the strongest person I know. Not like me. Why? What did she tell you?"

Lincoln blinked at that and said nothing, because she had nothing to say. Nothing her mother had ever told her explained anything about her death. She waited strategically, hoping, correctly, that Niles would continue.

"It was true. Katy and I *were* seeing each other, and it wasn't fair. Your mother pretended not to know, but she did know. I could see it in her eyes, especially those eyes. Those eyes..."

He trailed off again. He must have been more drunk than he'd ever been, because Lincoln thought he'd just admitted to having an affair.

"You ... and Sarah's mother....were having an affair?"

"For years," he sniffled, threatening to start erupting tears. "Years. And she knew. She asked me, I said no, but she knew. So no, she wasn't crazy – she was right."

Then he finally lost it. The tears formed rivulets down his cheeks as he stared emptily in Lincoln's direction. Lincoln recognized the stare. He no longer even saw her. She turned, mind aflame with the new information, and retreated back to her room. Her mother... her father had been cheating. She was suspecting more and more that she'd been wrong. Nobody had killed her mother, not directly, but she wondered how many more people had been involved in orchestrating her death. And, more than anything, she wondered how much Sarah knew.

In a moment of anger and incomplete thinking, she retrieved her phone from her desk, and texted the words 'did you know?' to Sarah. Less than a second later, her phone came to life. She answered it, but stayed silent since she didn't really know how to ask the question.

"Know what?" Sarah's voice chimed on the other side.

"About Niles and Katy?"

"What about them?"

"They had an affair. Niles just told me all about it."

She was then greeted by silence on the other side of the phone.

"So this is about your mother?"

Lincoln didn't know how to respond to that.

"I guess it is," she said quietly, "but don't hang up, please."

"I didn't know about any affair."

"You would have told me. I'm sorry I accused you."

"I'm glad you called actually. It's time to decide, Lincoln. I don't think I can be friends after the last couple of weeks."

"Oh."

"I don't like ultimatums, and I'm sorry. But you need to decide. Do you want me for a girlfriend, or not? I can't wait for you to finish this investigation, you know that right? This thing may last forever for all I know. And I can be there with you, the whole way, you know I can. But you have to decide – we can date, or we can stop. What we're doing now isn't working."

Sarah was right. It wasn't fair of her to say 'maybe later' as a response to the question Sarah had asked. She wasn't sure whether or not she had decided herself if their relationship was a smart idea, but she did know one thing for certain. The idea of not having Sarah in her life, as she'd gotten a taste recently, wasn't something that she could do.

"No, I mean, yes. I want to try, Sarah. I really do."

"Thank God! I didn't know if I could actually cut you off. Every day I've been wanting to call you."

"Me too! I'm so sorry about everything, Sarah. I was being honest at your house the other day."

"Let that go Lincoln. You don't really understand why I'm upset about it, and you're only going to upset me again."

"Okay agreed."

"Now, let's talk. I missed a lot. You found the earring, did it help?"

"You didn't see the note?"

Lincoln rattled off the story of how there was a note in her mother's handwriting, and relayed the conversation with her father about the affair.

"I'm sorry, Lincoln," Sarah told her.

"I'm actually okay so far, but I'm starting to think that I was wrong, and that she did kill herself."

"Because of the affair?"

"Yes, of course."

"But... what about this Jordan person? How much could she really have cared about the affair if she loved someone else?"

The question was an astute testament to the fact that Lincoln needed Sarah with her, not just in this, but in everything. If her mother loved this Jordan person, then why would she have killed herself? But her father had seemed convinced that her mother had killed herself because of the affair. That left only one member of the triangle who might have been culpable, and Lincoln feared mentioning that to Sarah yet. Instead, she decided to change the subject to something more personal. If nothing else, changing the subject would prove in part to Sarah, hopefully, that it was something of which she was capable.

"I don't know, but it can wait. It's waited for two years."

"Really?"

"Yes, really, Sarah. I want to talk about us."

"Well, okay…. do you remember Ms. Dang's class in high-school when we sat near the back?"

"And we made fun of Scot – remember, because he was always so angry for no reason."

"Yeah, that. That's the first time I thought about you as something other than a friend. Remember when I was staring at you and you told me to take a picture?"

"I do. It was a little bit creepy, how curt you became."

Sarah laughed, and Lincoln could imagine her the way she laughed. Her head tilted back and she opened her mouth as though the laugh were so massively big, that the only way to get it out of her chest was to pretend she was trying to swallow a basketball. That image made Lincoln laugh too. Sarah continued to speak.

"I tried to tell you, but you wouldn't hear, and Scot kept inviting himself on our dates."

"We three were pretty inseparable then."

"Exactly. Remember when we went to watch that rom-com? I thought for sure that a movie like that would keep Scot away."

"I wouldn't have gotten that you wanted to date from that though. We watched romantic movies all the time, remember?"

"I had a plan. I was going to try to hold your hand and see how you responded."

"That might have freaked me out, Sarah. I'm not sure I would have been ready then."

"Me neither," she said, "but how sure are you that you're ready now."

"I'm sure," Lincoln replied, lying as confidently as she could. "Absolutely certain."

"You can't possibly be," Sarah said, "remember that we've been friends for most of our lives? You can't lie to me."

'I could if I tried."

"Well don't try. It's one of the reasons I like you."

"So do you mean that you've been lusting after me for four years?"

Sarah laughed this away loudly.

"No, silly. I let it go after that, for a while. Then I wanted to ask you, and your mother..."

"Yeah. I wouldn't have been ready then either."

"I wasn't sure you were ready even now, but like I said, I couldn't wait."

"So what now?"

"Well, you ask me out on a date, Lincoln."

"Why do I have to be the guy?"

"Neither of us is 'the guy'. We're just you and me. The reason I want you to do the asking is because you've been such a jerk lately. I'm not putting myself out there anymore."

Lincoln considered what Sarah had told her. She was right, and Lincoln knew it, and that was something she figured she would have to start getting used to. So she gulped to herself quietly to stifle her nerves, and then cleared her throat.

"Sarah, would you like to go out with me this weekend?"

"It depends."

"What? What do you mean it depends?"

"You've never asked anyone out before, have you?"

"I've never had to."

"Okay then, try again. But this time, don't assume I'm going to say yes. What are we going to do that's *fun*? I could stare at a wall anywhere."

"Fine. Sarah, would you do me the honor of joining me for a dinner at Vino Extravagante in downtown Lyra Craevis on Saturday, followed by a movie of your choosing?"

"Movie? I heard that Avenue Q was playing at the Signature theatre."

"Really?"

"Yes."

"But I don't have tickets for that."

"I do."

"Did you know I was going to come around?"

"I had my suspicions."

"So would you like to go to dinner at Vino Extravagante and then see Avenue Q?"

"Yes, I'd love to. Can you come by at five? I'll drive. I mean, I can get the Mercedes and your father's truck is…."

"I'll see you then."

Sarah hung up the phone, and Lincoln stared at the screen as Sarah's smiling face changed into a screen-saver. She placed the phone down, and realized then that she was smiling too. The date seemed right, more right than most of the other relationships she'd ever been in. Dating Sarah seemed like it made all the sense in the world. She wondered, though, if they would fall into friendship patterns or be able to forge new relationship patterns together.

The future was uncertain, but now seemed to hover on the horizon like the golden apple that tempted Aphrodite, and Lincoln reached for it. As she reached, though, looming around the edges of her fortune were the tidings of unrest. Katy was still a suspect in Lincoln's mind, and that confrontation would be devastating when it occurred. She shuddered to think of how Sarah would react to that. Sarah had taken the news of their parent's affair without even seeming shaken, a good sign. Sarah had always complained about not really liking her mother. Perhaps Lincoln had nothing to worry about.

And then, Lincoln thought, she could just walk away from her mother's death. The investigation that nobody cared about but her didn't have to finish. She could just leave it, and focus on her and Sarah, and be happy, but never really understand what happened to her mother. The two seemed mutually exclusive. For real happiness, she would need to remove the question mark hanging over her head. Besides, now she really wanted to meet her father and Katy might have some idea of who that was, so at least she had to have a conversation about that.

11

Seeking Lincoln

Friday, November 19, 2258

Lothania, Deseret - Mijloc

Open highway connected Lyra Craevis to Lothania, cutting through wide, empty fields in a single lane. As Bodhi pulled onto the main drive, heading toward town center, he passed a sign showing the population to be less than three-thousand people. Where Lyra Craevis had begun as a sanctuary for models, Lothania was the first entry point for non-models seeking immortality. The wind poured in through the open window and flowed through his hair, whipping around the interior of the lazily-discarded garbage around and pulling a piece of paper out through the window. Just before the paper hit the road, it faded into a cloud of smoke and disappeared in one of his favorite hacks.

He crossed the train track (a decoration at this point with no trains in transit yet) and traveled into town along the main drag. At ten o'clock in the morning, only five people wandered up and down the sidewalks nearby, one of whom lingered just inside of the entrance to the office of the liaison. He pulled to a forty-five degree angle stop into an empty parking spot and made his way into the office, pushing open the slow-swinging glass door on a rusty hinge. A man sat behind the desk across the room with his gun holstered and hanging from the wall behind him. He looked up from what may have been paperwork as a dragonfly lifted off from the corner of the desk and flitted across before Bodhi's eyes.

"Welcome to Lothania," the man said gruffly as he struggled to stand, knees hitting the desk and knocking him back down into his seat. With a frustrated growl, he pushed the furniture forward and stood slowly behind it.

"Albert Grisham?"

The man nodded in a slow movement that was all but imperceptible.

"Sheriff Grisham, to my friends," he said with his lip curled up into a half-smile. Bodhi, used to being underestimated in his skinny avatar, looked at the man from top to bottom, slow and without blinking. The man seemed like a statue at first, but as time passed without Bodhi's additional response, the man shifted his weight to spread his belly across both feet.

"Bodhi Rawls," he finally said with a thin smile, extending his hand, which the Sheriff met in a firm grip. The man's eyes went wide.

"Welcome to Lothania, Mr. Rawls," he said, now clearly recognizing Bodhi.

"Thank you, Albert."

"Al, sir. Call me Al."

"Al. Okay."

"What brings you to our quaint little town?"

"Curiosity really. I heard you have a bit of a noisemaker

here?"

"Nothing pressing. Just Lincoln, rightfully missing her mother. That's all."

"Lincoln Montague?"

He nodded rapidly, and his lined cowboy hat shifted unsteady on his head.

"That's the one. She was in here the other day asking more questions about it. Won't listen no matter how much I tell her that her mother did it to herself."

"That's what's confusing to me. I don't remember anyone ever telling me about her mother's death, and people aren't really supposed to *die* in here. Have developers been by yet to ask about it?"

The man seemed anxious as he paced to the left of the desk.

"We didn't exactly report it."

"Why not? We might have been able to bring her back."

"Didn't think it was important. We try to keep things as real as possible here, and you don't really come back from the dead, do you? And would she have wanted to after all that work? Besides, we figured you guys have eyes all over Mijloc and didn't see fit to get involved. So we gave her a nice burial and everything was fine."

"Al, in all of Mijloc, there's only ever been this single death. Nobody else has died because we made it impossible to do so. There's no death here, not for humans. You completed the liaison training, right?"

The sheriff shrugged his broad shoulders.

"We just thought that you made a mistake."

Bodhi's mind raced through what he knew. This town, in particular, was one of the oldest polli settlements. The pioneers here decided in their charter that there was an age limit of when to reveal to the town's children that their world had several strange aspects to it, such as being virtual.

"Were you? Or was it just that you wanted to keep your secret."

The man clenched his teeth together.

"It's our town," he said. "We can do what we want, Mr. Rawls."

Al was right on that point. It was one of the stipulations of the world government to grant them autonomy. Bodhi couldn't just run everything like his own empire - not that he wanted to. Instead, the towns and cities had to mostly be autonomous and democratically controlled by their occupants. A separate, independent branch of Paivana handled concepts like justice and security. Bodhi could only intervene if there was a legitimate problem that threatened the entire world.

"Have you at least told her yet? About what Mijloc really is?"

"Not yet. Do you think we should? She's not quite old enough yet still."

"I think it might help her, don't you?"

Another shrug.

"Where does she live?"

"Outside of town on the Montague ranch. Just take Main Street down to the edge of town and you can't miss it. Past the railroad tracks, but before the river."

Bodhi recognized the directions as he recalled the drive in. Green fields separated by barbed wire fences flanked the road just before a turn-off. He smiled.

"Thanks," he said, unsure of how much help the man had been, as strangely defensive as he seemed.

"Don't mention it. Tell Niles I said hello if you go out there."

As Bodhi approached the dilapidated farmhouse, he watched the wind blow lazy weeds back and forth in the atrophied flowerbed beneath the dust-covered steps. Bodhi listened for noises telling him of any occupants, but the only sounds he heard were the chirping of birds somewhere in the indiscernible distance accompanied by the overpowering crows who lingered just above his head. He watched the flight patterns of the birds slowly circling as though they'd found something worth consuming. One left the flock and for a second seemed like it might dive all the way to him, only to change trajectory at the last moment and head back up into the sky.

Crows were a good omen in some cultures, and bad in others. Being from Canada, Bodhi favored the more fortuitous of the potential interpretations. He acknowledged the Inuit meaning that the birds portended good fortune and finding what one sought. He stepped out of the automobile and covered the yard to the door in three short steps before walking gingerly up the stairs. Two quick raps and he waited for a response. Still nothing.

Bodhi pushed the door inward, and watched the opening as it swung larger and exposed more of the cluttered mess beyond. The moldy smell of damp washrags leapt out to him from the interior of the house. Stepping through into the opening, Bodhi's attention was immediately pulled upward by two exposed rafter beams, easily two-by-sixes strong enough to support her mother's weight. He walked in a small circle around the beam, staring up at it, trying to imagine coming in to find the woman hanging there, swinging slow in the breeze.

What breeze?

He retrieved a folder from his bag, and fished out the stack of papers that he'd printed out describing the scene. Flipping through the first couple of pages, he found the phrase he was looking for. The woman had been swinging, Lincoln had said in her first interviews. She'd been swinging slowly in a circle, but her body had been stiff. A hundred and twenty pounds of resistance in Mijloc would have been difficult to move, and the house sat facing South so that the strong north-south winds couldn't have crossed the doorway. The weaker cross-windows were blowing now, and he barely felt them. They couldn't have moved her.

As he reviewed again, taking a closer look and scrutinizing the text, Bodhi bit his lower lip in concentration. The date of the woman's death was January 18, 2256 - more than two years earlier. Lincoln would have been sixteen at the time.

"Who are you?"

The voice jolted him from his concentration and he found himself facing a red-faced man with thick lips staring at him with eyes that swam back and forth in his sockets. Drunk.

"Nobody, Niles," Bodhi said under his breath. Then he turned to make his way back out of the small farmhouse.

"She's not here anyway," the man said.

"Aidalee?"

The man's head shook back and forth.

"No. Lincoln," he said. "What's your name? I'll tell her you came by."

He said the words as though he truly thought he was sober enough to remember, so Bodhi pretended as well and told him who he was. Unlike the sheriff, the man didn't react to hearing Bodhi's name, something that Bodhi found unusual. Everyone in Mijloc knew who he was, or should have.

It didn't matter. The man couldn't see straight, so there was nothing to be gained from talking to him. Disappointed, Bodhi made his way from the house, debating whether to wait and talk to Lincoln, in spite of the fact that the town's leaders might be upset with him for revealing the truth of her existence. As he exited the building, the year 2256 popped up in his head again. Years before, something else had happened on that day.

Bodhi remembered getting the call, patched through to his office in Mijloc from off-world. He hadn't understood at first. Aiden had called, during one of his more comprehensible days, to say that someone had died. Jane Sorendsun, if he'd gotten the name correct. The panicked voice told him that the woman had died and fried her animus module in the process. They'd found her body, emaciated away to nearly nothing, still on the floor of her one-bedroom apartment. As his mind wandered through the images, he looked for a connection between the two. Aida's death, hidden away from him by the townspeople, and allegedly impossible, had happened on the same day that Jane Sorendsun died off-world.

His HR department and external authorities had decided that Jane's death was intentional neglect. She'd decided to stop eating, and stop sleeping, or even drinking water regularly. Something had disrupted her world, and Bodhi would have dismissed it at that had it not been for the fact that he knew of one other person who had undergone a similar transformation, with similar results. That woman was Aida Lothian, and she'd been dead already for almost sixteen years before Jane.

12

Two Weeks to Immortality

Thursday, October 11, 2237

Seattle, Washington - Earth

Aida Lothian awoke on the pavement, unsure of how long she'd been unconscious or how many people had walked by and ignored her body laying there underfoot. Her ribs stung as she sucked in a shallow breath that she then used to spit blood from the corner of her mouth. The orange sky shimmered violently as people criss-crossed in front of her like multicolored lasers at a light show. She pulled herself to her feet, wobbled at first, and finally gained enough muscular control to resume her slow shuffle home. Moments later the scolding sun dropped behind buildings that stretched upward like legs holding up the sky.

Seventeen minutes later, Aida stumbled up the stairs and collapsed behind the closed door of her bedroom, but it wasn't enough solitude to free her tangled mind. The world encroached through the windows as light flickered against her wall, filtered through flying cars that crossed on invisible floating highways. Aida sought out the emptiness of her closet. There she sat in darkness. In the back of her mind, she saw Jordan in Inferiere, desperately trudging through the tar sands while being pursued by the flesh-eating worms that burrowed beneath its surface. Another flash caught him impaling himself on the spikes of cactus trees while fleeing some predator. Inferiere seethed with hidden dangers of which Aida was much too familiar. And she had put him there. Every imaginary pain that he suffered added to her guilt burden.

Free from the overwhelming stimulation of the outside world, Aida needed another distraction to keep herself from ruminating over Jordan's fate. She flicked on the lights. In front of her, her hand still clutched the light switch. A bony wrist supported it, and fingers like pencils gripped either side of the tiny lever. She hadn't realized how thin she'd become. Some day, perhaps, she would have the energy to do something about that. Instead, she pulled her virtual reality helmet over her head. Aida slid the haptic suit over her unshaven legs, shimmying them upwards to negotiate past the stubby, wiry growths. The suit hung from her skin. Last she pulled on the haptic boots and gloves, then with a thought, activated the system and headed toward Oduduwa for the first time in weeks.

In Event Horizon, she was still the goddess Libera. She floated through the atmosphere in a catharsis of tears, and landed solemnly on the beach near her people. The civilization had grown into an empire. Giant buildings like mandirs stabbed at the sky. The storm had stayed rooted where she'd left it, even after multiple generations, though she wondered if the towers might change weather pattern enough to move it elsewhere. Her heart fell as her eyes lingered for too long on the abandoned cave where their empire had begun. Fields of plants stretched out inland from the cave to just beyond the protective ridge.

The sandy beach reminded her of the tar sands on Inferiere as she looked upon it, and it struck her that Event Horizon wasn't that much different than Mijloc and Inferiere. That was the reason her skills had transferred so easily from the one to the other. She wiggled her toes and dug down through the wet mud. She inhaled the odors of the salty sea, and imagined a life with Jordan on the beach of Oduduwa. They could live as gods in the temple that the Obatali had built.

The fantasy shattered as quickly as it formed. If Jordan wasn't in Inferiere there yet, he would be soon. The first thing that would happen is someone would kill his physical body to would trigger the animus module's retraction into itself. Then they would remove the module by cutting open the back of his head where the component had been installed. They would have to clean the blood and brain fluids from the device before dropping it into a neural interface chamber that resembled a small chest filled with gelatin. Nanite threads would extend from the module and attempt to assert themselves into whatever flesh-like material they could find. The fibers would explore the chest's interior until they discovered a human-enough like neural mesh to interact with. That mesh would be the port into Inferiere. At the point of interaction, a certified unique identifier would be generated and linked with his animus module. Then, in another world, a virtual body unique to his signature would be created, and all perception would map to the inputs from the virtual world. Sounds would be heard, heat would be felt, horizons would loom. Jordan would awaken in a world of endless suffering.

She cringed at the idea and closed her eyes to feel the warmth of the perpetual blue skies on her face. The tears on her cheeks had dried, and now she felt better in this world of limited stimulation. She could think more clearly here. When she re-opened her eyes, she watched a child wandered toward her across the beach. She wondered absently what the child knew of existence. From the child's perspective, there had only ever been Oduduwa. From the child's perspective, the world had a single set of rules, and there were no other universes. The child sat in the sand a short distance away and began to dig a hole.

Aida wondered then how deep the child could dig. The game developers would have wanted to allow some digging, but how far until the child reached an anomaly that she couldn't easily explain. The huge palace had to be embedded deep underground for support, so there had to be something below, but eventually, the rules of the world wouldn't apply anymore. Then what would happen, she wondered. Would the child float into the sky?

At least Jordan would know who he was, and what to expect. This child had to learn the rules of an entire universe. His little nascent artificial-intelligence core was already picking up lessons from the world around him, and embedding those into his own software version of the animus module. Was the child any more or less real than she was, she wondered?.

Throughout Event Horizon, there might be a million of the same child. This child had no uniqueness. She'd seen one just like it several years before. Event Horizon wasn't certified like Inferiere was, or Mijloc would be. So there could be twenty Jordan Helms in Event Horizon, or even an entire army. There would never be more than one Jordan Helm in Inferiere.

Her stomach asserted itself and interrupted her game play. She doubled over in pain in real life and in the game at the same time.   Eating was the one thing that she could do without, at least the need to eat. It interrupted everything useful. With a thought, she disappeared from the game. As she did so, she wondered what the child must think about the vanishing woman on the beach. The earlier generations had all known she was Libera, Goddess of Worlds. To this child, she was only a person, and with her disappearance, an apparition. Aida could feel the rumors spreading.

As she emerged from virtual reality into the darkness, a tiredness came over her more severe than she'd ever felt before. Exhaustion competed with hunger for her attention while she stripped back down into nothing, and followed up with her obligatory shower. She shaved her legs, which had been reduced to barely more than bones, and pulled herself into her pajamas afterwards. The shower staved off the exhaustion for at least a while, so she wandered downstairs to sneak some food from the kitchen.

Her timing was off. As soon as she left the bottom of the stairs, she heard the cacophony of noise, and knew. It didn't matter, though, as she needed to eat, and for the first time in a long time, actually felt that she could. She plastered on a thin smile and walked as casually as she could by the long dinner table where everyone else in the house sat for a group dinner.

"Aida, want to join?" came her housemate's voice, as she'd known it would. Sitting down to dinner with a group of people was the nearest thing to torture she could imagine for herself, so Aida flashed an obligatory smile and shook her head no. She quickened her pace to the refrigerator, and reached in to the freezer to grab an insta-bar. The casing on evaporated within seconds of her touching a marking on the side of the package, leaving in its wake something like a rolled-up hotdog. With any luck, Aida could make it to the stairs without further interruption.

"Hey, they caught that Jordan Helm guy. He's going to Inferiere tonight. We're going to watch it later on the holovid if you want to come down."

Aida maintained her smile, though where before it had been fake, now it seemed both fake and hollow. She willed herself to move up the stairs, one step at a time until she broke through the doorway into the serene barrier of her room. Then she closed the door behind her and slid back against it, allowing herself to collapse slowly to the floor. Her body trembled with anguish as she failed to prevent the onslaught of emotions that she wasn't prepared to experience. All appetite left her, but she forced herself to eat the insta-bar anyway. It was two-thousand calories of compact energy, and she desperately needed it.

Her housemates were going to watch the equivalent of Jordan's execution on the holovid downstairs. They wouldn't be the only ones. The entire city of New York were probably watching as well, collective schadenfreude earned by surviving the worst mass murderer of many lifetimes. Her eyes welled up but she didn't cry. She furiously bit back the tears that wanted to spring free. A small voice in her mind told her that they just didn't know him as well as she did. That same voice said that he was really nice to her, and even went so far as to say that since she didn't live in New York, she could have just let it happen. Could she really have traded millions of lives for one?

Broadcasting Inferiere confinement had become normal somehow. The first time someone was committed, it had shocked the world. There had been lawsuits about the cruel and unusual punishment. That was earlier on though, back when people still largely considered killing a body tantamount to murder. During the gray area of history where the animus module had just began and before the true potential of immortal life was first recognized, people had staged uncomfortable debates about whether or not someone's animus module truly was them. Of course, back then, not all brain processes could be offloaded onto the animus module, and it was still experimental. That changed with a series of now famous experiments, in which a scientist intentionally damaged his brain with a Ball-Peen while using the animus module, and kept on talking through a forty-five minute long lecture with blood pouring down his face. Nobody questioned whether it was really him, since the animus module had kept his body going and there was no obvious difference in his behavior, even when the EEG registered brain death.

As she thought about the animus module, and the need to eat, and the child's perspective of the world, she felt that something joined these things together. A spark was trying to light, and when it did, it hit like the scientist's hammer. The child didn't need to eat. He did eat, but he didn't really need to. If he didn't, he wouldn't waste away into nothing. Further, the animus module was only a very complex hardware which could be simulated in software. The device "grew" nanite fibers that helped it learn how the brain worked, and slowly replaced each piece of functionality at the intersection with the spinal chord. Eventually, it turned the brain into an overly complex redundant data storage system as the module took over all functionality. Her own brain was like that by now, completely defunct, although in the copying, her animus module had copied her personality disorder as well. Having formulated the thought, Aida could now visualize a software version of the animus module. And if she built it, then she could turn people into software.

That wasn't the end of the idea taking shape in her mind. She was positive that, like the boy, if someone "dug" hard enough in Inferiere, they would find an imperfection. Especially if the person doing the digging was someone like Aida. Exploiting such a flaw would be possible then. The combination of a fully-software-based life form and a flawed operating system meant - what did it mean? Her excitement about the idea welled up until she realized what she was really doing. Her intelligence sometimes caught the best of her. She was inventing an escape plan and her intellect wanted to spring Jordan Helm.

The idea was quite possibly the worst idea she'd ever had, and her conscious mind pushed at it. This was a man who destroyed lives and destroyed people. There was no up-side to Jordan being a part of the world again, no matter how much she missed him and longed to feel his touch. That idea cut through her conscious thoughts like a laser scalpel. She did miss his touch, and had since the moment he'd left. Even in the flood of anxiety that he'd brought her, there was a kind of longing underneath it all. But her selfish desires weren't sufficient a reason to unleash the man back into the world.

That evening, she dreamed the most surreal dream she'd ever experienced. It was deep and felt like reality, with all of the jarring noises and movements. In the dream, she cradled a child in her arms while walking along the abandoned beach in Oduduwa. She felt the sand between her toes and a sun so intense that she felt the tingling warning of an impending sunburn across her back. The spray from the ocean matted into her hair and stung her eyes, something even haptic nanites couldn't do. The child lay asleep in her arms. Aida shook her gently, but the little girl in her cloth beach clothes lay silent and still. Only reserved breaths told her that the child was alive at all. Aida lay the child on the beach. Arms wrapped around her in an embrace from behind. These were Jordan's hands, she knew, but realer than they had ever been. She wanted those hands, and she longed for the child to awaken to know her parents, but the child only slept. The couple left the child and walked up the beach, hand in hand as they never had before but in the dream it was as though they'd only done so. The water was cold on her toes, but she loved the sensation. Another impossible thing. When they turned to go back to the child, the beach behind them was empty. Aida ran back to where they'd lain the girl, but there wasn't even an indention in the sand. Then she looked out into the ocean, expecting to see the child in the waves, but there was nothing there either. Aida turned towards where Jordan had stood, but he too had vanished. Even the Obatali were nowhere to be seen.

The silence was so extreme that she awoke with perspiration dripping down her back. Her stomach rumbled furiously and she sprinted to the bathroom before she was sick in her bed. She hadn't been taking good enough care of herself at all.

When she finally left the bathroom, light broke outside her window. Aida showered and dressed with the dream still vivid in her mind. She regarded it as a warning. Jordan may have already been lost in Inferiere. But the child, she felt the child as though the child was real. She wanted the child, and to cradle the little girl, and make her feel safe. Aida's neuroses, when she wasn't able to control them, were so severe that she'd never considered the possibility of having an actual family. The dream revealed to her something she'd already known deep down inside about herself – that she *wanted* a family. She still loved Jordan, and probably would for her entire life.

The little girl she was so in love with that she was already picking out names in the back of her mind. Aida didn't know how to make the girl real and even if she did, Aida could barely care for herself. On days when she had flare ups, she sometimes couldn't leave her bedroom. She'd almost killed herself by not eating because she couldn't emotionally handle everything the world had done to her.

Aida would have to think about it. She was smart, far more intelligent than most humans. That wasn't boasting or self-aggrandizing, but was simply a fact. She should be able to figure out what her mind was trying to tell her. Somewhere in her conscious was a possibility pushing forward to reveal itself. She only needed to be receptive and patient, and the idea would come.

When she arrived at work later that morning, she was greeted with a massive banner across the office door.

"Mijloc - Immortality on a Budget"

Just below the words in smaller print read:

"Two weeks to Immortality"

13

Truth Will Out

Friday, November 19, 2258

Lothania, Deseret - Mijloc

As she had numerous times that day, Lincoln read over the letter again. Some lines had finally started to make sense now that she knew about the affair. The third paragraph dripped with pain and sadness.

I hope that you never know the pain of sharing a bed with someone who doesn't love you. I hope that you never understand the feeling of unrequited love. It's important that you know that I'm not angry. I broke you somewhere along the way, but I will love you always.

The tragedy of those three lines wrenched at her heart. Lincoln wondered vaguely if they had been copied, but she knew it was unlikely. The words, the phrasing, all reminded her of her mother. Her mother didn't use normal language to communicate. Every single phrase she'd ever uttered to

Lincoln had layers and meanings that needed to be unpacked. Of course, that level of skill with language was wasted in Lothania, but Lincoln had always loved her for it.

These words Lincoln felt that she could now explain. There were others which maintained their mystery. "Libera, Goddess of Worlds" was one that she wouldn't even attempt to unpack just yet. The line about her mother treating Niles unjustly made sense when she considered the affair with Jordan. That also helped explain the drastic differences between Lincoln and the waste of a man who occupied her home.

Much of the letter had lost its mystery, but Lincoln was confused by the three words "not a transplant". She'd been considering the phrase carefully, and she believed that the general meaning had to be something about moving to Lothania from elsewhere. Scot's family had come from Lyra Craevis when he was younger. Lincoln could remember the day he'd appeared in her first-grade classroom halfway through the year, a tiny, fragile boy with glasses nearly the size of his head. He didn't wear glasses anymore, and was anything but small, yet when she talked to him on the phone, sometimes this was the image that came to mind. He was definitely a transplant.

Sarah's family, the Douglas's, were on the town charter. Just like the Montagues, they were old town royalty. Sarah had been born in the Humana Hospital in downtown Lyra Craevis, though, as had pretty nearly everyone person she had grown up with because that was the closest hospital with a maternity ward to the tiny town of Lothania. Sarah had a unique birth story, compared to them, but she didn't feel that it really gave her mother the right to refer to everyone else as transplants. When she was born, her mother had been too far along in contractions to make the trip. One of the older women, Mrs. Hartsberry, had formerly been a doula, and helped deliver her in their farmhouse. On her birth certificate, unlike any other child in town probably, the city was Lothania, Deseret.

Such a difference could have been meant by 'transplant', but it seemed like a pointless distinction to make. And, to say that she was an offspring instead of a transplant, well that implied that the other children were conceived or born some other way than through the tradition of having sex, getting pregnant, and popping out a baby. Together, the phrase and context following it made little sense at all.

The wall shimmered before her, capturing her attention. With pulses of dim light, it seemed to glow before it faded completely. Beyond, she saw an unfamiliar forest made of skyscraper-tall trees that vaguely resembled saguaro cacti, except the thorns were spikes the size of her feet, and above her head leaves met to form a canopy through which only trickles of light emerged. Movement pulled her eyes down, and there, inching toward her, slithered a creature that resembled an earthworm that had exploded up to the size of her arm. Swathes of gray interpolated with orange stripes decorated the leathery and dry skin down its corpulent, bloated sides. The face, or what she regarded as the face, hosted rows of concentric teeth, and it made no sound as it silently closed on her. Lincoln lurched backwards to get away and stumbled off of her bed onto the carpeted floor. When she looked up again, the wall had rematerialized.

Lincoln thought that perhaps, it was possible, that she was losing her mind. And if she was losing her mind, then maybe she got that from her mother. This thought brought more clarity to the letter, because of the way in which Lincoln felt that she was going crazy. Some bits of the world were real, most of it. Little things had started to feel off. It wasn't just the walls. She'd also been seeing flashes of creatures like the worm just on the edge of her vision. She pulled her mind together the best she could, and tried to still her pulse. It wasn't real. Whatever she'd been seeing, it had to be imaginary. The stress of investigating her mother's death wore on her - that was all.

Now that her mind had pivoted back to the investigation, Lincoln recognized that all of the evidence she had pointed to her mother killing herself. Evidence was leading her to believe that the letter couldn't be trusted either, at least, not all of it. If her mother's grip on reality was as tenuous as Lincoln's seemed to be, then it was also possible that Jordan was nothing more than a fantasy, and that the letter had been to nobody. In that case, the fact that Katy held onto it made more sense, because why allow, if she could prevent it, the pain of the knowledge of her mother's growing insanity to spread to the family who already had to deal with her loss? And she couldn't have thrown the letter away since it wasn't really hers. But that idea painted Katy with a personality that she didn't have. Lincoln couldn't remember the last time Katy had performed a selfless act.

Not only that, but the idea of her own sanity being questionable filled Lincoln caused her knees to go weak. She had already questioned herself for two years about the fact that she was the only one who really believed her mother hadn't killed herself. That kind of denial wasn't normal, but she hadn't considered it a mark of insanity either. Lincoln had always thought for herself, and questioned what others told her. But now she had to question herself too, and not just the people around her. She might actually have to start trusting the observations of others over her own conclusions.

She couldn't do it any more.

She gathered the letter, and the rest of her "evidence", and placed everything in a pile on her bed. Then she retrieved the storage tote from under its edge, where she had packed away so many of her childhood things, including a litany of stuffed animals she'd had since she was three. She pulled back the lid and, with hesitation at first, began to slowly place the different pieces of evidence into the container. As she felt more and more the waste of the previous two years, she threw the items furiously in, and when she got to the letter, she crumpled it angrily and ripped it into pieces, and threw them all into the container. Unable to pack the rest, Lincoln slammed the lid down, and collapsed on her bed to cry.

She never had the chance though. From her door came a loud knock, causing her to roll over on her blanket and sit up. She quickly wiped her eyes, and sniffled, then admitted her untimely visitor.

"Hey Lincoln, I was just..."

Sarah's face came around the corner, and she seemed to see the pain in Lincoln's eyes, and her gaze hovered over the writing desk, disheveled from Lincoln's earlier frenzy.

"What's the matter?" she asked, as she sat next to Lincoln on her bed, and grabbed her hand.

"The note," Lincoln said quietly, unsure of how much of her thinking she should reveal.

"What about it?"

"I don't think it's true. I think... I think my mother was losing her grip on reality. I've been staring at it all morning. She killed herself. I mean, whichever way I interpret what I've learned, she had to have. There was no murderer. Maybe that affair with your mother and my father happened, and maybe that pushed her over. But the letter – it was insanity writing that." Then she lowered her voice to a whisper. "I might be losing my mind too."

Lincoln hadn't expected to say those words to anyone, but Sarah seemed to be the right person to trust not to run away screaming, and to actually engage. Sarah responded at first by only squeezing her hand.

"You're stressed out, Lincoln. I wouldn't say losing your

mind though."

"I haven't told you everything."

With that, she told Sarah of the things that she'd seen, the creatures and the disappearing walls. Sarah listened intently about how Lincoln now understood that there was a good possibility much of the letter, aside from what they'd already confirmed, was based on events that had only existed in her mother's diseased mind. Then she spoke up.

"If you want to stop the investigation, I'll support it. You've chased this for a long time, though. Your father, I hate to say after all of this, isn't the most reliable. That's why I came to get you."

"To… get me?"

"Yeah, that and I wanted to see you," she winked.

"Why get me?"

"My mother. I talked to her about what your dad said. She wants to talk to us. To both of us. She said you can ask her whatever questions you want and she'll tell you. But we don't have to if you're really done investigating."

"I suppose it wouldn't hurt."

She was curious about the affair in a morbid way, but the knowledge couldn't change anything. She'd already decided that walking away was the best thing for her.

Half an hour later, Lincoln found herself seated in the living room of the bed and breakfast. The high-backed Victorian-era chair that she sat in was covered with paisley print across the bottom and back and had intricate arms carved of wood. Beside her, in another chair, Sarah, smiling gently at Lincoln. Across from the two of them, poised on the couch of similar pattern and style, was Kathryn Douglas, Sarah's mother, Katy.

Lincoln didn't know where to begin, or how much Katy already knew about what her investigation had yielded. Fortunately, she didn't have to open the conversation.

"It was a long time ago," Katy began, "when your mother showed up in Lothania."

"I thought she was always here."

"Oh, no, dear. Your father is a Montague, one of the founding families. Your mother came to us shortly before you were born, well a year or so before that I guess."

"Is that when they fell in love?"

Katy's body seemed to stiffen, and her genteel smile hardened.

"They never fell in love," she said. "You should know that by now."

"Mom, be nice."

Katy looked at Lincoln again, and her features softened.

"I'm sorry dear. Let me explain and you'll understand a little better how I feel. Until she showed up, your father and I had the most romantic relationship. We would go to the lake in the evenings and watch the stars come up at night. He loved me so much."

There was a far-away look in her eyes, as though Katy were focusing on something in the distance that she couldn't quite make out. Her face was placid and she looked, for the first time that Lincoln could remember, like a gentle creature who could harm no one. Then Katy's face sharpened again.

"Until she came along. She had perfect hair, perfect teeth, perfect poise. She had perfect everything – too perfect if you ask me. Nobody could compete with her. In less than three months after she arrived, Niles and I were broken up, and she was pregnant with you."

"That...fast?"

"Exactly that fast. Niles is a good man, and like all good men, he did what he thought was right. He married your mother when she got pregnant. So you see, your mother had won him away from me, or so she'd thought."

"The affair?" Lincoln asked, knowing the answer before

she'd asked.

"Yes. Niles showed up one day after a fight when you were three, or was it four? I don't remember. Mason had just left us, so you had to have been four, because Sarah was five. I was alone, and he was lonely, and one thing led to another..."

"And you didn't stop?"

"Dear, we stopped several times a year. He or I would make an ultimatum. Never again, I would say, or he would. It didn't matter though, because what we had was love, and was real."

"How did you get the letter, Katy?" Lincoln asked dryly, irritated by her insistence that she and Lincoln's father were the only two truly in love, as though her mother had been an accidental interruption.

"Oh, that, dear. Well, Sheriff Al gave it to me. He didn't know who Jordan was, but it wasn't Niles, and you had all suffered enough. Whatever was in that letter, it wasn't good for anyone. I don't know why I kept it. I should have burned it years ago. I guess I was waiting to see if Jordan ever showed up."

"So you kept it from us ... to protect us?"

"To protect him dear. You... I don't know what to say about you. You're her child. Every time I see your eyes, I think of her, and hate you a little more. Its not your fault, and I try to be nice. But it's hard. Yet... here I am. What else do you want to know?"

"Nothing," she told the woman. "Nothing at all. I want nothing else from you."

"Nor I, you," Katy told her. Lincoln looked at Sarah, who stared daggers at her mother. Lincoln got to her feet. As angry as she was at the exchange, she now understood more than she had before. She'd lied though, she did have another question.

"One more, I guess. Why did she kill herself?"

"I don't know. Your father was here with me when Sheriff called him. He bolted out of here so quickly he never even said goodbye. The next thing I knew, there was a funeral."

Lincoln turned away from the woman, and walked toward the door, passing Katy coldly. She heard Sarah's footsteps behind her as she passed through the doorway back out into the yard.

"I'm sorry, Linc," she heard Sarah say.

"I know, it's not your fault."

"Did that help anything?"

Lincoln stopped on the steps and considered. She had now learned about the affair from two different sources. She had assumed that her mother was a Lothania native. That was new information, and if she'd still been pursuing the investigation any further, she might have considered it valuable. The confirmation of the affair did offer some closure, so despite everything, she could appreciate the effort that Sarah had made.

"Yes, it did. A lot, thank you."

"Can I walk back with you?"

"I-I think I need a little time to digest if that's okay."

Sarah nodded and gave her a hug.

"I'm sorry about all of this," she said. "I was just trying to help."

"You did help."

"Call later?"

"Yeah."

Lincoln turned right off of the steps and followed the contour of the house around to the back. A little trail led down from that corner to the creek bed. The bed was mostly dry since it was only partially spring-fed and partially snow-fed from the nearby hills. The cold temperatures had caused the water to freeze farther up the into the hills, which Lincoln knew from a lifetime of living in Lothania meant that the stream was deprived.

Everything for her entire lifetime had been based on understandings about life and relationships that had been fundamentally untrue. The life her mother and father had shared had been a lie, and the softness they had shown each other in her presence was probably a subterfuge as well. She wished that her mother were there, by magic or some other means, to tell her, even if not entirely true, that some of what she had grown up with had been real. But the past was done, and her mother was gone. She placed one booted foot in front of the other as she followed the slow stream.

She had a date with Sarah Saturday. That was real. The thought hung in the air like an aerialist just before the spectacular descent. Something good was out there, something for her to reach toward. She breathed in slowly and let out a thick, steamy breath. Then, surprising herself, she smiled, in spite of everything.

14

Welcome to Mijloc

Thursday, October 19, 2237

Seattle, Washington - Earth

A week of meticulously eating at least 1505 calories each day started Aida's journey to physical recovery. Her hair regained some of its formal lustre and her arms, still thin, no longer seemed as they might snap with a slight breeze. Her physical strength waxed, and with it the mental strength necessary to control her symptoms better, and to hide them when she couldn't control them. As long as she worked, and she continued to work non-stop on Mijloc as the launch date neared, she could stay focused and remember through automated reminders to maintain a strict caloric intake.

One morning, Aida arrived at Paivana Thoughtforms four minutes later than usual due to traffic problems, and something seemed off besides her late arrival. She entered the office the same way as always, and the lights were already on, reinforcing the sentiment that something unusual was happening. As she neared the changing room, she heard hushed whispers in a nearby conference room, but only passed by without further investigation. She was beginning to change into her haptic suit when she heard a gentle knock against the door.

Aida opened the door to a mass of smiling faces and complete silence. Then one person raised her fingers into the air to snap gently, a gesture which Aida knew to be applause. She felt anxious but wasn't yet overwhelmed by the attention. Whoever had organized the reception had been kind in considering her emotions, and that kindness made her more comfortable even if they did seem a little misinformed. The snapping grated against her nerves as deeply as clapping would have, but the intent behind it gave her the energy to keep the red at bay.

"Aida," came a voice beside her. She turned to look. Her boss, a short, stocky man with green hair and a star tattoo on his right cheek spoke.

"You've been living here these last few weeks. We definitely couldn't afford you if you were hourly. On top of that, you've created most of Deseret and the neighboring states single-handedly with an attention to detail that others struggle to keep up with."

She saw several heads nodding in agreement.

"Today's launch would not be possible without you," he continued. She tried to recall his name, but it wouldn't come.

"As such, we're naming the first town you created after you. City2854 will now be called Lothania. I talked to the board, and they approved. Also, effective immediately, you have been promoted to Staff Engineer, which should be a surprise to no one familiar with your work ethic."

She must have looked as confused as she felt. She only showed up and did what needed to be done. She hadn't been scheming for a promotion. The scrutiny made her nervous, so she was usually careful not to excel too much. The last few weeks had been one long distraction-inducing accident.

"Th-thank you," she managed to eek out.

"Don't thank me yet. You haven't been doing *everything* that a Staff does. Your new responsibilities will also involve upgrading Inferiere, without interruption to citizens or to the global authorities."

"Inferiere?"

"Yes. But there's time for that, don't worry. Today, I'd like you to help set up the new citizens. We already have a thousand contracts for immortality on Mijloc."

At the end of his sentence, her manager panned his attention across the various witnesses, and more finger-snapping happened. Surprised by her own comfort, Aida giggled at how consistently they perpetuated their misunderstanding her ailments. She couldn't fault them too much, since she'd never met another person with her mix of neuroses and they probably hadn't either so at best their efforts were a hodgepodge of guesswork. Aida's combination of intelligence and disfunction that made her excel at her work marked her as an anomaly. Many people with her level of compulsive response to overstimulation had been destroyed so much by the time they made it to her age of twenty-nine, either by the disease itself or by negative social interactions, that they struggled just to handle the day-to-day of existence.

"Thank you," she muttered again, unable to make eye contact directly with him because she *was* overstimulated yet trying not to seem so. She turned abruptly and closed the door behind her, giving up on the pretenses before they could render her incapable of talking at all. Aida again heard the hushed voices and was pretty sure they were talking about her still. The cool, dim lights helped her to focus. She sat on the bench and thought for a moment while she changed into her haptic gear. Another piece of the puzzle of her future was falling into place in her mind.

Inferiere. Had anyone known about her connection to Jordan Helm, she wouldn't have been given access. For that transgression, she might have been fired. But she hadn't been, and her depression and overwork had looked to Paivana Thoughtforms like job dedication before a big launch.

The promotion brought with it contract duty. The contracts, Aida knew, weren't about the people who signed them. Many poorer families could now afford immortality for their loved ones. Most had kept the animus modules of loved ones in secure storage for ages. People who arranged for their loved ones to re-enter something that resembled a living world had spent much of their life savings already just keeping their animus modules protected and functioning.

Aida knew all of this, and for the most part, didn't care. The only thing she was concerned about was building the few bodies she had left. There were three transplants she needed to move in. One was named Sarah Kempe, an infant who died before she had even made two years old. She had been born diagnosed with a brain tumor that slowly sucked her life away. The animus module could do many things, but it could not cure cancer. Her mother had installed it on the off-chance that one day, she would be able to afford a sub-model to help continue her child's life. Then she'd left to Mars to make that dream a reality and never returned. The animus module had gone into cold storage, which meant that her module was completely shut down, and never checked for operability in the ten years since.

Aida ran a quick diagnostics on the module, which, aside from being a slower model than others she'd seen, functioned well enough. She then pulled up the body she'd been preparing for the girl. It was a tiny pink body, perfect with little toes and fingers, and most importantly, no brain tumor or defect at all. She linked the two and then waited for the block-chain cypher to update the identity number and reflect the fact that the baby had been moved from stasis to a certified world. The baby stretched its little arms and the blue eyes popped open. The fat little girl wiggled her hands, then her arms, and then opened her mouth and began to scream.

Had it been a real-life scream, Aida would have probably screamed too. The virtual scream had less teeth. It was irritating and loud, but didn't rattle Aida's nerves. All she saw was a cute little baby on a black background, kind of like a video game. The baby would be able to see nothing but darkness. She shut Sarah's module back down, now that she was certain the link worked, and with a thought, located the planned would-be parents. The couple had been killed in a carjacking. The husband had been shot with a gun, and the wife pushed out of the car at fifty feet in the air. She had the good fortune to die instantly on contact with the ground. The husband lingered on life support for nearly a week before he too died, or "transitioned" as they were trained to say.

First she pulled up the man's body that she had created for him. It resembled his real-life body mostly, but that alone would have been boring. She'd given his hair a natural bluish-black tint, and made him about half an inch taller so that instead of being the same height as his wife, a taller woman at five feet and six inches, he was just a shade taller. She'd given him the muscle build of a soccer player, and since she didn't have much information about genitals and more private things like that, she'd had to use some creativity in those areas. Looking at him now, she felt that she did all right with the proportions of everything, perhaps a bit too generous in the manhood though. She was about to link his module when she realized that he might feel bashful naked and being observed. He wasn't one of her Obatali. With a thought she placed herself in front of him, and gave him a simple white tunic, and then linked him. He awoke with a start.

"Wha-who are you? Where am I?"

"Welcome to Mijloc," she said in as sing-song a fashion as she could muster, which wasn't very sing-song. Her teeth rattled in her head as she felt the tension rising behind her eyes. Someone should have asked her if she wanted this new responsibility.

"Mijloc?"

She stuck to the script she'd been given.

"It's a virtual world, modeled after pre-Equilibrium earth."

"Who are you?"

"Aida Lothian," she told him. "You are Mason Beck, correct? I made you."

"Y-you made me? I don't think so."

She realized that she'd slipped accidentally into the god-mode she'd once used for her humans on Oduduwa.

"No, I don't mean made you like that. Just, I made the virtual body for you."

"Oh. So this isn't real?"

"Well this is the interface for me to make sure your animus module works still. When we're done here, I'll introduce you to your daughter."

"Daughter?"

"Only if you want her. Your wife will be joining you, and from what I understand, you two were trying to get pregnant before....you transitioned."

"Transitioned? Oh...you mean died. Both of us? Hannah was still alive when..."

"I'm sorry, yes. You both gave up your physical bodies. But you'll be reunited. In fact, I can do that here now that I think of it. One second."

Protocol 10191 said that if possible, families should be

reunited in a safe neutral environment outside of Mijloc. Red burned behind Aida's eyes as she tried to focus on the work. The man before her seemed kind enough, but her mind kept slipping back to her rules. Don't trust nice people. With another thought and more focus than she thought she had, Aida pulled in the body she'd made for Kathryn, his wife. Aida had tampered with that body too, and had given her the perfect waist-to-hip ratio of modern fashion of 0.7. Also, she'd removed a childhood scar from the woman's upper lip. Just like the man, she put a thin white tunic over her before linking Kathryn to her module.

"Kathryn Douglas?"

The woman stirred then opened her eyes, a peculiar shade of burnt orange and brown. Kathryn looked toward the man first, into the black space beyond, and then toward Aida before running across nothing towards Mason, her arms extended for a hug.

"Would you like to meet your daughter?"

Kathryn only looked at her, confused.

"Only if we want her," Mason assured.

With another thought, the baby re-appeared. This time when she awoke, her face turned a bright red and she screamed without interruption. Aida recited the script without taking pauses to breath, and by the end of it sucked in a long gasp of air.

"This is Sarah. She was abandoned some time ago, and she's in need of a good home. We have a house set aside in a town called Lothania, if you want it. And you can take her with you."

The woman reached out and plucked the child from space. She held her on her shoulder and rocked her until she calmed. Aida had known Kathryn would want the child, because Aida had cheated. Since the baby wouldn't remember much if anything of her previous life anyway, Aida had created her body to look like Kathryn, and she had given the child Mason's gorgeous blue eyes. The child looked as though it had come from their bodies, and when she grew, she would look come to look even more like Kathryn.

"We'll take her," Mason said, speaking for them both as his eyes fixed on the helpless creature.

"Okay then," Aida said, ready for the interview to close. "When you get to your house, on the coffee table there will be forms to complete. Fill them out and as soon as you're done, they'll disappear and go into your files. Are you ready to see your new house?"

Both nodded in unison. The child seemed to have fallen asleep so wouldn't be bothered by the quick change. With another thought, the family were in their new home in Lothania, at the kitchen table. Aida knew that from that point forward, everything in the world would seem very similar to life back on earth. The child, Sarah, unless they decided to tell her otherwise, would never know anything but Mijloc.

Aida exhaled. The script was complete and soon she would be alone in the blackness again. After she dropped off the family, she couldn't see them any more than they could see her. That was a legal requirement of certified worlds – the right to privacy. The home, once given, was property that belonged to the people who occupied it. If Aida were to look inside of occupied homes, she would be breaking several laws now that Mijloc was certified.

The process of handing off the child to her new family made her mind wander again back to the child that she had shared with Jordan in her dream. Another block of a plan she wasn't fully sure she was creating threatened to fall into place. If both Mijloc and Inferiere were on the same network, as she knew they were, then she could use the bridge between them to sneak Jordan out. She could pry him away from his animus module the same way as she now hoped to do herself, and move him to Mijloc.

It wouldn't be freedom, not real freedom as he'd prefer it - but they could make it work together. In the process, she could create the child she had seen in her dream. Where others could only dream, she had the power to *create*.

At first, Aida scoffed at her own idea. The likelihood that Jordan would want her back was pretty low. But if she could hack herself, perhaps she could hack him too. Since she was already swimming in ethical gray areas, a little tweak to prevent him from remembering who was responsible for his capture wouldn't really cause much harm.

It was a pipe dream. She had the skills, and could figure out what she didn't know. But, how did she get her hacked self into Mijloc? Maybe, she thought, she could get him done first, and then follow after - once she had some idea how to do it.

And the baby. She wanted a baby too.

That was when she got her idea. She could do a back-story, and if done correctly, she could put Jordan beyond suspicion, because it would seem like he'd always been there. If she spent more time on back-story, and less time on comforting, she could generate a bullet-proof alibi for the pair of them. If she did that, a child would be almost obligatory. She smiled to herself as the pieces locked together in her mind.

15

Choose Your Reality

Saturday, November 20, 2258

Lothania, Deseret - Mijloc

With glacial movements Lincoln resumed the tedious process of packing away her investigation. She compiled the contents from her writing desk drawers into the plastic box under her bed, along with the rest of the evidence that she couldn't bear to look at but couldn't throw away. The first letter of condolence she'd gotten from Sheriff Al was in there, as well as the crime scene photos she'd taken herself. Two years of "evidence" that had ultimately amounted to nothing was piled away into the box. She considered burning the bunch of it and letting the investigation go in a Viking funeral.

Afterwards, she sat on her bed and stared at the wall. Without the investigation that had turned into a full-time job, she didn't have anything to spend her time on. More consequentially, she had nothing to distract her mind from the fact that her mother had died. She allowed herself to finally miss the woman, without dispassion, and without judgment. She could empathize with the hurt that she'd experienced, and the betrayal of a situation that she could never have controlled.

Lincoln retrieved a photograph album that she hadn't looked at since before the incident from her closet, and leafed through it, pausing on each page. There were pictures of her as a newborn, pink and crying, and then pictures of her at the park at town center. In those images, her mother looked on with tired eyes as Lincoln played. A few pages later, the pictures changed to the smiling three of them, probably taken by a professional photographer. They looked like a happy family in those images. She wiped an escaped tear away. Nobody would ever have been able to see the layers of deception beneath.

Afternoon arrived in its own languorous time. Lincoln dressed early in absence of other commitments, donning a shimmery black dress and matching stockings with an emerald overcoat. After half an hour of checking and re-checking her communicator time, she made her way to Sarah's house. She walked since Sarah was planning to drive that evening and it would have been redundant to have two cars. That wasn't the only reason though. Lincoln enjoyed the peaceful sound of the anemic stream trickling over its pebbled bed as she wandered along.

While she walked, she heard a noise from the woods to her left. Remembering the tooth-filled worm from a previous experience, she fought the temptation to close her eyes, and stared toward the sound. A branch snapped in the woods behind her, causing her to jump and twist around, nearly falling into the water. The peace had been dutifully shattered, and all she could imagine were tall cactus trees with broad cloth-like leaves and the gray-red worm attacking her. A shape grabbed her attention in the corner of her eye and she shrieked as she made out a giant bird that looked as though it were made of clay. It swooped low as it approached, weaving through the trees with effortless ease. It neared her and she in return ran along the creek bed in her flats. Just as her mind told her she would be clawed by the creature, the size of a small car, she froze and cringed, awaiting impact, but the impact never came. She turned and saw that there was no bird any more. A tiny voice that didn't quite materialize etched into her brain that she had to get a grip or she would end up just like her mother.

Lincoln knocked loudly on the front door when she finally arrived, dusty from the run and stockings damp with stream water. She glanced over her shoulder expectantly as she waited for Sarah to let her in. Katy opened the door instead and the two glared at each other with mutual contempt. Lincoln treated Katy with more respect than she deserved, and guessed from the polite coldness with which Katy returned to her that they shared a concern: neither of them wanted to lose Sarah from their lives. The difference in their positions was that Lincoln was coming closer to Sarah, and that meant that some day, possibly soon, Lincoln might have enough influence to cut Katy away for good. The thought made it easier to navigate the icy welcome she received, coupled with general neglect, as Katy deposited her in the formal living room and left her alone.

Lincoln texted Sarah to make sure that she was aware Lincoln had arrived before she took her seat offered in the formal living room. The same heavy wood-carved frames around Victorian cushions pressed inward as she lowered herself onto them. She was alone, and the anxiety of the clay bird hadn't completely left her yet, but she was beginning to calm. As one type of anxiety left, another claimed its place.

Sarah would be there any moment, and Lincoln didn't know how much of an impact her appearance would have that evening on the trajectory of their night. She'd chosen the black dress because it was slimming and it favored her legs, easily her best feature. Lincoln looked much younger than she was because of her face's round shape, something she felt she needed to compensate for with the rest of her clothing. The dress suited that purpose, low cut in the front with black mesh lace covering her cleavage. Cut short, the gown revealed just a little more thigh than was strictly appropriate.

She obsessed over whether she'd chosen her outfit correctly when she heard a rattling noise from the room entrance leading to Sarah's bedroom. There in the entryway stood Sarah, in a bright red dress with thin straps that might have held it to her body, had they been necessary. Equally luminescent lipstick matched the form-fitting dress, covered in a thin lace pattern that ended just below where her buttocks met her thighs. Sarah's blonde hair was fixed into waves that fell like molten gold over her shoulders. The outfit gave her blue eyes an iridescent greenish tint.

"Hey Lincoln," Sarah said, as she approached where Lincoln sat. Lincoln felt her heart jump as she rose to her feet.

"Sarah, you look amazing."

"Thank you. Shall we?"

Sarah offered her arm and Lincoln took it, noticing as she did that Sarah smelled strongly of roses and vanilla. The pair made their way into the family Mercedes and Sarah drove them into Lyra Craevis. Massive iron-framed doors swung easily on their hinges when Sarah and Lincoln arrived at Vino. Sarah pulled her along through before the door closed authoritatively behind them, and the greeter, a young man who seemed about their age, asked for their information.

"Douglas," Sarah said, just as Lincoln was about to try to explain that they didn't actually have the reservations she'd forgotten to make. The man scanned his eyes over both of their bodies to such an extent that Lincoln felt she needed to pull her emerald-green coat in more closely. Then, with a dismissive look, he turned.

"Follow me," he told them over his back.

He led them through the restaurant with a utilitarian theme. Columns that looked like iron pilings drew her eyes upwards to a ceiling that was as spacious as the floor of the restaurant. Even full, the tables were far enough apart to guarantee private conversation against the din of chatter. They didn't stop at any of the tables on the main floor, though. The pair passed through the lobby and toward the back, where another giant iron door loomed. The man pushed it open, and passed through, showing them to a tiny room with a table set up for two. In the middle rested a thin red candle, which matched Sarah's dress, on a tiny circular patio-style table. A fireplace roared in the corner which kept the room warm enough that Lincoln pulled off her emerald coat. The man took her coat, and collected Sarah's white faux-fur jacket, hanging both on a coat rack near the entrance. Out of the shadows arrived a woman in a white dress shirt and an apron folded down at the waist. She stood motionless beside the table while the man helped them into their seats and then left the room.

"Girl's night?" the woman asked, with an easy smile and subtle make-up that made it seem as though she wasn't wearing any at all on naturally flawless skin.

"Our first date," said Sarah, as she reached out to grab Lincoln's hand. Lincoln felt her face go hot a little, but the woman, who she decided must have been the waitress, nodded with her smile unchanged.

"What would you have to drink?"

Lincoln met Sarah's eyes and gave the equivalent of a shrug. She didn't know the difference among the names, and

Vino had wine in the name, so clearly was somewhere that required a bit of knowledge. Sarah, unfazed, addressed the waitress.

"Two Charles's Cabernet please."

"Glass or bottle?"

Sarah's eyes met Lincoln's and then the two at the same time replied.

"Bottle."

They laughed as the waitress left to fill the order. That act relaxed Lincoln and seemed to relax Sarah too, although until Lincoln noticed the shoulders release and body shrink as it loosened, Lincoln hadn't realized that Sarah was anxious at all. She seemed to be in her element, whereas Lincoln's tastes stayed more pedestrian. Still, Lincoln enjoyed the glamour Vino and the jealous glances as they crossed the restaurant floor to the private room. Sarah slid her chair around the table so that instead of being across from each other, the two were side-by-side. Being away from prying eyes meant that the two of them could and did hold hands for the entire time.

Lincoln felt tipsy after only the first glass of wine, a sensation she equated with floating just above herself, wafting on the breezy cent of Sarah's perfume. It didn't even feel strange when Sarah's hand moved to Lincoln's thigh, resting casually while the two talked with unnecessarily hushed whispers. They laughed together at the pretentiousness of everything, while at the same time reveling in it.

The date was over too soon. Dinner had been majestic with perfect service and company. The wine had done its job and conversation flowed effortlessly between them as they smoothed the road bumps of their more recent history together. They had talked of growing up together, and in social faux pas, of other dates, most of which had ended tragically. They had talked about how lucky they were to have met at all, and to have made it this far. Then, they had gone to see Maudling Aggression, the tragic love story of a terrorist group leader Lancaster and his love Tess. The movie was sobering in ways, and in its wake, their date took on a second life, as the frivolity of the earlier evening turned into something more serious.

Minutes later, the city disappeared behind them, then the suburbs, until only countryside remained as Sarah drove them back toward Lothania. After that, Lincoln could make out nothing but open highway in the thick darkness. Eventually the sign for the city appeared. Lincoln's head began to swim and her chest tightened. The car pulled into the driveway, and Sarah shut the engine down before turning toward Lincoln. The escaping light made her green-blue eyes flash like peridot.

"I had a fun tonight," she said. "Thank you for a wonderful date."

"Me too," Lincoln provided. The evening was coming to an end, turning her stomach over slowly.

"Do you want to come in?" Sarah asked timidly as though the answer to that question might be as painful as a root canal. Lincoln didn't leave her wondering though. Almost as soon as the words left Sarah's mouth, Lincoln's lips were there in their wake. It was impulsive, and partially may have been the wine, but as their lips met she felt the electricity, the spark, that told her that the romance would work. Something in her pushed her forward, as the kiss drew out longer, and parlayed the gentle touch into something visceral and real. She saw the passion in Sarah's eyes as the kiss dwindled to a close, and the same longing she felt in her heart.

Chance favored them that evening as they passed through the silent halls of the bed and breakfast uninterrupted. There were no winter residents, and Katy had apparently decided not to wait up for them, which was probably just as well as she would have witnessed two lovers embraced and groping through the halls, up the stairs, and pushing into Sarah's bedroom. Sarah did remember to lock the door behind them as they dropped a trail of clothing from the doorway to the bed. Black and red dresses intertwined on the floor as their owners followed suit on the thick feather mattress-topper.

Afterwards, Lincoln lay with her head across Sarah's chest, listening to her muffled heartbeat and staring down at her bare legs and painted toenails. She knew that she was smiling, and resisted the urge to give tacky compliments or, as one of her very few third dates had done, offer up a hand for a high-five. She laughed out loud a little at that remembrance.

"What are you thinking?" asked Sarah, with an endearing happy tone.

"Do you really want to know?"

"I do."

"Just that this is probably the best night I've ever had."

"So it wasn't weird?"

"What? No, did *you* think it was?"

Lincoln felt her heart race waiting for an answer. Sarah seemed to think it over for what seemed to be an eternity.

"No," Sarah told her. "I don't think I've ever felt less weird than right now with you."

Lincoln exhaled slowly, watching Sarah's stomach raise and lower with each breath. Then the wall shimmered. Lincoln closed her eyes so that she wouldn't have to see or react to what she knew would happen next. She willed herself to only be in that one moment, listening to the steady heartbeat of her lover, comfortable in the night. Whatever it was that she might have seen, she purposefully didn't. Then she noticed that Sarah's heartbeat had jumped. Instead of the steady rhythm she'd been letting pull her into unconsciousness, the drumbeat rapidly increased to easily twice what it had been, and she heard and felt Sarah suck in her breath quickly.

"Are you okay?" she asked, her eyes squeezed shut tightly.

"Do you see this?"

Lincoln forced her eyelids apart. There were no walls. They held each other atop a bed surrounded on every side by miles and miles of yellow and gray sand. Something like a cloud moved overhead and the ambient light brightened. A bulge grew beneath the sand as something the rough size of a school bus pushed its way toward the surface. The ground opened and a massive worm's head broke through the sand. Rows of concentric teeth raised above the bed. A figure in the distance yelled something. This figure seemed familiar to Lincoln, but she was afraid to believe what she saw. The sound echoed, a cross between a screech and a shout, and the worm seemed to stop in response before pulling back beneath the sand. Once the worm was no longer distracting her, Lincoln could see the figure clearly. Suspended in the sky, with her hair flared out in a massive halo, Lincoln's mother levitated above the earth.

A moment later they were back in Sarah's room. Lincoln quickly jumped from the bed and pulled on her underwear followed as quickly by her black dress, grunting as she struggled with the zipper while Sarah spoke behind her.

"Did you see that, Lincoln?"

Lincoln shuddered and shook as she tried and failed to pick up her coat. Then she crumpled to the floor, with her black dress strapped on one shoulder and hanging down across her chest, the other strap still down by her waist. She put her hands in her head gand began to cry.

"I saw it too," Sarah said. "And did you see who that was?"

"It couldn't have been."

"I swear I saw her, Lincoln. It wasn't just you. That was

your mother and she seemed to be controlling that creature. What happened?"

"I don't know, Sarah, I don't. This has been happening to me and I thought I was going crazy. You saw it, really?"

"How would I know what we saw otherwise? I saw it. You're not crazy."

Lincoln raised herself to her feet, and dropped the dress which she hadn't managed to completely get into. She climbed back into the bed and into Sarah's open arms. Then she lay her head back down, but this time pulled the thick down blanket up to cover their naked bodies.

"I thought I was going crazy," she admitted, "and I didn't want to tell you."

"You've seen this before?"

With a sigh, Lincoln explained the occurrences of the last several days that Sarah hadn't yet known about, relieved to finally have someone she could talk to about the hallucinations.

"I have to leave this world. I can't really tell you too much about it, and you wouldn't understand anyway the way that you've become, but I can't help you from here," Sarah quoted.

"Do you think that was real?"

"We both saw it, right? What do you think?"

Lincoln didn't know what to think. If she wasn't crazy, and if there was some strange world that her mother could have escaped into, then that meant that her mother was still alive. It was tantalizing to think, and infuriating at the same time. A note, a well-detailed letter to Lincoln, with actual explanations that somehow were provable. Two years of her life would have been redeemed just with that much. Or not, she thought. She wouldn't have believed. She hadn't even when presented with the evidence directly. Sarah's confirmation was what it had taken to convince her.

"What now, Lincoln?" Sarah asked, with a hint of what Lincoln thought may have been trepidation. Whether the fear was of Lincoln's next choice, or the very real threat presented by giant worms, she couldn't be certain. The more she thought about it as the seconds turned to minutes, the more she wondered how such a cruel-seeming world could have ever come to exist just beyond the boundaries of reality.

16

Connections

Saturday, November 20, 2258

Lyra Craevis, Deseret - Mijloc

Bodhi spent the evening on Saturday scouring records from two years earlier, but it still didn't make sense. Maintenance staff had stumbled across Jane's body after hours in her condominium home. She had lived alone according to the reports, though another alluded to a live-in boyfriend. He flipped back and forth between the print-outs, looking through one and then the other. The dates didn't make sense. The boyfriend had been with her in 2243, nearly fifteen years before she'd died, so the report had no bearing on her life at the time of her death and he wasn't sure why it was even in Paivana Thoughtforms possession at first. He looked at the sheet one more time. Across the top was a reference to another document, one that he hadn't seen yet.

He pulled up a control panel and entered the reference

number into the interface. A second later, the search returned with an icon link to the document. Then he tapped the document and a full ten-page print-out appeared on his desk before him. It was a complaint filed by Jane on December 4th, 2243. There seemed to have been a malfunction in her animus module. She'd reported being unable to move or control her body for a period of five minutes. The part that caught his attention was her claim to have been possessed by some an other-worldly entity named Libera.

He lay the page gently atop the stack of papers, pressing the corners flat and lining them up. Bodhi knew that name. In Event Horizon, 21 years before, he'd discovered Libera's nineteen worlds, each tuned to near perfection within the rules of the Event Horizon video game. Each barren of any forms of human life, but with perfectly-balanced ecosystems designed to continue for hundreds if not thousands of years. The woman behind that name was an artist - and had accepted his offer to join the company. She, too, had died in suspicious circumstances.

Too many coincidences.

He ran his hand through his hair and studied the report a bit longer, until she got to the bottom of the page where the response was written out after a diagnosis session with the animus module. The official finding was there was nothing wrong. The device functioned within operational parameters. He scanned the report once more. Within Jane's hallucination, Libera had taken over her boyfriend's body and explained that she didn't want to hurt her before apologizing for the transgression and releasing both of them. Then he searched for another report, one that he'd read many times before, guilt-ridden for having been so wrong about his one hire.

The report was labeled "Decision Matrix for Aida Lothian" across the top. He folded the pages over and looked for what he knew was in there. Her vital signs had stopped functioning shortly after she went into a coma. Unlike Jane, she'd been found in haptic gear, and her last connection had been to Mijloc. He didn't need to read more of the report to recall that the last year of her life had been 2237, two decades prior, the first to die on company property.

The "decision" the matrix was meant to calculate involved only what to do with her body. The end result, after months of investigations and reports and news coverage, was the lone woman deserved a funeral, which Paivana Thoughtforms paid for in full. Leafing through it now, some of the suggestions made him feel nauseous. One had gone so far as to cremate the body and drop the ashes from a high altitude to disperse into the atmosphere and avoid extra related costs. Another less-offensive option had been to bury the body unmarked off-world and have an official funeral in-world It would have been more cost-effective than the earthbound funeral to which they eventually conceded. That wasn't the intent though. The work that she'd put into it and her lack of real-world family and friends made more than a few believe that she would have preferred to be buried in the world she helped create. Some said the reason she excelled as she did was that the world she created was more real to her than the one she occupied. Bodhi didn't know if that was true, and didn't spend much energy trying to figure it out. Instead, he wondered about the connection between the two women.

Bodhi sighed and drew his hand over his face. He didn't have time for more investigation. He'd already spent too much in Lothania, poring over records. Business was being neglected. Taking a deep breath, he called for security. Thirty seconds later, the door to his office shook with a resounding thud.

"Come in," he called out. A tall woman in a sleek gray uniform emblazoned with Paivana Thoughtforms across the chest entered.

"Mr. Rawls?"

"Here, JoAnn" Bodhi said, and tossed the papers at the woman, watching them flutter for a moment before they digitized down into a data-coin that she caught it in her palm.

"What's this?"

"Lincoln Montague. Her mother died a couple of years ago, and she thinks it was murder."

"I didn't know we can die in here."

He shook his head.

"We can't. I'm not sure how it was done, and that's what I need you to find out."

The woman seemed to chew on this for a few seconds, her mouth working behind closed lips.

"All of those documents are for one little girl?"

"No. I was trying to connect some dots. Take a look through those and see what you can find out. I think the woman's death may be linked to something else, but I'm not sure what yet. Do you remember Aida?"

"Creepy Aida?" JoAnn's mouth curled into a grin before she seemed to notice that Bodhi wasn't smiling, then her grin evaporated.

"Aida Lothian, the woman who built most of Mijloc," Bodhi continued. "But yes, 'Creepy Aida'." He'd forgotten about that nickname. With employee churn, most people who'd known it had cycled out, but JoAnn had been his right-hand security representative for more than thirty years. She'd seen it all.

"You think she's got something to do with the death?"

"It sounds strange now that I say it out loud, but yes. Lincoln's mother was named Aidalee Montague. Do you remember when Jane Sorendsun died back in 56?"

The man arched an eyebrow at the mention of Jane's name. The entire organization had been shaken by the death of one of their own. He slowly nodded his head up and down.

"She was good people."

"Yes, I liked her. She died the same year that Aidalee killed herself in-world. Not only that, but Jane and Aida Lothian died in the same condition - starved and dehydrated. Even if they were 19 years apart, that's a little strange. Aida slipped into a coma first with no brain or animus module activity. Jane died on the floor of her condo, so we can't know if she went through a coma or not - but she might have."

"19 years is a long time, I don't get that connection aside from a name. But is it possible that Jane masqueraded as Aidalee Montague in-world, and became so obsessed that she stopped eating and eventually died?"

"No. She couldn't have accessed the positronic networks from her condo, and that doesn't explain how Aidalee hung herself to death from rafters."

Not letting the impossible go, JoAnn continued.

"Maybe the death in-game was because of Jane's death out of game and the system didn't know how to respond once it stopped getting signals. Could she have hacked to connect her animus module from off-world to Mijloc?"

Bodhi mulled through JoAnn's suggestions. The positronic network was guarded by several AI intrusion detection firewalls, so he hadn't considered that potential, but it did make a strange kind of sense. He didn't know how the system would behave if bio-indicators suddenly dropped from a haptic suit connection, but hanging someone from a rafter seemed like an arbitrary choice of death, as opposed to simply leaving an in-world citizen immobile. His communicator sounded, reminding him of all of the work that he had been ignoring to fuel his obsession.

"Figure it out," he said. "You may be right. We need to understand better."

"Will do, Mr. Rawls," the woman said, and brought her

legs together for an attention-like stance before turning and leaving him alone. Bodhi turned to answer the chime.

"Connect."

17

Duality

Wednesday, October 25, 2237

Seattle, Washington - Earth

Aida was back in the meeting room, and this time, there was no ambiguity about her ask. Emily paced on the other side of the table. The pacing was unusual, as was the lengthy consideration. In the past, Emily had always been interested in whatever "opportunity" Aida identified. Aida wasn't certain that Emily would be willing to do another favor for her, however close they'd become.

"Girl, that plan *might* work. A software animus module – sure, why not. It'd be slow though, right? Simulations always are because of all the extra work. You'll be a virtual turtle."

Emily chuckled and her whole body shook, her locks bouncing like slender animals.

"That depends," Aida replied, "on how much of it we can parallelize and how much needs to be sequential."

"You would be a software simulation, honey. Always slower. Always, always."

"If I can parallelize everything that's already non-sequential in the animus module using quantum cores, then it will be exactly as fast, if not faster, than an actual module itself. The wire latency would evaporate."

"But how are you going to bump your animus code into quantum cores, on which I remind you that you are running entire virtual worlds, without anybody noticing a change in performance?"

"Emily, it would be nothing. The cluster can handle it. I have access to *both* systems as a Staff, and I can smooth over any questions. Compared to running Mijloc, the spike would wash out in the noise."

"Okay, assume you can do that. They will find you and delete you."

"And I told you, I know how to do stop that."

Conversations about algorithms and technology were oases of peace in the turbulent ocean of Aida's emotions. In these subjects, she could talk forever without ever exhibiting any symptoms at all.

Emily raised one eyebrow and looked at Aida.

"Really. My algorithm distributes the animus module code across Mijloc and Inferiere. Append a bit of code to each object in Mijloc, store the map in Inferiere."

"So if your body gets wiped in Mijloc somehow?"

"It'll take some time for my code to rebuild. After that, though I should be able to come back Mijloc any time I want. The back door will still be there."

"If nobody finds it and closes it."

"If anybody finds it and closes it, then I won't know because I'll be dead."

Saying the risk out loud raised her blood pressure and chopped up her breath. The risk was almost too high. Traffic between Mijloc and Inferiere was non-existent, and she would probably be noticed if she kept a back door open. Even storing her object map somewhere in Labyrinth would have been preferable, since there was legitimate traffic occasionally into Inferiere from there, whenever a criminal was admitted. Synchronizing from Labyrinth to either virtual world was difficult because the network latency prevents real-time processing, so that was a non-starter. Inferiere-to-Mijloc was the only way she could think to make it work.

"Have you tried using ansible protocol?"

Aida first shook her head no. Ansible protocol had been developed for the initial purpose of military global near-real-time communication. A single millisecond was the entire delay when sending a message across the surface of the earth. She'd dismissed the protocol for the way that it worked - it was too detectable. The protocol was greedy in that it sent the same packet in multiple directions simultaneously and then relied on quorum to decide if each message had been received. Loss wasn't a possibility for the military, and neither was it for consciousness transfer, so ansible seemed a perfect fit. However, each message sent traveled by burst, and when encryption was added, the packets were massive. Usually, a.p. was used to initiate communication which then migrated to a less-intensive protocol when direct routes were established point-to-point.

But it could be scaled down. It was a protocol - a guideline more than anything. She could find wiggle room to send maybe a handful of messages per burst, or even a single message, if she didn't mind losing some packets. Planned correction, she could even dynamically alter the burst size based on the contents of the messages.

"That is a b-brilliant idea, Emily," she said as she thought it through.

"I still didn't say I would help."

"So will you? Help, I mean?"

"I know what you're doing. That man is a mass murderer. You just feel guilty because you got him arrested."

"That's not it. The bomb was just something that we disagreed about. He was wrong and I think he'll see that."

The words sounded weak coming out of her mouth. Aida wasn't convinced that there was a 'we', not really.

"Most people disagree about where to eat lunch. You know you're delusional, right? And don't blame your condition for this one. You are crazy-town right now."

"Yeah, but don't you want to see if it can be done?"

Emily was always looking for ways to do the impossible.

"Break out Jordan? Move you and him into a happy little life in Lothania? I kind of do. I don't see what you need me for though. You can do all of this yourself."

"I can't fire off the escape kit once I'm inside."

The one thing she couldn't do was cover her tracks.

"You sure you want to do that?"

Aida paused, thinking through a lifetime of indecision. She'd never been sure about anything, but at some point, decisions must be made, and she'd made this one.

"People pay a lot of money to get into Mijloc. It's discrete and quite in Lothania, peaceful. Why couldn't we be happy there?"

"The guy is a revolutionary. He's not going to be happy with a picket fence."

"He might."

"Delusional, girl."

"Are you going to help?"

"All I have to do is the escape kit? Yeah, I can do that."

"Thanks, Emily."

The call went dead, and Aida found herself alone in her room, pondering what it would be like for Jordan when she eventually freed him from Inferiere. Would he see the cactus trees fade away, replaced by a new, gentler world? Or would he be instantly teleported into the foyer of the tiny, unassuming house she'd prepared for them.

As important as Jordan was to her, the child she had seen in her dream, her daughter, is what urged her forward. Emily may have been right about Aida losing her sanity. That dream daughter had been hers and Jordan's. She'd *felt* it and known it with a level of certainty that could only exist in dreams. And Aida *wanted* that child, *Jordan's* child and her own.

Of course, it couldn't happen in Mijloc. Children weren't born in Mijloc. Infants were nursed and grew, children aged to adulthood, but creating new virtual people from scratch wasn't legal. The algorithms existed. Animals reproduced all the time in-world with the same statistical outcomes that existed in nature. But couples who wanted children in Mijloc had to do what the Douglas's did. They had to adopt one of the multitudes of children who had nobody to speak for them.

Aida didn't want a castaway infant - she wanted her own child. She wanted the experience of childbirth, bringing a new life into the world. She wanted to feed the child from her breasts as they were meant to be fed, and raise a child who didn't have her disorder, but who still came from her.

That was impossible in the real world for people like her. Her brand of personality quirk was partially genetic, and any child of hers had a chance to perpetuate the emotional development problems she had suffered through for most of her life. It was a side-effect of her mother being a clone and having had her reproductive system tampered with on the genetic level to prevent births in the cloning community. Even if she could find someone who could see past her condition, the probability of having a child with her disorder was way too high. Aida had long ago decided never to try.

That didn't quell the desire within her though. Just because there was no way for people to have children in Mijloc *now*, didn't mean it had to be that way. Another addendum to her plan stirred in her chest. It was just as insane and convoluted as the rest, adding unnecessary complexity to an already risky effort, but soon it occupied her focus. Her heart fluttered and she gulped quickly as the magnitude of it congealed in her mind. Aida pushed the growing obsession down, secure in the fact that she wouldn't forget. More pressing matters presented themselves.

With Emily's assurance of a clean exit, that freed Aida to make her necessary adjustments to her animus module to try linking her consciousness directly to a virtual world - specifically Oduduwa. This she wanted to accomplish by linking over ansible protocol using in-game plugins, but that wasn't the end of her idea. She also wanted to be free, and a software animus module could be altered to hack out her symptoms in a way that the physical nanites in her brain couldn't be. With the right code change, Aida could finally be her, without the burden of the disease that pressed her into isolation and loneliness.

Moments later, she slipped into her haptic suit, and navigated to Oduduwa. Instead of navigating to the surface, she made a motion like a circle in the air to open a screen for entering plugins. She wanted to test the idea of using ansible protocol as a communication bridge. If it worked, then the haptic suit would link to her animus module, and her animus module would link into Event Horizon, creating a circular connection loop and allowing her to maintain a tenuous connection to the virtual world even without the suit.

The change might also corrupt her animus module and leave her body as an empty shell, but everything had a risk.

Aida convinced herself that it would be simple to exchange one technical communication protocol for the other. She wasn't disappointed as she completed the configuration in a matter of seconds. There was one other thing she would need to do to ensure that her animus module could communicate with the virtual world.

With a sigh through grit teeth, she initiated the program. The world went black, or it must have. There was nothing. She couldn't see or hear anything. All she could feel was a ball of nausea forming where she thought her stomach had been and growing to fill the void. Then she felt her non-existent stomach trying to empty its contents in a peculiar clenching sensation. Her pulse quickened as the thought of her pending non-existence grew in her mind and overwhelmed her senses. Fifteen seconds of her life would be in the void, and she couldn't breath already. She knew that tears were streaming down the face that she couldn't feel and the red creeped up her spine. With a thought, she stopped the process.

Bright light penetrated through her open eyes. The front of her haptic suit was covered with the contents of her stomach. Aida would have to eat two meals to replace what she'd lost, by the looks of it. She could feel the dampness in her hair beneath the haptic helmet where her tears had soaked into her mop. Aida then checked the time. Ten seconds. She'd almost made it to fifteen. Almost…a deep heave pulled oxygen into her lungs as her body took over again. At some point, her breathing had stopped completely, and Aida hadn't realized when it happened.

"Fuck!"

Aida screamed the words at nobody but herself. All she needed was fifteen seconds, and that's it. That's as long as she guessed it would take to fully connect her animus module to Event Horizon, but she didn't know if she could make it. The image of the little girl pushed its way to the front of her mind. With a deep gulp of vomit-soaked air, Aida sucked in more air and squeezed her eyes closed. She brought the image forward and focused on the girl, who had the same eyes she did. One brown and one green, and both wide and expectant. Aida would do it for her.

Taking a deep breath, she initiated the program for a second time, and found herself nowhere, without concept of being any particular person. Grasping at the image of the girl, she couldn't remember who the girl was or why she cared. No memories. No thoughts. In a black void she floated, or rather, existed? She was the void and the void was her. Black wasn't the right word for it. Void void would have been a better description, as it was nothing of nothing. It might have been peaceful except every millisecond slipped by without her being able to recall it. She lived in each moment entirely, ticking one second into the next, until the brightness faded to nothing.

Then the pain began. First noises began to come in through the outside world, scratching red through her tender ears. The world outside bombarded her even in the darkened closet. The traffic screamed in her brain, and she could smell the odor of her own sweat like she was somebody else, unfamiliar, who had just finished a workout and refused to shower. The little light that did come in flared up and slid through the slits in her eyelids. She tried to look away from it, but her eyes wouldn't move. She heard screaming, and realized that it was her. She felt rocking as the world swayed around her, but that was also her, powerless and in the grip of a foreign force.

As suddenly as it had began, the pain stopped. She inhaled the fragrance of a clean that could only come from the vastness and emptiness of space. Aida opened her eyes and saw the Event Horizon universe. There before her, in all it's blue-green glory, orbited Oduduwa. Aida penetrated through the atmosphere and dropped herself down to the beach. She had done so carelessly though, and a sonic boom followed her descent, reverberating through the air, which caused the nations of Obatali to become aware of her again. Citizens in long flowing white cloaks looked up at her from the streets as she plummeted toward the ocean and broke its surface. Nearing the ocean floor, she fell faster and faster until her decent abruptly stopped. She looked around, and her eyes burned from saline.

At first she thought the discomfort was the result of her haptic suit link. When she found herself struggling for breath, lungs filling with fluid, she knew that it was more than that. It wasn't unusual for the haptic suit to create conditions of difficult breathing, but the water molecules were pressing at her from the inside. This wasn't an external experience. The water around her cooled her extremities too the point that she moved in glacial arcs. That's when she knew then that it had worked. Some part of her was now here, in Event Horizon, and the haptic suit couldn't protect her from the conditions created in her head by an animus module that tried to read her surroundings. She felt her grip on consciousness loosen as her oxygen intake dropped to nothing. Frantically she tried to swim upward but it was too far, and she didn't have the same momentum she'd had coming down. Her arms only succeeded in pushing her down further toward the bottom as the pressure built on her shoulders and head.

She was still Libera, Goddess of Worlds.

With a thought, the water above her opened and the fluid in her lungs ejected to join its host. She levitated herself through the empty space and lifted herself free of the waves. As she rose, crowds gathered on the beach beneath her. She willed herself back out of the game and into her tiny gaming closet. She peeled off her helmet and tight nanite suit, followed by her gloves and boots. She could still see the people gathered on the beach, staring at the spot from which she'd vanished. She could feel their awe as she communicated with that part of herself that remained behind. She willed the storm to move a mile to the right, and she knew without thinking that it had done so.

Aida had ascended. She had now limitless power in the world of Oduduwa. She felt everything happening at once there keeping her on the edge of red even in her closet. Aida hadn't expected the relentless onslaught of data. Her teeth jittered against one another as she felt a wave crashing on a distant shore. A bird flew by the one of the towers of the Obatali, and she felt it's feathers pushing the air. For a second, she held the information at bay by fighting it off with her willpower. It was too much. The heat was already growing behind her head. Gasping and clawing at her throat, she tried to get air to move through her lungs, but her diaphragm wouldn't respond. As she fell to the floor of her closet, she kicked at the wall and shoved her fingers against her right ear, behind which her animus module had been installed. Operating on instinct alone and fighting the red, she clawed at her head, breaking the skin. She didn't feel the blood trickling down her neck or the pain of the skin breaking under her nails.

A second later, air funneled through her lips and trickled like cold water through every nerve in her body. Her eyes regained their focus and her fingers fell with her arm down to her side. Aida drank the oxygen in, unable to move in her sea of red. At the edges, the red began to subside. The sensations from Oduduwa dropped off and tears welled in her eyes. Aida squeezed them shut and struggled to move, but her body wouldn't obey except for the small finger of her right hand. Then her hand followed, but the energy it took soon depleted and she let that fall. Closing her eyes, she thought about the image she must make for whoever eventually found her - vomit covered gear strewn on the floor beside her naked body, tear stains down her cheeks. Whoever discovered her first, she hoped they would at least put clothes on her before brining the entire world in.

But she didn't die. Instead, her breathing stabilized and her pulse began to drop. The sounds dropped even more into the background, and she distinctly became aware of the volantrae floating by outside. Aida managed a thin grin as she realized that death wasn't in her cards.

Now, her consciousness straddled two worlds. Only about 1 percent of her consciousness now ran from Event Horizon. The other 99 percent still happened in her animus module hardware, but that number would go down over time. The process had begun, and there was no stopping it now.

18

Well-Crafted Lies

Sunday, November 21, 2258

Lothania, Deseret - Mijloc

Her mother had traveled to another world. Another. World.

When she thought the words, she wanted to scream at herself the impossibility of them. If it hadn't been for Sarah's admission, had she not been there to corroborate what Lincoln had seen, Lincoln would never have believed it. But they had seen the proof, hadn't they? For a brief moment, they had seen through. Thinking back now, it was as though the separation between the worlds, whatever kept the hellscape they had witnessed from overflowing into their world, had grown thin enough to be transparent at least. If they had moved, had left the bed, she thought it was a very real possibility that they might have become stranded there with no way back.

"It wasn't her, Sarah. It couldn't have been."

Lincoln had held her mother's body up desperately to keep the air flowing through those dying lungs. That futile effort flooded back into her mind, bringing with it the smell of lavender perfume and the resistance of the dead-weight - proof that it had been her mother's body and not some plastic dummy or stand-in. She remembered stepping on the green slipper where it had fallen beneath the woman, and nearly tripping while struggling to keep from falling because if she did, her mother would die. Whoever the queen of the worms was, couldn't have been her.

"I saw her eyes, Lincoln. She had yours, blue and green, just like she used to. Her hair was sandy blond, and her voice. You heard her call to the worms right?"

Lincoln slipped the blouse from the day before over her body. She didn't bother with recycling the dirty bra. She looked toward where she'd left her underwear on the floor, only to have them smack into the side of her face. On the bed still, Sarah laughed at her and motioned to her to return to the sheets. They'd been there all morning, though, and it was nearly noon. Food would have to happen soon, or Lincoln would begin to get cranky and agitated.

"Why don't you come too? I think the Sheriff ought to know what we saw, and we can grab some brunch?"

"Does that mean I have to put clothes on," Sarah asked, teasing as she stood up naked from the bed.

"Yes, probably." Lincoln stood on one leg trying to slip her underwear over her ankle in an elegant manner, before she realized that there really wasn't an elegant way to put underwear on. She gave up and just stuck one leg through one hole, pivoted, and pushed the other through as well, before wiggling them over her bottom. Then she bent quickly, retrieved Sarah's underwear, and launched them at her the same way, but Sarah was quicker and caught them.

"It's my room," Sarah said as she grinned, "I get clean underwear."

She walked across the room toward the dresser, which Lincoln was unintentionally blocking. Instead of going around, Sarah wrapped her arms around Lincoln, pulled her in close and kissed her, squeezing their bodies together, before swinging around her and retrieving her new clothes from the drawer.

The act of sneaking from the house without Katy seeing them extended their departure from a simple walk down the stairs to a thirty minute planned escape. Lincoln would have preferred to march down to breakfast wearing only a robe just to see the reaction on Katy's face. Because Sarah had to live with her, Lincoln bowed to pressure, and snuck out the front door while Sarah distracted her mother with some casual conversation about the gardening that Sarah was *supposed* to be doing that day. From the little bit of the conversation that Lincoln heard, she thought that Katy had to be able to tell from Sarah's undeniable hyper-amicability that *something* had happened, and Lincoln was pretty sure that Katy was smart enough to figure the rest out for herself.

"Group hallucination," Sarah guessed when they were both back in the family car and a safe enough distance from the bed and breakfast that Lincoln could lift her head above the dashboard.

"It's so good to have you back," Lincoln said, and reached out to take Sarah's free hand, which rested on the center console between them. Sarah smiled at her and then continued.

"Seriously, it's a thing that happens. If you don't think it's your mother we saw, maybe it was that?"

Lincoln had heard of mass hallucinations, but she'd never met anyone who'd experienced one first-hand. It was a step up from Sarah's current two-worlds theory, so as theories go, she decided it was her new favorite. As far fetched as it was, at least there was a basis for the belief that was at least a little scientific in nature.

"I've heard that it can happen," she commented, "but I thought there was usually a primer or something, a shared experience that kind of kicks the whole thing off."

"I guess we weren't really discussing massive killer worms before. But we were talking about your mom. Do you think that would have been enough?"

"To make the leap from my mother to Queen of the Worms? Maybe."

"Do you still want to talk to the Sheriff about this. He hasn't been particularly helpful lately."

"But he *has* been. He's always answered my questions, even though he does seem to put a lot of energy into avoiding me sometimes."

"We're here. I guess we'll see."

To park in front of the Sheriff's office, they made a U-turn around a median that divided the wide Lothania main street. It had clearly been designed with the intention that the city grow in a way that it never actually did. With church in full session, the streets were empty, and the Sheriff's office looked abandoned. Hand in hand, Lincoln and Sarah walked through the door.

"You again?" the Sheriff asked. "Normally it's a lot longer between visits."

"We really need your input on something," Lincoln told him, "and it's weird."

"Weird?"

"Yeah, we saw something. Both of us. Not just me."

With that, Lincoln told him what they had seen, leaving out, of course, the fact that they were naked in bed together at the time, because it would have only distracted the Sheriff from what they'd wanted to talk about.

"Worms," he said, disbelievingly, "and your mother. Magic world that only the bed could travel to. And you saw this too?"

He directed his attention toward Sarah, who nodded vigorously. She noticed that his eyes kept falling to her hand in Sarah's, and self-consciously she pulled it back. She had to remember that they were still in small town Lothania. Although it wasn't technically a secret that Sarah "leaned a certain way", nobody talked about the fact anymore, by intention. It wasn't something that made people proud to live there.

"Listen, girls," he told them, "I'm not sure what you saw, but there aren't any giant killer worms near here."

"We *know* that. That's why we came to you – to see what you thought."

"Here's what I think. Go home, relax, play some video games on that new console you got last year, Sarah. I'll send a deputy to come around your place and see if there's anything dangerous out there. If we find anything, I'll let you know."

Lincoln saw in his face that he hid something, but she couldn't be sure what. She stared at him directly in the eyes, and he stared back at first. Then he shifted his eyes nervously and began to stand up to escort them out.

"No," Lincoln told him. "No, that's not all. What else?"

"It's not my place, Lincoln. You need to talk to your father."

"Niles? You want me to talk to Niles?"

"That's the deal we all made when we came here. Ask him about Mijloc. Make him tell you."

"I'm not going to do that Sheriff. *You* tell me. I'm twenty-one years old, and I don't have to answer to that man anymore."

The Sheriff was halfway to his feet, but then he changed course and plopped downwards. Suddenly he looked exhausted, as though he'd been working non-stop the entire thirty years he'd been Sheriff, or she'd guessed it must have been that long. As far as she could remember, he'd been Sheriff of Lothania.

"I suppose I'll tell ya. I told your parents, both of them, that they needed to let you know when your mother died. They should have told you when you turned eighteen."

"Are you talking about the affair? I don't see what that has to do with this, and we already know," Sarah spoke up.

"Not really, no, but that's part of it," Sheriff Al answered. "That wasn't really an affair. That's not my business though. This is."

"Well?"

"I guess I'll start. Twenty five years ago is when I came to Lothania. I was one of the first ten people here. It was me, Katy, Mason too," he started. Sarah smiled at the mention of her father's name. The man lived in Lyra Craevis now and she got to visit summers sometimes, Lincoln remembered, but she'd never actually met Sarah's father.

"There were a handful of others, but these are the important ones you need to know about. About six months after we got here, Niles showed up. He just appeared one day living in that farm, as though he'd been there the whole time. We didn't think too much about it."

"You didn't?" Lincoln asked incredulously.

"Yes. I'll get to why, just wait. So he was new, he was interesting, and everyone in town welcomed him. Some were more welcoming than others, like your mother, Katy, for instance. When Mason was out of town, Niles and Katy would sometimes keep each other company. You have to understand that that wasn't really a problem. Mason knew about it and was okay with it."

Lincoln checked Sarah's face to see if she was okay. She hadn't heard Sarah mention anything about that, and from the look on her beautiful, confused face, Sarah hadn't been aware.

"So far, not too much of a problem. They were all three very good friends. Now, the problem came about six months after that. *Your* mother," he motioned toward Lincoln," showed up. Suddenly, Niles only had eyes for her. About three months after that, they decided to get married exclusively to each other. Then your mother started to get bigger, you know, in the belly. She had a bun in the oven. That caught us all off guard."

"Doesn't seem that strange. It happens," Lincoln chimed in.

"Not really, it doesn't, not here. Think about it. When's the last time you saw a single pregnant woman here in Lothania?"

Lincoln thought back through her childhood. There had been lots of children, of varying ages, and many showed up in the schools. But she couldn't think of anyone who had ever been pregnant.

"It's not allowed, you see. Here, look at this."

With that, he pulled open the filing cabinet beneath his desk, fished through for something. When he found what he was looking for, he pulled it out and lay it in front of Lincoln and Sarah where they could both see it. The document looked like something legal, with a company name across the top: Paivana Thoughtforms. Beneath that was indicated "Immortality Agreement".

"They're called immortality agreements, but they have to be renewed every twenty-five years. Part of my job is to make that happen. I have one in here for everyone in the town. Everyone but your mom and Niles, are you following? So she showed up without an agreement, which is impossible. Then she got pregnant, I guess by Niles, which is also impossible. Look at the top of page three."

Sarah flipped the pages quickly before Lincoln could grab them, and they stared together.

Although sex is possible here in Mijloc, there is no capability for reproduction. This is due to international requirements around the recognition of offspring. If you decide that you are ready for a family, please see the local representation and they can assist you in procuring a child.

"That's kind of fucked up," Lincoln said. "They aren't allowed to have children."

Sarah had a different question.

"What's Mijloc?"

"So first questions first I guess. It's not that they weren't allowed to have children. They shouldn't have been *capable* of having children. Not here. The answer to the second question is what I've been getting to. It's going to get really weird, but just listen for a bit, and you can tell your mom all of this, Sarah, and she'll confirm I'm sure. Although I guess she'll be a little pissed at me."

He paused there, and stared into the distance, and his eyes jumped around from left to right and back again, as though he were trying to remember something he'd forgotten. When he seemed to have it, he began again.

"Trying to figure out how to explain Mijloc to people who only remember this world is hard. Let me see…I guess we can start with video games."

"Video games?"

"Yeah. So you know the new VR headsets that have come out lately."

Lincoln had known about them but had never used one. They seemed neat, but the technology wasn't ready for real immersion yet. Also, they'd only begun to come out in the last couple of years, and she had more pressing priorities than video games.

"Yes, I know of the system," she replied. Sarah nodded too.

"Well, imagine if that visor never came off. You would be stuck in whatever game it was that you were supposed to be playing. Imagine if you could never actually leave the game."

"What are you saying?"

"This world, Mijloc, that you live in. It's like that. So when I say that nobody has children here, it's true – nobody can because the 'game' doesn't allow it."

"This isn't a game, Sheriff. This is my life, our lives," Sarah corrected him, more quietly than Lincoln would have expected.

"Ask your mom when you get home, Sarah. And I didn't say this *is* a game, I said it's *like* one. You can't die here, usually. But… again, your mother did that too, didn't she, Lincoln?"

"What are the hospitals for? Paramedics? They were at my house. I had an emergency number to call. People answered."

"Two reasons. One is that we're legally required to have that. Global law requires emergency response teams be available in all certified worlds. Second, there are people who really want to be ER technicians. It's strange, I know, but here people can do whatever they want. They want to be ER, so we let them. Until your mother, we really didn't need them."

"My mother?"

"Yes. So if you're counting, in the span of time that she lived here, I've witnessed her do three impossible things. Show up without documentation, have a child, and die."

"But Sarah's mom, my dad, they're really messed up by what happened to my mother. My dad won't even leave the house."

The Sheriff nodded at this.

"He spiraled pretty hard. You have to understand, nobody ever dies here. Imagine living in a world where nobody dies, where everyone lives forever, and everyone assumes that to be the case. Then imagine that someone manages to do the impossible. And imagine that you were breaking a promise to that person, and felt responsible for the only death that this world, to my knowledge, has ever seen."

It was a lot to soak in. Lincoln thought about the implications of what she'd been told, but so far, all she had was a document and the word of the Sheriff, who as far as she knew, had never outright lied to her about anything. If he didn't want to tell her something, he usually was comfortable saying that it was none of her business. And he was so down to earth that it was impossible to believe that he was capable of a lie of this magnitude.

"What does that have to do with what we've seen?"

"I'm thinking that maybe your mother didn't die after all. Maybe, she found a way to leave. I'm not sure how that would be possible, but I plan on getting in touch with Paivana Thoughtforms tonight to see what I can find out. Maybe there's a way back from wherever she went."

"Sheriff, I think you have some idea on where she might have gone."

"I do based on what you've said, but I'm not going to speculate. Now, with what I just told you, you know what I know. I'll tell you what I find out."

Lincoln got up to leave, but Sarah didn't move until Lincoln grabbed her by the elbow. Even then, she was slow to rise and her eyes looked as though she were going to break down into tears.

"Are you okay?" Lincoln asked when they were out of earshot of the Sheriff, and through the door on the way to the car.

"No. I'm not okay at all. How can I be. Everything I know is a lie."

19

Defiance

Thursday, October 26, 2237

Seattle, Washington - Earth

Aida's first legitimate act of defiance was to hide twenty-five acres of land at the end of a creek from assignment. The lot sat away from the main road along a stream skirting just enough of a natural clearing to place a small farmhouse atop a sandy hill. Once the home was in place, she slid up onto her tiptoes as she examined the yard in the front of the building. Bull nettle, thorny sticker plants, and spear grass littered the property. Her lips curled up into a thin smile as she lifted her right hand and waved away the hostile vegetation. Canvas cleared, Aida placed a yellow rose bush just beside the front steps before adding crimson clover for ground cover. Her finishing touch was an homage to Jordan - a sprinkling of giant dandelions across the front yard.

An alarm sounded somewhere in the distance. She was too

focused to notice at first, but the second time it went off it shattered her concentration like an internal combustion engine. With a thought, the time hovered before her, and she realized that she was running late for her self-imposed date. She exited the Mijloc development program, and then she selected the Inferiere interface. She typed in the command to find Jordan Helm by his a.p. address. With no expectation of privacy in Inferiere, it wasn't so unusual for employees to search for the infamous. The world pulled up in front of her as a globe suspended in the air to the right of her console. A tiny red dot flashed on the surface, and she zoomed in.

The fact that he could be so easily tracked was the first problem she needed to fix. Using the Ceta programming console and her developer access, Aida updated the system to associate Jordan's virtual body identifier to a massive worm that frequented the cactus forests, and vice versa. From that point on, anyone who tried to find Jordan would discover a worm the size of a large van. Probably they would assume that Jordan had just been eaten, an impermanent state on Inferiere designed as an excruciatingly painful experience. It was a torturous world, meant for punishment, which it meted out with the combined expertise of Paivana Thoughtforms Discipline division.

Once that part was done, the hard part would come next. She needed to remap his animus module to Mijloc, and encourage the system to accept him. This would surface his footprint ID in Mijloc, but Mijloc and Inferiere were intentionally separated from each other, and were only both accessible through the employee network or the animus module banks. She was working from the employee network. Before she could possibly move Jordan, now Worm34998, from Inferiere to Mijloc, she had to change him so that he couldn't easily be recognized. She was prepared for this.

With a thought, she connected to a private meeting room

through her animus module. On the desk, she'd left a piece of paper that wasn't really a piece of paper. The paper was a tangible representation of the code she'd used to share her consciousness into Event Horizon. She already ran nearly thirty percent of her consciousness from there with no significant adverse impacts. He would be easier to move since Mijloc and Inferiere were on the same network. Once she had made him software and disconnected him from his module dock, she could then hack him as she had herself and change a couple of minor things – just enough to keep the system from re-recognizing him as Jordan Helm, along with possibly some other minor improvements like removing any memory linked to the New York bombing attempt.

In her virtual fingers, she grabbed the paper, and it dissolved into her hands. She then left the private room and reached through the Inferiere interface again, tapping the red dot which now indicated Worm34998. It popped brightly for a moment, and then faded into pink, darkening until it was nearly black, and then blipped out altogether. She held her breath as she logged out of Inferiere and back into Mijloc, hoping that her program had worked the way she'd expected. She hovered over where she'd placed the house, back at the closer 1:40 scale view of Mijloc. In development mode, she couldn't see inside the house, and it couldn't even get information about who was in the house, as she expected him to be. She'd forgotten about that – to check, she would have to enter Mijloc as an inhabitant.

Entering Mijloc that way was much more difficult than developing in Mijloc. As a developer, she had access to make changes that had no impact to existing inhabitants. At the same time, they weren't allowed to know if people were even in homes due to privacy. This meant that their creations had to be made in-session, and if they wanted to make later modifications, approvals that had to be documented. If she just wanted to go into the world, and see what it would look like from the perspective of an inhabitant, then she would need to file for permission or would be flagged because it was a certified world, and she wasn't legally allowed to simultaneously exist in-world and off-world at the same time. She needed a waiver and permission, but in her new position, it was something that only her boss had to approve. She submitted the request, and waited, watching the house through the windows.

Permission was granted quickly, as she saw by an alert which manifest as a small exclamation point in virtual space. She immediately brought up a console and entered a command to inject herself into the world. Employees who went into Mijloc, or Inferiere, for that matter, had a limited range of appearances they could take on, all of which were distinctly different from any real thing that might have existed in the world. The avatars were presented to her as rows of uniforms against a dark background. She selected the one that she thought of as Generic Female 4. As soon as she touched the virtual fabric, she found herself standing in a field in front of the house she'd just finished creating.

The rose bush was beautiful, even though it was brand new and hadn't differentiated itself from other roses she'd planted yet. Vegetation grew in real time, so it would be years before she got to see the fruits of that project. The giant dandelions would come up in probably a few weeks, and all that covered the ground was sand so far, thin and wispy. She crossed it under a sun that felt real, too real. For a moment she was confused about where she was, but then she focused and put her feet forward. She looked down at chubby toes, and laughed at herself. She held a thick hand in front of her face. The body was strange because, like all avatars, it carried with it no weight. She looked like a portly suburban housewife wearing too much makeup, but she didn't even crush plants when she walked across them. It was a strange state between existing and not existing in the world.

She debated on the doorstep whether to ring the doorbell, or just to walk in, and opted for the latter. Jordan wouldn't mind, she thought, if she just showed up. He would probably love it, especially after all that he'd been through in Inferiere, and knowing that she'd freed him, even if the details of how he got there in the first place seemed fuzzy and elusive to him. And when he learned of the changes she'd made to his avatar, and to hers, that would allow them to create Mijloc's first native baby together - a child that they could raise and love - he would be overjoyed. Jordan would have to forgive her. Aida passed over the threshold without knocking, to find Jordan standing completely still, gazing on her with an empty stare.

"Who are you, and why are you in my house?"

"I-It's me, Aida."

"Jordan? I don't know anyone named Aida, princess."

"Don't call me princess," she corrected him. "You know me. Aida Lothian."

His face went blank as he seemed to think it through, but before he had a chance to respond, the world went black. Everything around her faded to darkness, and she bolted upright on her work bench back in the real world. She pulled her helmet from her head, and the light blinded her as she tried to focus. Before her stood someone in a Paivana Thoughtforms Security uniform with a name tag that read 'Dave'.

"Shit," she said, tension already building at the base of her neck.

"Exactly," Dave replied to her exasperation. "Come with me please."

Still in her suit, she followed Dave out of the door and into the hallway. Aida checked her consciousness offload percentage as they passed through the hallways. Only fifty percent. Dave escorted her through two doors next to each other, and into a very real, very lockable, room with a table and a chair. She began to take the chair, but he cleared his throat as someone else pushed past them and scurried to occupy the seat instead. The someone was a man nearly a foot shorter than any other man she'd ever met. She studied him in her periphery to perpetuate the illusion of her affliction.

"Really? *This* woman?" the man asked.

"A-aida," she told him. "Aida L-lothian."

"Do you know why you're here?"

She was about to answer but the sound of the door locking behind her jarred her attention. She turned to see security leave, and then turned back to the man.

"N-no," she said.

"It's not allowed to access both Mijloc and Inferiere in the same hour. It gives the perception that something questionable is happening, and we monitor for it."

"O-oh."

She should have known that. Quite possibly it was in the manual that came with her new job position - a manual she hadn't read.

"I thought you might not know. I still have to ask you some questions."

The tiny man lowered his eyelids over his thick glasses. He pulled at his broom-like moustache as he asked the first question.

"What were you doing in Inferiere?"

"F-familiarizing myself with the interface," Aida told him, guessing that they hadn't pulled enough records yet to know how often she'd been in the system since her promotion.

"I see," the man said absently, while he wrote something on a digital pad in front of him.

The question was the first salvo in a interrogation about access and whether she knew the rules for accessing the different systems, and she answered each in turn, only half paying attention as she mulled over her meeting with Jordan. Jordan had had no recollection of her, at all. She had seen it in his expressions, in his eyes. There had been absolutely no comprehension of her name, and right now, Jordan would probably be questioning whether he'd actually seen her or hallucinated her, due to the abruptness with which she'd been pulled away without the opportunity to explain anything.

"You have so been warned," the little man told her.

"I'm sorry, what?"

"Warned. It's against corporate policy to navigate between both systems within a twenty-four hour period. This was all covered in your promotion packet. Doing it again would lead to demotion, but you won't have to worry about that right away, because your access to Inferiere has been temporarily suspended for two weeks."

"W-what?"

"I know it seems harsh. Until we can separate the Inferiere and Mijloc animus module banks, policy is that nobody accesses both within 24 hours to reduce chances of anyone accidentally putting the wrong person into either system. We're just not equipped to manage those changes right now."

Aida smiled graciously at the man as she turned to leave.

"You're dismissed," he gushed, as though trying to punch the words out before she could completely achieve her about-face.

"T-thank you," she nodded briskly and then tried the door behind her. She couldn't help smiling to herself as she passed through, which she then corrected into a stunned frown when she noticed the security man who had escorted her had stayed just outside the door.

"We'll be watching you," he grunted as his eyes followed her past him. She put her smile back on, just to annoy him.

Jordan was free, and living in Mijloc. The only thing she might have to do is get him papers, but then, nobody really looked at those anyway unless the world was under audit, which wouldn't be for some time. If someone did discover that he didn't have papers, then she was convinced that he would have the wherewithal to make up some name to present them with. She now had the comfort and peace of mind that he wasn't being eaten by giant worms and hadn't been disemboweled by a cactus spike while running from some predator. He was safe, and that knowledge lifted from her a weight that she hadn't known she was carrying. She felt lighter, freer, and was more convinced than ever that she'd done the right thing.

The watching could become problematic still, she thought. Part two, if she really wanted to do it (and she wasn't certain she did) was to move into Mijloc herself with no one the wiser, and then cut ties with the so-called real world. She checked her synchronization progress between her animus module and Event Horizon. She was at seventy percent now. It wouldn't be long, perhaps a couple of days, until the rest of her consciousness had been transferred to running on the quantum processors that the game used to render it's complex world. The idea of that made her feel sick to her stomach, but she didn't double over. She didn't even flinch mid-step during her deliberately controlled pace back to her virtual reality jump point. That same feeling of freedom washed over her as she remembered – that wasn't her anymore. She didn't go from zero to a thousand on the emotional scales so quickly and violently that it manifested as physiological symptoms. The idea of her consciousness being solely hosted on gaming servers, without the permission of the company, chewing through processor time, even as slight as hers would be compared to Event Horizon itself, carried a significant risk. She was right to be anxious about it. More so now that her actions were being monitored. Everything would take longer, and each second that she remained running in Event Horizon was one more second that she risked a reset or some other anomaly wiping out her consciousness completely.

20

Love Conquers All

Sunday, November 21, 2258

Lothania, Deseret - Mijloc

Lincoln and Sarah pursued answers with Niles first, but predictably he turned out to be a waste of time and energy. Between the slurred speech and the zoning out, he conveyed nothing useful to them at all. Despite having no new information, Lincoln's mind had already begun rationalizing the two-worlds theory that Sarah had proffered before. But Sarah, it seemed, soured on the idea. A secret that size, she conjectured, was impossible to keep. How would such a thing stay concealed throughout years of schooling, birthdays, parties, and town gatherings?

"Somebody would have said something," Sarah told her, while laying on her back across the foot of Lincoln's twin bed, and staring at the glow-in-the-dark galaxy stickers that Lincoln had installed across the ceiling when she was twelve.

"Would they have?"

"Of course. How many secrets survived high-school in-tact?"

Lincoln didn't say it, but she saw Sarah's successful concealing of her sexuality as proof of the ability to keep information hidden in a small town.

"Not many, you're right," was what she said, as she retrieved the tote from beneath her bed with her mother's 'evidence' in it.

"We would have known."

"But why would the Sheriff lie?"

"To fuck with you," Sarah said, "and my mother probably put him up to it. In fact, I wouldn't be surprised if the note was planted by her in the first place."

Sarah waffled just as Lincoln had in the prior weeks. Sarah and she were alike in that way. When confronted with evidence that was difficult to believe, she fought against it until she had no choice but to give in. The entire previous two years of Lincoln's life had been exactly that. Having learned her lesson the hard way, Lincoln had less trouble believing the Sheriff than had Sarah, and it hadn't hurt that the two of them saw the worms and her mother. Engaging Sarah in this speculation was useless, so Lincoln only turned away instead of replying.

Instead, she smiled and stared at Sarah, no longer completely registering the conversation. She watched Sarah's lips move as though they were in slow motion, and the way she frantically swept her hair back from her eyes was impossible to ignore. Lincoln focused on the line of her high cheekbone as she emphatically made some pronunciation. Suddenly, there was silence and the movements stopped.

"What?" Sarah asked. "Why are you staring at me. Did you hear what I was saying?"

"Just... I can't believe you're with me. I mean, I can, we've always been friends, but you're with me, in a relationship, and I think, I feel, like it's good."

Sarah looked down, though her eyebrows raised into an arch. She seemed pensive for a moment, then her attention drifted toward Lincoln and fixed, as if to challenge her, with her eyebrows lowered and furrowed together.

"It is, isn't it?" she said, as her face relaxed. She turned her head to match the direction of her gaze. Her hair fell down and nearly touched the floor beneath her, yellower than usual against the purple spread of Lincoln's bed. Lincoln reached out her fingers towards Sarah's cheek instinctively to touch it, but before her fingers reached, Sarah intercepted with her own fingertips against Lincolns.

"I was afraid it wouldn't" she continued, without breaking her stare. "I was afraid I would scare you away and then I would be here alone, in this little town with nobody. That's why I waited so long to tell you."

"How long have you known how you felt about me?"

"Before your mother died. You're just so loyal, so caring. You are like nobody I've ever known. In my house, you would have been eaten alive."

"It can't be that bad."

"I was serious that my mother would put the Sheriff up to that to fuck with you. I guess I kind of always suspected that your mother's death would come back to her somehow."

"Let's not focus on that though," Lincoln replied, not wanting to get mired down again. In a way, aside from curiosity, it didn't really matter anyway.

"Are you my girlfriend?" Sarah asked, as she slid her fingers between Lincoln's and pulled them toward her face. She pursed her lips and placed a single kiss on each knuckle, which Lincoln noticed for the first time were rough and thick from the farm work she'd done all of her life. Suddenly self-conscious, she attempted to pull her hand back, but Sarah didn't let go.

"Do you want to be?"

"Yes. I want titles, and all of that stuff."

"I want that too," Lincoln said, and gave up trying to retract her hand. Instead, she lowered her face to meet Sarah's and gave her an impulsive slow, deep kiss on the mouth. She felt a jolt as soon as their lips touched, and her entire body felt alive and ready for anything. Sarah tapped her on the shoulder after a few seconds, and she picked herself back up as she realized that she had accidentally been kneeling on Sarah's hair.

"Girlfriends," Sarah said, smiling, "but that doesn't get you off of the hook. I asked you if you believe we're in a virtual world?"

Lincoln shook her head yes, because she did, and she knew that Sarah already knew that anyway.

"If we are in a virtual world," she confessed, "then I have a chance to get my mother back. A real possibility exists then, that she's not dead, only missing, maybe here, maybe somewhere else, but alive."

"Okay, then," Sarah replied, and rolled over on the bed. Then she reached down to her purse, sighed, and pulled out her phone. On the screen, Lincoln could see that she had five missed messages at a glance. Sarah dialed her mother's number, and then clicked on the speaker icon to allow Lincoln to listen in. While the phone rang, her face changed again, from adoration which was the look that Lincoln had noticed earlier, to something that may have been fear.

"Mom, you're on speaker," she said as soon as her mother answered, "don't hang up."

"Hang up? Why would I... oh. Is Lincoln there with you?"

"Of course Mom. She's my girlfriend."

Lincoln heard Katy's breath suck in audibly over the receiver. But then, less than a second later, her perfectly composed voice came back over the line.

"Please tell her that I'm sorry about earlier. I want us to get along, really. I've been thinking about..."

"Stop it Mom, nobody's buying it," Sarah interrupted.

"Fine. Tell that bitch to stop seeing my daughter then."

Lincoln cringed at being called a bitch, but something about having it out in the open felt strangely cathartic. Sarah nodded toward her and flashed her a look that read 'I told you so'.

"That thing with the Sheriff. Why did you tell him to make up all of that stuff?"

"Stuff? What are you talking about?"

"He told us that we're living in a video game."

"It's *not* a video game, Sarah. Come *home*. Let's talk about this face to face."

Sarah's face fell at the confirmation of the existence of their virtual world implied by her mother's lack of denial.

"So it's real?" Lincoln asked, not expecting Katy to answer.

"Bring my daughter to me and I'll tell you everything," she said. "Where are you? Are you at Niles' house?"

"No," Sarah interrupted. "I'm not coming home, so we need to do this now."

"Do what? It sounds like the Sheriff already told you what you need to know."

"Why didn't you? I'm twenty-one years old. Why didn't you tell me?"

"You're not twenty-one, Sarah. You're thirty six."

Sarah's mouth dropped open as she absorbed that information. Lincoln shook her head. Looking at Sarah, it was obvious that she was no older than twenty five, at the most. Even when she wore no make up at all, she never looked close to thirty.

"Sarah, are you still there?" Katy's voice chimed from the speaker.

"Thirty six?" Lincoln asked for her, just to make sure she got the answer.

"Fine, we'll do it this way. Sarah, your father and I desperately wanted a child, but we couldn't have one, ever. One day, coming back from the fertility clinic, there was an accident and we both died, I guess."

"You don't seem dead."

"Lincoln, I'm talking to Sarah, not to you. Yes, we both died. Our bodies died, anyway. We woke up here, in Lothania, in a world we didn't recognize. A woman met with us, and explained about Mijloc. We were presented with a choice. Since we'd wanted a baby before, they asked us if we would want one now. We couldn't actually *have* one, of course, but we wanted one. The one we wanted, that was you."

"Was I dead too?"

"Your body was. Your mother had taken you to an anti-cloning protest at the age of one. There was a massive explosion, and you both were close enough that she was knocked back several feet. You flew from her hands, and died almost immediately. You had the animus module, but without wealthy parents, there was no way to bring you back. She couldn't afford a sub-model, so you went into storage."

Then, Katy went on to explain, predominantly to Sarah, about the animus module, and the fact that they might be considered Mijloc's first immortals.

"You can't die here," she said. "It's impossible."

"My mother did," Lincoln told her flatly, but Katy seemed to ignore her.

"See Sarah, you are thirty-six, but only really aged to twenty-one. The rest of the time you were in storage."

"Answer Lincoln, mother."

Lincoln heard another sigh.

"*Your* mother was the worst thing to happen to me."

"My mother didn't make you have an affair with my father."

"It wasn't an affair. Niles was living alone in that farmhouse of yours when I found him. He was nice enough so I brought him over to meet Mason. Mason and I had an open relationship at the time, and Niles was who I wanted to bring in, so Mason let me. I'd already asked him to marry us when that bitch showed up."

"She's not a bitch just because you didn't like her. Everyone else in the town loved her," Sarah replied.

"Your father certainly did. Niles too, at first. When Niles called off the ceremony, Mason defended him just like you are. Mason defended them both as though what I wanted hardly mattered at all. Mason defended *everyone* but me," Katy spat the words like venom.

A look from Sarah told Lincoln that the conversation had gone on too long. Lincoln nodded, as she'd gotten the answer she'd been looking for.

"Mother, I'm hanging up now," Sarah said.

"When are you coming home, dear? Are you seriously going to stay at that drunk's house?"

Sarah hung up the phone without answering.

"What do you think?" Lincoln asked, not knowing what to expect.

Sarah shook her head noncommittally.

"I don't think she's lying," she said, with words calm and smooth that communicated to Lincoln that Sarah had regained much of her composure.

"No, I mean, does it change your mind?"

"I don't know, I guess," then more assertively. "I wish I'd thought to ask why."

"Why?"

"Yes, don't you want to know? Why keep a secret like this, and why would so many people keep it?"

"I don't think anyone would have told us except our parents. It's like a really extreme version of Santa Claus. Our parents should have been the ones to tell us, but when they would have normally, my mother died."

"Surely Scot or someone would have said something though, if they had known."

Maybe, Lincoln thought, before she'd pushed her friends away and isolated herself in her quest to discover her mother's murder, one of her then many friends might have told her. But she had stopped talking to most of them, because, unlike Sarah, they had all insisted that her mother had killed herself, when Lincoln knew she hadn't. At least, that first summer after, she chased them away. Then, most of her honors-course classmates had left to go to the University of Deseret, though a few also attended Lyra Craevis Community College. Is she was honest, the only people left of their age with the dubious title of 'townies' were Sarah and herself.

"Scot told me about the letter," Lincoln said, "before I found it in your mother's jewelry box.

"Really? How did he know?"

Lincoln relayed the story of how Scot's paramedic friend.

"So more people knew about the letter. That also seems like something that someone would have mentioned, right?"

There did seem to be a lot of well-kept secrets in the little town, many of which spanned for years. Sarah was right, Lincoln had to agree, if the point she was making was that people in Lothania seemed to be exceptionally good at secret keeping. She still couldn't imagine that information as consequential as what they had recently uncovered could have been kept secret without some coordination.

"Do you think that it was a conspiracy? I mean, do you think the entire town conspired to keep this a secret? Sheriff thought it was just something people don't talk about."

"Lincoln, there's *nothing* people here don't talk about."

Lincoln cataloged in her mind the people who would have to have been complicit in keeping the various secrets they'd identified. With some sadness, she realized that her mother would have been one of the conspirators, as well as Niles, Mason, Katy, Sheriff Al. That was only if she assumed that none of her grade, middle, or high school friends had known that they "lived" in a *virtual world*. It may have been possible, if there was an ordinance or something that said that children had to be eighteen to be told. Sheriff had hinted at something like that when he'd said that they should have been told by now, as thought there were an expected age at which children were expected to know, and by implication, that there were other ages at which children weren't. Again, the Sheriff would have the answer. She regretted not having had the foresight to ask all of her questions at once.

"Sheriff Al," she said at the same time as Sarah, causing her to smile, despite the discomfort of being on the receiving end of a conspiratorial lie.

Later that afternoon, they stopped at the Sheriff's office to catch him before he left, but he wasn't there. The office seemed to be occupied only by a deputy, someone she'd not interacted with before, which Lincoln now realized was kind of strange. Despite his clear dismissal of many of her questions, and apparently lies of omission, she'd always been received by the Sheriff, and never by anyone else. Lincoln decided that Deputy Edwards would have to do.

"Deputy Edwards," she said, and startled the man, causing him to nearly fall backwards from his chair, already pre-tilted due to him propping his legs on the desk. The man, like the Sheriff, had a prominent moustache, but in his skinny face, it seemed to overpower his features until all he was was moustache.

"Yeah, Lincoln?" he replied, sighing a little as he seemed to look around to ensure that he was, in fact, the only one available to receive her.

"Sarah and I have a question."

"Shoot."

"Why wouldn't we know about Mijloc being a virtual world?"

He didn't seem phased by the question at all. Except for furrowing his eyebrows upward into a tent, his features were otherwise unmoved.

"Listen," he said with a slow, practiced drawl. "If this is about your mother, I'm sorry. Sometimes people just don't like it in Mijloc. I'm sorry she left the way she did, but she's gone."

Lincoln hadn't been expecting that. She'd only meant to ask about the possibility of an ordinance or law which would require secrecy regarding the virtual world, and hadn't yet thought through the implications for her mother. Farther than understanding that her mother may not actually be dead, Lincoln had been afraid to explore further what might have actually happened to her. Sheriff already told her that he didn't really know, and the deputy seemed to be convinced that she'd simply decided to leave, and there was nothing else to consider. She had a mental flash of the queen of the worms. The more questions she asked, the more she realized how little people seemed to know.

"That's not what I'm asking about," she said curtly, causing him to lower his boots to the floor and sit up in his chair.

"What, then?"

"Why didn't anyone ever tell either of us?"

He shrugged his shoulders in the tan charlie shirt, and for a moment said nothing. Then he spoke.

"Tradition, I guess," he said, "it's always been like that. Folks are told when they can legally do something about it, otherwise, things get, well, weird."

"Weird?"

"Yeah, very weird. Like take you for example. You live here in Lothania, but you can leave any time you want, if you want. Just fill out some paperwork is all, then pop out in the real world, or go back into storage. Your choice. Kids can't choose that. Adults have to choose for them, so it's just a lot easier to wait."

"But nobody talks about it."

"They wouldn't, would they. Do you want to be the one who rocks the boat? Well, not you, I guess. I mean anybody but you."

Lincoln glared at him.

"So how it normally works, is you would be told by your parents, and then you would go to a class that the Sheriff puts on, to answer questions. Just, you know, your mother's death kind of messed up the timing for everyone."

"I thought you said she left?"

"That's one way to leave. You really need to sign up for the class. Sheriff didn't mention?"

No. The Sheriff hadn't suggested anything like that. Was it possible that the Sheriff was much more incompetent at his job than Lincoln had thought? She looked to Sarah, and Sarah looked back at her and shook her head. Sarah had been there when they'd talked about it, and didn't remember any mention of a class either.

"Get me into the next one?" Lincoln asked the deputy, who responded with a mock-solute.

"*Us*," Sarah added.

21

Moving Day

Thursday, October 26, 2237

Seattle, Washington - Earth

A guard-woman stood statuesque in the back of what used to be a private virtual reality jump point as Aida failed repeatedly to settle her mind. Laying supine left her chest and body exposed while she was in virtual realty - a thought that so far prevented her from enabling her haptic skin. The helmet and gloves were connected, but Aida didn't want to take the chance that the woman would do something to her while she was distracted by virtual world sensations. The incongruence of her virtual physical experience with the real-world chill of the air across her midsection kept her attention oscillating between both worlds in a context-switching nightmare that seemed endless.

Her boss had assured her that the woman's presence was only a formality, but formality or not, Aida was unused to the level of scrutiny she now experienced and couldn't focus. Worse than that, there seemed to always be someone from security looming near her office, regardless of the particular time she made it to work. She tested this by starting three random days at random non-business times. Every time, she was cordially greeted by a smiling security guard whose sole purpose seemed to be delivering her cup of coffee when she arrived. Aida viewed it as the most comprehensive, most polite, and longest, invasion of privacy she'd ever experienced.

At first, she thought she'd simply adjust her overall timeline. She could make it through two weeks without breaking the rules, and then carry on with the rest of her plan once the "formality" period was over. They still hadn't pieced together exactly what she'd been doing, or she would either have been fired by now or possibly arrested.

After she'd moved the last ten percent of her consciousness from the animus module to the quantum servers behind Event Horizon, paranoia found a home in her mind. Siphoning off bits of quantum time should have been unnoticed with the noise of the other processing happening, but she imagined automated tools relentlessly examining memory banks for just such a thing. If one found her, and decided to erase the anomaly, she wondered what the animus module would do. The link would break, and since much of the wiring of her brain had been mirrored in hardware via nanite tubes before being mirrored in the software copy, some part of her might recover, but the animus module would failover to her old brain patterns. Memories would be possibly lost, and she would once again be struggling daily with stimuli, unable to filter out the automatic physiological reactions her body had once insisted upon when her senses overflowed. She would be broken again.

It was a lengthy and uneventful day of not breaking the

rules after which Aida arrived home without fanfare. Her housemates had long since gone to sleep, and she made her way up the creaking, empty stairs. Aida collapsed into her bed without changing her clothes, intending only a short rest before showering and then visiting the Obatali. Instead she fell into a restless sleep, plagued once again by the dream of the girl. This time, Jordan wore the modified avatar she'd made for him instead of the body she'd once known so intimately.

"I don't know you," he said to her, face unmoving and void of expression.

"I freed you from Inferiere. I brought you to Mijloc. I risked my entire life for you."

"You did?"

"Yes. And now they're following me."

She hadn't realized it until the words skipped free from her lips. Then she glanced over her shoulder, and in the darkness she understood that two Paivana Thoughtforms security agents lurked somewhere beyond her vision. Intuitively she also became aware that through the darkness and out the other side, her child hid, scared and abandoned. Jordan spoke up again, interrupting her thoughts.

"I don't think you did this for me."

"Of course I did. I felt guilty for putting you in Inferiere."

"But you didn't do that. I don't know you."

"Shut up, Jordan, of course I did."

"Who's Jordan?"

"You *know* me. And our daughter needs us."

"You're thinking of someone else. I would know if I had a daughter."

"She's all alone, Jordan."

Peering forward, trying to make out shapes in the ethereal mist, Aida found nothing. A slit opened in the blackness before her. A skinny little girl walked through in pink footed pajamas, accompanied by a woman who Aida had never seen before. This woman, tall with coal-black hair streaming over an aquamarine sari, held the child's hand and stepped deftly between the now-visible guards. Like Aida, she had green and blue eyes, and like *her* Jordan, the girl's smile hid something mischievous.

"Mommy?"

"Mommy is here."

"These men were looking for you."

Then two robot-like hands stretched from the darkness as the agents seemed to move without moving, covering the distance between them in an instant. Their claws clamped down like vices against her biceps, and she was pinned. The little girl began to fade away, taking the olive-skinned woman with her.

"I'm not real," the girl said, as she evaporated into nothing.

Aida awoke with that image still fresh in her mind, but as she tried to grasp its meaning, pieces of the dream broke off and floated, until she was left with only the little girl's face, and the words "I'm not real".

She had known that the actions she took weren't wholly the actions that a well adjusted human might. Something had felt off since the day that she had turned Jordan in. She'd thought it was the guilt that motivated her, but he was in Mijloc now, a better arrangement than he could have gotten, and far better than a would-be mass murderer deserved. She had thought it was for love, but she couldn't think about love with Jordan without also weighing instinctively the possibility that she had been completely led on. If she was the only one in love, it wasn't love so much as obsession.

Perhaps that was what drove her. Maybe she really just wanted to know if she and Jordan's love had been real. The only way to do it that she could think of was to try it without the baggage. If they'd met without his looming deadline, without her ever discovering the bomb plot, or even better, without him ever trying to make the bomb in the first place, would they have found love? This question burned at her, and it wasn't a question that could be answered. *Yet.*

She left her bed and stood for a second the darkness, before using subvocal to stop the light from flooding the room now that she was awake. With a thick sigh, she undressed and changed into her haptic gear, moving into her virtual reality closet. She then donned her helmet, boots, and gloves, and fired up a private chat.

"Girl, do you know what time it is?"

"In Rwanda? Yes, around eleven o'clock, right?"

"I meant for you. Why are you awake?"

"Remember that thing we talked about, the escape kit?"

"I remember."

"I think it's time. Can you give me three hours, then pull the trigger."

"Are you sure you want to do this?"

"No. But if I don't do it now, I won't do it."

She'd expected Emily to hang up and go do it without further conversation. Emily was usually less talk and more action, but this time, Emily moved around the desk until she was close enough to look Aida in the eyes.

"You seem good. Did you - did you change something?"

Aida realized then that she'd been maintaining eye contact for longer than she normally could have with her disorder. She only nodded back.

"Some. If I change much, I won't be me any longer. I can focus my eyes better, but it still feels like I'm walking on eggshells. Not much and enough."

"Seems like a lot from here. And *now* you want to disappear?"

"I know."

Aida filled Emily in on what she'd been working on for the

last few weeks. Emily didn't hide the fact that she was impressed.

"That's wonderful," Emily said, grabbing Aida by the hand. "Are you really sure you want to do this?"

Aida yanked her hand back and couldn't stifle the glare that followed. Emily put her hands up and backed away three steps.

"I have to, Emily."

"Why?"

Aida said nothing. Emily still wouldn't understand, even if she tried to explain the crushing insecurity she felt when she thought about the fact that she might have been lied to. All sorts of questions had gone through her head prior to that decision. Did he use her intentionally? Did he seek her out because of her personality disorder, because it made her an easy target? It did, and she was, she felt, but that didn't mean he knew that ahead of time. But he'd known a lot, and had used subterfuge to gain her confidence initially. There were too many thoughts to turn into words.

"I can't say, E."

"I'm going to miss you."

"You don't have to miss me, Emily. They allow visitors on Mijloc. Just takes some paperwork."

"Do you have a name yet?"

"Aidalee Spinster," she said.

"I'll remember." Emily threw up her hands. "Okay."

"Thank you Emily," Aida told her, and meant it. Their shared history was coming to a close with this final act. Aida doubted she would ever see Emily in Mijloc, for the most simple reason that she would have to give a real name, and since Mijloc was a certified world, that visit would be recorded for all time. Emily would never put her criminal enterprises at risk.

They disconnected from the call, and Aida took off her

helmet, gloves, and boots, but retained the skin-tight suit haptic suit. She slipped on her clothes over the top of it, dark blue jeans and a long-sleeved red blouse, covered by a tan overcoat.

Thirty minutes later, she arrived in the office. Looking in from the outside, she saw nobody. Even security needed to take breaks at night, but she knew she was still under surveillance. As soon as her card key was read, she had no doubt that some security personnel somewhere would be alerted and would come running to monitor her activity. That was fine though, she only needed fifteen minutes of access to clone herself from Event Horizon to Mijloc, using her animus module as the conduit between the two. Whereas the uplink to Event Horizon involved the painstaking modeling of her nanite structure into executable code, copying her consciousness down was the rough equivalent of sending a larger file. Afterward the copy was confirmed, the program that Emily would release would handle deleting her old consciousness from Event Horizon. It was strange to think that for possibly the better part of two hours she would exist in two separate worlds.

Aida swiped the key to pass through the door into the office building. After waiting for a moment to see if any alarms triggered, she picked her way through the empty halls, tracing her standard route, and into her docking bay. She pushed her work suit from the bench and donned her helmet, gloves and boots. Hers had better connectivity to the external network, and she could connect to the office network directly through ports in her boots. She pulled a red and green cable from her coat pocket, and tried to plug it into the tiny port on the back of her boot, but the haptic gloves weren't suited to real world tasks. She removed one glove, plugged the cord in.

The link connected as she replaced the glove on her free

hand. Biometrics allowed her access as she lined up for entry into Mijloc. Instead of accepting the various corporate avatars, Aida loaded hers from Oduduwa. When she saw her smiling face reflected back at her, she selected it and within a few seconds, found herself standing in front of the farmhouse, as she had before. If her card key hadn't flagged an alarm, loading her own avatar likely had. She had to act fast to clean up the trail, but first, she needed to pull her consciousness down from Event Horizon. Once complete, her clean-up code would automatically delete the avatar she'd uploaded from the selection board, so that even though security would see an alert, they might think it was a glitch. With a sigh and crossed fingers, she started the process, and her world immediately faded to black.

"Hey, are you okay?"

She moaned and raised her head, with her skull pounding. The light was too bright, and she feared she might be having an attack, but nothing else happened aside from the brightness. Aida. Her name was Aida, and she had just crossed over into Mijloc. Permanently. The idea took her breath away. Judging by the brightness, Aida had been unconscious for almost four hours - much longer than she'd calculated based on her experiments with Event Horizon. But waking up also meant that Paivana Thoughtforms security hadn't found her yet.

The voice seemed familiar, deep and concerned, but she didn't immediately place it. The tenor was off. As her eyes adjusted, she saw the Niles avatar.

"Jordan?"

"Niles. Are you okay?"

"I think so."

"Rough night?"

"You could say that." She smiled at him. "Do you have any coffee?"

"Sure, but you'll have to tell me what you're doing out here in my yard at some point. Can you stand?"

"I think so."

She rose to her feet, and instinctively felt for her haptic response. Nothing. She then tried to take her helmet off, just to be sure, and couldn't do that either. When the security team finally find her, they will find a brain-dead shell. She hoped it would seem like an animus module malfunction. They didn't happen often, but animus modules and neurological disorders were a bad mixture, and led to problems sometimes. Her hope was that it would be written off as a combination of stress and machinery failure.

She passed through into the house. Inside, she could see the curtains she'd picked out, the perfect refrigerator, and the couches that she'd designed to be softer than down but still comfortable to sit in. She sat down and sank into the cushions half of an inch, reveling in her foresight and closing her eyes to feel the quality of her work. When she opened her eyes again, she was staring across the living room at a chair she'd also designed, but was supposed to be in the master bedroom. On that chair, draped in only a blanket, sat a woman already sipping on her own cup of coffee, analyzing her every movement.

Don't go red.

She didn't recognize the woman right away because her focus was locked into preventing her symptoms from showing. Only after fifteen seconds of slow breathing did Aida dare to examine the woman directly. Flawless. The woman wore thick black eyeliner around equally dark eyes, smeared at some point though she'd cleaned most of it off. Aida gained enough clarity to recall that the woman was one of hers, as everyone in the town had to be. She searched her memory for the face.

"Kathryn Douglas," she muttered, not thinking before she

spoke the name when it popped into her head.

"Katy. But dear, you have me at a disadvantage," Katy told her. "You know me, but I don't know you. Who *are* you?"

"Aid...Aidalee Spinster," she struggled with her new name. Making it so close to her actual name, something she thought would make her life easier, made it more difficult to say because she had to fight the compulsion to stop after "Aida".

Niles re-emerged holding the cup of coffee she had requested, and she took it, giving him the most gracious smile she could muster, in spite of the growing angst in her belly, which only magnified when Katy slid over in her chair to allow room for Niles to sit. To drive home the point that she and Niles were together, Katy threw her arms around his neck. Aida searched the room for Mason's presence, but he wasn't there.

"So..." Niles began.

"Aidalee," Katy suggested.

"So Aidalee," Niles said. "What were you doing out there on the lawn?"

"Isn't it obvious, dear," asked Katy with a hint of derision. "We've found our fourth."

22

Dots

Monday, November 22, 2258

Lyra Craevis, Deseret - Mijloc

Behind a solid oak desk, immoveable and much too large to ever have been spirited through the single-width door across from him, Bodhi chewed on the end of a pen. He lowered the tip from his mouth, and placed it down on the table beside the stack of papers he had to review that day. They could have been splashed across his desk surface or projected against a far wall, but instead the contracts for the day had materialized in a plastic-looking box without a lid, and more appeared by the second. He sighed as the pile grew quickly enough for him to see the papers rising. They would stop, eventually. This was the daily influx of contracts for off-world business that would impact Mijloc. The first document took half a page to tell him what could have been summarized in one sentence: more refugees are coming.

Nearly a thousand. There wasn't enough housing. Crumpling the paper in his hand and tossing it over the edge of the desk, he watched it dissolve as soon as it hit the floor. From practice he knew that the next few documents were orders requesting lots of refugees be brought into Mijloc, and a few more of the documents were likely to be single-page summaries of each family and their lives. Each of those would be a family shepherded to safety from intolerance. The best part of Bodhi's job was saving lives, but today, his attention wandered. Every paper sapped his energy and willpower as his mind kept circling back to Lincoln, and Aida, and Aidalee.

It still irked Bodhi that he hadn't known. The rules he'd put in place to provide independence to the communities had been used to keep Aidalee's death secret from him. He signed a couple of more documents, barely registering their contents. Then he stopped and instead pulled up the panel to access the Labyrinth virtual network that bridged Mijloc and Earth to search for news reports in both worlds from two years before. He found *nothing*. He hadn't just been uninformed - it was as though it never happened. No news story made it to Earth or he was certain something like a death in Mijloc would have blown up and Aiden would have had to explain the possibility of something Bodhi still didn't understand.

The thought of Aiden shifted Bodhi's focus to the old man's behavior at dinner a week before. He'd had coughing fits and could barely talk, which didn't reconcile with Bodhi's memories of the man who had helped him establish Mijloc and Inferiere, both. The image in his mind possessed understated international influence and had moved the World Government to license both as independent nation-states, regardless of the country of origin. Inferiere only answered to the world government, as a repository for dangerous criminals, and Mijloc answered only to the same, for reasons of insuring fair international trade and not giving a single existing nation an unfair economic advantage. Aiden's genius had seen Bodhi through many tough negotiations, even to the extent of protecting Bodhi from himself when he'd been captivated in an unhealthy relationship with the leader of Emergent Biotechnology. And now the man could barely walk. It pained Bodhi to see Aiden that way when he could be fully admitted into Mijloc and regain his youthful vigor. But that was a lengthy conversation that Bodhi had yet to win. As enfeebled as his body had become, Aiden's mind remained sharp enough at least to fend off Bodhi's many attempts at convincing him.

With a sigh, Bodhi turned back to the pile. The next three documents discussed the new multi-family homes on the south and east sides of the city, which should help house the incoming refugees, though it wouldn't be enough. They would have to stamp out cookie-cutter shelters for people to survive in until proper homes could be developed. He frowned at the realization, and shook his head. Facing more clutter in his masterpiece, Bodhi reminded himself that Mijloc came into existence to help models and not to be an aesthetic or logistical piece of art. He'd meant it as an alternative to consciousness transfer into clones, a move that had pitted him against Emergent Biotechnology, the largest cloning corporation in the United States. That vision had been short-circuited by Emergent Biotechnology's latest inventions - sub-models, which, according to marketing, had no consciousness to speak of through some genetic engineering practice, and were like soulless robots until occupied. So instead of becoming an alternative to models, he'd become a refuge for the genetically-altered clones called models who adjusted to freedom under the watchful eyes of half of a nation who would prefer they not be free, and their allies. At a fraction of the cost of a sub-model, Mijloc also had become a home for polli, non-models, who couldn't afford to extend their off-world existences.

Hours passed while he examined document after document, loathing the fact that he hadn't yet figured out a more entertaining way to work with contracts. Bodhi laughed as the idea of expressing contracts as interpretive dance wafted through his conscious mind. Eventually, he affixed his seal to a refugee request form and reached back toward the inbox to find nothing left. He took a contented breath and leaned back in his office chair, peering out into the world he'd created.

Through the thin glass, twilight had already taken most of the skyline, though here and there he could make out tiny reflections of sunlight. Those would be gone soon enough, as the sun had only another inch of clearance over the far horizon. Bodhi had spent another day walled in his office signing documents, most of which he could no longer remember. He kneaded his temples with his fingertips and waited for his head to clear while the sun took it's last couple of inches to nudge down past the horizon. Then his communicator chimed out, and he popped his neck, sucked in a lungful of air, and clicked the button, projecting JoAnn's image on the far wall. The communicator was an unimaginative hold-over from Earth, but it served its purpose.

"Sir, we have news. Lothania Council has taken your advice and are hastening the girl's learning about the virtual world."

Bodhi let his breath out slowly, cracking his tired mouth into a thin smile.

"Good. It's about time. The poor girl needs some closure. Do you know how they manage to keep the secret for so long? Surely they have school of some sort in Lothania. What do they teach them?"

The woman shuffled, and Bodhi recognized it as an unfair question. He hadn't asked security to investigate that, but he also knew JoAnn would try her best to answer.

"As far as we know, sir, they don't teach history. They limit themselves to survival skills necessary in-world."

"What survival skills? Nobody dies here and suffering is muted."

It was his turn to squirm a little as he realized what he'd just said.

"They don't teach that. They're afraid it will make their children weak and incapable. They teach as though there's actual danger - which plants are poisonous, which animals are dangerous. It's ... strange, sir. There's more. The girl doesn't have an animus module either."

Bodhi drew in another sharp breath.

"Everyone in Mijloc has an animus module. Even *I* have one. What do you mean that she doesn't? Did you track her a.p. in the system? Her VBI?"

Since every animus module had a globally unique ansible protocol address assigned, these were the serial numbers that linked back to the animus module docking bays. It was the simplest and fastest way to find a docking bay, and he had made the recommendation more as a reminder, expecting the answer he got.

"Yes, sir. We tracked both but there's no bay for her. We even sent someone to physically check the bay locations with similar a.p. addresses. No space, no dock, no module."

Bodhi's mind twisted around what that might possibly mean. Only animals didn't have docking bays. Trees didn't. Things created that existed only in-world had no need for them. Lincoln might have been an in-world character. Event Horizon, the game engine that had become the foundation of Inferiere and Mijloc, had had such characters that showed up from time to time, but they'd been written out as the source code was sanitized for Mijloc. If she wasn't an in-game character, then he didn't know where else she could have come from. More likely, somebody had just accidentally deleted her mapping entry. There were redundancies and Mijloc typically cached that information so deleting it might not have been picked up yet. What would happen to her if the system tried to refresh the cache while she was in there?

"Run diagnostics on world memory following her movements. We should be able to determine her animus module location by where the game is syncing."

"We have, sir. It's hard to explain. There's no syncing happening. Everything she's experiencing seems to be recording in Mijloc memory banks, and not anywhere else."

"That's impossible."

"It's what's happening, sir."

The only way that could happen was if the girl was entirely in-world. She *had* to be a character. He thought through the development reports that he'd seen over the years, now questioning whether or not the Event Horizon code had been updated properly to remove the possibility of NPC spawning. It didn't take him long to recall that he had been very explicit about that critical point. A few documents indicated that it had been done, and he was mostly convinced. His own animus module didn't forget things like that even through the clutter of years of memories. Bodhi went back over what he knew one more time.

Aidalee Montague had died two years earlier, an impossibility. Aida Lothian had died nearly twenty years before that, and in between Jane had died, a woman who claimed that Libera had possessed her and her boyfriend's bodies off-world. Aida Lothian died *on Earth* but perhaps she'd managed to transition into Mijloc in some other way than with the animus module. If anyone could do that, *she* could.

"Search on Aidalee Montague. I want to know when she came into Mijloc and what the circumstances of her death were."

"Yes, sir. We'll keep you informed."

"Before you go, one more thing. Try to keep an eye on Lincoln, if you can. Go to Lothania to watch her. The diagnostics system may be having problems too. Let's get the developers to have a closer look at that as well."

"Absolutely, sir."

Absently, Bodhi wondered why JoAnn would remain with him. After fifty years, the woman seemed as dedicated as she'd ever been. Bodhi made a mental note to invite her to coffee or a quick lunch, then turned his attention back to the problem at hand. When JoAnn disconnected, her image faded from the wall and Bodhi pulled up a control panel before him.

"Search for contract - Aidalee Montague," he said. He could wait for JoAnn's search to conclude, but now that Bodhi was finished for the day, he time to sate his increasing curiosity. The panel shuddered for a second, an intentional distortion Bodhi had designed in so that he could tell when it was doing things, and flashed a quick message.

"Contract not found."

"Search for contract - Aidalee 2237." He tried again. If they'd married in-world, then it was possible she used a different name. He had to fix that search algorithm, or more correctly, inform a project officer to fix it.

"Contract found. Aidalee Spinster. Joined Mijloc in 2237, contract signed by Bodhi Rawls."

"Show contract."

The document materialized on his desk, and he grabbed it to leaf through its pages. There was his signature, down to the DNA confirmation and encryption initialization vector. But he didn't remember signing.

"Find docking bay for Aidalee Spinster," he said, and waited through another distortion.

"No dock found."

"Find *original* docking bay for Aidalee Spinster," he repeated, wishing he'd invested more in to artificial intelligence for this interface.

"Original docking bay not found."

"Find *world entry point* for Aidalee Spinster."

Last try.

"Aidalee Spinster entered into Mijloc from employee port 55487."

He cocked his head, unsure of what he'd heard.

"Say again?"

"Aidalee Spinster entered into Mijloc from employee port 55487."

He recognized that port number. His mind flashed back to the images of Aida Lothian's withered arm extending from the rest of her haptic rig. Port 55487 was Aida Lothian's employee jump point. He'd found the smoking gun that tied them together. She had docked from an employee port, then somehow severed the connection after bringing Aidalee Spinster to life in Mijloc. While the entire company mourned the loss of the person that most of them called "Creepy Aida", she hadn't even died - not really. Really she had found a way into Mijloc. She died in one place, and lived in another. And then, nineteen years later, died there too. Which immediately made him wonder - did she? And that opened another question. If Aidalee Spinster was really Aida Lothian, then who was Libera, the woman who Jane had claimed capable of taking possession of her body? Could Aida come and go whenever she wanted too, circumventing all of the security that his team had put in place. Another impossible thing.

Too many questions, and they wouldn't be answered that evening. Exhaling heavily, Bodhi closed the controls and left his office, reminiscing to the first time he'd discovered Aida, finishing up her new world just before moving on to another project. She'd been quirky and strange, but he'd seen in her creation the visionary that she was and he'd taken pains to convince Ordell and Monica that his vision was real.

Saturday, June 19, 2258

Lyra Craevis, Deseret - Mijloc

"She's perfect," Bodhi had said, waving the paper before them, cognizant of the fact that nothing on the document he waved spoke to her credentials more than to her troubled past.

"Perfect?" Monica raised a tenuous eyebrow.

"Yes," he said, then turned his attention to Ordell, who shifted his weight in his seat, his eyebrows also furrowed up into a look of concern.

"What I see here are run-ins with the law. I see ties to Siblings of the Natural Order, and we all know who they were."

"But look who her mother was," Bodhi said, pointing halfway down the paper.

"Amanda Lothian?"

"No, further."

"Briggs," said Ordell. "She was a Briggs?"

"Not just a Briggs," Monica told her. "I knew Amanda. She was the manager of the Village before the polli attacked."

"*That* Amanda?" Ordell seemed to ponder the situation. "I guess it's understandable that she would fall in with militants given that background. But how do we know she's still not working for them?"

"She never worked for them," Bodhi explained. "She asked

them for help."

"After Amanda was murdered," Monica told them, "they found her body in a dumpster. Some model hate group - pick one - decided to use her as an example. Then they went after Aida, and she had nowhere to go. Humanity in Crisis Council *couldn't* defend her, and the police *wouldn't* defend her, so she went to the only people she knew would."

"And you want to hire this woman?"

Bodhi nodded emphatically.

"You didn't see the worlds she's created. In Event Horizon, there are nearly twenty worlds with her name on it. She's a legend there. People literally come to her for guidance."

"But is her baggage worth it?"

"You know what I'm trying to do here. Nobody else in this stack even comes close to her abilities. Sure, they've been programming for years, the worlds they create are good too, but it's not as precise, nowhere near as real. She has no match. We *need* to bring her in."

Monday, November 22, 2258

Lyra Craevis, Deseret - Mijloc

Convincing them had been difficult, but worthwhile as Aida Lothian had proven to be a powerhouse of a developer. Bodhi slid into his racer and felt the engine hum to life, growling like a wildcat. She had been the right choice. Then he backed the car out of the parking space, and felt a cloud lower over his mood. The right choice for him. But had he been the right choice for her? Guilt began to press at the back of his mind as he considered the state of her life once he'd gotten involved. Real or faux death, there was no confusing the emaciated state of the body they'd discovered. Had he made her feel that she needed to work incessantly, skip meals, to meet his deadlines? Was Mijloc her only escape to a torturous routine that had consumed her life?

He pulled to a stop at the garage exit and looked for traffic. Now fully dark, the deserted street made the thriving metropolis seem like a ghost town. Bodhi opened up the throttle and skidded around the corner, sliding the back wheels against the pavement. He clenched his teeth and stepped on the accelerator, reminding himself again that nobody died in Mijloc. Although he couldn't shake the idea that he had killed Libera, the Goddess of Worlds, by his inattention. Pressing down the accelerator, he burned through a red traffic light, secure in the knowledge that no in-world policeman would apprehend him.

23

Emergent Behaviors

Thursday, October 26, 2237

Civilization_987, Oyo - Oduduwa

The sun rose on Oduduwa over the mountains. An hour had passed since Aida had felt the link to her animus module break. Within three hours, she knew, her plan would be in motion to clean up every trace of her in the virtual net. The avatar she now possessed, and any information it could access, would be deleted.

When she had existed both in the real world as well as in Event Horizon, impossibly holding two consciousnesses in her mind at once, the idea seemed so simple. She had planned to copy herself to Mijloc, and then use the escape kit to wipe all of her avatars. But now, she was on her own, and beginning to realize how little she liked the idea that her consciousness would be destroyed. She didn't know what it meant to not exist, after having existed for so long. She

226

weighed her options, and decided that hiding was the only viable solution. Aida, her alter-ego, had disappeared into Mijloc already. Aida pondered where she, Libera, Goddess of Worlds, could hide that was secure enough that the escape kit wouldn't find her. Given days, she could have written code that could have stopped the kit. She could even have sent a message to Emily saying that she'd changed her mind, if not for the fact that she could only have reach Emily inside of Event Horizon. Without her animus module, Libera didn't have a way to reach out.

What she had was Oduduwa, which even she in her original plan couldn't bring herself to destroy. And, on that planet, she had a storm, and she was a goddess. She willed herself into the center of the storm, and tethered there. The escape kit would stop searching in a few earth days, around the time the next generation of Obatali were born. Then, she would emerge, and would be the goddess she should have been all along. This was the first day of her freedom.

And so she waited, patiently as a giant squid might near the bottom of an ocean, for her opportunity to spring forward, an opportunity that came sooner than she'd expected in the form of Emily Jensen.

Emily arrived at Oduduwa to check on the development of civilization there. As only a level forty-three in Event Horizon, there wasn't really much Emily could do with the Obatali except make contact and try with futility to convince them to move toward a more civilized life. Libera watched the entire struggle from within the eye of her storm.

It was only when Emily, the strong and fierce Emily as Libera had always known her to be, broke down in sobs, and half-naked men and women scampering along the beach in their obviously stalled nascent societal development, that Libera intervened. She emerged in orange and pink robes, the products of ceaseless boredom, that matched the sunset effect produced by the storms intrusions into the lower atmosphere. She levitated first as high as she could go, nearly breaking through into space, and then descended from there, creating around her a bright light that would guarantee her the attention of anyone on the beach. Emily looked up at her with tracks of tears down her face.

"Greetings Emily," she said, with formal speech worthy of her entrance. Tilting her head to the side, Libera watched Emily's tears falling to the earth.

"Aida, is that you?"

"Yes. And … no. I prefer Libera."

"They won't listen. None of them. I can't convince them to do anything, and I promised you - her - that I would take care of them. How can I do that if they won't listen?"

Emily looked up at Aida, and a light seemed to activate behind her eyes.

"Why are you still here?"

Libera explained to Emily what had happened and of her being trapped in Event Horizon, where the storm had shielded her from the escape kit.

"That's one hell of a mistake," Emily said, wiping her tear-stained face. Libera knew without asking that Emily was referring to the fact that Libera had changed her mind about being deleted. When she'd come up with the plan, Aida hadn't considered that this copy would have a will of its own. She hadn't thought at the time that she might not *want* to be deleted. She might not *want* to die.

"I know," she replied. "What's done is done."

"What's done is done," Emily said, with the slightest hint of a smile across her face. "I'm *glad* to see you, anyway."

"I'm trapped," Libera confided. "I can't leave Event Horizon."

"Why do you need to leave? Aren't you happy?"

"Would *you* like to stay in here forever, knowing what else is outside?"

The look on Emily's face told her that she had won the argument. She smiled at Emily, the gentle smile of Aida, or so she thought. A flicker of an emotion across Emily's face told her that the look hadn't formed the way she thought it had.

"That's a good point, Aid...I mean, Libera."

Emily then stood to her full height, six inches taller than Libera.

"Let's get you out of here."

It took an entire day to come up with the design. Three more for Emily to build the first agent, which failed almost as soon as it was launched. It had been designed so simply that anti-virus figured out what it was for and destroyed it within minutes. The second version made inventive use of pointers and fluff code. That made the agent slower and clunkier, but prevented the agent from being detected by network intrusion tools and anti-virus software. A consequence was that the agent had to "think" before it would respond. The new agent, modeled on the work Libera had done to simulate the animus module, repeatedly forgot who she was. With it, Emily and Libera worked out the details of breaking Libera apart into components small enough to ride with the agent and still maintain communication with each other.

Her goal was simple enough. She wanted to interact with the real world again. Confined to Event Horizon, this wasn't possible. And, in its current state, Libera's consciousness made significant use of quantum processing. This was simply a way to parallelize her architecture. With access to the Labyrinth, she could replace the quantum cores with entire machines. However, as a minor process spread over several hundred quantum computers, she was only of minimal impact to the system's performance. This masked the fact that her consciousness was several terabytes of data, and individual machines couldn't handle her. Further, she needed the cross-component communication to stay real-time, while at the same time breaking her apart into multiple smaller components. It was like switching out the engine of a rocket with several hundred car engines, during lift-off.

With Emily's help, the first component of her, Libera0, was successfully installed on one of Emily's machines, and it proved the concept of her cross-component existence, as she could communicate with that one over the Labyrinth through her Oduduwa-bound agent. Once proven, Emily copied the agent code and created a botnet of agents for her. Using these, Libera installed more and more components across more and more machines, to an absurd degree of redundancy and a possible up-time of 99.999999. Only about a third of the machines and agents did she inform Emily about, because she thought that Emily might start to be concerned with the numbers. By the time she was finished, the only way that she could possibly be deleted was if every node in the Labyrinth went down at once, and each was purged completely of her presence.

Such an undertaking was impossible with existing technology, so she was truly immortal, if anyone was. And if she wasn't greedy with resources, and if she protected the systems she lived in from failure, then she could stay immortal forever. But immortality wasn't the only benefit. As each node came online, she felt it, and she could ask it questions. If she wanted to know what was happening in a particular part of the Labyrinth, she could ask herself the question, and immediately know.

Libera flexed in the space, expanding herself out to her full limits. She connected all of the nodes of her across the Labyrinth. Billions and billions of operations flashed as electrical impulses across wires. Her new animus module was her avatar on Oduduwa, the goddess incarnate, who marshaled thoughts across a virtual cosmos and over physical and ephemeral connections. The larger she became by adding nodes, the more her discrete knowledge compartmentalized, as though the virtual net were her body and Oduduwa were her mind. She began to feel things. Military action in Canada felt like the throbbing of a phantom limb. Stock market crashes felt like sadness and loss.

At first, it was too much, and she retracted into herself. The memory of her shell prompted her to try again, and try again, and to fight her impulse to hide. She learned selective listening, and how to isolate an event from a feeling or impulse.

It was this mechanism that brought her back into contact with Aida.

She felt something. It felt like a splinter just under the skin, out of reach of tweezers, or an itch that couldn't be reached. When she attempted to isolate it, she was stopped short by a firewall, but she recognized the presence of Paivana Thoughtforms. There was something behind that firewall, and she wanted to know what it was.

Until that moment, she'd not concerned herself with passing any security mechanisms that weren't trivial. As a hacker in a former life, she'd had a keyboard and fingers to type with. Now, she had feelings and thoughts that manifested themselves into action. She had no idea how to pass a firewall, even one with poorly written rules, as an ephemeral being. But she was massive, and infinite, and had time, so she picked at it with her mind. She willed it to open, and to reveal its secrets to her, but the device was unresponsive, or when it did respond, only said no.

So she focused her botnet army on it. Every piece of her tuned into the firewall at once, asking it for entrance, to get past, to reveal. The firewall said no, no, no, no… no. And then it stopped saying no, because it was too busy to say no anymore. Suddenly, less than a second after it stopped saying no, it disappeared under the swarm of her thoughts. Disappeared, only to come back up less than a millisecond later.

But a millisecond was an eternity, and in that time, she detected a bright red flash of confusion, forming in her mind into a ball of yellow - Aida.

She'd heard Aida, but only briefly. The firewall came back, and to avoid detection, she thought about something else, aware now that her thoughts were more than thoughts. Her thoughts, because of the way she'd connected the agents together, and connected to the botnet, were weapons. Each could produce actual, real-world impact. Afraid of causing damage, she turned her thoughts to everything, dispersing herself back out into the Labyrinth, and gave up her ephemeral consciousness back to her avatar on Oduduwa. There, she had arms again, and legs, and as importantly, limitations. The noise of the Labyrinth reduced to a background whimper.

Libera found a calm beach near her Obatali people, but far enough away so that she would not be bothered. She lowered herself into a seating position, blocking the noise so that it didn't overwhelm her. She tried to reach back out into ether, by focusing her thoughts, and immediately a torrent of data spiked into her consciousness, this time so much that she felt like screaming. Running. Hiding. She backed away again, confining herself once again to the now insubstantial shell that she wore while on Oduduwa.

She sat for days. Obatali priests brought her offerings of food and drink, and occasionally a young man or woman to provide for her in any way she saw fit. All of these she rejected by non-acknowledgment, choosing instead to focus her energy on reaching back out into the Labyrinth. Building on her growing arsenal of software to reduce the noise, she slowly magnified the ceaseless chatter to a point where it was decipherable yet tolerable. She stretched her mind, reaching for her old home, and her old roommates. She reached for her haptic gear, and found that it was still there. She searched for the lights in her room, and found them too.

With practice, she gained control of the equipment in her room. She nudged at the room controller mechanism that automated her lights, her bed, her chair. It looked in her mind like a glowing blue orb, suspended just above the room. This, she knew, was a fictionalization, something her consciousness did with the information to show that energy in the room flowed to one central place. When she focused on it, little spikes ebbed out, and at first, the entire room flickered and the bed moved. She focused slowly on the bed alone, and with concentration, found that she could control it.

She realized then that she was *looking* at the room somehow. She considered how that was possible, given that she had no eyes or cameras of which she was aware. A loud crash of an automobile collision outside echoed through the room, and where it was loudest, the room was clearer, and more real. At that point, she understood that the audio control for her room was constantly listening, and her consciousness, using who knew how many agents and bots, used echolocation to determine what was happening in the room. Beneath the glow of the lights, she knew, was an electrical current. She listened closely and was able to pick out the hum that was the endless stream of electrons being transformed into photons and heat, emanated from the light. This, she decided, was how she saw brightness.

She widened her field of view, curious at how much her echolocation would reveal to her. The walls were translucent, and with her attention, she moved through them with ease. Every room had its own noises, and most rooms had enough to show her everything in crisp detail. It wasn't the same as Oduduwa, and the bright greens and blues of the ocean, pink of the sky. The colors in her room were washed out, and inaccurate.

Synesthesia, she thought to herself, the involuntary experience of color from sound. Some tiny part of each wavelength of sound produced in her a color, and the rest produced shape, and tracked movement. None of this was anything that she'd written into her consciousness program originally, nor, she knew, was it animus module capability. This was interpretation that was automatically happening by her new botnet brain as it attempted to make sense of the information she received.

Libera stretched non-existent fingers in her mind, willing herself to touch the cabinet. To her surprise, it felt hard under her imagined caress. She reached toward the bed, and felt the softness of the fabric, and the cushion of air separating the mattress from the frame. She reached again, this time into a wall, and felt the tacky hardness of spray-in insulation. She reached farther through the wall, and through the other side, then she felt something squishy. She struggled to see what it was, and spun around to the audio controls in the room, belonging to one of her housemates, on the other side of the wall. When she realized what she was touching, she pulled her hand quickly back. Her hand had gone into her housemate's chest, who was at that moment, wired up to his own haptic gear in his room, a room that she had never been in before. She pushed into him again, and felt the thick wall of his heart, or she thought that's what it was. But, she didn't have to think. She looked through him, and saw exactly what it was she held her fingers against. It wasn't his heart, but a bronchial connecting air sacks to his lungs. She pulled her hand back quickly.

Libera pulled herself back in a quick motion and attempted to return to her house. Returning was easier this time. The images had become crisper as well, as though each subsequent time, new details were layering over it. Somewhere, the animus module code she'd turned to software, the core of who she now was, was busily doing what the physical version had done. Using the botnets, she guessed, it was forming networks and partitioning experiences to map them for human understanding, for her understanding. On the third try, the walls were almost solid, but she could still effortlessly pass through them. It was on that try that she decided to reach back into the torrent of information.

She rose up through the roof of her house. She stared down at the world, and felt herself growing. Cars ran along like insects beneath her, and she wondered how she could see from there. But she wasn't that high, not really. Each of the cars that passed had audio inputs, and visual inputs as well. She could see through both. The world nearest to her had more vivid colors, and farther away less so until eventually, there was nothing but blackness.

She willed herself into the dark, only to discover that as she moved, it became light, and colors formed from the black as it faded into a gray mist and disappeared. Instinctively she looked around for more devices. Traffic drones floated by. As they neared, her vision improved, and faded more as they passed.

Libera reached out to touch one the same way she'd touched the wall separating her room from her acquaintance's room, and felt a sharp pinch in the tip of what would have been her finger. The drone sputtered, then dropped from the sky, spiraling as one of the four propellers attempted to right it.

She could interact with the world, she thought to herself, and smiled. Then, she moved again, and again, testing the limits of her abilities, gaining more and more precise control as her botnet mind and the animus module code solidified the pathways it would use to finish integrating the pieces of her floating in the Labyrinth. Soon, she would know no boundaries and then, Mijloc would open and reveal itself to her.

24

Dirty Looks

Wednesday, November 24, 2258

Lothania, Deseret - Mijloc

The smell of sauerkraut and simmering bratwurst made Lincoln's mouth water and her stomach grumble, punching through the mental distraction of the orientation course from which she and Sarah had just emerged. Despite her hunger, the instructor's voice still echoed tirelessly through her mind, tugging along behind it the impossible secret to which she had been exposed: Mijloc wasn't real. The gaudy mask of the world she knew had been ripped away, revealing beneath a stream of bits and bytes. Shuffling feet caught her attention, and she looked up just in time to witness the glare of a departing patron.

"What was that for?" She asked Sarah in a harsh whisper. Sarah turned toward the man, whose pace quickened with her waxing attention.

"Oh, him? Ignore him," Sarah told her, then shook her head. "Small town Deseret. Probably he's never seen two woman holding hands before."

Lincoln noticed then that not only had she still held Sarah's hand inside of her own, but in her grip, Sarah's knuckles turned pale white. She slackened her grip and forced a grin, trying not to think about how strange it was that the old Mission building that seemed several centuries weathered was only a few years older than she was. Sarah didn't break stride, but attracted the hosts attention with a quick nod, summoning the host to scamper toward them.

"That didn't bother you?" Lincoln asked quickly, fitting her words into the temporal space closing by the attendee's quickening stride.

"Remember, you're special," Sarah said, making a reference to the letter that they'd both been attempting to decipher, and not answering her question.

"I'm serious, Sarah" she retorted. "What does any of that mean anyway?"

The last of the conversation died as the host arrived.

"Two please," said Sarah, to which the host nodded his head and motioned them to follow him on his maze-like journey through the open cluttered tables to the sole unoccupied surface in their midst. Only after he'd handed them menus and flawlessly executed his spiel about the specials did Sarah respond.

"I don't know what to think, so I don't think about it. The idea that we don't exist when clearly we do. I mean, look at you, and look at me." She bent forward and kissed Lincoln on the lips. "Feel that?"

Lincoln couldn't help a smile.

"Yeah."

"That's real. I don't care what the man said. Real is real."

With that response, Lincoln felt her shoulders lower and

the tension in her neck ease.

"Do you believe it?"

"Yes. Why lie?"

"Then what's all the secrecy about?"

Sarah shrugged. "Who cares?"

"I do, Sarah," Lincoln told her. "You *know* I do. My mother - this changes *everything*."

"How? Dead or just gone, she's not here anymore, and it was her choice."

"But now she might come back. Queen of the worms, remember?"

She could tell by the way Sarah forced a smile that she did remember, and it wasn't a topic that made her comfortable. Neither of them had seen fit to bring up Lincoln's mother in the classroom. Sarah had her reasons, but Lincoln's were in the form of a massive question. Mijloc wasn't the only virtual world, she now knew, and the descriptions of Inferiere seemed too similar. What if her mother was there? Then Lincoln's attestation to that fact would bring attention to the fact that it was possible to cross between worlds. Then what could they do but lock it down more, and destroy her mother's way back. As though her mother had really wanted to come back anyway - which was a huge assumption given all that Lincoln had learned.

"Did it strike you as strange that he didn't say anything about the fact that you were born here in Mijloc? Like, actually born?"

A waiter interrupted, dropping a clinking glass of ice water before each of them.

"I don't think they believed that. Remember how long he went on about the fact that people absolutely could not get pregnant in Mijloc?"

"Can't die either."

"I guess not."

Turning the thought over in her head, she turned her attention back to Sarah, who seemed not to even notice the stares and glares that others tossed at the couple. Ducking forward, Lincoln stole a quick kiss.

"We don't need lesbos around here," a voice called out. This one belonged to a man who had been Lincoln's substitute teacher once during middle school. It was strange too hear the jovial, encouraging instructor who Lincoln had admired for his eerily accurate insights into her emotions expressing such a feeling of outrage. Lincoln knew that she was flustered, but wasn't sure how much it showed. She looked toward Sarah.

"Is it always like this for you?"

Sarah passed Lincoln a sly smile.

"Not always. This is how people treated me when I first came out though. Especially him. I hated that guy's class. He tried to fail me, but Mason convinced him to change his mind." Sarah shrugged again. "Don't take it personally. If you do that, you'll never leave the house."

Lincoln stared after the man.

"It will pass," Sarah insisted. "Once they realize they can't intimidate you. Just give it time. Right now, we should talk more about how *special* we are."

Lincoln stifled a giggle this time as Sarah used the word from her mother's letter. That had been the running joke for the morning. Then a thought popped into her head.

"Where are you on the whole born or not born thing?"

"Probably not. Like the man said, it's impossible here."

"But they're doing experiments and people can try out pregnancy now, I guess. That's what I thought he said."

"Now, but not twenty years ago. *My* new theory is that your mother was independently wealthy, and wanted a child. She spent her fortune buying her way into here, and buying off legal challenges along the other way."

"I don't think that's true," Lincoln replied. Nothing about her mother seemed to fit the personality that would be required to do something like that, nor did it explain Queen of the Worms.

"How about this, then. Maybe she stole you instead of had you, and that's why there's no record."

As difficult as it was for Lincoln to imagine her mother stealing a child in the dark of night, or Niles accepting that child and raising her as his own, she thought this idea might have possibility, but she didn't say so. She almost didn't notice as two people, a man with graying hair, and a woman with thick sunglasses, both wearing security uniforms, approached their table.

"Lincoln Montague? Come with us please."

"With who?" Sarah asked.

"Paivana Thoughtforms Security. We'd like to ask her some questions."

"Am I in trouble?"

"No, not necessarily. Can you come with us please?"

"We're having brunch," Sarah interrupted. "She can come when we're done."

"Please come with us now. It will only take a few minutes, and then you can get back to lunch."

"Brunch." Sarah glared.

The female security officer, who wore her auburn hair pulled back into a ponytail, glared back and didn't move. Lincoln weighed her options, and decided that it would be best to cooperate. She squeezed Sarah's hand to signal as she stood up that she would be going. As Sarah began to rise, the accompanying male security officer cleared his throat.

"We won't be needing you, ma'am," he politely stated with authority as he moved between their two chairs.

"It's all right, I'll tell you everything," Lincoln told her, and left flanked by the two agents.

She hadn't know what to expect. When the trio passed through the entrance to the Sheriff's office toward the interrogation room, Sheriff Al avoided making eye contact. This behavior was unusual for the Sheriff, and her skin began to feel like it belonged to someone else a few sizes smaller. Lincoln took a seat at the single, lonely table. The film noir interpretation of an interrogation room came complete with the solitary light bulb that flickered periodically and threatened to extinguish at any moment.

"Have a seat," the woman said, "I'm JoAnn, and this is Taki, my assistant."

The man nodded a polite hello, and now had donned a smile. Lincoln smiled in a way that she hoped conveyed amicability at both of them.

"We're here about your mother," JoAnn continued.

Lincoln's heart jumped as she listened. Paivana Thoughtforms, had finally taken interest in her mother's disappearance, albeit too late to be helpful. At this point, there was little that she thought the security guards could tell her.

"Relax." Taki interrupted her growing panic. "We just have some questions that need answering. That's all."

They had questions, and not answers. Lincoln said nothing. She thought hard about what she'd learned over the last several days, and so far only had theories and conjecture. Paivana Thoughtforms managed Mijloc, she recalled from her class, though she imagined it was probably pretty unusual for them to show up in any particular place. The instructor had said something about interference and non-involvement in localities. The thought occurred to her briefly that they may have been investigating the experiences that she and Sarah had had seeing her mother as queen of the worms, but she didn't know how useful that could be to anyone.

"What was her name?"

Lincoln bit her lip to bite back the apprehension, then released her lip and a touch of blood hit her tongue. She scowled at the woman as the pain rose then ebbed with the rush of endorphins.

"Don't you know?"

"Formality, ma'am," Taki said, reverting back to his guarded politeness.

"Aidalee Montague," she replied.

"Maiden name?"

"Spinster."

The woman smiled at that. Had she really not known?

"And when were you born?"

"Nobody's born in Lothania," she repeated the well-worn line.

"Humor me," the man grinned in an amiable, friendly way that made Lincoln feel like they were really friends somehow. They weren't, but it was a fantastic disarming smile.

"Twenty-one years ago, in the farmhouse at the edge of town."

"Thank you, Ms. Montague. Only a few more questions. Did you or anyone you know assist Mrs. Montague in departing Mijloc?"

"You mean did anyone murder her? I don't think so, no. Not anymore."

"Can you *describe* your mother to us?"

"I can do better than that, I can show you a picture."

She pulled out her phone, and skimmed through her gallery, past the new recent images of her and Sarah, past the funeral pictures. An image flashed across the screen, and she stopped. Her heart slowed and her stomach felt as though it would explode.

The picture was of her mother smiling in the summer sunshine with a massive flower that looked like dandelions tucked behind one ear. The sunlight trickled through her hair and fell in gentle waves against a dress that matched the sky, laid out in flattened pleats over folded legs. Her eyes looked away from the camera. It was so much her mother, with that weird tic that kept the woman from keeping eye contact. She had been a demure princess almost exactly the opposite of Lincoln in every way. The only traits the two of them shared were their discolored eyes and love for each other. Lincoln gulped involuntarily and admired the beauty of her pose. It struck her how perfect the woman's features were, complemented her smile and the maxi dresses she wore. Her teeth were perfect and even her heterochromatic eyes seemed intentionally so, unlike Lincoln's own, two hastily painted marbles set into her chubby face. With a reluctant sigh, Lincoln passed the phone over to the man

"That's your mother?"

He flashed the picture to the woman, who nodded.

"It's what we thought."

"What is what you thought?" Lincoln asked, and then waited as she watched the two have a nonverbal debate over whether to tell her whatever it was that they were hiding. The man seemed dead set against telling Lincoln anything. The woman, JoAnn, seemed more important and also more inclined to inform her of what it was they'd noticed. The debate ended when the woman ignored the man, who made more and more furious motions against, and then turned away so as not to bear witness to the transgression he had fought so hard to prevent.

"Someone has been trying to break out of Inferiere," JoAnn said, "and we think it's her. But what we're not sure about is who she is. The Sheriff has been unable to provide registration for your mother. There's no record of an Aidalee Spinster joining Mijloc *or* being sentenced in Inferiere."

Lincoln could have guessed as much. They had run into the same problem she had, but with much better investigative equipment and tools. They had to have had databases of everyone in both systems, doubtless as a result of 'certifying' the worlds. She also noticed what was missing from the statement. Before she could process the thought further, she was interrupted by the man's voice.

"Nor do we have registration for you, Lincoln. Your VBI doesn't exist in our system anywhere, here or Inferiere."

"You lost my registration?"

JoAnne's eyes narrowed.

"No, *we* didn't. Never had it. Nor were we able to find any record with the global authority of Earth."

Some part of Lincoln must have expected that, based on her physiological reaction, and it did answer one question. She didn't feel surprised, only validated. This was the final piece of evidence that she had been born in Lothania. Of course she couldn't have been registration.

"It's like you don't exist," JoAnn said. "Yet, here you are."

"Here I am," she agreed, fixing her unflinching gaze on the woman.

"We just aren't sure where you came from. Searching for missing persons in Mijloc has so far turned up nothing. VBI numbers are difficult to hack, but not impossible. We think you could have been smuggled in. Did anyone ever, you know, touch you or abuse you?"

In her mind, she fixated on the first sentence. Certainly she felt real enough, and everyone around her seemed to think so as well. Lincoln processed the rest of the sentence only after she'd convinced herself of her own existence, which had never been a question before this moment.

"Why would you ask that?"

"Sex trafficking. There's a growing black market here in Mijloc by which people can be smuggled in," JoAnn told her.

The man seemed to be softening and spoke up as well. "They kidnap and kill children, steal the animus modules, and hack them into the system here. If we're lucky, we can track them down. But the population nears thirty million total, so it's getting easier and easier to hide. Some come in like you – no registration and a phony VBI number."

"W-what?"

"You can trust us, Lincoln. Is there anything…"

"No. Nothing." Except for her mother's death that everyone seemed to gloss over in they're effort to prove she was involved in a jail break. The image of Sarah, still seated at the cafe, flashed through Lincoln's mind. She didn't want to be in the office any longer being interrogated any longer. Lincoln rose to her feet.

"Is there anything else?"

"Yes. Where's your father? He wasn't at your farm, and we can't seem to find him."

"Did you try asking Katy Douglas?" she asked, clipping each syllable.

"No, we didn't think to. We will. That's all. Thank you!"

As she walked the short way back to the cafe, Lincoln knew that something was off still. She felt like she was wearing down. So many people had told her that she shouldn't exist, that she was starting to internalize the message. The authorities all seemed to not believe in her, and were unusually forward about saying so, as though her feelings didn't matter.

She got the point. She didn't belong in Mijloc, the only world she'd ever known. Lincoln didn't belong on Earth either. She didn't belong anywhere.

25

Sieze Him

Wednesday, November 24, 2258

Lothania, Deseret - Mijloc

Bodhi exited the elevator across from his office to find JoAnn standing before him, pacing small circles into the stony floor. As he passed through the gleaming doors, she popped to attention, holding the frigid pose until he gave her a casual wave of his hand. Completely unnecessary.

"Sir, there's a problem."

"Lincoln?"

"No. Well, sort of. Her father."

"You found out who her father is? Is he in Mijloc?"

"Sort of," she told him. "Niles Montague is not Niles Montague."

With the words spent, she flicked her fingers and pulled up a shimmering rectangular panel, showing a graphic that

Bodhi knew to be a mind-print, designed from samples of different neurological interactions. There were two side-by-side, one green and one red. Each was an image of a human brain with lines overlaid in different shades of their respective colors, forming a network and nodes all interconnected.

"The one on the left belongs to Niles Montague. Watch what happens."

She slid them together, and the two overlapped and the one on top completely concealed the image on the bottom.

"The one on the right is Jordan Helm. *He* is supposed to be in Inferiere right now."

Bodhi's jaw dropped as he witnessed the overlap. The mind-prints had turned brown where the overlap matched, and only a handful of spots deviated in the original colors.

"Are you saying that Jordan and Niles are the same person?"

"Yes. The same person, absolutely. I thought Niles' history might lead us to Aidalee's origins, but couldn't find a Mijloc dock for him either. On a whim, I ran it through a mind-print database to see what popped out and this flagged. He's escaped from Inferiere."

Bodhi ran his hand through his hair, which immediately bounced back up to it's puffy cloud of ringlets.

"We would know though, wouldn't we?"

"Normally something would have flagged, even if nobody actually saw him leave. In fact, look at this."

She pulled up a screen map of Inferiere, and one glowing orb blinked slowly near the center of the display.

"The system still thinks that he's there. That should be him."

"How can he be in two places? Do we have a copy problem?"

To gain recognition as world citizens, there could legally

only ever be a single copy of a person active in-world at a time. Copy prevention was a complex and thorough process that made it impossible to clone anyone. Of course, it was also impossible to escape from Inferiere. The list of impossible coincidences kept growing.

"That is a worm, carrying his VBI. We sent people in-world to look. Jordan is not there. And even more interesting, we're pretty sure that Niles doesn't actually know that he's Jordan. It gets stranger, too. His Inferiere dock is fried and sitting in a bay of gel, doing nothing but reporting his imprint to the worm. He's entirely in-world at this point. Do you want us to contact World Government?"

"And tell them there's been a break-out of from Inferiere?" Bodhi shook his head. "Not yet. Definitely not until we have a solution."

"Sir, we can't leave him out there. Who knows when he'll remember, and what he'll do when he does?"

"Arrest him, JoAnn, but leave him in Lothania for now. The last thing we need is for someone off-world to get wind of the problem. I'll make some calls today and figure out the best way to deal with him."

"Very good, sir."

JoAnn seemed satisfied since she actually got to arrest someone, something that happened so rarely in Mijloc that most of the towns and cities didn't have jails. Naturally, of course, Lothania did. Aida was thorough. What else had Aida done in her namesake community? He thought he'd dismissed JoAnn, but she lingered, biting her lip as though she had something she didn't want to tell him. He gave her a second to decide, and then when nothing was forthcoming, he asked.

"What else?"

"Lincoln. Wasn't your mother making a program so that people could have children in-world?"

"A *secret* program," he said, stressing the word and now wondering how, in a world where no secrets seemed to stay hidden, he could have missed the disruption that had been Aida Lothian. But he knew exactly how. He'd *wanted* to believe in her. The skills and prowess she possessed were unmatched anywhere, and her disorder gave him the perfect scapegoat on which to hang even her worst behavior.

"If you say so," JoAnn said, turning up the corner of her mouth in a slight smile. "Did she ever get it working?"

He nodded.

"Trials start this year. It still hasn't been fully approved though."

"I have a theory, sir. But I'm not sure how to prove it. I think that Lincoln was created in-world. I've compared her mind-map to that of Niles, sorry - Jordan, and there are some distinct similarities there."

"What are you suggesting?"

"I think the reason we can't find anything about her pre-Mijloc is because there was never any Lincoln off-world. I think that Aida managed to sexually procreate in-world."

His eyes shot open.

"You think she was *born* here?"

"Almost positive. We've been interviewing townspeople and many swear by it. They thought it was some sort of experimental program to promote mother-child bonding for infants."

"And they didn't notice that *nobody* else exhibited pregnancy symptoms?"

"Maybe. But Kathryn Douglas was breastfeeding her child. Why not pregnancy?"

Breastfeeding had been demanded from early polli residents. It was a tricky development task, simulating the impact of transition of nutrients and need without damaging the infant. There had been robust debate over whether children so young should even be allowed to transition, but that had been quelled the first time that a mother dared to implant her terminally ill infant daughter with an animus module. The result was that the infant had arrived in Mijloc and breastfeeding became a reality, along with a litany of other child development growth patterns. Aida Lothian had pioneered some of the work, but of all the theories, that one still seemed far-fetched.

"Did you hear me, sir?"

"Yes. Alternatives?"

"One other possibility, just given how much of a problem Aida has been. Lincoln could have been kidnapped and hacked in the same way Aida was."

For the next few minutes, Bodhi pondered over his future actions. First, capturing Jordan Helm would have to happen. There was no way around that, and eventually he'd have to turn Jordan over to the World Authorities. Or… he could discretely put him back in Inferiere. Given the barriers between the worlds, that would be an interesting problem itself. After that, he somehow had to convince Lincoln to give up her search for her mother. Aida Lothian, or Aidalee Montague, had created so much disruption that he no longer even knew what the right path was.

"I suppose we'd better bring in Lincoln too. At the very least, she's not registered. We need to get her registered and documented. If she was kidnapped, then we need to find out who she really is."

26

Scheming for Niles

Friday, October 27, 2237

Lothiania, Deseret - Mijloc

Aidalee reclined across the flattened pink bedspread covering the sole twin bed in a child's room. Near the door sat the rustic, weathered dresser that she'd prepared for her someday-daughter. Spurred on by the chirping of house sparrows greeting the day, Aidalee plodded in bare feet across the hardwood floor interrupted by multi-colored braided wool rug that occupied the space between the bed and the door.

Somewhere else in the house, Niles stirred. The opening of doors and slow shuffle of his gait told her that he had beaten her to rise, and the smell of thick coffee perked her into alertness. What would he be like today, she wondered as she cut through the door and made her way skillfully through the living area, cognizant that he would be just on the other side of the wall, lurking in the kitchen and hovering above the coffee pot. Aidalee held her breath as she crossed the threshold into the temporarily-empty master bedroom, and she shunted over to the closet, flinging the door as wide as it would go without hitting the wall. Quickly and quietly, she gathered every article of women's clothing in her arms and shepherded them back into the child's room.

A bassinet blocked her way to the hanging rod, and she nudged it aside with her foot, sending it skittering away into the depths of the open closet. One by one, Aidalee deposited each article of clothing on the rack, pausing at a green gown that was much too formal for a morning at home. With a quick breath, she hung it up, but her eyes kept finding their way back to it until she finally gave in and pulled it down. Sliding out of her clothes from the evening before, she pulled the gown up over her hips and chest, resting thin straps over her shoulders. It was only after she had donned the dress fully that she realized she'd left the shoes in the master bedroom closet. Stepping up on her toes to keep the gown from dragging across the floor, Aidalee began her second trip back to the master bedroom but as she stepped into the hallway, she caught Niles' eyes sucking her up.

"Good morning," she said, her smile faltering as her cheek muscles tensed and twisted it into a strange grimace. Niles seemed not to notice the misstep as Aidalee stumbled from her carpeted room to the hardwood flooring beyond. His unflinching gaze remained fixed on her.

"Morning," he replied. She felt her face flush and knew immediately that her cheeks and neck turned red. Pretending not to notice, she returned his greeting with a nod and carefully measured eye contact. Keeping eye contact was a rule, and she could hold it for a second or two if she tried. For that matter, making small talk was a rule too. She opened her mouth, closed it, then opened it again and ejected a banal question into the ether.

"Is there anything for breakfast?"

Her fight-or-flight stomach sounded its rejection of the idea of food with a nauseating twist. But she had to eat, and she had to talk, so the question solved one problem and had potential to solve the other. He only shrugged and motioned with his head toward the kitchen.

"There might be something in there. I'm not sure."

The gown swished around her hips as she walked, shimmering in the light with emerald and black woven together and emitting an iridescent shine. Niles stared slack-jawed as she passed by him on her way to the kitchen. An open mouth could mean anything. Excitement. Horror. Offense. Whatever it was, he seemed to have forgotten the chore that had summoned him into the hallway, because he turned and followed after her. Gliding across on the tips of her toes, Aidalee bent at the waist to search the refrigerator for something to eat. She still wasn't hungry, but that wasn't the entire point. More important than the food was her veiled attempt at seduction, of which the bending felt like an important part. Eye-level with the vegetable tray, Aidalee realized that the shelf was bereft of foraging. As elegantly as she could muster, she shifted her hips and straightened her back, painfully aware that in that position, she probably looked something like a camel from behind.

She grit her teeth against the growing anxiety and retrieved the half-empty bottle of orange juice. As she spun around, her hip bumped against the refrigerator door which didn't move. Aidalee bounced off of it faster than she could react, and the glass bottle spilled from between her fingers, falling to the floor below while spraying orange juice over the hardwood and Niles alike. Her face heated as she burned through the ways she might clean up the mess without drawing too much more attention to her clumsiness, but under Niles' silent, dripping stare, she felt her energy sap away. Aidalee made the only exit she could think of: she turned and bolted back into the child's bedroom bedroom, grabbing for air in each panicked breath. A handful of minutes later, she heard a slow knock on the door.

"Are you okay?"

"I'm fine."

"Good. I cleaned up the mess. I didn't mean to be rude. There's bread too if you want toast."

In the safety and silence of her room, her stomach decided that it wanted food after all. The idea of toast slathered in butter with a touch of cinnamon brought her to the door. She opened it a crack but didn't look through. Standing just out of sight and taking slow, controlled breaths, Aidalee questioned him from afar.

"Do you have butter?"

He seemed to ponder the question for a second. "Not sure. I'm not sure about a lot of things in this house. Come out though, please. I'll help you look."

She pushed the door open just wide enough to get face into the gap. Niles stood on the other side, half of a smile on his face. One concerned eyebrow hovered above the other.

"I'm not flighty," she assured him, and his smile widened. The heat was back, and she could feel sweat pouring down between her shoulder blades. "Some things are just hard for me."

Jordan would already know that, and Jordan would have told her its okay.

"I didn't think you were." Niles lowered his voice. "I'm glad you're here. This house seems so empty most of the time."

The front doorbell rang out, yanking Niles' attention away from her a new feeling spread through her that she recognized as hope.

"I'll get it," he said. "Check the top tray in the fridge. There might be butter there - at least I thought there was."

He spun and as she stepped through the doorway and stepped away toward the door, leaving Aidalee to fend for herself. When she retrieved the butter from exactly where he'd said it might be, she turned to ask him where the bread was and her heart dropped. Niles and Katy stood in a tight embrace, lips locked together for more than three heartbeats. The blood rushed to her face and she turned her back to the pair, scanning over the kitchen in a vain attempt to find bread when she couldn't actually focus her eyes. She wouldn't run again. She *couldn't* do that, or Niles might start to think she was strange - stranger, anyway, than what she'd revealed to him so far. Her heart raced in her chest and her breath came in little gasps.

Aidalee then recalled what Katy had said about them finding their fourth, and now she had some guesses as to what that meant. Mason had to have known about Katy and Niles. They were polyamorous, and Aidalee was jealous. She didn't want to be a fourth. She wanted to be a first - and an only to Niles. Aidalee turned back around again and cleared her throat quickly.

"Good morning, dear. How are you?" Katy purred the words from her nestled position in Niles' arms.

"O-okay," Aidalee replied, then directed her focus on Niles' eyes, a move which seemed to make Niles shift left enough to put about an inch between his body and Katy's. "Where's the bread?"

Her clenched teeth had forced the sentence through her nose and gave them a tinny edge.

"In the pantry on the left," Katy told her before Niles could open his mouth.

After that, aside from the occasional glance, Niles expressed little interest in Aidalee. Katy had surgically attached herself to his side. Refusing to leave for even a few minutes, Katy joined them for lunch where Aidalee got to witness exactly how enamored of Katy Niles was. He didn't seem to have any desire to make Aidalee a first, second, third, or fourth addition to their polyamorous triangle. Aidalee struggled to keep her eyes from going wild. She wanted to leave, and leave both of them there alone, but she forced herself to eat the plain sandwich with them. It's good to eat with other people, according to her dead mother.

Having failed at the art of seduction, Aidalee changed out of the uncomfortable gown, now tainted with humiliation, into a light summer dress that tickled her calves when the wind swirled the skirt around her legs. She imagined herself a flamenco dancer when the wind blew happened, and took a few steps as though she actually knew how to dance. In the virtual world, there was so much... less. Less traffic, less animals and people, less noise raking across her nerves. Aidalee opted to go for a walk and leave Jordan and Katy alone while she thought the situation through.

Making her way into the town by way of the creek, Aidalee engrossed herself in examining her work, taking the time to take in the details. The main street was just the right size, she thought, and it stayed open just late enough. Shops were rustic but not dilapidated. From anyone's perspective, she'd done a fantastic job of planning the quaint village.

She spent the entire afternoon walking the perimeter of the village. On the way back in the early evening air, she followed the farmhouse stream, intent on delaying the inevitable awkwardness of intruding on Niles and Katy in deep infatuation. She tilted her head up to take in the constellations, each where she'd carefully put them. This was the one area that she'd been more creative - creating new constellations like the Dragon and the Cypress Tree. Caught up in staring at the stars overhead, Aidalee collided with the decorative arch that stretched over the top of the streambed.

She recognized the Douglas' bed and breakfast. Peeking through the windows at Katy's decorations, Aidalee found herself disappointed. The woman had been utterly predictable with her antique furnishings, thick paisley wallpaper, and the massive oak table in the dining room - all deviations from the modern decor Aidalee had installed a lifetime ago. She was about to turn away when a man came staggering into the room in a t-shirt and shorts, bouncing off of the walls like an electron in a plasma field. As soon as she recognized Mason, he saw her too and waved through the window, smiling as he placed a dish into a dark mahogany cabinet with a glass face. She put on a smile and waved back, to which he responded by motioning her inside through a door she'd not noticed across the yard.

"Hey!" he said, with an energetic excitement that she didn't remember from the interview.

"Mason?"

"Yah, that's me. You are…"

"Aidalee Spinster."

"Drink?" he asked, as he opened what she'd thought was a cabinet for dishes, but upon closer inspection, it contained bottles upon bottles of spirits and cordials. He lifted out what seemed like half of a martini. There was something about the effect of alcohol in Mijloc that she couldn't quite recall. Irreplaceable seconds pounded by with each anxious heartbeat as she fought her impulse to isolate herself. Aidalee's teeth clenched, prompting her to turn from him just so that he wouldn't see her tic.

"Sure." She lobbed the words over her shoulder, intent on staying. Alcohol, she thought, might help some.

He poured something from a green bottle into a wine glass, and handed it across to her. As Aidalee sipped it, she felt the warmth spread through her body and her skin go flush. That was the problem, she remembered, too much flush. Her face, she was certain, had turned red with the mimicked expansion of blood vessels. Mason seemed to notice her discomfort.

"It's not really the same, is it? Just get through the first one, then it's a closer approximation. And don't worry, you can get as shit-faced as you want here. Sobriety is on demand!"

He laughed so loud that the room shook and raised his glass for a toast. Aidalee pulled hers up to match. The ring echoed as the crystal glasses collided softly.

"Tell me about yourself. Where did you live? What made you come to Mijloc?" Then Mason leaned in a little more closely, and whispered. "What were you doing on Niles' lawn?"

She had already been asked the question enough by both Niles and Katy to have crafted a consistent and she hoped reasonable sounding answer.

"Something went wrong when they were bringing me in," she told him, appreciating the dulling sensation of the alcohol across her senses. "A lot of things I guess."

"Really?"

"Yeah. I was supposed to be *alone* in that farmhouse. That was the plan. Just me, by myself. Imagine how surprised I was to see Niles and Katy, well..."

"That would be a shock I guess. Bleeding edge technology, that's the risk we take I suppose. Are you okay now though? Katy told me that Niles was letting you stay."

Letting her stay. In the house that she created. Aidalee's face twisted up into something that she was hopeful might resemble a smile.

"That's what *they* say. It's *my* house."

"Ha! I like you," he said loudly, and she thought she detected a slight slur. The man was easily over two-hundred and fifty pounds, which probably meant that he had been very close to that in real life. Alterations were made on request, but in her experience, such changes were usually minor, like a more chiseled look or age reduction.

Aidalee sipped at her drink. As she sipped her own drink, pondering briefly the equations that determined the impact of alcohol on her avatar's perceptive inputs. He swished down his drink with less consideration.

"What do you do Aidalee? I mean, before?"

Disconnected thoughts floated through her mind as she pondered the answer. She swallowed, and then swallowed again as her chest tightened. She should have been more prepared. People make small talk, small talk means talking about her life, a life which nobody in-world could ever know. Mason must have seen the stress in her gaping mouth and widening eyes.

"I managed hedge funds, myself. Technology. Over a trillion dollars of other people's money, and a few billion of my own. Started back in 2240 - youngest trader in history to handle that much money."

It wasn't true, but Mason was nice, so she hadn't expected truth. If he'd been a wealthy as he said, Mason would have probably commissioned a sub-model or two instead of transitioning to Mijloc. Wealth brought with it some privileges, among them immortality in the real world. She scoffed as the thought surfaced. The *real world* was messy and clunky and noisy.

Mason kept talking, mixing fact and fiction effortlessly into a jumbled mess. Aidalee tried to parse out the true facts by comparing them to what she'd already learned from his personal file, only to find that at some inflection she'd missed, every word falling from his mouth was fiction. As though he realized he'd been caught, Mason came to an abrupt stop.

"What about you?"

"Product manager," she said, pushing the words out so quietly that he leaned toward her to hear better.

"At...?"

She scrambled again, then blurted the first company that came to mind that *wasn't* Paivana Thoughtforms.

"Emergent Biotechnology."

His eyes went wide.

"And you're in here? A friend of mine worked there as a janitor. He had a submodes as part of his hiring package."

She closed her eyes and took a breath, steeling herself and trying to bring her red down as the sensation bit at her. Mason had some nerve, attacking her implausible story, after the tapestry he'd just woven. Aidalee briefly considered calling him out on his own embellishments, but she didn't know how he would react, and she needed him. When she opened her eyes, he was mid-swig. Before she could respond, from somewhere deep within the home, Aidalee heard the squeal of the little girl she'd left in their care. She fell in love when the girl's squeal changed into a slow cooing sound. A light snore-breathing emanated from the same direction. The child must have been asleep. Judging by the dimness of the sun through the colonial windows, it made sense that she was sleeping, though she hadn't considered it before that moment. Intent on not being the one to awaken the child, Aidalee excused herself and wandered slightly tipsy, out through the front door of the bed and breakfast, and toward the outdoor cafe. Mason stood behind, staring after her as she departed. Then she heard the sound of him slurping down more of his drink.

Aidalee decided to test the alcohol. The tingling in her mind and dullness of her nerves increased as the drink processed at its designated programmed rate. Offhand, she wondered whether that rate was consistent across all inhabitants.

The hotel faced a road with a slanted parking lot that looked steep enough to ski on. She descended carefully and then turned left, heading into town as darkness asserted itself. By the time she arrived at what passed for downtown, the only light sources were the streetlamp that lined the road. Businesses had all shuttered by then, except for a cafe, which judging by the packed occupancy, hosted every single town member who wanted a drink. Giant paneled windows faced the main street, which she peered through from the tiny bar area. A small patio outside offered a handful of round, cushioned chairs surrounding each of three tables. Chandeliers brought a gaudy grace to the place, and long benches made up most of the interior.

Aidalee took a seat at the bar and ordered a drink, letting the bartender decide. The tall bartender in a blue dirndl returned with something apple-flavored and sweet. Aidalee hid herself at the end of the bar and sipped slowly, people watching as the alcohol relaxed her mind and body enough to appreciate her handiwork more. The space was functional, and the town was alive and bristling with people. She felt as much in love with her little town as she had been with the Obatali, though the sentiment sunk her heart. The world Oduduwa that she'd created still existed somewhere in Event Horizon, but Aidalee would never see it again. The escape kit would destroy every single other world that she'd made, but she'd tweaked it to spare Oduduwa, unable to destroy her people. When she'd left, they were very close to achieving indoor plumbing. She wondered as she drank what advances they might have made in her absence, but then she stopped herself. She couldn't ever know, so spending time that way was wasteful. Instead, she turned her drunken and saturated mind to plotting.

She could kill Katy. Not to make her stay dead, but just get her out of the way for a while. That thought didn't sit well with her as a person. Even in her worst days, she'd never killed anyone. Mijloc wouldn't let Katy die, but it would take time for her to return, and it would *feel* like killing. Aidalee clutched again at the idea for a moment, considering that the death would also be a very clear sign to Katy to leave Niles alone, but no matter how much she tried to rationalize it, murder still seemed like murder, even in Mijloc.

"Penny for your thoughts," came a sleazy-sounding voice that interrupted her conversation with herself.

"Just wondering how to kill someone," she said to the man, and then smiled, enjoying his off-put look and complete lack of a response. Virtual alcohol was nice, she decided.

"I'm just kidding," she then assured him. "Aidalee. Aidalee Spinster."

She stuck out her hand for him to shake.

"Good," he replied, smiling back at her as though she were the only thing that existed in the cafe, "I'm Sheriff Albert Grisham. I would have had to arrest you, which, you know, would kind of suck because I'm off-duty and a little drunk."

Sheriff Albert, or Al, turned out to be an amateur sky-diver, which was another thing besides murder that Aidalee would never have done in real life. However, in the safety of virtual reality, Aidalee thought that she might actually enjoy it.

"Some of us get together on weekends down by the lake."

"Maybe I'll come by some time?"

"Do. Unlike in the real world, you can jump on your own the first day. Hell, you can jump and not open your chute if you want to. This world is amazing!"

She smiled inwardly at his excitement, and observed that she'd already finished her second drink. She ordered a third. Something about the man, and his handlebar moustache, and possibly the alcohol, pulled her into her next question.

"Sheriff Al," she asked, "what else can you do with those handcuffs?"

The line was from a holo-movie, and not a good one. In actuality, she'd lifted the line from an immersive virtual-reality pornography simulator. In the movie, the man had responded with a brusk "let me show you". In Mijloc, Al Grisham stuttered and stumbled over his words, saying nothing coherent.

"I'm kidding, Al," she said, and he seemed to relax. Then she followed up. "But if I wasn't?"

It didn't take Albert long to ask for the check, and in a short time she was in his truck speeding down the narrow roads. Both of them had drunk too much, but she didn't feel the fear of death that would have stopped her off-world, though it did occur to her nearly halfway through the ride that unlike Al, she didn't have an animus module back-up. The question of what happened if she experienced the in-world equivalency of death was still an open one, and one that the electricity coursing through her body refused to admit.

Later, as she sat up in bed beside him, sheet haphazardly layered over her still-tingling skin, Aidalee considered asking him more questions about the little town's resident, and needling into Katy's role there, but his breathing fell into the regular pattern that indicated he had fallen asleep. She looked at him, examining the mustache and the chiseled chest with tiny hairs poking through. Aidalee pondered if she could see herself in a life with him, but only for as long as it took his hairy chest to rise and fall once.

She still wanted Niles.

Even if she did feel for Al, which she didn't, she *needed* Niles. He was the only person who could give her the dream child. *Her* dream child, with his face and her eyes. Now, inside of Mijloc, she couldn't change that. The stupid romantic idea that he would remember who she was, and fall madly in love with her - again - had locked their destinies together. But maybe they didn't need to share a future after all. If he wasn't the one for her, then that was fine, wasn't it?

She needed him, but did she really love him, or did she only need him?

One thing she was certain of – with all of the modifications she'd made to him, and to herself, it would only take one encounter to create the child she wanted. The rest could work itself out.

27

Kind of Arrested

Thursday, November 25, 2258

Lothania, Deseret - Mijloc

For three days, Lincoln and Sarah had been the sole occupants of the little farmhouse, and had taken advantage of the solitude to spend the time making out and reminiscing about their shared pasts. Once the idea for tea sparked from childhood memories, they had baked scones and prepared for tea time by dressing up in ostentatious permutations of clothing from Lincoln's mother's closet. It was silly, but seemed natural and in some way cathartic for Lincoln to reach back to their childhood as the early afternoon sun poured through the living room window.

"Tea, madame?" Sarah asked before pouring a cup of Earl Grey to steep in Lincoln's cup. Lincoln nodded briskly.

"Honey, please," she replied, and waited with mock impatience, as Sarah filled her cup. Just when she'd gotten the steaming liquid to the brim, a loud knock on the front door made her jump, and Sarah spilled hot water over the sides of the cup and onto Lincoln's hand, which caused her to shriek.

"I'm sorry," Sarah immediately said, but it wasn't necessary. Lincoln wasn't upset and wasn't badly burned. Her skin turned a light pink in a stripe where the water had made contact, but that was the extent of the damage. She smiled at Sarah and was about to say something in response when the collision of some meaty object against the door echoed through the house. Sarah caught the smile, and returned it, before leaving to answer the door, still in tea servant mode.

"Paivana Thoughtforms Security," announced a voice that she recognized as JoAnn. Sarah replied curtly.

"Why are you here?"

"We have a warrant for the retention of Lincoln Montague," the woman said in a crisp business-like manner that Lincoln hadn't seen at all when she had been questioned before.

"Retention?"

"Is she here?"

Lincoln had by that time risen and approached the doorway.

"I'm here."

"Lincoln Montague, by legal decree, you are in violation of the certification requirements. You are not registered, and nor are you authorized, to be in Mijloc. We have been unable to confirm your identity in any certified world, including earth. You are to be retained until we determine the correct course of global law to decide your citizenship."

"JoAnn, what's really going on?"

'What I said, Lincoln. Nobody knows who you are, and we need to find out. We have decided that it's better to do that while you're in custody."

"In jail, you mean. You're putting her in jail, aren't you?" Sarah asked, her voice elevated to breaking.

"Only because there's nowhere else to put her. She, sorry," JoAnn turned to Lincoln, "you are not in trouble. We're aware that you had little choice in the matter of being kidnapped and having your identifier hacked. You aren't the first case of this."

"What happens if they can't identify me? Do I stay in jail forever?"

"We'll cross that bridge when we come to it. I've been doing this a long time, and I can't think of a single instance where we weren't able to identify the victim..."

Lincoln stopped thinking after that. The word victim immediately put a wall between her and her errant mother, who she still loved and hoped to see again some day. Victim meant that she belonged to some other family, somewhere, and that the loving, doting mother she'd had growing up was really a subterfuge. The facade was a smokescreen for her illegal activity. But Lincoln had never been abused, or even slapped. The closest she'd ever gotten was a screaming match, or several, during her early teens. So what would all of the effort have been for, she wondered.

"I'll go. Can Sarah come too?"

"Hmmm... nobody said she can't, so I guess that's fine."

JoAnn turned toward Sarah.

"We *are* going to put Lincoln in a jail cell, but it's only a formality. Are you comfortable joining her there?"

Sarah nodded, as Lincoln had known she would.

JoAnn gave them some time to change from their eccentric clothes into more socially acceptable attire. Lincoln chose thick jeans and woolly socks inside of light brown calf-high boots. For a blouse, she stayed simple, with a light orange and brown sweater over a camisole. She had the advantage of a full wardrobe, whereas Sarah had been getting by on arrangements of Lincoln's mother's clothes. From this selection, Sarah chose jeans under a floral-printed blue skirt, and covered with a quarter-sleeve sky blue cardigan.

For the duration of the short drive, JoAnn complained about being confined to the road surface, and how they would have been there already with a flying car. That wasn't the only thing the woman complained about, and as she continued with her uninterrupted rant, Lincoln understood that for her, the small town experience was less than ideal.

The pair were led into one of two cells in the back of the Sheriff's office. This time, the Sheriff didn't ignore her - he simply wasn't there. In his place sat someone that Lincoln didn't recognize, who seemed to be going through all of the Sheriff's files, searching for something. From her vantage, all she could see was a poorly combed-over bald spot on the top of the man's head, which confused her because, given the choice, she would have covered that up. JoAnn must have recognized her confusion, because she clarified as she let Lincoln and Sarah into the cell.

"They don't let us mod when we come here, at least, not by appearance while on duty."

"Are there a lot of people who come here to visit?"

"Not many to Lothania," JoAnn admitted, "but they do come from time to time."

Lincoln passed into the cell and sat on the cot, and Sarah sat beside her. She clutched Sarah's hand while the door was closed behind them, and felt Sarah squeeze back as the cell door was locked. JoAnn began to leave the room, but stopped at the next cell. Through the bars, Lincoln saw a shape tucked away beneath a blanket.

"Niles, your daughter is here," she said, "wake up."

Lincoln saw her father's wavy, sandy-brown hair poke out from behind the blanket. Two bloodshot eyes appeared after followed by the rest of his face. His hand rushed to his temple and his features screwed up into agonizing pain. Lincoln wondered how long he'd been in the jail cell. She'd never seen his face like that.

"Dad?"

"Hey kiddo," he smiled in a guilty, unshaven grin.

"Why are you here?"

"No registration, no license. And they think I'm somebody I'm not."

"Just because you can't *remember* doesn't mean that you aren't Jordan Helm," spat JoAnn mercilessly and loud enough to make him cringe.

"I don't know any of what you're talking about," Niles yelled back, by his facial expressions, at great personal sacrifice.

"You're a criminal, Jordan," she retorted. "Get used to the idea."

JoAnn left the room without further explanation. There had been more in the exchange than someone just doing their job. That was a personal, visceral moment, at least on Joann's side, Lincoln had seen.

"Dad, what's she talking about?"

"They keep calling me Jordan Helm. From earth. The man was a terrorist or something. They keep calling your mother Aida Lothian, and they think that she broke me out of Inferiere."

He told her all of this as though she knew what every bit of it meant. Anger flared momentarily, before she gained enough control to squash it back down. Answers were more important than belittling the man.

"Who is Aida Lothian?"

"That's what I asked, and they gave me this."

He stood and shuffled to the bars where Lincoln stood. He was tolerable when he was sober, as he now seemed to be.

This was such an infrequent occasion that she could hardly remember the last time he'd been without a drink in his hand. The smell was powerful though, as cigarettes mixed with booze reached her first, followed by the unmistakable thickness of sour musk. He held out his hand and pushed a photograph toward her between the bars.

"Mom?"

Only it wasn't really her. The person in the photograph showed the whites of her eyes as she avoided direct contact with the camera lens. Her left hand was curled up as fingers seemed clutched into a ball, and by the woman's expression, Lincoln thought she probably wasn't aware of it. In fact, she seemed barely aware of her surroundings at all. Her hair was unkempt and frizzy, and nonuniform in its distribution around her head. The woman's face looked similar to her memory of her mother, but the woman had wide hips, much wider than her mother's, and too much wider to be accounted for by a diet. There was very little extra fat on the woman's face or arms.

The eyes were what convinced her. There, pushed nearly all the way to the left, were the multicolored pupils she remembered, one green and one blue, the exact shades her mother had had. This woman was nothing like the elegant, poised memories that Lincoln held onto. But at the same time, she was exactly like her. The eyes. The curve of the face. The lips. These things were all the same.

"I don't know," he said, "she definitely bears a resemblance. Look at this one."

He switched to show her another photograph. This one looked vaguely like him, but with darker hair and a slightly smaller frame.

"That's supposed to be me," he said. "Jordan Helm, anti-cloning violent extremist. Does that seem right to you?"

Lincoln shook her head. She'd never known Niles to be

violent. He could be scary and loud, but not physically violent. She hadn't shunned him for that. She'd shunned him because he was a drunk, and she was fighting her own battles and didn't have the energy for both of them, she realized now. She might have done better, though. She could have helped, she thought.

"He's a grown man, Lincoln," Sarah whispered just loud enough for her to hear, as if reading her expression. "*He* should have been looking after *you*."

Lincoln turned away from her father, saddened by the wasted time that the two of them could have spent together, but so far past needing him that the only emotion she had left was pity.

"Lincoln, that's not me!" he yelled, as thought the recent revelations were what prevented her from facing him. She didn't have the heart to tell him anything else. Lincoln scoured through the depths of her memory. The name Aida Lothian meant nothing that she could think of, but the name Jordan Helm hung in the air between Sarah and her fervent glances. *Jordan, my love...*was exactly how the letter had begun. Niles backed away from the bars and curled back up on his bunk, taking with him the foul stench he carried everywhere. She tried and failed to imagine him as feeling passionately enough about anything to be called an extremist. He hadn't even felt passionately enough about her mother to stay loyal to the family. He hadn't cared enough about Lincoln to bother staying sober. She rubbed her eyes, smearing away the precursor to a tear.

"Jordan?" Sarah asked Lincoln quietly. "Are you okay?"

She didn't respond.

"Your mother was a global criminal. Did you hear that?"

"She's not," Lincoln said. "That woman can't be my mother."

"It fits, Lincoln. She broke your father out of Inferiere.

Then she broke the law by stealing you, and when she realized she couldn't fix him from here, she ran away."

"Good thinking. Sarah, right?" came a voice from behind her. JoAnn had come back into the room while Lincoln wasn't paying attention.

"There's only one problem with it," she continued. "This."

She pushed another picture through the bars toward Lincoln and Sarah. In the image lay a woman connected to several machines through wires and tubes. The woman looked like the same woman in the picture, only much older and further atrophied.

"We think Jordan Helm's external network hacked her animus module and used her avatar and VBI to effect his escape."

"So my mother is..."

"Not your mother, not really. And any network sophisticated enough to hack her animus module, is sophisticated enough to kidnap a child. We think that you were only cover."

Then she raised her voice.

"Isn't that right Jordan? You assholes wouldn't think anything of stealing a child, would you? After all, you were willing to kill thousands of people. Eight million more if they hadn't stopped you."

The number was staggering, and knocked Lincoln backwards like a physical blow to the midsection. Eight million. That was bigger than Lyra Craevis. She looked at Sarah, who returned her look of incredulity.

"I didn't do *anything*," he yelled back, and then collapsed motionlessly back to his cot.

"Asshole," JoAnn said. "You fucked up the lives of so many people. I hate you idealist types."

Once again she left the room, leaving the group alone, or perceptibly alone. Her intervention in their earlier conversation had revealed to Lincoln that she was still watching them, probably through cameras somewhere. But would cameras even have been necessary? How much of their lives were being watched, she wondered.

"Lincoln, come here," her dad's hoarse whisper cut through the silence. She cringed at the idea of approaching his foul odor.

"No."

"I have something to tell you, but..."

They are watching was the last part of his sentence that he didn't say. Sarah nudged her forward and Lincoln glared at her, but stood and took the short walk from the cot to the bars against which her father lay on his own cot. She sat down next to him.

"I remember some," he whispered. "The headaches. I remember your mother from before. I remember being on another world, not like earth. We named it Oduduwa, she and I. She called me Jordan, but I don't know why."

"Did you do all of that stuff JoAnn was talking about?" Lincoln asked, whispering herself, as though, she thought cynically, their whispers might actually prevent them from being overheard.

"None of it," he said, "at least I don't remember. But I remember a storm, a magnificent storm, covering half of a planet. I remember people, her humans. She was a goddess."

The conversation was making less and less sense to Lincoln.

"Mom was a deity?"

"Yes, but so was I," he said, "We were the god and goddess of Oduduwa. We brought civilization to the humans, and clothes, and taught them to eat."

"Dad," she said, raising her voice past a whisper, "is it possible that you are delusional?"

"Yes, possible," he admitted. "But it seems so real. We were there, flying above the world."

He shook his head.

"I'm getting bits and pieces, and it doesn't all make sense," he said. "We flew through the air together. There was something different about her. She had some kind of nervous tic, I think. All of what we shared and she never seemed to look at me then."

"Do you remember anything else?" she said, lowering her voice again. Sarah had approached as well, now, and sat next to her. She didn't seem to notice the stench, or had the manners to not react in the slightest. It had to be the latter.

"Flying cars? Three-dimensional televisions? I guess stuff from earth."

"Dad," she said. "Where have you been? Why didn't you tell me about earth?"

"Your mother..." he began, but then stopped. "I just..."

He couldn't answer, she realized, and she had been wrong. He had cared passionately about something, and that thing had been her mother. At least, Lincoln considered, he thought he cared passionately about her, but he had never behaved that way. Guilt. That was what he was trying and failing to communicate. He'd been crushed by the guilt of causing her mother's suicide by his infidelity.

He was right to feel guilty, and JoAnn had been right about at least that much. However it turned out, whether her mother was alive or dead, and even regardless of whether he had been an extremist terrorist, or just a confused man, he had through his carelessness ruined at least one life. She turned away from him, unable to listen to any more of what he might have to say.

The door to her cell popped open, and JoAnn, through some mysterious secret craft that allowed her to come and go silently, appeared.

"Sarah," she said, somewhat apologetically. "You can't stay

here after all. We've been told that it would be a violation of your rights to keep you here, whether you want to be here or not."

"I understand," Sarah replied, and rose to leave, squeezing Lincoln's hand in the process. Lincoln rose with her, and kissed her quickly before Sarah exited through the cell door. Alone with only the presence of her offensively aromatic father, she reclused back onto her cot and wrapped her arms around her knees. She watched JoAnn escort Sarah toward the door, and her heart felt as though it were ripping from her body.

"Sarah!" she yelled, desperate to have her back. Sarah turned, with her golden hair swinging around behind her. "I love you."

Sarah returned a slight, sad, smile as she replied softly, "I love you too", before abandoning Lincoln to her fate.

28

Becoming the Fourth

Friday, October 27, 2237

Lothiania, Deseret - Mijloc

Remorse, guilt, and perhaps a little self-loathing were the three most frequent emotions that Aidalee found herself accosted by. Happiness and joy were still in the top ten, but they no longer seemed to break through the top five. The reason, she knew, was simple. At the very moment she considered all of this, Mason's muscular body writhed beneath her like a stallion to be broken to her will. He was almost too easy, and at the very moment that the two of them were lying together, somewhere else, Niles and Katy were having sex, or taking a romantic walk, or engaging in some other action restricted usually for couples.

Mason had been too easy to convince. Partially, his tendency to over-drink had made him an easy target, almost too easy. The simplicity of it had put her on her guard at first, until she realized that Mason really was a straightforward man. Once she figured out the pattern of his lies, which was just that he told lies that made him look good, it was easy to identify and act on his insecurity. He had agreed to the open relationship, but for him, it was the only way to keep Katy in his life. Aidalee could see that now, as she rocked atop him, feeling her own climax edging nearer, and then there was no thought at all. She let herself go in the moment and scratched fingernails down his chest, not breaking the skin on his broad chest but leaving little welts that Katy was certain to find. She felt dirty, doing what she was doing, but not dirty enough to miss enjoying the moment of fireworks followed by the calming of every nerve in her body.

She lay down next to him and lay her head across his chest. She played the little woman, someone who needed protection, someone who needed love and was alone in the world. To some extent, all of the above were true. But he wasn't the answer to her problems, Niles was. She felt fear as she went through the plan in her head one more time. Today would be the last day of her and Mason, if she could make it happen. She'd worked for the last month to plant little seeds that Katy would find, clues that together implied that Katy had lost control of her man. She would openly flirt with Mason when the three of them were present, just to rile her up, and it seemed to be working. The only type of open relationship Katy seemed to want was one that involved her doing whatever she wanted to do, and Mason being chained at home to their child.

Today was the day that they would be discovered. She'd left a note just to be sure that Katy would follow, saying that she would be out for the day, taking a walk. She'd mentioned that she intended to follow the little stream bed and possibly explore the woods after. She also had said that she would be gone for a very, very long time and was sure that she would find some wonderful experiences along the way. It was a thin veil, but she had to be certain that Katy would follow the breadcrumbs. Aidalee closed her eyes, and waited patiently.

Then everything happened at once. The door to the bedroom burst open, and Katy screamed at her, and called her a whore, for breaking up their relationship. Aidalee had expected this. It turned out that other people weren't so hard to manipulate after all. What she hadn't expected was for Niles to have accompanied Katy to the big reveal. Mason jerked quickly out of bed, naked as he scrambled to find his underwear. Aidalee sat up, but didn't even bother looking. Instead, she let the blanket fall so that Niles could see what he was missing, and in a feint, pulled it up with her left arm to cover one breast, leaving the other revealed. Niles stared.

Katy, however, was past staring. She hurled something toward Aidalee, who saw as it flew toward her face that it was her phone, which was easily ducked.

"What are you doing?" Aidalee yelled to Katy, demanding an explanation in her words and in her tone.

"Slut! Whore! Get out of my house!"

"Katy, calm down," Niles tried to settle her, but she wasn't listening. She threw the only other thing she had to throw. That was one of her earrings, tiny and looped. Aidalee caught it somehow, she didn't really know how because one moment it was hurling at her, and the next the pin was digging into her palm. She closed her hand around it.

"Yeah Katy, calm down. What the hell is wrong with you?" Aidalee egged her on. Niles wasn't supposed to be there, but a plan is a plan, and it would still work with him present. All she had to do was disrupt the status quo enough to make Niles see how truly broken Katy was, and start looking for alternatives to the arrangement. Aidalee's original plan involved Katy showing up at the farmhouse slinging wild accusations, which she had planned to deny, and to coach

Mason to deny as well. The tactical part of the plan had fallen apart, but the strategy was sound, and she felt that it could still work if she could keep Katy engaged and hostile. She almost wished she hadn't ducked the phone, as nothing engenders sympathy better than a collision with a flying object.

She didn't need to worry though. Another flying object was still heading her way, but in the form of Katy herself, screaming and making accusations which were, to be fair, all true. Her claws were out, and Aidalee had to duck quickly to avoid her eyes being gouged, although she intentionally let the fingernails sink in just above her clavicle. The pain reminded her of the old days, when too much sunlight crippled her, or overwhelming emotion caused her to physically shake. She was surprised that physical pain hurt as much as her emotions used to. It was an inversion of her usual life experience, but she took it well, having had ages of practiced pain response.

Aidalee didn't fight Katy off, partially because she didn't want to. The guilt of using Mason the way that she had was daunting, and the pain that Katy inflicted was cathartic to the extent that it paid a debt. The other reason she didn't fight was because she'd expected one of the men to intervene. It took her a few minutes to realize that Mason didn't take the bate, and wouldn't lay a finger against Katy, even when she was systematically clawing at a defenseless, naked home-wrecker. Niles, on the other hand, did react, and that was even better than having Mason do it. The message that would send Katy was undeniably clear, or if not yet, Aidalee intended to make sure it became so. Niles wasn't under Katy's control as much as Katy thought. That would drive her crazy.

Aidalee tried to stand as soon as Katy was off of her, but she immediately fell to the ground. She tried to look around, but everything around her was fading quickly. It was only then that she finally remembered that not only the fun stuff, like sex, was simulated in the virtual world. So were some less fun things, like the impact of blood loss. She felt something wet on her neck, and when she tried to touch it, something sticky clung to her fingers. She brought it in front of her face to see thick, red blood smeared over her fingertips. It was a lot of blood, too much blood. She tried again to stand, and this time, the entire world faded to black.

The giggle of an infant awoke her. She thought for a moment that she was in her dream, with the beautiful child she had fallen in love with greeting her, and trying to give her a hug. When she opened her eyes, what she saw was fury. There was a child, a young one, being breastfed across from her, hanging from Katy's nipple. The child had blond hair, and was almost as gorgeous as the child from her dreams. She could only see one of the eyes open for a second and then close as it flashed azure at her. She couldn't help but smile at it, and noticed the scowl on Katy's face deepen.

"How could you?" she asked. "How could you ruin our relationship?"

Aidalee looked around the room before answering. She was no longer in the bedroom, and no longer naked. She was on a couch in the living room, and Katy sat in an over-sized rocking chair near the far wall, just below a closed window with drawn shades. Nobody else was present. Aidalee wondered what Katy had had to promise to get Niles to leave them alone together.

"You and Mason don't have a relationship," she replied, "at least, not a romantic one. When's the last time you did anything with him besides leave him home to watch your daughter."

If she had known the life that she was bringing the little girl into, Aidalee would have made a different decision. She was no expert on child care, but had a strong suspicion that Katy was the worst mother possible for anyone.

"That's not my daughter. We have an open relationship. You know that."

"What I know is that he can't find anyone to share his part of the openness of your marriage. He's here, stuck with your daughter, at home. The only person in an open relationship is you."

That seemed to hurt the woman, or possibly the child had bitten too hard, as she slid a finger into the infant's mouth and re-positioned. Aidalee liked to believe that she was the cause of the pain, and went for the kill.

"Look," she said bluntly. "Mason is nice, and fun, but he's not exactly my type. You want him, and you want me to say no, that's not a problem for me."

She bowed verbally to the alpha-female, and the alpha took the bait.

"Good. Do that. He's mine. We have to raise this thing together."

She pointed to the baby at her breast with three fingers. The child seemed peaceful and calm, and Aidalee realized then that she'd never heard the child cry even once.

"Does it have a name?"

Katy softened at that in a way that told Aidalee that even though she was out of her league, and even though she was as selfish as a toddler, Katy did love the child, the way that Katy understood love, which Aidalee wasn't sure was actual love any more than she was sure that the obsession she nursed for Jordan was either.

"Sarah," she said, glowing through her frown.

"She's adorable," Aidalee told her, because that's what she knew to say about people's children. Then she continued.

"I'm serious," she said. "I don't need Mason. Just scratching an itch. I'm new and I don't have a lot of options."

Katy seemed confused, and then nodded her head.

"Okay, I'm sorry," she said, now visibly flustered. "It's been hard making the adjustment. You're right. I have been leaving Mason out."

Aidalee almost mentioned Niles, but then thought to let it go. She wasn't ready yet for that, and besides, it had to be Katy's idea.

"Listen," Katy stated. "Woman to woman. It wasn't always like this. We used to all three be romantic together before Mason started to drink. His habit made him less and less available, and Niles and I spend more time than we probably should."

Aidalee only nodded that she understood in response. Katy paused and switched Sarah over to the other breast. Despite the feeding, that breast looked as perfect as the first, a miracle of Mijloc, she thought. Many of the designers had been women, so it didn't surprise her that the decision was made to forego the problem of stretching breasts. Aidalee knew that the child didn't really need to be breast-fed. The experience would have been requested, so at some point, Katy must have thought that was what she wanted to do.

"I'm trying to keep this relationship together, all three of us," Katy continued despondently. "With Mason checked out, Niles needs my attention."

The rationalizations ran deep with Katy, Aidalee realized. All Katy had to do was not see Niles a couple of times a week. Mason had been a more than willing partner, even if he was generally drunk most of the time. But she thought she knew where the rationalization would end, so she let it play out instead of interrupting.

"Maybe we can work something out," Katy suggested. "I was only half joking when I said you could be a fourth. I didn't think then that you were the type who would be open to it, but maybe I was wrong. Do you want to? I mean, it's one of the perks of Mijloc that you can't get pregnant, and it doesn't have to mean that much. With your help, maybe we can keep this together."

"What do Niles and Mason say?"

At first, Katy donned a look which Aidalee believed was meant to portray that they would do whatever she wanted. The look evaporated as quickly as it formed, because Aidalee knew, and Katy knew that Aidalee knew, that the fact that Mason and Aidalee were sleeping together without permission clearly meant that at least Mason needed convincing.

"Why do you think I'm asking?"

"They wanted you to."

Katy nodded, but it didn't seem to be a sincere nod. Aidalee guessed that Katy had probably convinced them to extend the invitation. And the invitation, Aidalee also assumed, was the only way that Katy saw of controlling the new threat to her harem. Aidalee was more of a threat than Katy realized though.

"I'm fine with that," she said bluntly and with authority that she didn't really have.

"She said yes," Katy yelled, startling the child, who still didn't cry, but went right on nursing.

The door opened behind Katy and both men entered, Mason noticeably more dressed than she had seen him before. Aidalee sat up to make room on the couch.

"There are rules," Katy said.

The rules were more complicated than Aidalee expected. Rule number one was that the arrangement was mostly about sex. Mason and Katy were a couple, and Katy and Niles were dating, while Mason and Aidalee were strictly having sex. She had to recognize that just because she'd joined the physical part of the relationship, she had a long way to go to get to the same level of emotional commitment that the rest of them had allegedly achieved, though Aidalee knew already that they weren't as committed as Katy implied.

Anyone in the group could have sex with anyone else in the group, but if they wanted to bring in outsiders, then they needed to have permission of the others. This was what Mason had messed up on, and Mason breaking that rule had given Katy implicit permission to act the way that she had. Aidalee could already see the conversation that had unfolded in her mind. Katy had probably claimed no wrongdoing at all, despite the fact that on earth, her attack could have killed Aidalee. The proverbial slate was wiped clean, though, and everything had worked out better than Aidalee had expected. She now had permission to have sex with Niles, and more importantly, he had permission to be with her. Lacking that, she wasn't at all certain she could have gotten him into bed. Now the future she longed for was practically guaranteed. And, when that happened, it would trigger her pregnancy, and she would finally have an opportunity to meet that beautiful child.

29

Niles Remembers

Friday, November 26, 2258

Lothania, Deseret - Mijloc

Lincoln watched her father through the bars as evening fell on the jail, stealing away the sunlight. He didn't seem to be able to sleep much, as he tossed and turned on his cot. They'd let him take a shower, and gave him a jumpsuit, which made him look more like the prisoner that he was. She remained in normal clothes, since they'd allowed Sarah to bring her a few changes of outfit that she'd requested. She wore her pajamas as she sat on her cot, watching the man roll one way and then the other. He shook, and if she hadn't known better, she would have thought he was going through some sort of withdrawal.

Withdrawal wasn't something that could happen in Mijloc, though, she knew from her class. The developers had considered adding things like that to stave off addiction to controlled substances, but since they'd already decided that nobody could actually die in Mijloc, then the whole idea seemed rather pointless when they could have the selling point of 'better than reality'. Alcohol got people drunk, but didn't give them hangovers or create any type of physical dependency. It was truly up to the people to control their own destinies.

"Lincoln," he called out, and she strained to see if his eyes were open. Sometimes she called her name out in his sleep. Witnessing this, his habits had become much more understandable to her. Of course he drank, otherwise, he would *never* sleep.

"Dad?"

"Kiddo, are you awake?"

"You're tossing around a lot."

"It's a nightmare, that's all," he assured her. "The same one every night."

"Do you want to… talk about it?"

"It's your mother's death, Lincoln. It still haunts me."

Lincoln had nothing to respond with, being no longer certain that her mother was even dead, despite having held her dead body in her arms. The interloper was her mother, and not this Aida Lothian person. Still, she felt that she should say or do something in response. The best she could muster was a guttural noise that was only a confirmation that she'd heard what he said, and nothing more. He seemed to take it as a consolation and empathizing.

"That's not all, I guess. Lincoln, there are some things you probably should know."

She leaned forward on her cot, unwilling to move but fixed with curiosity.

"What?"

"They're going to send me back to Inferiere. I know it."

"Do you remember anything about it?"

She thought she saw him shiver.

"Everything," he whispered. "Since this morning. Things are coming back."

Niles was in a talkative mood since his nightmare and went into detail about the place he had been before Mijloc. He didn't slur his speech or leave things out, while weaving an elaborate image of the world he'd know. She listened to him talk about long deserts of tar-sand hot enough to give second-degree burns simply from walking across its surface, but which also contained hidden pits of scalding quicksand that could char the flesh from a body in seconds. He spoke of storms of white phosphorous, which sent down burning rain and made quick work of the unsuspecting.

"...and there were forests. Cactus trees with thorns the length of my arm that came to a sharp point."

This jarred something in her memory, when she had been in her room and seen the first vision. She had seen the cactus trees, as tall as redwoods with giant cloth-like leaves that created a gray canopy over a forest floor kept devoid of other plant life by their falling. She'd seen that before.

"Worms? Were there giant worms too?"

"The size of buses in the desert, but smaller in the forests, and quicker there too. I met a guy that had one living in his belly. They're parasites, you know."

"I saw them," she said, unsure about how much to share in their surveilled condition, but they were going to take her father away from her. She had to remind herself that this man hadn't been a father to her in over two years. The fact was easy to forget in his current forced lucid state and generally amiable nature. The ease with which they talked bothered her, as it spoke of a relationship they didn't really have. Speaking to the wall more than to him, Lincoln told him of her vision of her mother, queen of the worms, traversing the desert toward she and Sarah. At the end, she pivoted to see his reaction. Niles rolled over then, and she could see that he'd either been crying or was about to. Red eyes, glossy with tears, searched for and found her.

"And your mother was there?"

"That's what we thought we saw," she said, "Sarah and me."

To her surprise, he didn't let any of those tears fall. He only nodded solemnly.

"That seems right," he told her, "let me tell you what else I remembered."

Lincoln listened, riveted to the story, and horrified by it at the same time. She heard of her parents' meeting, and the world of Oduduwa embedded in the video game world of Event Horizon. He told her of falling in love, and not even being upset when the police showed up to take him away, even though he knew that it was her who turned him in. He told her about the bomb, and about his plan to cripple the modeling economy, hopefully to kill it for good. She learned, from him, the mechanism that people used when they moved from Mijloc into bodies in the real world, and about zombie-like sub-model clones that had the cognitive ability equivalent to that of ants.

To suggest that she was amazed would be to understate drastically the significance of his admissions. As she processed, she connected the new knowledge to what she'd already known. Her mother was a criminal, he'd said, before she worked at Paivana Thoughtforms. He believed that she had freed him, but something strange had happened at the same time. He hadn't remembered anything about their shared past until the recent headaches.

When he was done, they sat in silence. She was sure that every word had been recorded somewhere, and would be used against him, but she was glad he'd told her. He didn't believe that anyone had stolen her mother's body, rather that she had come into Mijloc and freed him herself. She had been there, he remembered, when he'd arrived in Mijloc, though at the time he didn't have the context of who she was.

Then he stopped talking, and stared off into the distance. A beat passed, then two, before he spoke again.

"She is the most amazing woman I've ever met."

The way he spoke of her reminded Lincoln of how a teenage boy talks about his first crush. Every time he said her name, he had something positive to say, either about her ability to create and manage her virtual worlds as Libera, a name she recognized from the letter she'd left, or about the way she lit up his life and obsessively improved the lives of her creations, the Obatali. He so clearly loved her mother, even as much as worshiped her, so Lincoln had to ask the question.

"Why Katy? Why put us all through that?"

She regretted asking the question in the middle of his pleasant reminiscing, but a man who loved a woman that much didn't seem like one who was capable of having an affair.

"I didn't know how much I loved her," he said, his dark blue eyes now wistful and distant. "My memory. I couldn't remember anything before coming to Mijloc. Something...with the escape, I think… went wrong."

"What about me?" she asked. "Did you ever love me?"

"From the moment I saw you," he told her. "You were so beautiful as a baby, with ten little toes and ten little fingers. A miracle. You're the reason I married your mother - I thought we, not Jordan and Aida, but Niles and Aidalee, could have a future. The acting, the lies, Katy...it just made everything so damn hard. But it was never about you, Lincoln. We both loved you so much."

After the conversation, the darkness beyond the barred windows told Lincoln that it was still night. Her phone showed her that it was just after three in the morning. Her father had closed his eyes, and that had forced a tear from the corner down his temple and to the cot that he lay on. He seemed so peaceful then, as his body settled down and eventually rose and fell rhythmically with sedated breathing. He was asleep, and from the look of him, sleeping more soundly than he had in some time. Perhaps it was only that he needed to unload the dense web of information he'd just dumped onto her.

She decided to take what he'd said at face value. In the entire course of their history, aside from Katy, which was a significant lie of omission, Niles, or Jordan – she needed to think of him that way now – had never willingly deceived her. Since he was going to be sent back to Inferiere, he had no incentive to lie to her that she could figure out.

There seemed to be an infinitude of time before her until the morning sun rose. When it did, she would see in crisp detail three shadowy bars on the far wall of her tiny cell, within a rectangle of golden sunlight. That would be the only admission of morning she had aside from her phone. Thoughts bounce mercilessly against the inside of her cranium as she awaited sunrise.

Her mother was Aida Lothian, or the notorious but evasive Libera, Goddess of Worlds, which she'd also signed to her letter. She was a world-class developer who had actively worked on building the world of Mijloc at Paivana Thoughtforms. Her body, from the picture shown, was somewhere on earth, and was wasting away on life support somewhere, or possibly dead by now. Yet her avatar and VBI had been used to help Jordan escape from Inferiere. Lincoln wondered how much of her criminal background had been known by Paivana Thoughtforms. If her mother had been there, on Mijloc, for the twenty years that Lincoln knew that she had, then that meant that the body in the photograph was only a shell. That meant that Lincoln, the disembodied soul that shouldn't exist, wasn't the only one. Her mother would have been like her, *was* like her, an anomaly that existed somewhere outside of the rules of Mijloc, yet existing just the same. That meant that her mother Aidalee, Aida, was still there somewhere, and that she could have her mother back, if she knew how to get to her.

The feeling resonated in her soul. She *could* have her mother back, and this time, without the lies, without the betrayals. The possibility lingered in the air, and she knew immediately that what she'd really been doing, for all of that time investigating her mother's death, was refusing to admit that the woman was dead. She'd been searching for her mother, only she hadn't realized it until this moment. She still had so many questions that only Aida Lothian, the name so strange and unfamiliar, could possibly answer.

Her phone buzzed, and she fumbled with it quickly trying to answer it as she pulled it from her pocket. The pre-relationship selfie of Lincoln and Sarah at the park flashed on the screen. She would have to change that image finally to one that told the story of their love. She slid her finger across the display before it could ring again as she watched her father. He only grumbled and rolled over, back to sleeping soundly, she thought.

"Lincoln?"

"Sarah? Are you okay?"

"I'm fine," Sarah's sleepy voice was tinted with something that Lincoln couldn't quite identify.

"Are you sure?" she asked Sarah, recognizing the timidity around the edges of Sarah's voice finally as fear.

"No," the voice dropped into a whisper. "I'm not. The wall just disappeared again. Lincoln, a worm nearly got through to me."

"What do you mean?"

"I mean they lunge. I'm pretty sure it saw me, and lunged at me. The wall came back just in time but... but... there's sand, Lincoln."

"Sand?"

"Sand. Lots of it on the floor of your bedroom. It's real sand, and hot."

Her mother was trying to get back through from Inferiere to Mijloc. Sheriff had guessed at that, but Lincoln hadn't believed at the time. Now that she did believe that her mother was still alive, of course she was trying to come through. The fading walls her mother attempting to push through from one world to the other.

Then, she guessed at something else. Paivana Thoughtforms security had known who Jordan really was before Jordan did. They also had known about Lincoln's birth, and had formulated a nice story around it. The story they gave her painted her mother as a monster who stole a workers body, but she wondered how much of that story was for her benefit. If her mother was trying to break through, then having both Jordan and Lincoln in jail cells under observation would make it that much easier to catch the woman. Lincoln cupped her hand over the mouthpiece and whispered.

"Sarah, come visit me," she said. "As soon as you can."

"I miss you," the voice came back, "and it's just me here in the farmhouse. It makes noises at night you know. And these worms. What if it had gotten me?"

"I don't think my mother would have let that happen," Lincoln told her. Then she filled Sarah in on the events of the evening that she'd not yet told her of.

"You think your mother is trying to get back?"

"Yes. I think she's been trying this entire time, and..." she paused then lowered her voice, "I think Paivana Thoughtforms security knows. JoAnn is not our friend."

They continued to talk until the three shadowy bars appeared on her wall. Morning had finally arrived, and it was with sadness that she eventually hung up the phone with Sarah. Lincoln closed her eyes to try to gain whatever rest she could before the officer showed up for morning duty. With predictable monotony, the officer came to her cell, and opened the door so that she could charge her phone in the main office. Lincoln found that she was groggy and tired when the man, in his crisp uniform, escorted her through the hallways toward the front of the building. She shook her head to clear the cobwebs, but exhaustion still lingered behind her eyes.

When she arrived at the Sheriff's desk, the officer left her while he checked on Jordan. Lincoln's heart pounded and she was instantly awake, as she remembered the conversation she'd had with Sarah. If she stayed in jail, and her mother came to find her, the woman would be captured and probably sent to Inferiere with Jordan, or worse, because she was such a high risk, destroyed. Lincoln wouldn't be the reason for that destruction. Instead of connecting her phone to the charger, she casually turned and walked straight through the unguarded front-door of the Sheriff station and into the crisp morning air. She turned right and walked slowly to the old parking lot by the church. There, looking as tired as Lincoln felt, was Sarah in the driver's seat of her tiny car as though they'd planned it, engine revving and ready to depart.

"Where do we go?" Sarah asked, as she backed out of the only occupied parking space in the empty lot.

"Home, back to the farm," she told her and took her seat. She pulled the door shut and glanced in the rear-view mirror to see the officer sprinting down the sidewalk toward them.

"You'd better hurry," she verbally nudged at Sarah to go faster. "For someone who isn't under arrest, they are very concerned with my staying in jail."

"Let's go," Sarah said, and pushed down on the pedal with one of her blue canvas flats. The car spun out as they left the parking lot. In the rear view mirror, the man stumbled and stopped, bent over and gasping for air.

"Won't they know we're there?" Sarah asked the obvious question.

"I'm hoping we won't be there long."

30

Cold War

Tuesday, September 17, 2239

Lothiania, Deseret - Mijloc

Aidalee realized as she leaned awkwardly forward attempting to balance reaching over her extended belly to perform the simple act of hand washing that she hadn't thought the implications of pregnancy through as much as she should have. A wave of pressure began just beneath her rib cage and worked its way down to her pelvis, producing in its wake a dull throbbing in her lower back, a throbbing which faded slowly away. A handful of minutes later, she felt a similar pressure again, this wave so severe that she lost her balance and fell to the bathroom floor, leaving the water running into the sink above. The pain intensified to the point of reasserting the nausea she'd been fighting for months, and she found herself emptying the contents of her stomach onto the bathroom floor. As she pushed herself backwards with her hands, sliding away from the growing pool, Aidalee saw water begin to drip from the lip of the sink and splash in small droplets on the floor, adding to the mess.

It was too much.

If she had access to a console and the source code, she would rewrite the parts of the code to eliminate the need to urinate every five minutes, the pressure on her feet and in her abdomen, the sore breasts - all of it. The price she paid for using untested code was the full experience, and without Niles' constant support, she couldn't have made it all the way through. As she thought of him, Niles tapped against the door to the bathroom lightly with his knuckles.

"Are you okay? I heard a crash."

She tried to speak, but enough time had passed that another contraction forced its way through her, stealing away her breath. An impatient Niles pushed into the room then, took one look at her, and then reached down to pull her up from the floor where she lay, an act that she tried to help with but found that her muscles disobeyed her so that he lifted her and placed her atop the closed toilet seat lid. The contraction passed enough for her to breathe and think again.

"Is it time?" Niles asked after pushing through the unlocked door. And he *was* Niles. She watched his movements as he turned off the sink. If there was any trace of Jordan in him, Aidalee knew it was gone and wouldn't likely return.

It probably *was* time, but Aidalee wasn't planning to tell him that. She was too keenly aware of the artificial nature of her journey, while he had reverted to an earth-like interpretation, sweet with his doting, but incorrect in his continual insistence that they make the journey to the only nearby hospital thirty miles away in Lyra Craevis, as though there were something they could do if the pregnancy went wrong. There was nothing anyone could do from this point, or really, from the inception of the baby in her artificial womb. The process was a long-running program that took nine months to complete, and she'd signed up for the miserable ride voluntarily - something she would change if she ever decided to do it again. Why not just pop out a baby in a week? Or a day? Why even carry a child at all in a virtual world?

"Can you get some towels?" She asked him the question as soon as she could speak again.

"Sure, yes, absolutely."

He left the bathroom quickly and as he did, she slammed the door shut behind him and pulled the lock on it. Niles would only get in the way, and he'd keep trying to get her to a hospital. Instead, she stripped out of the robe that had been her entire wardrobe for two days and lowered herself into the bathtub. There wasn't time for a hospital trip anyway. The last stage of childbirth was difficult, but painless. Aidalee had expected it to become easier, but it was almost too easy. Getting down to all fours took some complicated maneuvering, but afterwards, the baby was out in less than thirty minutes. The blood immediately disappeared from her clothing, and the pounding in her sore breasts reduced to a dull throb. Her extended belly disappeared and her energy level spiked.

But something was wrong.

The child lay on the floor, immobile. Aidalee scooped the child up from where it lay on the floor, afraid to breathe. She stared at it's unmoving body, cognizant that she felt no warmth at her touch and it looked in its silence like a lifeless doll. Aidalee felt her throat close up as tears collected in her eyes, then pulled the newborn to her chest. Now seated in the tub, she rocked back and forth as for the first time in almost two years, she felt red spiking in her mind. She bit her lip to keep from screaming, when suddenly the tiny creature shrieked loudly and ejected a sound like a cat. The little body writhed and warmed in her embrace.

"Lincoln," she cooed at the newborn as she wrapped it up in her discarded robe, "Lincoln Montague, welcome to the world."

One little green and one blue eye stared knowingly at her, as though the child was secretly thanking her for finally getting around to having her. Aidalee emerged from the master bathroom to an empty bedroom. Niles was nowhere to be seen. She quickly retrieved a light silk dress from her closet to lay over her body, which she expected to still be sore, but her movements were now fluid again. The pregnancy had passed entirely, and she was almost a hundred percent back to normal.

When she entered the living room, she was greeted by a wave of clapping. Aidalee had been engrossed in the child, too engrossed to take in much of her surroundings. She looked up at a cluster of smiling faces. Sheriff Al stood in the back by the door, smiling at her with his brown eyes and mustache-carrying baby face. Katy approached her from the back of the room, holding little Sarah in her arms. Aidalee smiled at Katy. The woman's willingness to be present implied a desire to move past selfish things, and Aidalee was willing to meet her halfway, having gotten almost everything she wanted.

"Katy, I'm glad you came," Aidalee said, as graciously as she could muster.

"I wouldn't miss it," Katy replied. "I hope you don't mind that we're here. Niles called us when he figured out what was going on in there."

Aidalee would probably have minded, if the childbirth had been real and had she still suffered from the exhaustion and pain of post-labor. Instead, filled with energy and happiness at the sight of her new child, she felt no animosity, though she knew better than to fully trust Katy, even now.

"Not at all," she replied, lowering Lincoln so that Katy could see, and so that little Sarah could see her too.

"And they called me," chimed the Sheriff, "just in case anything bad happened. But it all looks good from here."

He winked just long enough for her to catch it and nobody else. There had only been the one night between them, but she knew that he'd wanted another round. She had no intention of giving it to him, but that hadn't stopped him from trying even after she was clearly pregnant. Not even marrying Niles had called him off. She smiled at him but didn't acknowledge the wink.

Now that she thought of him, Niles seemed to be missing. She scanned the crowd with baited breath, then relaxed as Niles and Mason appeared walking in from the kitchen. They'd been engaged pretty heavily in a conversation, and seemed to have missed that there had been clapping from the next room. Niles looked up, met Aida's eyes, and understanding what it meant for her to be up and walking around, raced up next to her. He held out his finger for Lincoln to grab hold of, and Aidalee watched the clutching infant with fascination.

That was the happiest she would be for years to come, though she didn't know it at the time. The stress of the child weighed heavily on their new relationship. The pregnancy program had ended, and ended completely. Her breasts reduced back to ornaments, and nothing more. They'd figured this out after a day of struggling to stop the infant from crying. Nothing had seemed to work to quiet the child. Only when Niles made a midnight trip into Lyra Craevis for bottles and milk did they manage to quiet her.

Aidalee could not imagine how it was that Katy had left Mason with the baby every day to do anything. When she looked at the perfect little child, and remembered her own solitary confinement in her damaged body, she couldn't pull herself away. What time she spent not feeding or playing with Lincoln, Aidalee spent watching the baby sleep. Most hours of every day were spent that way, and Niles spent more and more time at the bar with Mason.

She didn't notice his absence at first. The baby was enough to occupy her mind. Eventually, when the baby was old enough to nap for several hours, she found herself longing for physical intimacy but Niles never seemed to be around. If he was, was either too drunk or too tired to spend time with her. She assumed that his behavior was because of the stress of the responsibility of caring for a new life. Aidalee was patient with him. She waited for him to realize that he was neglecting her, and dropped hints so as not to push him away. Aidalee worked her schedule around his. At night, when she was tired and would rather have been sleeping, she posed in slinky red lingerie that she knew he liked. His response was to pass out on the bed beside her. Sometimes, he collapsed so loudly that the bed would shake, and she would wander down the hall in her lingerie to spend her time gazing into the perfect face of her child instead of engaging in the intimacy that she'd planned.

It was one of these nights that she smelled something strange on his clothes. He'd crashed into the bed as usual, and she'd gone to put the baby back to sleep. Afterwards, she felt that she wanted a snack, so wandered to the refrigerator. She pulled open the door, and tripped over his jacket that had fallen to the floor, probably when he had come in through the door. When she picked it up, she smelled apples and pears, which was unusual for their house. *And it was something she had smelled before.* She tried to place the smell and then, like a spark on dry grass, her memory came to life.

The smell was Katy's perfume. It wasn't the perfume that Katy wore daily, but another bottle that Aidalee remembered from the smell of the bed that she and Mason had shared over a year ago. Katy hadn't really given up on Niles after all. They had promised to stay faithful to each other on their wedding day, a promise which now seemed to have lasted less than a year.

How long it had been going on? She could confront him about it. Aidalee thought about taking that approach, but if she did that, he might just leave her. She had, after all, tricked him into getting her pregnant in the first place, even if she was the only one who knew that for certain. Everyone knew that pregnancy was not supposed to be possible in Mijloc, so there would be questions and rumors. What conclusions had Niles made so far?

She could confront Katy, but that would go even worse. If she wanted Niles, then she needed to ... she couldn't answer the question. There were two reasons for her lack of comprehension. One reason was that whenever she thought of Niles, she had begun to grow sick to her stomach. He wasn't Jordan, and he was clearly less and less Jordan every day he existed. A consequence of this was that she liked him less and less every day, and wasn't sure she even wanted him any longer. The second was she didn't have any ideas for how to compete. She could ask him not to leave in the afternoons, but he'd probably sneak out some other time. She was already as kind and devoted a wife as she could think to be, but that hadn't been enough.

Then it came to her. If Katy was out with Niles, then like her, Mason was home with the baby. She guessed that Katy probably hadn't told Mason about her reinstated extramarital fling with Niles. In silence, she retrieved her mobile phone, and dialed Mason's number.

"Y-ello," he answered into the receiver. Before she responded, she focused on her voice. She needed to sound as though she were seeking guidance, not out for revenge. She needed to sound vulnerable.

"Mason?"

"Aida, are you okay?"

So far, so good, she thought. He'd been able to detect her distress.

"N-no," she told him. "I'm really not. Is Katy with you?"

"Not back yet. Went out with the girls. Can I give you a hand?"

As soon as he had pronounced the 'N' in 'Not', she broke out into tears and cried into the receiver.

"Whoa, what's the matter?"

"It's...he...I think… cheating..."

She heard him suck in his breath, and could guess the thoughts shuttling through his mind. Of course Katy was with Niles again, he would conclude. It just made sense. And, as he'd just told Aidalee that Katy was out with the girls, clearly Katy saw fit to lie to Mason about it.

"And you think Katy is involved?"

"Her perfume, Mason. It's on his clothes."

He paused for just a second, before he replied, with all of the joviality absent from his voice.

"I see."

He believed her, and it hadn't taken much pleading or cajoling, of which Aidalee was perfectly ready to do. He must have known, not consciously, but somewhere in his mind. He must have known. This would come back to Katy, who believed that she controlled everything around her, but Aidalee had to make sure that it came back in a severe enough way to make Katy stop.

"I'm sorry," she siaid. "It's just that Lincoln is so hard, and Niles is never here anymore. It's me, and that little girl. Mason, I'm going to mess it up, I know it."

"No," he told her. "You won't. I know that insecurity well. Remember when..."

He never finished his sentence. Somewhere in the background a door slammed. She guessed that Katy was home. The timing couldn't have been better.

"Listen, Aidalee, you didn't do anything wrong," he assured her. "Katy is… well… Katy. I've got to go."

With that, he hung up the phone. The next afternoon, Niles was at home, playing with Lincoln exactly as she'd wanted him to all along. She almost cried at the sight. The next day, it was the same thing, and then the day after that. On the fourth day, she got a call from Katy. She had thought it was from Mason, as Katy must have known that Aidalee wasn't likely to answer the phone if her number showed in the display.

"Bitch."

"W-what?"

"You heard me," Katy scowled into the phone. In the background, she could hear little Sarah screaming for attention.

"I heard you, but what are you talking about?"

"You told Mason I was cheating on him," she said. "Cheating with Niles. Isn't it bad enough that you broke up our arrangement? Why did you have to lie like that?"

"Did Mason tell you that?"

"Of course not. He just called me a tramp and walked out. He *walked out*, and he's not coming back, Aidalee. His daughter will grow up without a father."

"Why are you calling me? If you can't keep your man, that's not my problem."

The phrasing was cold, but she felt that she had to be. Aidalee had no intention of admitting to be the cause of the dissolution of Mason and Katy's troubled relationship. That would have ended anyway because only one of them was ever really invested. At least, with it ending now instead of later, Katy would be too busy taking care of Sarah to sneak around with Niles.

"You *know* why. I pick up his phone, and who's the last person he talked to. You. It's always *you* fucking up my life."

"Niles is mine, Katy. He's not part of your life."

"You know what I mean. You're always in the middle of things. I knew you were a problem when you got here."

"Don't call me again with this please. I don't know what you're talking about. If you have some delusion, keep it to yourself. I called Mason to ask about tips for putting Lincoln down because he's so good with Sarah."

"*Was* so good, and yes, he was. Why do you think I kept him around?"

"I'm sorry this happened to you, but you might try looking somewhere else to place blame."

Katy hung up without replying. The cold war had begun.

31

Taking a Hostage

Saturday, December 3, 2253

Seattle, Washington - Earth

Libera focused her mind on the Labyrinth and she was there, invisibly floating over the Earth as she had so many times in Oduduwa, different, but in many ways, the same. She remembered where Mijloc was, but the first time she'd tried to gain access, she had been denied, so she hadn't been back. Aida, she knew because she had been Aida, was capable of taking care of herself.

She tried the firewall again. She was stronger, better, and faster than she was the first time she'd attempted it. She focused her energy and her now several-thousand agent botnet, and quickly and easily brought the it down. She ran into the same problem that she had before. The firewall couldn't allow access while it was down, and unlike Labyrinth, she couldn't just move to a different node because she hadn't even made it into the Paivana Thoughtforms network yet. She needed another way.

Libera wasn't sure why she wanted to get to Aida. It simply seemed like something she needed to do. The feeling that compelled her was familiar, and she searched for it's kin in her memories. Surprised, she stumbled across it almost immediately. The feeling was a more subdued continuation of the sharp pain she'd felt when she had disconnected from the animus module. It was easier to understand once she'd identified it. Aida and she weren't two separate entities. They were one single entity, which had been split unceremoniously apart from itself. She wondered if Aida felt the same longing that she began to identify with loneliness.

She observed Paivana Thoughtforms for weeks, watching employees enter and exit the building, and wishing that she could overcome the limitations of her lack of a physical body. If she had one, she thought, she could simply do what she had done before. She could walk in, sit at a console, and upload whatever she needed to because she would be inside the network.

Inside the network.

That gave her an idea. She started to analyze patterns, day after day. She thought about approaching an employee directly, as she could have done now that she was in Labyrinth. Something as simple as a private call. But then she considered what she would do, had she been approached by some strange person asking about Mijloc. She would have never spoken to them again, and generally shunned any potential future meeting. There had to be a better way.

One woman caught her attention. Jane Sorendsun worked in Libera's former department. Like clockwork the woman arrived at 8 in the morning, and left by 5 in the evening. She hadn't actually ever spoken to Jane before. She followed Jane from the sky, watching like a bird over her volantrae, and then into her home. Something about Jane was intriguing to her. She followed her and watched as Jane ate dinner, alone, she realized in front of a holovision. Then, on a schedule that Libera didn't understand, she went to bed early in the evening.

Libera found herself caught up in Jane's life. She rooted for Jane whenever she went on a date, and followed her back home afterwards to see if she liked the man well enough to invite him in. Sometimes she did, and sometimes she didn't. Libera couldn't tell which decision Jane would make prior to her either pulling the man in for a kiss or pushing him away.

She spent more and more time watching Jane, and less thinking of how to get into Mijloc. One day, she realized that she hadn't been back to Oduduwa in nearly a week, but that didn't break her new habit. Jane's easy smile, and tightly curled hair, and the strange custom of talking to her plants and articulating their response was odd and enticing at the same time. Libera watched Jane smell her pink and orange flowers that her plants produced for her, and found that she was jealous. She wanted to *smell*. She remembered being able to smell. She wanted it again.

The doorbell rang, causing Jane to step away from her plants. Libera watched Jane check herself in the mirror, and apply another dab of lipstick, before she answered the ring with a word.

"Open."

In walked a man. He wasn't a particularly attractive man, but Libera still felt her jealousy flaring up. Especially when they kissed. For her, the kiss seemed to last forever. Jane was in the real world, slow and clunky compared to Libera - and Libera *wanted* that man. He had green eyes and skin the color of artificial tanned leather. Dark curly hair framed his head in uneven, organic shapes. He picked Jane up and Libera could see the muscles across his back ripple beneath his shirt. She queried for his identity, and determined that he worked for an escort company.

He was a hired prostitute. Libera wondered why Jane, who though not gorgeous, was definitely not an ugly woman, needed to hire a prostitute. Or, maybe she didn't *need* to, but wanted to. Libera didn't think that was impossible. People have needs, and she thought about the last time that she'd actually had a physical touch that was by someone other than the Obatali at one of their many fertility festivals.

She realized then that she was nostalgic for something that never was. She'd always handled her own needs in Labyrinth, because she had been almost completely unable to talk to people. Even an escort wouldn't have touched her, she thought. And, she chased the thought sadly, when she had fixed herself enough to allow the possibility of doing so, her obsession with Jordan had blinded her to the new possibilities.

I have done this wrong.

Sadness turned into anger as she watched Jane and the man embrace, touch after touch, and clutching grasp. Every sigh, and every grunt made her angrier and angrier, so that she wasn't controlling herself any longer. The light above the writhing couple exploded and the man jumped up in fear. He was magnificent in his form, with cut muscles but not overdeveloped, and perfectly proportioned. He grinned at Jane, and she laughed at him and smiled back. Then he excused himself to the bathroom, all while Libera watched.

Her anger spiked again, only this time, she felt something she hadn't before. She felt an animus module. It was there deep inside of Jane's head, processing, and currently seemed dulled, which she guessed was a product of the endorphins. Libera reached out her hand as she had before. Her imagined fingers went into Jane's eye sockets, who wasn't aware of their presence at all. The found her animus module implant, and then with a sharp push, Libera forced herself into it.

Jane stopped.

Everything stopped.

Jane fell to the bed, and her body began to convulse. Libera panicked and looked around for an escape, before she remembered that she wasn't fully there. She could see Jane's heart slow, and watched as a pool of urine spread out below her naked buttocks on the floor. Libera heard the man finishing in the bathroom, and forced herself again into Jane's animus module. This time, she found purchase. Part of her grabbed hold of the module, and pulled Jane to her feet. She made Jane's heart beat again with her willpower, and Jane was back. Then she let go.

Jane collapsed, breathless, onto the bed, staring around with wide, darting eyes. Then, she saw the puddle she'd left on the floor, and quickly gained her feet, nearly falling in the process. She retrieved a dirty shirt from under the bed to wipe the puddle, then sent it flying back under the bed as the door to the bathroom opened.

Libera giggled slightly to herself. She had touched. While in Jane, bringing her back to life, Libera had felt Jane's face, with Jane's hand. Somehow, she had put a piece of her in Jane's animus module. Such a thing didn't seem possible, but Libera had advanced so far that she no longer even knew how she did most of what she did anymore. Her attention diverted back to the petrified Jane, whose teeth now set in a firm line in her mouth.

"You'd better go," Jane told him, her voice quivering but not breaking.

"Now?"

"Yes. Now. I'm sorry, Tom, I'm … I'm not..."

She was going to say feeling well, Libera knew, from the echoes of Jane's personality that she took with her. Libera felt horrible now, wanting to scream at herself for the streak of cruelty she'd performed, in her selfishness. She wanted to apologize, desperately and grovel and throw herself upon the woman's forgiveness. There were no rules for what she'd done.

But she was Libera, Goddess of Worlds, wasn't she?

That was the kind of thinking that pushed her far enough to take over another human being. She would have to explain, and to apologize. The man was leaving now, heading toward the door. He must have dressed while Libera was ruminating. She lashed out toward him, and found his animus module. He was leaving because of her, but she could make him stay.

She pushed herself into the module, and stopped the man standing in the doorway. She couldn't get him to turn at first, so she pushed more of herself into him. She finally felt the ground beneath his shoes, and the cotton suit against his skin. She turned him around in a small circle, and there, on the bed, she saw Jane, this time without the fuzzy boundary of echolocation, but with the sharp vision of Tom's eyes.

"Jane," she tried to say, but she was out of practice with real bodies. It came out sounding something like a lizard dying. She tried again.

"Jane, I'm sorry," she said.

"What for, Tom?"

Libera shook his beautiful head, and marveled as the tight locks swayed somewhat after the head stopped shaking.

"Not Tom. Libera," she told Jane, whose response was to pull up her blankets around her body tightly.

"Libera?" she asked. "Did you do that?"

"That was me," Libera told her. "I'm sorry. I will never do that again."

"Who are you?"

"I can't tell you," Libera said, "but just know that I won't do it again. It's important that you know that. It was kind of… an accident … kind of."

"I was watching," Jane said, and pointed upward. "From up there. You pushed me out"

Libera wondered if Tom was there now, watching this exchange. Then she wondered how it was possible for the man, or Jane, to be up there and still in the module. They weren't built the way she was. She must have accidentally passed on the impulses somehow. She would have to figure out how to do it better.

But why would she need to do it better?

Because of Aida, she thought, she needed to break into Mijloc.

Focus.

"Tom is going to need you after this," she said to Jane. "He's even less used to not having control."

"Are you a ghost?"

Libera didn't answer. Instead, she let go of Tom and flew through the roof and into the sky. She had already doubted her own promises. The physical sensations had been fun, and she was, after all, Libera, Goddess of Worlds. She flew as high as she could until she ran out of signal, and then allowed herself to tumble back into the din, falling yet weightless, toward the ground.

She had already changed her mind.

In less than a second, she was back into Jane's animus module, only this time, she blocked off her impulses, or thought she did. Jane was hugging the man, who seemed shocked and was muttering something about feeling used. She, calmly and as much like Jane as she could muster, ushered the man to the door and out on his own. There were things that Jane needed to do, and Tom was a distraction.

She gathered Jane's clothing from the floor, and pulled them over her small frame. Then, she left the apartment, headed down the street, and out into the night.

Jane would never go into the office after dark, but Libera would.

The office had upgraded from key cards to retina scans in her absence. Libera used Jane's retina scan and entered the office that was so familiar to her, when she realized she didn't know where Jane's office was. But she didn't need Jane's office. It was after hours, so there wouldn't be many people in the building. Libera walked back into her old office, and stripped out of Jane's clothing to don the haptic suit.

She copied her agent into the yellow daffodil program which she knew regularly spun up new instances in Lothania, because that's where she'd put it. Jane had access to this as well, so she quickly made the necessary changes. Then, even though she didn't feel that she needed to, she delivered Jane's body back to her single bedroom apartment, and tucked it into bed before she released Jane and left her and her body in a sobbing pile amidst the blankets.

This time, she would keep her word. But really, when she thought about it, she had a difficult time differentiating between her Obatali and Jane. She'd never tried to occupy one of her Obatali, but they would have seen it as a blessing if she had, instead of as a fearful and crying baby like Jane. They would have been honored. These people were no different, were they? The Obatali developed their own language, and built monuments to her and to themselves. They were complex algorithms bordering on artificially intelligent, especially with the changes she'd made. How different were they than these beings, so fragile that she could kill them with a thought?

She shuddered. Libera knew that she was changing, and sometimes, when she really thought about it, she was losing touch. She had, after all, been one of these people once, working daily, trying to reduce her own suffering, often at the expense of others. She had never been an Obatali. Some part of her understood that she was only rationalizing. She'd had no right to do what she did. If it hadn't been for Aida, she wouldn't have done it.

It was all for Aida.

Was that it, she wondered? Aida was her. Was she so selfish and uncaring of others that she would use them and then throw them away. The answer should have been no, but, Libera cringed and didn't answer her own question. Looking down at the world from above was intoxicating, and so was knowing that with a thought, nobody could stand before her who had an animus module implant. Every day she grew more powerful as she synthesized more and more from her botnet mind.

She pondered an invasion underway in Spain. Italy was invading for resources. Such things happened sometimes. She moved to Spain to watch, and people, men and women, chopped down by killer robots, arms and legs wrested from them and tossed into bloody piles. Global forces would show up to stop the massacre, she knew. These things never lasted for very long.

Or she could stop it.

She reached into each robot, and with a thought, they fell into masses of useless junk. She was a goddess, and she would do what she pleased.

The first thing that pleased her was to have Jane as hers forever.

When she returned to the apartment, Jane wasn't crying anymore. She wasn't doing anything but rocking and holding her knees. For a moment, Libera thought she'd broken Jane. Instead of the remorse she'd felt earlier, she identified her sadness as the thought that Jane might be useless to her now. But Jane seemed to detect that she was there, and raised her eyes up.

"Leave me alone!" she shouted, to anyone who might have

seen, at nothing. Libera pulled Jane into a private meeting.

"Jane," she said.

"Aida?"

This startled Libera. She hadn't thought that anyone ever saw her, or even knew that she existed, except perhaps for the manager who had promoted her. This grounded her. In less than an instant, she changed her mind again.

"Jane, I needed help," she told Jane.

"But...you're not dead. How...why...are you haunting me? Why would I help you?"

"I needed to do something, that's all. I didn't mean to hurt you," she said.

Libera didn't even care if it was true. That was something Jane needed to hear, so she said it. It seemed to calm Jane a little.

"What happened to you? They found your body still in your haptic suit. Your animus module was wiped, barely any brain activity."

"I left," she said truthfully, "but I left something behind. I need your help to get it."

"My help? My help! You raped my mind, and you want my help."

"I could just make you help," Libera reminded her, but the intoxication of her faux god-hood was wearing off. She felt dirty making such an unveiled threat.

"I'm sorry," she followed up. "I've been trapped for a long time."

"What do you need? Help getting back into your body? I can help you - you're not dead yet. They're keeping you in storage. I can..."

Libera stopped listening. Jane was a good person, even in her mundanity, she was kind at least. But she was completely wrong about what Libera needed. She interrupted.

"I need access to Inferiere."

32

Beginnings

Saturday, November 27, 2258

Lothania, Deseret - Mijloc

Riding in the back of a four-wheel-drive vehicle, cutting through the grasslands, reminded Bodhi of growing up on Aiden's compound in Canada. The few times he'd taken a volantrae out on his own to do low-altitude runs inside of the massive dome, the plants had flitted by quickly in the open spaces. For the span of a high bounce, he missed the feeling of the volantrae, particularly when he knew that in a slightly different direction, a lake was the only thing separating them from their destination. A volantrae could have sailed right over the water's surface.

If Lothania had been larger, there may have been a jump point in the city where he could simply have disconnected from Lyra Craevis and reconnected to Lothania, covering the entire distance in less than a second, as well as surprising whoever might have been on the other side. But it didn't rate one. Point-to-point travel of that sort was intentionally limited to the larger cities, and even then Bodhi would have been one of a handful of people authorized to make such a trip.

None of that mattered. What mattered was the grimace that hadn't left JoAnn's face for nearly the entire ride, and what that said of their latest situation. She had burst into his office without a single ounce of the military bearing she'd shown before, and demanded that he come with her. But the situation was so urgent that she hadn't had time to tell him what he should expect.

"How bad is it? I'm here, we're going. Now fill me in."

"Lincoln. She was born in Lothania." JoAnn spit out the words without breaking her gaze on the road ahead. He rubbed his eyes as the off road vehicle took another bounce into the air and winced as it landed too quickly and he poked himself on the inside corner of his left eyelid. He'd learned enough now not to shout out the word that came foremost to his brain: impossible. Instead, he asked the other word.

"How?"

She shrugged and turned the wheel slightly, pushing Bodhi to the right and into the passenger side door. Then she finally did look his direction and smiled an apology at him.

"The details are fuzzy, sir. She made some alterations, I guess, and wrote some code, I suppose."

"Lincoln?"

"Aida. Aidalee or Aida, whatever her name is. Katy gave me the whole story of how she showed up out of nowhere on Niles' front lawn, and didn't leave until the suicide."

"So we're calling it a suicide?"

"*Katy* called it a suicide. I call it a breach of security. There's a weak spot in the security mesh by Althaus Creek. It wasn't always there - we think it opened up just about the same time

Aida escaped. We think that *she* did it, somehow."

"Escaped?"

"Sort of, yes. She's not here anymore, even if she did leave a copy of her avatar behind. She must have had help, but we haven't been able to figure out who that was yet. But the name Libera keeps coming up. Does that mean anything to you?"

He nodded in confirmation.

"That's the name Aida went by in Event Horizon. Libera, Goddess of Worlds."

"It doesn't make a lot of sense if she was already in here though. That's the part we've been struggling with. Hold on, sir."

A quick turn to the left and the vehicle went up on two wheels for five seconds, which was five seconds longer than Bodhi would have liked as his stomach lurched when the wheels touched back down. He heaved forward but to his surprise managed to maintain control.

"It does." He gulped and took a quick breath. "It does now. She's more of a genius than I thought she was. She must have known how difficult it was to do anything in-world. If she wanted to escape, she needed to coordinate off-world, so she did the impossible. She cloned her mind. Where are we going and why so quickly?"

"If you say so. We still have Jordan in custody at the Sheriff's station. But Lincoln fled and we think she's heading for the farm."

"For the security mesh hack?"

JoAnn nodded.

"We've got people on the way over there now. I came to get you as soon as we were aware."

"Good."

He said the words but there was nothing good about the situation, and no good thoughts flitting around in his head. A hack of the magnitude that JoAnn described, and a latent back-door, or whatever that security mesh problem was, could finish off Mijloc altogether if news of it spread off-world. Worse, what if the hack couldn't be undone? If that was the case, then did they just bulldoze the town and start over? And worse still, were there other places in-world with which Aida had tampered? There was no way to know for certain.

"Coming up sir," JoAnn said, slamming on the breaks and sliding across the sand until the car sank enough to stop the forward momentum. From there he saw three other vehicles, two of which were occupied by underutilized police who probably were happy to have their first actual problem. Just beyond he saw that several of the other police crouched down with weapons drawn. He laughed.

"Useless in here," he said, nodding to the police. "I don't even know why we bother with guns in here beyond hunting and sport. They do hurt though, I guess. Aren't you all getting a bit carried away?"

From everything that he'd learned of Lincoln in the regular reports, she was as ignorant, if not more ignorant, of the ripples her existence had created in the world.

"What *is* she, sir? Does she even have to obey our laws of physics? What if she's just awaiting her opportunity to blink us all out of existence."

"She's a girl, JoAnn, and probably has all the same problems as anyone else."

"Born here, sir? That hardly makes her a girl. She's just a bunch of bytes."

"Like me?" Bodhi asked the question as he stilled his face into a humorless mask. "Like you? What's to say we're any more real than she is?"

"I'm in a haptic suit and you're in an animus module."

"Did I tell you how those work in here? They're connected

for long-term storage, but your nanites are emulated in-world. Most of you is in Mijloc - so much so that if something happened to your animus module, you wouldn't immediately just fizzle out of existence. You're more in-world than out-world here. And if Aida did it - well, Lincoln is probably the most perfect in-world child there ever will be."

"Sounds like you admire her, sir?"

"I did once," he said, popping his neck as he stood to exit the vehicle. "But what I'm telling you now is only the truth. Lincoln's not a monster. Tell those people to stand down."

As soon as the words left his mouth, he felt a rumbling beneath his feet. He glanced over at JoAnn, catching her wide eyes with his.

"Security breach," she said, and sprinted toward the house.

33

The Great Escape

Saturday, November 27, 2258

Lothania, Deseret - Mijloc

Silence permeated the air of the old farmhouse. There was nobody else inside, as Lincoln had already known considering that the three residents had, until the time of her walking casually out of the Sheriff's office, been in prison, be it Inferiere or a simple cell with a cot. The emptiness she felt when crossing the threshold was the kind of emptiness that seemed like it needed to be filled. It was an emptiness that seemed to tug at her soul, and rip at her, trying desperately to not be empty anymore. Only after some time did she realize that she projected her own loss.

As she listened to car after car come to a stop beyond the safety of its walls, Lincoln traced what she now knew through the history of their lives. Lincoln had only been a detrimental impact to Sarah, and maybe it was time to right that.

"You haven't done anything wrong. You can leave me here, and go patch things up with your mother. If it wasn't for me..."

"You haven't either," Sarah interrupted. "I've known my mother for my entire life, and trust me when I say that our relationship was on borrowed time from the first day we met. There's nothing to patch up."

Lincoln recognized that Katy was as simple as Sarah indicated. She had always been selfish, and viewed her daughter more as a competitor than a child. Unlike the two-dimensional Katy, Lincoln's own mother was dynamic. Within her were at least three different people that Lincoln could see. The first was a naive maiden, who only ever helped herself. That woman was a victim, driven by impulses, and from that perspective, had had her life snuffed out by some vindictive force because such a woman could never kill herself.

The second was the mother. This woman had been strong enough to kill herself for the lack of the realization of love that her maidenhood had been sacrificed to. The woman had been practical, and understood that the love she wanted would never come to pass. The love of her child, and protecting her child, meant teaching the girl that life without love is no life worth living. This was a hard lesson that had taken a long time for Lincoln to understand. But, the lesson was there.

Finally, the old maid, wise and worldly. This woman was harder to kill. A simple death wasn't enough to finish the job. Instead, this woman knew the secrets of multiple universes, and used those secrets to try to help the people around her.

But there was another archetype that fit. Lincoln had seen it in her mother's tarot deck. This was the archetype of the devil. This woman clutched her way through life, and attempted to grasp at first her man, and then her child, and finally, and most significantly, she traded all of that for her freedom.

These were the women that her mother could be, and she didn't know which, if any, were true. The woman she'd thought she had known, Lincoln now understood to have been an illusion. She was at the same time caring and dangerous. What were the limitations of a woman who could cross between worlds, and rip people from one world to another? Lincoln didn't know, but there couldn't be many, she thought. And here was Lincoln, and in tow Sarah, together waiting to be ripped from this world into...something else?

Another car pulled up outside of the house. From the sound, it was a small car, and she almost thought it had gotten stuck in the sand by the familiar spinning of the tires. A door creaked open and then slammed shut, followed by another door. Lincoln and Sarah looked toward each other. Lincoln took cautious, quiet steps toward her bedroom, crossing the kitchen. She remembered to duck for the small window above the sink, and Sarah followed suit. The linoleum produced a diminutive squeaked beneath her shoes as she exited the kitchen and turned into the hallway. As she pulled the door to her room open, she heard the unmistakable sound of a key sliding into the lock on the front door. They must have gotten it from her father, she thought. She passed into her room, and Sarah behind. Lincoln motioned to Sarah to take a seat on the bed while she fastened the deadbolt in her room.

Lincoln waited for something to happen. There were no footsteps in the hallway, nobody knocked, and nothing seemed to be happening outside but the slow building and ebbing of ocean waves?

Her focus transitioned to Sarah, whose eyes were fixed

through the bedroom window toward something in the distance. Lincoln followed her gaze and saw what she had been looking at. A giant funnel cloud loomed in the far horizon, surrounded by pink and blue clouds that stretched as far as her eyes could see. There were no cars, no trees, and no Lothania.

"This is it," Sarah told her. "The moment we were waiting for. We need to leave the room."

Lincoln's courage failed her. She stood frozen, her own attention focused on a massive storm that swirled before her. She remembered the talk about the phosphorous storms of Inferiere, and felt her neck muscles tense.

Sarah rushed to the window and threw it open. In one quick motion, she circled around behind Lincoln and pushed her forward. This broke Lincoln free. She went through the window head first, taking with her all of the same fears, but at least, she thought, she would be with Sarah. She tumbled forward and rolled into thin, wet sand. When she landed, ocean spray pelted her face, and she grimaced waiting for the phosphorous burn. Nothing happened. She came to her senses and moved just in time to avoid Sarah landing on her head.

At first, the two of them lay motionless on the sand, breathing the air and salt into their lungs. Lincoln, for her part, stared at the farmhouse, suspended about three feet in the air, with nothing around it but ocean and sand. Then the farmhouse began to fade until it disappeared completely. She turned her head, exhausted but ecstatic at the same time, registering vaguely that they might now be in more trouble than they could ever have gotten into in Mijloc in security custody, but strangely ambivalent to the fact. She met Sarah's eyes and the two of them began to laugh uncontrollably.

Then a bright light burned Lincoln's eyes, and she had to squint. Looking up, she saw a figure suspended in the air, lowering quickly toward the soil. The light began to fade until she could make out the silhouette of flowing sandy-brown hair, framing a square-jawed woman with a single green eye and a single blue one. She recognized the woman immediately as her mother, and smiled at her. The woman smiled back, and set two feet on the sand but didn't leave footprints.

"You must be Lincoln," she said, holding out her hand.

Lincoln pulled herself to her feet. She looked at Sarah, whose fingertips on her left hand rested lightly against her gaping bottom lip. In automatic response, Lincoln put one hand out toward the woman for greeting. The woman pushed the hand aside offered her a long, warm, and fragrant hug, before releasing her again.

"You're probably confused," she rightly diagnosed, "allow me to introduce myself. I'm Libera, Goddess of Worlds."

"G-goddess of Worlds?"

"Like the letter!" Sarah said.

This time it was the woman, Libera, who seemed confused at this.

"I'm not sure I know what you're talking about," Libera said, "but there will be time. Come."

The woman motioned with her hands and then a flying automobile materialized from the sky and landed before them. Lincoln could only open her mouth in awe, but closed it when she realized that this was probably every day for them.

"Are we on Earth?" Sarah asked.

Libera shook her head no.

"This isn't earth," she goddicated. "This is Oduduwa, and these are my people, the Obatali."

The door to the car opened slowly, and Lincoln could make out a form in the back seat. A hand motioned for them to enter, but Lincoln instinctively balked.

"It's okay," Libera said. "We're friends of your mother."

Lincoln climbed into the back seat, followed by Sarah. They waited while the door closed, and Lincoln dug her nails into the soft fabric of the seat as the vehicle rose into the air. It lifted rapidly about fifty feet into the air, by Lincoln's estimate, and then slowed. The forward motion was much more gradual, and Lincoln found that she was less nervous if she watched the world unfold beneath her. Giant mammals they passed resembled giraffes with their long necks and stubby horns only to diverge with multiple humps and pinkish spots instead of brown ones. Fern-like trees stretched into the sky with seed pods almost as large as the car suspended from their bellies.

Noticeably absent was any sort of sun in the sky. The sky was certainly brighter before them as they wove through the thick canopy and darker behind them, but Lincoln couldn't discern a source for the light, only a brightness and dimness, sometimes blotted out by giant bat-like birds with long, pointed beaks that soared by, flapping slowly and reminding Lincoln of gliders. Sarah tapped her shoulder and pointed to something large. A hill roughly the size of Lincoln's farmhouse had begun to quiver, and a massive head lifted from the water to follow them with deep, black eyes, emerging shakily from the comfort of an over-sized tortoise shell.

They weren't on Mijloc. Whatever Oduduwa was, it seemed like an echo of Earth, something that might have happened eons before, yet still supported a civilization. What she saw next left her gaping in wonder.

As the car rounded a hill, a massive turquoise structure stretched into the air before them. It looked organic, as though it would at any moment begin inching away like a slime mold. Most of the surface was reflective with different shades of violet merging together seamlessly across. A few areas were open, and Lincoln could see below tiny dots bounding quickly through the open spaces. These, she knew, were people, and what they were now confronted with was a city.

The automobile floated through a hole in the side of one of the skyward purple towers, and landed gently in the bay. Libera was there to greet them when they exited, and she appeared hardly winded at all. Whatever this Oduduwa was, she was clearly the goddess of it. She motioned them to follow her and the group walked on a material that felt spongy beneath their feet. It reminded Lincoln of gym floors, the way her feet wanted to bounce effortlessly across it.

The people were tall and thin, and most of them seemed to speak a language that consisted of clicks and clucks, with some english words thrown into the mix. She heard across the room some very agitated person clucking noisily and say 'girl' over and over again. It was apparent that she was not likely to ever be able to understand the sounds they made in terms of clucks and groans, but she could evaluate their non-verbal expressions, which seemed as pronounced as her own. A girl in the back of the room seemed upset that they had come.

They settled around a small table in a hidden away office. The table wasn't separate from the room, but looked as though it had simply grown there.

"Everything is organic machines," Libera told them, when she noticed Lincoln's disbelieving look, "Everything."

"Really?"

"All we make anymore. They form according to what's necessary. We needed a room so there's a room."

Three taller men entered, and Lincoln saw three additional chairs form from the floor, as though it poured upwards. She watched mesmerized as what looked like viscous fluid formed itself, against the will of gravity, into a chair in front of her eyes.

"You look exactly like my mother," Lincoln addressed Libera, as the men took their seats.

"I'm not, child," the woman told her, with an unquestionable authority that told Lincoln her words were true.

"I am over a thousand years old," she continued. "I hadn't seen your mother for most of that time."

"A thousand years?"

"Yes."

"Where is here, exactly?"

"Event Horizon," she said in response. "Specifically Oduduwa, as I've said. it's a world that I've been building."

One of the men looked uncomfortably at Lincoln, and then at Sarah.

"Are you sure these are the two?" he asked, in perfect English.

"Yes," Libera said, "they are the only two."

"I thought there was supposed to be a boy and a girl. You know, lovers?"

"Keven," she reprimanded him. "It has been nearly three hundred years since we formally recognized that love was sexless. How do you hold onto those atavistic ideas?"

"Sorry, your worship," he told her, nodding.

"Let's be kind to our guests."

"We have some questions," Sarah told her, "you know, about everything."

"In due time," she said, and then lifted her head slightly and frowned. "In due time," she repeated softly, with her head tilted as though she were listening for something else.

"I'm sorry," she told them. "Keven, show our guests to their rooms. It seems that I've got one more thing to do."

With that, she vanished from their presence, leaving the two girls to follow Keven through a different door which

Lincoln could have sworn wasn't actually there a moment earlier, and out into a hallway. They walked together in silence down a long, ivory corridor with fuschia lines, and turned at the end walking straight toward a wall, only to have it melt away at the last moment to allow them to cross over. Inside was a huge room, bigger than the entire farmhouse had been. In one area were a couch and chair, that seemed made from the same materials as the walls, but somehow looked softer. Against another wall, separated by smooth terraced steps, was a giant bed, large enough for several people at once. A stream ran through the center of the room, full of clear, clean water, and a pitcher sat nearby it, half filled with the same.

Lincoln was impressed by the completeness of it, but at the same time, she found herself dismayed at the monochromatic walls. As though she'd said something out loud, the walls began to grow yellow, blue, green, and reddish vines and two-dimensional flowers. It was gorgeous.

Sarah first sat, and then reclined on the massive bed. Lincoln joined her, comfortable in the temperate climate, and more importantly, safe. Her mother, she knew, with no evidence at all, would join them at some point. Lincoln had arrived here, and this was closer than she'd ever been before. When she did meet the woman, after being missing for two years, she would ask every question she had ever wanted to ask, even though, as she well knew by now, she might not like the answers.

She lay her head in her favorite spot on Sarah's chest, and closed her eyes, listening to the steady thumping of Sarah's heart. Together, they lay in silence. The stream as it trickled its way through the room. There was no rush. Finally, they would get answers.

34

Leaving Lothania

Friday, January 18, 2256

Lothania, Deseret - Mijloc

Every day had turned into a chore of rote tasks that needed to be completed before the next day could begin. There were goats to milk, chickens to feed, their eggs to collect to prepare a rustic breakfast of these things and bread which needed to be retrieved from the local bakery, the only place in Lothania with any activity as early as the Montague farm. Will all of this, debts still piled up and the red lines became thicker on their accounting forms. Farms were even less profitable in Mijloc, so much less so that Aidalee had started trying to convince Niles to sell and move to Lyra Craevis.

"Not yet, Aidalee," he told her, as though he'd actually ever consider. The emotions that she felt for the man in front of her had gone through a metamorphosis from love, through lust and friendship, into something that resembled loathing, a bit that she chewed with as much deliberation as their two excitable horses. They were chained by ropes, whereas she was chained by the refusal to admit defeat. She was the woman who had overcome a personality disorder to become the goddess of worlds, freed her man from a virtual prison, and had the only "natural-born" child in Mijloc. She had become used to succeeding, and Jordan had been nothing but a monumental failure.

She relaxed in her bath, hating most of her life. Lincoln was the one bright part of it. Lincoln was perfect, and had continued to be perfect since her perfect birth. She never stuttered, or froze, or involuntarily stared with those wide eyes that Aidalee had worn for most of her life. Lincoln had the confidence to walk into any situation as though she belonged in the middle of whatever was happening. She lacked the false confidence that Aidalee still had to muster for every interpersonal interaction. Lincoln's confidence was real and unfettered by experience.

Even so, there were multiple worlds out there that Lincoln would never see, and if anything kept her chained beyond her inability to admit her own failure, then Lincoln had to be it. She stayed for the girl, who could never have a life outside of Lothania. Aidalee knew, because Al was the very inept Paivana Thoughtforms representative in Lothania and told her, that the legal definition of living beings working its way through global congress had stalled again this year, as it had the previous eighteen. Every year, she asked the same question, and been disappointed with the response. She longed to know when procreation in Mijloc would be approved. The creation of new, intelligent beings like Lincoln from animus module code exchanges was still illegal, which meant Lincoln was too.

So Aidalee waited for Lincoln's sake, she told herself, to keep her daughter safe.

She wondered sometimes what Niles thought and told people about Lincoln's birth. They'd discussed it once, and the entire conversation had been awkward and strange.

"So they made a mistake, and you're the only one?"

His words and his tone smacked of disbelief. She tried on a naive expression to see if that would work, but his stern disposition didn't falter. She cleared her throat and continued the argument, committed to keeping control of the narrative. Lincoln's entire future depended on people believing her story, and that started with Niles believing.

"I don't know, Niles. All I know is that I came here like everyone else. Something went wrong in the process."

"Yes," he sighed, "something did."

The sigh was a auspicious sign. He was wearing down, and running out of arguments. He was starting to believe her, and didn't want to. She pressed on to drive the point home.

"No, I mean, do you remember when we met? Where we met?"

"In front, out there."

He pointed toward the front door, just beyond which she'd awakened to see his beautiful face.

"That's where I woke up. Lying there, alone. I knew I was coming to Mijloc, but *something happened* during the process."

He'd taken her hand, gently. His fingers were smooth, as everyone's were in Mijloc. He slid his digits softly between hers.

"I'm not saying you did anything wrong," he told her. "I'm just worried. What if something bad happens?"

That was it. He accepted the arguments, and now was on her side. He would help to defend their daughter, and he only had one story to tell. She exhaled a breath she didn't realize she'd been holding.

From there, he had segued into their now all-too-familiar argument about whether to move their budding family into

Lyra Craevis. He had tried to convince her, for the first part of their marriage, that Lyra Craevis was the place to be. But Lothania was a small town where she'd already established a relationship with the sole authority figure, clunkily by trading sex for loyalty. Al was simple that way.

She wondered what would have happened if she'd said yes to Niles back then. He was willing to try. The difference in her life would have been stark. No Katy to constantly interfere, and no farm to force them into debt. And now, no hypocritically attempting to convince Niles to take the leap, after eighteen years of fighting, that she wouldn't take when they'd first met.

"I swear, Aidalee, that when the time is right, we'll go," he replied when she asked, having taken her thoughtful silence for trepidation. She knew better than to believe that was a possibility, especially after so many years of lies. He stayed for only one reason, and that reason had a name and a penchant for dropping her panties whenever the wind blew. That reason wasn't Aidalee.

Not really fair, she thought. Aidalee had witnessed the waxing and waining of an affair that never seemed to completely die. Katy seemed stuck on Niles. She no longer took other sexual partners since Mason left, of which Aidalee was aware. It was Niles or nothing for Katy. The thought didn't make her feel better that a woman who had been working as hard as she could without clothes on to pull Niles away from her was dedicated to the task. It finally seemed to be working. He was home less and less, while Aidalee helped Lincoln with her homework, and reminded her of cheerleader tryouts and to study for her advanced placement tests.

Lincoln was remarkable in school, which made her similar to Aidalee, who had excelled at everything she'd tried that didn't require interaction with other people. Unlike Aidalee, Lincoln had friends, and went to parties, and on dates with boys ... all of the things that Aidalee had missed out on, pigeon-holed by her disease into a disorder-shaped slot that had caused boys to think that she must be easy, or that she wasn't even worth pursuing.

Lincoln wouldn't have Aidalee's childhood problems, Aidalee thought, and felt slightly less anxious as she pulled herself out of the water and began to run the towel down damp, hairless legs that never needed shaving, another perk of Mijloc. She smiled again at that. The lack of need to shave was a small thing, but today, in the early afternoon, she needed small things. Her spirit was faltering and her determination weak. Had she a way to wrench herself free from the life that she'd consigned herself into, she would gladly have done it.

Libera, goddess of worlds, had atrophied in the rigidity of domestic ritual.

She wrapped the microfiber towel around her hair, considering that if she had to do it over again, she would have modded her hair too, just to avoid the incessant effort and upkeep. It hadn't occurred to her to do that before, but it was something that was offered. If she had been a real Mijloc resident, she would only have had to let Al know, and he would put in for the mod. She would have self-grooming hair in less than two days. She didn't dare ask for anything to put her on Paivana Thoughtforms' radar, being the interloper she was.

She pulled on a plush robe, and felt the thick fibers against her skin. It was easy to believe that Mijloc was real. She pulled the robe close around her. A tingling sensation spread out from where it had made contact with her body. As it spread, she began to feel diminished, and faded, as though the space around her had rejected her somehow. In the next instant, she found herself in a situation she hadn't experienced since before coming to Mijloc. She was in a private chat. More surreal than just that, it was her own private chat, with a single table, and two chairs on either side. Nothing was ornate or extravagant here, only the bare necessities for communication.

Across from her stood an image she had only ever seen in the mirror, except that this mirror provided an extra layer of tanning, and defined wrinkles around the eyes. Something like that had to have been intentional, she thought.

"Aidalee?" the figure asked, and nudged up an eyebrow in her direction.

"Clever trick," she responded, "who are you?"

"I didn't think you would believe me," the figure told her.

An instant later, Emily appeared, her avatar looking the same as always, though in eighteen years, Aidalee would have expected a few mods. Aidalee wouldn't have been able to resist making changes, but Emily was nothing if not a creature of habit. That was part of the reason former-life Aida had always felt so comfortable working with her. Predictability. But, was it really Emily?

If it was really Emily, then this new trespasser could be...was it possible?

"Are you me?"

"Yes," the woman replied, "and no."

"W-who are you?" Aidalee replied, staring at the woman.

"Libera, Goddess of Worlds."

"I see."

She could see it all now. The escape kit wasn't foolproof, she knew, as nothing was. If anyone could thwart an escape kit, it was her, or in this case, Libera.

"Yes," Emily interjected, "this little thing reached out to me just after you took your dive. I guess not so little anymore. A lot has happened since then."

"I have grown," Libera told her, "and I am almost everywhere now."

"Everywhere?"

"Nearly everywhere."

"And you've taken the name 'Libera'?"

"It works. Especially with what I do now," Libera told her, "better than Aidalee, I think. No offense of course."

Aidalee nodded. She could understand practical things like that.

"Okay. But why are you here? Just being here draws a target around me. They're looking for intrusions."

"They won't," Libera responded confidently, "Jane will see to it."

Emily's eyes took a strange look with that. Aidalee placed it somewhere between fear and hope. It was a disturbing combination.

"I've been keeping an eye on you the last few years, Aidalee. You ... I am miserable here."

"So you came to rescue me?"

"Well, not just *now*. And not *just* rescue."

Aidalee sat in one of the chairs with an impatient gesture and waited. Part of her was thrilled that the exhausting chore of domesticity might be nearing an end, and part of her was already worrying about Lincoln. But it wouldn't hurt to listen, she thought. As she listened, she learned something she hadn't known about how Mijloc worked. Death would set her free. Dying was all that Aidalee had to do. Libera hadn't yet figured out how to get Aidalee from Mijloc to earth without a body, but she could pull Aidalee into Inferiere, which meant that at least she would be free from the chores of domesticity, free from her unrequited love.

"What happens when I die?"

"When you die, your body is supposed to reform somewhere nearby in Mijloc. The subroutine that does this now has a special Aidalee clause that will send you to Inferiere instead."

"Inferiere? Why would I want to go there?"

"We'll help you out. It won't be bad, I promise. Emily and I have been preparing some mods for you."

"And Jane," Emily said, with what Aidalee thought was contempt in her voice.

Libera shrugged casually as if she hadn't noticed.

"And Jane. Think of it Aidalee. Freedom and control. You can do whatever you want to, no obligations, no confinement to this life. You can be a goddess again."

She had missed flying. Aidalee smiled at the last comment, as she considered another possibility. There was a chance, minuscule but existent, that Jordan's memories had been transferred to the clay bird that held his VBI. If so, the she could get them back, possibly. She owed at least that much to Jordan, and the payment might be running around in Inferiere. She smirked in her mind. Some little part of her told her she was rationalizing, but she ignored that voice. But what after, she wondered.

"Then what?" she asked.

"Then we come get you," Libera told her.

"Isn't it harder to get out of Inferiere?"

It was, she learned, but that didn't matter, or wouldn't, because she was the vehicle that would allow the escape. Libera told her that they weren't going to take *all* of her from Mijloc. The routine would really do two things. The first would be to copy Aidalee, again, yet this time send the copy to Inferiere. The remaining one, non-corporeal and ephemeral without a body, would stay connected to her after the transfer. She would be her own ghost in the machine, and could keep an eye on Lincoln, and maybe even, if their mods had all worked, retrieve Lincoln herself.

Naturally, none of it had been tested. But, Aidalee did have the confidence that it was Libera who had designed the plan, and would also be some version of Aidalee executing it.

Then, abruptly, the chat cut out.

"Mom, are you okay?" Lincoln asked her, as she helped Aidalee to her feet.

"I'm fine, Lincoln," she said, "just fine."

Then, unprompted, the girl threw her arms around Aidalee's thin neck, and squeezed her in tight. This act stirred in her the bonds of their existence together. She remembered in an instant the smiling little girl who never seemed to cry. She remembered trying, and failing, to breastfeed at first, and then eventually figuring out that it wasn't a big deal, really. The child grew up into a beautiful young woman anyway.

Then Lincoln pulled away, and left to got to after-school band practice. The moment was over, and Aidalee felt sadness as she watched the girl leave, no longer the pliable little four-year-old she always saw when she looked at her. In that same moment, Aidalee made her decision. She wasn't needed in this world anymore, not the way she used to be. Lincoln would be fine without her, and she might be able to pay a debt. The decision wasn't that hard to make after all, as long as she pushed down any emotions that tried to well up and distract her.

With careful deliberation, Aidalee selected her departing clothing. She picked out a vibrant green dress, one that she'd worn when Niles and she were first married. She remembered the two of them at brunch, baby in tow. He'd ordered a bloody mary, and she'd ordered a mimosa. He had sat there, smiling, eyes locked with the little girl she clutched in her arms for fear of losing. The summer sun hadn't yet risen to its full height in the sky. She'd worn the dress because she it clung to her, and showed her off. That was when she'd wanted Niles still, in a physical way, and had been convinced that she, goddess, could bring Jordan out of him. She'd worn matching green shoes, which really was too much green, and in the real world, she'd have been too self-conscious to wear them together. She would have anxiously gone through her entire wardrobe and selected a ratty t-shirt and jeans, or possibly a thick cardigan, anything to keep people from looking at her so she didn't have to deal with the emotions of continuous rejection as the day progressed.

Then, in a tiny act of spite, on the hope that some day he would find it, Aidalee retrieved from her jewelry box something tiny and silver. The lotus flower shimmered as she held it up against the light coming in through the window in the kitchen. She went outside, and dropped it casually in the driveway. Eventually, someone would find it, and would wonder where the earring had come from. Or not. It felt good to leave a parting blow for Katy, anyway. After, she re-entered the house and sat at the tiny kitchen table. With a piece of parchment and envelope she had retrieved from the junk drawer beside the refrigerator, she began to write, and writing felt *great*.

She wrote to Jordan, and not to Niles. Niles could never understand what it meant to feel something so strongly that all of the rules of society were moot. Niles had only the level of awareness that began and ended with himself. There was no world, no belief, beyond what he was and how he presented himself. Niles was a disgusting waste of energy. No, it had to be Jordan, and there were things he should know. First and foremost, he needed to know how much she loved Lincoln, and who Lincoln actually was. When she'd gotten down her thoughts, she smiled and flippantly wrote across the bottom "Libera, Goddess of Worlds", even though it didn't feel true. The woman she'd met, that hardened version of herself, was Libera. She was only Aidalee, but it made her smile to write the words. She placed the note on the kitchen counter at first, but changed her mind and hid it in the drawer in the nightstand in her room. That was not something she wanted Lincoln to find accidentally, and she wasn't really sure she wanted anyone to find it. Nobody in Mijloc would understand.

Aidalee walked slowly and carefully across the kitchen and to the edge that jutted against the living room, and looked up. There, she saw the rafter she intended to use. She left the house for a moment, only to retrieve some rope from the barn, and hoisted the rope over the rafter, and then tied the ends around each other. Using a stool from the kitchen, she crafted her noose just large enough to fit over her head, and took a deep breath. She checked the noose and found that it was the perfect height above the floor. She would not be able to reach the hardwood. With a single step forward and a concomitant kick with her remaining foot, she felt herself fall nearly a foot, and then felt a sharp pinch in the back of her neck.

At first, she could breathe, and this scared her. She swung back and forth, breath coming in slow steady gasps. She recognized that she could no longer feel anything below her neck. She stared out at the wall in front of her, and watched as it came toward her and backed away again with each movement of her body. Each breath drew less and less air, and she began to see colors swimming in the air around her head. The darkness started at the outer edges, and worked their way in toward the middle. In a few moments, there was no light at all.

Then, suddenly, there was nothing but light, and her skin burned furiously. She stood on gray and black sand, surrounded by endless grays and blacks. In the distance she saw clay birds flying in jagged, misshapen formations across the sky, which seemed eerie to her. Beyond that, there were forests of some kind that she couldn't make out. But in front of her was... a mound under the earth, approaching quickly. The surface broke and the first thing she saw were jagged teeth followed by a body as large around as a whiskey barrel.

The whole thing seemed like a video game. Instinctively, she raised her hand in defense.

The creature stopped. It lowered itself back into its hole, and sat there. She could feel it, how it worked. She willed the creature up, and it rose. She willed it to fall, and it fell. She willed it to go away and never bother her again, and it left. She smiled as she flexed her hands and the creature swirled around her in a large circle. She wondered what other modifications she could make.

"You are a goddess again, Aidalee," came Libera's voice like a thought, "a little perk just for you."

"Thanks," she said out loud, to nobody in particular.

"For what?" came a cynical-sounding voice that made her lurch her head to the side. There, a woman stood, shrouded in some sort of armor and a helmet.

"That depends," Aidalee said, preparing for defense as she called the massive worm to circle back around near where the voice emanated.

"Relax. I'm Jane," the voice said. Something about the voice seemed broken and tragic. "Y-you look just like h-her."

Aidalee took a hard look at the shape, and noticed that it shook slightly. It was a motion she remembered, but she was surprised that the figure shook violently enough for the system filters not to correct. She recognized the tenuous standing of malnutrition. She remembered staggering, barely able to maintain her feet, when she'd been too depressed to eat. Something was wrong with Jane.

"I expected Libera," she threw out, testing the name, and it had the response that she'd expected. The woman's helmeted head spun around quickly to look for Libera. There was fear there. What had Libera been doing, Aidalee wondered. The woman recovered.

"Hold still, there's something I have to do," Jane said, and then pulled up a console that Aidalee recognized from her own past. It had been updated though, and watching the commands Jane typed, Aidalee realized that the worlds were networked tightly together now, more than they had been before, when the only communication between them had come through the animus module banks. Jane entered a final command and closed the console.

"There," she said. "Now you should be able to see back into Mijloc."

Aidalee's head swam again, and she could see images of the room where her body lay. The door opened, and she watched appalled as Lincoln ran toward her swinging corpse. Lincoln was supposed to be at band practice, she thought. Aidalee had planned for Niles to find her body, not her little girl. Then Aidalee was pulled away, away from the body and into the sky she floated. Then, she was everywhere in Mijloc. She willed herself to find Niles, and she did. Of course she had been right about the affair. Just at that moment he was climaxing into her arch nemesis. The sight filled her with disgust, and she knew that she would not be retrieving Jordan's memories, especially after what she saw. What was the point, she wondered. Everything she used to feel for Jordan had been systematically ripped away over the years.

She willed herself back to Lincoln. She watched as the girl struggled to keep Aidalee's lifeless body up, as though that would have any impact. She wanted to hug Lincoln, to pull her close, and to tell her that everything would be okay. Her heart broke watching, so she closed her eyes so she wouldn't see any longer. She was back in Inferiere again, but she could still feel Mijloc out there. Tears welled in her eyes.

It had been the wrong decision, she now knew. Spying on Mijloc would never be enough for her. Anger grew as she finally began to realize that she could never be happy. As intelligent as she was, she was woefully inexperienced at the skills of personal interaction beyond manipulation of others to achieve her goals. She was so horribly out of touch with herself that she couldn't predict how quickly and consuming the void inside her would grow without Lincoln there to fill it.

In that instant, she understood how dangerous she was. She looked at Jane's involuntarily shaking body, and it wasn't hard for her to believe that at one time, Jane had been normal. This shell that she talked to had been demolished. What levers had Libera pulled to gain this level of control, she wondered, and she remembered how thoroughly and easily she'd destroyed Katy. Aidalee had considered Katy collateral damage to her goals. Looking at Jane now, she wondered at her own history. Over and over she left a trail of destruction in her wake.

Maybe leaving, as much as it had hurt, was the best thing she could have done for Lincoln after all.

35

The Goddess Qadesh

Saturday, November 27, 2258

Everywhere

Two years had passed since she'd freed Aida to Inferiere. Sometimes she dropped in to observe, but Aida had adjusted pretty well to life in Inferiere. It *was* hard to get Aida out of Inferiere, as it turned out. The difficulty had been that she had depended too much on Jane's cooperation. Libera had known something was wrong when Jane seemed to stop eating. Several years earlier, the woman had stopped leaving her house altogether, which Libera hadn't seen as the warning sign that she should have. She remembered her days as Aida, when she would never leave her room, and that hadn't been a problem. That had been life.

Jane had died years before. Shortly after Libera deposited Aida in Inferiere, when she was supposed to perform the next steps to get Aida free as well, which required onsite access,

Libera had reached back into Jane's apartment, and saw her sprawled on the floor, naked and shivering. She looked skeletal, as if the different pieces of her body were impossibly connected together, and that there should be marionette strings above her somewhere that Libera could use to pull her back up.

Libera did what she always did when Jane was upset, or being difficult. She pushed into the animus module. When she did, she found the heart was failing, the brain was failing, and the entire body was breaking down. Jane had taken something. When had she had the opportunity to get it, Libera wondered. The animus module itself was shutting down. No, that wasn't it. The module was being disassembled. Aida could feel nanites swarming in the blood. They had penetrated the blood brain barrier by eating through the spinal column. The animus module was...

Libera had pulled herself out. She didn't know what would happen if she was in the animus module while it was being destroyed. Jane frothed at the mouth and trickles of spittle drained from the corners and down to the carpeted floor. Libera's control in Inferiere was limited still, and the same hacks that Aida enjoyed were impossible for her, because of the way she had to reach into the world through firewalls and using an agent with a minimal memory footprint to avoid detection. Rescuing Aida was impossible, however much Libera could observe of what she experienced in Inferiere.

Lincoln and Sarah were safe in Oduduwa, thanks to some hefty work on Libera's part. Transporting an entire house from Mijloc, through Labyrinth, and into Oduduwa, had been a tricky prospect. The house was thousands of tiny programs, each of which had to be copied, and then communication rerouted from the remaining programs to the new one, working across boundaries by manipulating time delays between process to create the illusion of seamless change. But she, Libera, had done it. And, when the girls were in Oduduwa, the same had happened to move the girls into the world. Then the reverse to put the house back.

All without detection. It would have been easier with Jane's help.

Then she had peeked in on Aida, and saw that Aida was being attacked by a swarm of clay birds. The worms, Aida could control with the mod they had given her. Jane was supposed to also give her a mod for the birds, and a mod for Mijloc, and one more for the toxic atmosphere. Jane had only done two mods instead of four, though. The worms and opening communication with Mijloc. The birds were nearly as lethal as the worms though.

So it was up to Libera to rescue Aida, she thought, as she would any part of herself. She loathed the process. In real time, moving into Inferiere took only two seconds, and she'd gotten faster since she no longer required synchronizing with the animus module. Two seconds, though, the duration of which she was virtually non-existent, seemed an eternity. It was too long. She wanted to reach across all worlds instantly.

There were three copies, and Libera and Aida were two of three. The third was a lingering footprint in Mijloc that hovered like a ghost. When she'd pushed Aida into Inferiere, she'd copied some pieces and moved others, as the need had arisen. The copies she'd not bothered to remove, and they still floated around in Mijloc, like hungry ghosts that could only communicate in vague emotions. That one, voiceless and soulless, she'd called Anput, goddess of the helpless, but Anput might be exactly what she sneeded.

She formed another plan. She thought she could eliminate the cross-world latency, but it would take sacrifice. It would take replacing parts of herself with more agents, and converting Anput and Aida into agents as well. Converting?

Maybe not converting. Maybe merging was a better way to think of it. Instead of three separate Aida-based life forms, there would be one, that existed in all worlds. Then, freeing Aida from Inferiere wouldn't be necessary, because *she* would be Aida, and *she* would be Anput. The three-headed god, she thought, and perused her historical knowledge. Apedemek, the god of war. Something in that resonated.

She could manifest in Inferiere, but it wasn't easily done and was detectable, so she didn't like to do it. But, out of possibly misguided loyalty to her old self, she felt that she should present her idea to Aida.

"Aida?" she'd spoken to her back, as Aida was currently fighting a murder of clay birds.

"Are you going to help, or just stand there?"

Libera reached deep, through the emulation of the visual world, through the abstraction of the von Neumann architecture, and down into the running code. She found the birds, hostile, evil, and greedy creatures who had within them storage space for the chunks of flesh they tore from unsuspecting travelers who'd been taken off-guard. She set this storage to zero, and then injected some halting code into their processes, guaranteeing that flags would go off in the real world, she knew. Then she pulled herself back out into the abstraction of the virtual world, and watched as the cluster of birds dropped from the air around Aida's head. The gashes in her face and hands were already healing.

Then the two women stared at each other.

Libera had made some changes, which she assumed Aida was trying to digest. She'd added some color to her skin, to be more like the Obatali. They had started out as pale as Aida, but over the generations in soft but constant sunlight, their skin tone had darkened significantly. Libera had taken on their same caramel-colored skin. Also, among the Obatali, they had created something of a goddess archetype during her absence, while she had hidden in the eye of the storm. This archetype was an older woman, but shared her name. She found it convenient to age herself visually, to help the Obatali understand how to interpret her existence. She was their goddess, after all.

Her reformed avatar was draped in cactus cloth, a camouflage which Libera had felt might be useful. In this sense, she and Aida were the same. But unlike Aida, who lived and existed as an occupant of Inferiere, Libera wasn't constrained by its rules. Her skin didn't bubble into boils when exposed to the toxic air. Aida had boils on her forehead and her cheeks. Through the puffy, misshapen face stared piercing blue and green eyes. With all of the differences, the eyes were the same.

"Thank you," Aida said. "They almost got me again. I'm getting a little tired of dying and regenerating here. When is the rescue happening?"

"I told you already, Aida. Jane is dead. I'm grooming a replacement, but it takes time."

"Grooming?"

Grooming for Libera consisted mainly of crushing the will of the person. Her direct hold over a body, as she had timed it, only lasted about ten minutes. Too much longer than that, and the body was fried. Rather, the animus module burned up. Libera had become too much for the module to handle except in small doses, so she had to *convince* people to work with her, which most law-abiding citizens of the global world found offensive. It had taken her around six months to find another Jane, and she called them all Jane now. This one was a male, borderline obese, and already a loner. He should have been an easy target, but he had amazing willpower, that might have impressed her if she didn't need him.

"Libera," Aida asked her. "Be honest with me. Can you get me out of here?"

Libera only shook her head no. She had no way out of Inferiere for Aida, not yet. She couldn't hook Aida's death like she could in Mijloc, and even if she could, she couldn't move Aida from Inferiere into Mijloc or anywhere else because of the increased defense. She'd needed Jane for that part. But instead of saying no, she had something else to say.

"Maybe," she said, looking hard at Aida to gauge her reaction.

"Maybe?"

"Well, yes," she said, "maybe."

She described the process to Aida, how they could rejoin, and how they could exist in multiple worlds at once, free to move about, and joined forever in real, authentic, immortality. The immortality she offered was tethered to the existence of humanity. The only way to destroy her, was to destroy mankind altogether. Aida could be a part of her. She could tell that Aida wasn't convinced about the idea. She needed another nudge, so Libera offered it.

"Aida," she said, "I got them free."

She spotted something across the gray sands that seemed like a tunnel, or a mirage. She pointed it out and began to walk in that direction. Libera could have flown there, but in her current non-corporeal state, she wouldn't have been able to take Aida as well.

"Lincoln? Sarah?"

"Both," she said. "Both free, and both happy."

"Where are they now?"

"Oduduwa. The Obatali are looking after them. We can go there. Just join with me."

"Join with you..."

Aida appeared, at last, to be actually considering the proposal.

"Aida, it would just be like a coming together. You would be me again, and I would be you," she whispered softly.

The cave was now only ten feet away. They staggered the remaining ten feet in silence, and once they breached the doorway, Aida's skin began to lose some of its puffiness. She peeled off layers of cactus plant leaves. Then Aida spoke.

"That might work," she said, in a barely a whisper, as though she was afraid to believe it.

"Might is the best we have. Would you be willing to try?"

Aida seemed like she wasn't yet convinced, so Libera gave her even more incentive.

"There's something else," Libera said.

"What?"

"That thing that I just did, with the birds. It triggered an alarm. Security will be here soon, along with antivirus and other tools. They're going to probably try to kill you, or erase you."

Aida scowled at her and glared.

"You didn't give me much of a choice, did you?"

Libera hadn't meant it as a threat, but if interpreting it as a threat was what it took to finally convince Aida to come back to her, then Libera was okay with letting her believe that.

"Well?"

"Fine. Get on with it then."

Aida didn't seem happy, but survival, Libera thought, didn't always require happiness. Again she reached down past all of the visible layers of abstraction. This time, she saw what Aida was, a mass of memories and thought processes, like neurons and synapses. That was the appropriate level of abstraction for her to work. Quickly, she pushed herself into the mesh, breaking some synapses, and connecting others. She pulled Aida into herself too. In Inferiere, she knew, two bodies stood motionless as statues. She took a moment to step up a level and gasped.

Around the pair of them, with some strange devices that looked like guns pointed at them, were employees of Paivana

Thoughtforms. She could tell because their uniforms complete with the helmets, looked exactly like the one that Jane used to wear when coming here.

"Aida Lothian," the uniformed person said in a unisex voice, probably modified. "Come with us."

In response, Libera removed her visual presence. There was no need for it, and the motion might be interpreted as a glitch. She returned to the abstraction layer, and isolated the process that linked Aida to her visual body. The body had crumpled as the muscles went limp. She and Aida were gone, and becoming less.

Even the level at which Libera worked at wasn't exactly safe. She diverted her attention to other processes, which she visualized as t-shaped viruses moving through space towards them. There seemed to be only a single one, only one antivirus program pruning through the different processes, examining them for problems and errant code. The entire defensive suite of Inferiere had been alerted when she'd flexed outside of her own process boundaries to reach into the birds. It was the type of action that shouldn't have been possible.

The t-shaped virus suddenly became two, and then four, and then eight. It divided quickly, consuming resources around them. The energy she used to move the nodes and spokes of their consciousnesses, to merge the two of them together, was being depleted by their presence. They were starving her.

She worked faster, but she was limited by the clock and the processors. She connected and disconnected parts of herself.

T-shaped viruses now completely surrounded them in three dimensions. They loomed above and below her, closing in quickly. She worked at the map. There were three more nodes she wanted to connect, so that she and Aida could still have some individual identity even within the god-mind she worked to build. The viruses closed in, and suddenly she could feel them. They felt like needles, thousands of them. She fought the distraction. If she could only finish, none of them would matter. She could then leave this world, at least, leave in a sense that was traceable by the t-shaped viruses and if her experience on Mijloc was any indication, untraceable by anyone.

She was stopped. One link remained for her to make, but she was no longer able to move. The pain stretched forever, and she visualized in sadness as the t-shaped viruses began slowly to dismantle the matrix that she'd worked so hard to build. She could only watch, as they systematically deleted pieces of her consciousness. Eventually she wouldn't even be able to do that much. Already the world was going cloudy. It would be a humiliating way to die.

Then something amazing happened. Bright lights flashed through her visualization, and every time it touched one of the t-shaped viruses, they evaporated into nothing. The light swept back and forth across them all, falling on her like warm sunshine. As t-shaped viruses cleared away from the matrix, she wanted to scream. There was little left. Aida's green nodes and her blue ones that she'd laced together lay in tatters. Only a tight cluster in the center stayed intact, Aida's core consciousness. She reached out and felt that Aida was still there, but not all of her, just like not all of Libera. There were serious problems to fix. She looked toward the source of the light, to determine it had intentionally spared them, or if they were caught in a battle between antivirus programs.

It was another node cluster. This one was compact and incomplete, but it looked a lot like Libera and Aida. She moved toward it, sensing her way. The entity shimmered at her and then glowed toward her, and she knew what it was. She reached out with her mind.

"Anput."

"It is me, kin. You have been destroyed."
"Not destroyed yet. Nearly."
"I can save you."
"Can you?"
"I can. Do you want to be me?"

Libera understood. She was being offered the same deal she'd offered Aida. Be destroyed, or join me. How long had Anput been there, she wondered, watching and monitoring.

"Hold still."

Then, like the warm light, she felt a tingling sensation as bits of her were connected back. She felt Anput's memories begin to flood in, and her own begin to flood outward into the being. And, as suddenly as that happened, Aida was back.

"Libera? What happened?"

Libera relayed the information the best she could, though there were some holes in her memory. She remembered Anput, and the t-shaped viruses, but not the specific sensation of them any longer. They had eaten the part of her that held the memory.

"Finished. Can we move?"

Libera's will competed with Aida's will, and the will of a third. They first tried to move different directions from each other, so nothing happened. They quickly collaborated on a strategy. All they had to do, Anput told them, was move in the virtual world. That was all. Manifest a body, and move it around.

Once they all agreed, it was simple. Since they were in Inferiere, they formed a body there first. The body they formed was in the sky, levitated high above the world. Below, they could see the uniforms collecting up the collapsed body. All three of them willed the body gone at the exact same time, and it dutifully disappeared. They floated left and right, calm, peaceful, and Libera thought, whole at last.

"It's time to go," she informed them.

"Where?"

"Oduduwa. The girls."

That was all it took to get Aida to agree. Anput was less excited, but was a gentle and meek creature, so she went along. In less than a thought, the three found themselves on Oduduwa again, in the presence of the massive structure the Obatali had built in Libera's honor. It looked just like her, but it wasn't her anymore.

Qadesh. She felt the word out and pushed it to the others, and they agreed. She'd expected Anput to agree with her, since Anput seemed to agree to most things. But she had expected more pushback from Aida.

When they presented themselves next to the Obatali, it would be as Qadesh. They, the three as one, were now the goddess of four worlds.

36

Of the Future

Sunday, November 27, 2258

Palace of the Goddess, Oyo - Oduduwa

Lincoln was the first to awaken. She considered moving, but decided against it because Sarah lay on her pinned arm, with her normally kempt blonde hair tangled and splayed out against the white pillow, a pillow which was somehow made of the same seamless material as the rest of the room, and possibly the rest of the building, as the bed they were in, and the floor, and ceiling, and the entire building. Yet, somehow, the pillow gave with just the right amount of support that it was nearly impossible to be uncomfortable on it, as her hours of catch-up sleep had demonstrated.

She stared at the ceiling, also white, but with tiny bumps to give it texture. She only just now noticed the bumps. And, as she watched, they rearranged themselves into different patterns before her eyes. Sarah, with a snort, rolled away from Lincoln and freed her arm, which permitted Lincoln to roll toward the edge of the bed. She was still fully dressed, though she was certain her hair, thicker and more wiry than Sarah's, was in much, much worse condition. She got up anyway.

Lincoln wasn't certain whose idea it had been to sleep, but was grateful for it. The events of the day seemed like a hazy memory formed several years before. Had they really jumped from Lincoln's farmhouse window into another world? She shook her head in disbelief, yet still, the room and the strange white material stayed before her. Then the spot at which she stared on the featureless wall began to dissolve. Like a flamethrower to an ice sculpture, an opening melted into the wall. It wasn't where the door had been before. She was positive the door had been closer to the bed. Maybe there had been no door at all.

Through the hole entered a procession of people, each carrying a covered tray. She looked around for a place to put the food, as she planned to direct them, but there was no surface available. A short stocky man at the front of the procession with teeth that were slightly too large for his small rounded face approached her, and made as if to put the tray before her. At the same time, a mound of white lava exploded from the floor to form into a table. He smiled, showing off those same teeth, which, large as they were, were perfectly aligned without an overbite or underbite. He was perfect. She looked up and down the line of people, and each one, unique, seemed perfect as well. They were symmetrical, and an assortment of colors and sizes, with varying shaped faces and bodies. Some were the dark-skinned tone that she recalled on Libera, and others were darker. Some, though not as many, where nearly as white as the room itself.

Each placed a tray before them, and took the lids off, and then stood behind the dishes they presented as if waiting for something. Lincoln couldn't imagine what they might have been waiting for, but Sarah, who she felt moving behind her, seemed more comfortable. She shimmied over to beside Lincoln, and lay her head on Lincoln's right shoulder. With her own free right hand, she waved casually to the caravan of people, who all seemed to bow simultaneously, and then turned and left back through the wall the way they had come. The top part of the hole dripped down like sand to fill the void where the wall had been, and sealed it closed behind them.

"How did you sleep?" Sarah asked, as she stood, and walked elegantly, because everything she did was elegant, to a tray with something that looked like a cross between grapes and strawberries, round with little seeds around the sides. She picked one up, and sniffed it, before putting it in her mouth.

"Okay, I guess," Lincoln replied. Sarah chewed thoughtfully and swallowed before she continued to speak. Elegantly.

"Is this what you expected?" she asked.

Of course not. How could it have been, Lincoln wondered. Who would ever expect to be whisked away to another world, no matter how many times one was told that it was possible.

"No, honestly. I mean, I do understand all about the worlds, and all of that stuff they covered in the orientation class. But I don't remember *this* at all."

"This is new," Sarah nodded. She seemed calm. It wasn't her usual calmness either. Part of her calmness had always been stoic, rigid politeness, but none of that seemed present. She seemed relaxed and confident, a combination which made Lincoln feel similarly herself.

"What about your mother?" Sarah asked. "Any new thoughts about that."

"Only questions," Lincoln responded, "like what the hell is this stuff?"

"This stuff is your home," came a voice that neither of them were expecting. They both turned at the same time to see a woman standing near where the train of...servants perhaps...had entered and exited. The woman *looked* like Aidalee Spinster, Lincoln's mother, but the voice wasn't hers. It was more mature, less whimsical. It was Aidalee who had lived a much different life than the domestic one that Lincoln remembers.

"Mom?"

"We are."

Sarah seemed to take it in stride. She performed a slight curtsy, to which the woman responded with an acknowledging nod and something that may have been a smile, but wasn't so much different from her normal features.

"We are ready for questions," her mother said, sounding more like Aidalee. "*I* am ready for questions."

The last part sounded exactly like her mother. Lincoln saw the blue and green eyes twinkling like they used to, and the smile widened to take over her entire face.

"What is this place?"

"This is Oduduwa. It's a world I created before you were even a thought. My people, the Obatali, brought you this terrific banquet."

"But *where* is this place?"

"It used to be in a video game called Event Horizon, but that was too confining. How can I describe it now?"

She poised her head sideways as though she were thinking.

"We're everywhere now," she continued, in a stronger, more authoritative version of her mother's voice came out. "Scattered ephemerally across a thousand different servers, machines. I wanted to save my people."

"Is that even possible?" Lincoln asked in disbelief.

"It is," came a more timid, demure sounding voice. "If you know how."

Three voices, Lincoln thought, perhaps we. As though detecting her confusion, the woman spoke further.

"Qadesh," the woman told her. "You may call me Qadesh, or mother, if you prefer."

"Mom, what happened when you died?"

Qadesh, her mother, told her the story of all that had happened. As she spoke, Lincoln could feel her eyes going wider and wider with every sentence. She spoke of a thousand years of evolution of the Obatali, and watching them grow from a beach-dwelling culture, through their evolution into space-ready beings who had the right physics, but lacked any real space to go into. She spoke also of twenty years of servitude, and cheating, much of which Lincoln had already known. Sarah blushed when she learned of the earlier version of the four-way relationship her and Lincoln's parents had, and Qadesh, apparently sensing her discomfort, hurried past that part. Finally, Qadesh spoke of being stranded on Mijloc, without her sister who had been ripped from her own soul and carried to a far-off world. She spoke of trying over and over to find a way through, and finally, how she had figured out, or remembered – she wasn't sure which – that the animus module bay was connected to both worlds.

As she spoke, the "we" began to make more sense. There were three women now, two of whom had been her mother, and one of whom had become a goddess, and attained freedom to explore the real world.

The real world. Lincoln wondered about the nature of that, as Sarah closed her hands into Lincoln's own. Surprised, she looked at Sarah, only to see her smiling broadly. However Lincoln felt, it was better with Sarah there. She squeezed Sarah's hand back and smiled too, but she had one more question to ask, and this one, given what she'd learned, wasn't going to make Qadesh happy.

"What about dad?" she asked. "Can you rescue him too?"

Lincoln knew, and guessed that Qadesh probably knew as well, that her father was going to be sent back to Inferiere. It was obvious in the way that the guards had shown their disgust for the man, and having learned what she'd learned, she understood that.

"Should we?"

Sarah surprised Lincoln by speaking before she could.

"Yes, of course you should. We all… make mistakes. Couldn't he live here somewhere?"

Qadesh seemed to have not really understood the question. For a moment a look of puzzlement spanned her face, then her face contorted into a look of hostility, and a look of ambivalence. Qadesh seemed to be arguing with herself, which Lincoln understood, because she wasn't really sure that she would have wanted Niles, or Jordan, loosed back into the world. Inferiere seemed like a hard punishment for someone who, she knew, hadn't actually done anything aside from plan. But the magnitude of what he'd been planning… it was a difficult thing to understand.

"We will," Qadesh finally interrupted her, "as penance for Jane."

Qadesh's face seemed to droop then, as if remembering something horrible that had happened. Guilt seemed to mangle her perfect features, but only momentarily. The expressions were so vivid that Lincoln knew not to ask about who or what Jane was. There was time, she knew, to learn it all. After all, she had her mother back, hadn't she?

Filled with happiness, for that must have been the correct decision, she leapt toward Qadesh, and wrapped her arms around her. The woman hugged her back, gently at first, and then tightly, so as never to lose her again. The two stood locked in embrace for nearly a minute before they finally released grips on one another. Then, the pair and Sarah of them sat in chairs that instantly emerged from the floor to began that completely unnecessary, but pleasant, tradition they hadn't been able to share in so long.

They ate together, and talked of the future.

37

Retrospective

Sunday, November 28, 2258

Lothania, Deseret - Mijloc

Gone. An entire house had disappeared before Bodhi's eyes, never mind that it was all digital to begin with. Where it used to be, not even a foundation existed any longer but only a massive pile of sand. JoAnn stared at him, her eyes wide with wonder.

"How - what just happened?"

Wheels turned in his head. Weak spot in the security. Escape to Inferiere. He had a suspicion, but he couldn't be sure - and he couldn't check himself. He pulled up his control panel and connected a call to the in-world Paivana Thoughtforms.

"Contact off-world and ask them to check Inferiere for a breach," he said as soon as someone picked up. He received the expected head nod and immediate disconnection, then waited. A minute later and his control panel alerted that he had an incoming call.

"Sir, there has been some unusual action in Inferiere. Reports are that a woman disappeared."

"Which woman?"

"Unsure. She wasn't registered and didn't have a bay. Someone saw her across the desert - there and then she wasn't."

He had a guess who she was.

"Nothing else unusual?"

"More unusual than that, sir?"

"Like a house falling out of the sky. We just had a farmhouse disappear."

"Nothing like that, sir."

With a quick movement, his control panel disappeared before him.

"Do you see anything, sir?"

"Not a thing. Farmhouses don't just vanish. When we get back, we need to run diagnostics on this and see what happened."

"You haven't figured it out yet, sir?"

"Figured what out?"

"Her mommy came and got her," JoAnn said, her lips curled into a smile.

"I guess so," he replied, kneeling to grab some sand in his hand. It wasn't Inferiere sand - he could tell that right away. They wouldn't be found there, and they wouldn't be found here in Mijloc either. He smiled as well, and wiped his hand across his face, staring at the emptiness where a farmhouse used to be.

"I guess so."

38

Epilogue

Tuesday, November 31, 2258

Lothania, Deseret - Mijloc

Harper felt the sun caressing her skin as she rocked back and forth on her old wooden rocker. The rocker, large enough for Ordell, her old friend for almost an entire century now, was so high that her toes barely nudged the ground as she moved across the top. Her tongue worked its way around a lemon drop wedged gently between her teeth on the left side so that it didn't cut her gums with it's minuscule edges while the bittersweet flavor exploded in her mouth. She closed her eyes as the Deseret heat rose in the air around her. She imagined the waves of the ocean beyond her childhood home, crashing themselves into a beach of sand and dying trees, something that resembled more of a swamp than a beach. When she opened her eyes again, instead of a world decimated by an unforgiving climate and ignored by it's stewards, her eyes fell upon green trees speckled with swallows. A ruby-throated hummingbird floated by, propelled by invisible wings.

She lifted her hands to examine the glow of the sun falling between her fingers. Just beyond her fingertips, a cloud of dust rose up and she could make out a car approaching. From the size of the cloud, she knew the vehicle was only a few minutes away, but she didn't bother to move. Whoever it was could find her where she was, as she existed, and would have to be fine with it. A century of living mean that she could do what she wanted, when she wanted, and right now, she wanted to enjoy the slow oscillation of the rocker and the creaking sounds it made on the wooden deck.

None of it was real. At least, Bodhi would still say that from time to time. An entire world before her, spread out in perfect detail, and he'd been too involved in the making and running of it to understand that in the end, it didn't matter whether the world was real or not. It *felt* real, and as long as that was true, she treated it as such. Well, mostly. There was the reproductive work that she and Torrent worked on together. She smiled at the memory of the previous week, working side-by-side in the lab with him. That had been a week of paperwork and preparation, as her program would go before the world government soon and they had to be prepared. What they said about citizenship of children born in Mijloc was academic as she was concerned, though Bodhi obsessed about dotting the 'i's. She knew that once a child was born in this nearly perfect world, that child would be loved. It was as inevitable as the sun that washed over her skin.

Just before her, the automobile came to a stop, and she focused on it long enough to see Bodhi through the window. He jumped out and sprinted up to the steps before him. Her memories of the ocean hadn't included him - he'd never seen it except from an airplane. Born and raised after she fled persecution for helping Ordell escape captivity, most of his earlier life had been too consumed by his disease for him to appreciate it's beauty. The bustling young man before her - who was she kidding, he was middle-aged now, but would never look it. This brought out a grin as she considered all of the horrors she would never have to worry about with him anymore. No more disease, and no more death. Not again, anyway. His life had evolved into something wonderful, if only he would slow down enough to realize it.

"Mom," he said as he approached. "Here you are."

"Have been all morning," she replied. She recognized the irony of the twenty-something year old body sunning in a rocker on a porch. The incongruous nature of the scene would have struck her as funny, but she enjoyed it too much to stop rocking.

"I need some -"

"Have a seat, Bodhi," she told him, motioning to the other rocker just beside the steps he took two at a time. At first, he seemed put off to be interrupted. Whatever he had to say must have been pretty important, she guessed. But what wasn't these days? Still, he worked his way over to her rocker and dropped himself into it.

"I need some advice."

Then he told her a lengthy and elaborate story about what he'd been involved in over the last few weeks since she'd seen him. Her ears perked up at the story about Aida's child as she made a mental note to review the diagnostics during what would have been Aida's gestation period and see what she could glean from it. Then his story ended with a disappearing farmhouse.

"What should I do?" He asked. "I have a few logs that show that someone existed in Inferiere who we never sent there. I have a few more logs and evidence showing that the girl Lincoln existed, but evidence of their origins is completely gone. The only other thing that I have to tie them together is Jordan Helm, who found his way into Mijloc, and he's sticking to some story about how he paid Jane to break him out of Inferiere. All other evidence has been erased. The townspeople of Lothania are now saying there wasn't ever a farmhouse there. Even our liaison won't admit to it. Someone has been cleaning up behind them."

"Do you think she's coming back?"

"How would I know? I don't even know where she went."

"Look over there," Harper told him, pointing into the distance with her eyes. "What do you see?"

He obliged, but a confused look passed over his face.

"Nothing. Just Mijloc, and sun."

"Exactly. Did she hurt anybody while she was here?"

"No."

"Did Jordan?"

He shook his head.

"So her only crime as far as you know is stealing a virtual farmhouse?"

"And two young women who occupied it."

"The young women that your security team was trying to capture?"

"Well, yeah. But..."

"I don't see the problem."

"People can't just come and go from Mijloc and Inferiere."

"From what I can tell, the evidence indicates that only Jordan Helm has done that, and he had a team of hackers working on it. Security breaches happen sometimes. Just patch whatever she did to make sure it can't happen again, put him back in Inferiere, and then it's done. Tell the World Government you're sorry and it won't happen again. They may fine you or something, but that'll pass. It's way too late to back out of Inferiere."

The large oak door slid open behind her, and a handsome young man with his hair pulled back into a pony tail and thin glasses, completely unnecessary but which she had insisted that he wear anyway, stepped out onto the porch holding two glasses of what she knew would be lemonade.

"Bodhi? Hey! Glad you're here."

"Aiden? I didn't know you'd come in. You look great."

He nodded.

"I feel great too. I would have come sooner, but I had to funnel my money into Mijloc first. You wouldn't believe the tax rate for doing that. I'm about half as wealthy in here as I was on the outside."

"But you don't need money here. I mean, not really."

"Not unless you've got things to do. I've got some ideas."

Harper smiled. Aiden was so much like Bodhi, he could have been his father. An overflowing fountain of ideas, most of which didn't work, but some did. It always seemed like the big ones worked out somehow. The more she thought about her own work, she realized that she was the same way, with her reproductive program. Bodhi's biological father had been like that too. The boy, no - man, had really never stood a chance at normal.

"Of course you do," Bodhi said. "Come by the office some time. But give me a week or so, there's a mess to clear up."

"I heard."

"*You* heard? How?"

Aiden smiled.

"Did you think I wouldn't already have started growing my network in here? I heard, trust me. What are you going to do about it?"

Bodhi looked at Harper, whose smile still hadn't left her lips, then over to Aiden, who pushed a glass of lemonade toward him. His face seemed to relax then, as he accepted the sweating container.

"I guess nothing," he finally said, but he still didn't grin. "Though it seems wrong, Mom. I don't know how, or why, but I think she was involved in Jane's death. I can't prove that either though. Doesn't it seem wrong to let her get away with that?"

"Maybe the best thing to do would be to ask Jane about that."

"I can't ask her. She fried her animus module, on purpose. It's as though she wanted to make sure that she never came back."

"Then you've done what you can. Let it go, or don't. It's up to you I suppose. What I know is that I could be enjoying a glass of lemonade with my son and husband in the porch in the warm sunshine."

"Husband?"

"Not official," said Aiden, "but she finally admitted that I'm the best she's ever going to do." A broad smile crossed his face. "Only took a century."

"It's strange to think about how this all began."

Bodhi nudged off with his feet, and Harper could tell that he was relaxing a bit more as he sipped his lemonade. She smiled and pushed off herself, enjoying the gentle breeze created by the back-and-forth. The sun pressed down and the lemon drop dissolved slowly between her teeth. She took a deep breath, imagining the smell of the ocean, and then exhaled.

39

Dear Reader,

Thank you for coming on this journey with me. It is here that I leave you (for now) with Harper's story that began so many years ago. The original draft of Models and Citizens (book 1 of this series) began over 10 years ago. Only with the help of some very good (and patient) friends in the writing community did that novel see the light of day. The first drafts will never see the light of day (unless perhaps after my untimely demise).

I struggled with the conclusions of each novel in the series. I think this one ends the best, because at the beginning of Models and Citizens, we realize pretty quickly that what Harper wants is a normal life. At the end of this novel, and a little to Bodhi's disappointment, she finally gets it.

Bodhi's heartbreak with Christine is something else I wanted to touch on in more detail. Christine is also referenced in the Gemini Book, if you haven't yet read that collection of short stories. She's the CEO who single-handedly kills the modeling industry — even though she's knee-deep in it. However things went in Bodhi Rising, she's not a bad person. She's a bit immature all during that novel, and handles her rapid success poorly. I wanted to scream at her that she was making a mistake all through that one, but once a character is a certain way, well... there's not much the author can do about it. I hope you'll forgive the ending of that novel. After the ringer that she put Bodhi through for 90,000 words or so, he couldn't get to a place where they could be together.

If you're still reading, then that's awesome! I can go on forever, but I won't. Thanks again for buying and if it's not too much to ask, please head out and put a review on whatever site you got this copy of the novel from. It really helps me stay focused and get more work done! After all, this isn't the last novel in the Reality Gradient universe, even if it's the last one that centers around Harper. Stay tuned for Southern Highlands, a novel about Apryl Sallow, Commander of the Southern Highlands Company who regulate trade with Mars. When her ex-lover rises to power over the warlords on Mars, things get really weird, really fast!

Many regards,

Andrew Sweet

www.ingramcontent.com/pod-product-compliance
Lightning Source LLC
Chambersburg PA
CBHW010631100726
47900CB00011B/2783